DANA RANSOM

TEMPTATION'S TRAIL

ZEBRA BOOKS
KENSINGTON PUBLISHING CORP.

ZEBRA BOOKS are published by

Kensington Publishing Corp.
475 Park Avenue South
New York, NY 10016

First Printing: February, 1994

Printed in the United States of America

BS

TEMPTED BY PASSION

"Why, Miss Amanda, I can't believe you're at a loss for words."

"Oh, I'm not, Mr. Bass. I was just fumbling for the right ones."

"What might those be?" he coaxed with a huskiness of voice.

Amanda drew a tight breath. Her gaze swept over him once more, and she plunged on recklessly. "That you are the most exquisitely gorgeous thing I have ever seen in my life, Mr. Bass. And I suggest you put something on before I'm tempted to forget myself."

He couldn't resist. Her adoration heated him up to a steady boil. His words were provocatively soft. "Just what might you be tempted to do, Miss Duncan?"

She touched him, first with fingertips, then with palms, sliding over the flatness of his belly in slow appreciation. Amanda took a step closer. Her hands moved up the hot slickness of his chest, fingers pausing over flat male nipples until they, too, stiffened with arousal.

Unbearable sensations shivered through him. He reached up, catching her hands, pulling them down. She swayed against him, her cotton blouse adhering to sticky flesh. He felt her mouth press to his shoulder and the startling rasp of her tongue on salty skin. He speared the fingers of one hand into her golden hair, pulling her head back.

Her eyes were mere slits through which passion glimmered. . . .

For John,
Forgive me for ever saying,
"What does a man know about romance?"
Looking forward to a great
editorial relationship.

Prologue

There.

Just a shadow on the ground. Only an Apache would have seen it.

He knelt down, little more than a shadow himself, to examine the faint impression bending the sparse stems of gamma grass. A twitch of movement played about his immobile face. It might have been a smile as he snapped off a single blade and put it to his lips. He sucked on it, testing the natural juices left in the bruised spear of grass, tasting the mild sweetness.

Close. He was very close.

Casting the stem aside, he rose in a fluid ripple of grace, standing next to naked beneath the hot West Texas sun. The only heat he felt was the fire warming his blood. It was a steady simmer of anticipation. He paused long enough to take a small sip from the jug of water he carried, then set off in the strong shambling gait that had seen him over thirty miles since morning. He didn't notice the distance. His legs were like steel wire, conditioned for abuse. All his senses were focused out of body, on the quarry ahead.

He found the horse. It struggled weakly upon the ground, its hide streaked with lather, a jagged spear of white protruding from its foreleg where the bone had been broken. He paused long enough to jerk his blade through the animal's throat, ending its misery. He kept his knife in hand. The man he hunted would be on foot now. No match for him at all.

He found a sign immediately. The bright splotch of crimson stood out against the Big Bend dust like a brilliant flower. Just as he'd thought. He'd wounded his prey that morning. He would be weak and terrified, in pain. Good. And he would be careless, which would make his task that much easier.

He moved faster now, sure, gliding low over the hard-packed ground like a stalking wolf hungry for a kill. The trail was obvious, made by a floundering man. A soon-to-be dead man.

Then he was upon him.

The cowboy had fallen into an arroyo and was scrambling frantically in the loose soil as he tried to climb up the other side. He'd dropped his rifle in his haste. He was bleeding from a shoulder wound. He was panting in fear. Sensing the presence of the silent ghost that had tracked him mercilessly, the cowboy flattened himself against the crumbling bank and stared up in blank terror. And he cried out in a raw, panicked voice.

"Who are you?"

The dusty warrior smiled, a baring of white teeth against swarthy skin. "You'll remember me. Before I'm done, you'll remember who I am."

Chapter One

He was tall and powerfully built, with a preponderance of muscular development and animal spirits, broad and deep of chest framed by square iron-cast shoulders and limbs like bars of steel. Faultlessly garbed, except for the burn of wind and Texas sun, he might pass as a gallant of the drawing room, grace and culture refined by every motion, word, and look. Beneath a broad-brimmed hat of the finest gray felt shone a brave countenance and eyes of the fiercest black imaginable. Few could stand their terrible glance when anger stirred this proud, true knight of the wilderness.

Amanda Duncan had memorized his description and there was no doubt in her mind that the man who stepped from the outer broil of West Texas heat was none other than Harmon Bass. A particular breathlessness overcame her, along with a certainty that in coming here she had done the right thing. Here was a man who would know exactly what to do.

The surrounding noise and squalor was forgotten as she lost herself in the study of him. He paused just inside the doors, assessing the dim and crowded corners of the hotel's public room. A sigh escaped the young woman's lips. Oh, my. He was everything she'd hoped for, everything the pages promised. Hard and handsome, a polished gemstone in this rough setting. Even in the oppressive heat, the starched white shirtfront beneath his black velveteen coat was unwilted, and not a hint of dirt smudged the snug fit of pale buckskin breeches tucked within high boots of varnished leather. And on one lean hip rode the mark of his trade, the forward-facing butt of a massive Colt .45. A deliciously dangerous chill swept through her.

Those glowing, coal-black eyes paused as they touched on her where she sat alone, conspicuous in her eastern travel clothes, and a faint smile moved the groomed perfection of his moustache. An elegant, long-fingered hand rose to the brim of his hat for a brief salute. Then, abruptly, his attention was pulled away when a small, dark, and very dusty cowboy bumped his arm in passing. She could imagine the threat in those piercing eyes as they cut to the offending person. His hand eased off the pearl handle of his gun when he saw the other was unarmed.

"Watch where you're going, breed." It was a low hiss of contempt as he shoved the smaller fellow aside, then meticulously brushed at the nap of his sleeve.

With bared head bowed in obvious awed respect, the trail-soiled cowboy murmured a soft, " 'Scuse me," and faded back between the close grouped tables toward the bar.

Amanda held her breath suspended as the princely gunman turned her way once more. He started across the room with a lethal stride, drawing more than a few cautious looks. Oh, yes, he was the perfect man for what she had in mind. A truly dangerous man, she thought with a wild exhilaration. Hands clutching the worn novel in her lap, she forced a stillness in limbs that wanted to quiver. An expectant smile bowed her moistened lips. It wasn't every day a woman met the man of her dreams, a man immortalized by his own heroic deeds. However, instead of joining her directly, he sank fluidly into an empty chair at the next table and drawled for the men at cards to deal him in. She expelled her breath in confusion.

It had been a long, exhaustive journey from New York to the desolate plains of Texas. Amanda had come all that distance, anxious and alone, and now the man she meant to hire seemed more intent upon the ascending order of his playing cards than in the terms of their agreement. He glanced her way again and again, he smiled thinly. Her excitement faltered only slightly when those intense eyes caressed along the bodice of her close-fitted jacket. As unfamiliar as she was with that dark, undressing look, it woke an immediate discomfort. Nonsense, she told herself firmly. He'd meant no insult with that bold, hot gaze. Harmon Bass was a man of noble thought and chivalric heart. She had no reason to fear he would act improperly toward her. The only ones needing to feel fear were the villains he brought to justice. Amanda bit back her impatience. She would wait for an audience with Harmon Bass, and then she would see justice done.

She didn't have long to wait.

"You're a liar, mister. A liar and a cheat."

That harsh claim was followed by the scrape of chairs and the unavoidable grab for sidearms. As Amanda stared in wide-eyed horror, pistols were drawn and discharged. The thunder of them was so deafening, her hands clapped to her ears to still the roar. Clearing smoke revealed the unexpectedly savage consequences. And the devastation of all her plans.

"Ma'am?"

It took all her strength to wrest her stare from the bright smear of crimson that grew from a small round hole to a circle the size of a dinner plate upon a snowy shirt bosom.

Deep in a daze of disbelief, she gazed up at the slightly made cowboy who'd backed down from a confrontation with the legendary gunman.

"He's dead." The words trembled upon her lips.

A disinterested glance canted down toward the sprawled figure. "Yes, ma'am. He most certainly is, and I don't guess he'll mind me borrowing his chair."

Using a dusty toe to nudge the shiny boot from its resting place upon the seat, the soft-spoken cowboy drew the chair around and sat facing a stunned Amanda. Her mind was reeling in shock. At the next table, the men went back to their cards and drinks, the shootist setting his yet-smoking pistol next to his pile of tattered chips. Noisy talk and laughter resumed throughout the room. No one seemed the least bit bothered by the crumpled form bleeding on the floor. Or by the identity of the corpse. No one seemed to care that a life had been taken cruelly, even callously, or that the deadly deed brought all her hopes to ruin.

"Isn't someone going to do something?" she whispered in a strained sort of panic.

"Do? Out here, we pretty much mind our own business and aren't too interested in them who don't mind theirs."

The enormity of it made her stutter stupidly. "B—but that man just k—killed Harmon Bass."

The cowboy's attention turned back to the corpse and he drawled, "Now, I don't rightly know who that fellow is, but I know who he's not. Might you be Miss Duncan?"

Amanda blinked, struggling to drag up a regular breath from the constriction of her lungs. "Yes."

"Then you'd be looking for me." When he was met by a look almost as blank as the black eyes gazing heavenward, he reached into the front of his rumpled shirt. "You sent me this letter."

Amanda stared at it, recognizing her handwriting in a

dull disconnected stupor. Two things struck her all at once with a force more stunning than the killer's .45.

The gentleman laid out on the floor wasn't Harmon Bass.

The man sitting across from her was.

"No."

"Ma'am?"

"You can't be." Amanda shook her head. She drew out her dog-eared copy of *Harmon Bass, the Texas Tracker; or, Bordertown Bounty Man.* She knew every word, having read the one hundred pages of fast-paced action, gunplay, and thrill-a-minute excitement over and over on the tedious train ride west. From the bold woodcut illustrations and inflated description, she knew Harmon Bass as well as she knew her own brother. She'd staked everything on a tall, experienced, gun-hung hero of larger-than-life virtue and strength who enforced justice single-handedly. He was a man of dashing physical appearance, flashy attire, and exquisite social bearing depicted vividly in each sensational scene. She'd come all this way to hire the gentleman painted upon those cheap pulp pages. And the unassuming man watching her so patiently was not him.

Just then, two men knelt down beside the inert figure on the floor, one of them tucking the pearl-handled Colt in his trouser band and the other relieving the corpse of his diamond stickpin, before they lifted him up with the casualness of a worthless sack of spoiled goods to haul him from the room. No one bothered to scrub the dark stains off the floorboards. Amanda felt her last meal roil dangerously. Heat suffused her face. Blood pulsed loud and fast between her temples until she was dizzy from the hurried beat. She'd never swooned in her life but she realized the threat of it unless she could get away from this hot, stifling room hung with the odor of death. For the first time, she doubted the wisdom of her impulsive trip.

"There's been some mistake," she murmured faintly. "I'm sorry. . . ."

As she started to rise, his hand closed around her wrist. It wasn't a painful or aggressive grasp, just a firm, controlling circle of rough, dry fingers. She stiffened all over as he spoke, softly, with a steel-threaded quiet.

"I've just ridden a hundred miles for the promise of pay. I'm thirsty, I'm hungry, I'm tired, and right now I'm getting more than a little annoyed, so you just sit yourself back down."

Amanda dropped into the chair without so much as a whimper. She wasn't cowed by the command, but she was properly cautious. "Who are you?"

"I'm the man you sent for."

"How did you get that letter? I posted it in care of the Texas Rangers."

"And they sent it to me." One corner of his mouth crooked up wryly as he tapped a dirty forefinger on the cover of her dime novel. "You wanted the heroic Harmon Bass bad enough to offer up a thousand dollars, and here I am to collect."

She studied him candidly for a moment. The violent shock was wearing off, returning her usual brash spirit. "Please don't take this the wrong way, but I don't plan to offer up that money to just anyone and I don't believe for a second that you're Mr. Bass."

His amusement had affected the rest of his mouth by then, shaping it into a small smile. "And why's that, Miss Duncan?"

"If you could read, you'd know perfectly well that you are nothing like Harmon Bass." She sized up his insignificant appearance with a clear eye and a cool word. "Why, you're too young. You can't be much more than twenty years old, you don't carry a gun, you don't dress like any gentleman I've ever seen, you let yourself be pushed around by a stranger, and you're—you're shor—you're not tall."

"No, ma'am," he claimed calmly in the face of her fierce blush, "tall, I'm not. But I can read. And I can tell the difference betwixt fact and fiction. Whether you like it or not, I'm the man you want. And just how old are you?"

"Seven—" She broke off, wishing she'd been smart enough to add a few years to the obvious. Too late. His unexpected question had caught her off guard. Pridefully, she stated, "I'm seventeen."

"Ahhh. Such a ripe old age to be calling me too young." Then he smiled, baring strong white teeth, and Amanda realized something else about him. Beneath the grime, he was very nice to look at. But that didn't make him any less a disappointment.

"I'm sorry for your inconvenience," she began, not unkindly. "I'm afraid you just don't—"

"Measure up?" he supplied mildly. Her face grew hotter but she didn't back down from her assessment. He smiled again, and engaging creases scored weather-browned cheeks. "Depends upon what kinda' fit you're looking to find. If you were counting on some steely-eyed, quick-fingered fool like the one in that there book and like our dear departed neighbor, then no, I'm not what you want. I'm no gun-handy hero. But in your letter you said you needed a tracker, and ma'am, I'm the best there is."

He said that with a quiet modesty, as a piece of fact and not a point of bravado. It made her think, but it still didn't convince her.

Until he said, softer still, "I need the money."

15

"Is there any way you can prove who you are?"

His black brows arched in surprise. "I've never had to. I suppose any of the Rangers could vouch for me, but it'd take a couple a days to get word back from Ysleta. You figuring to wait?"

"No. I can't afford to, Mr. . . . Bass."

"Then I suggest we get right to it, Miss Duncan. You'll just have to trust me."

What choice did she have? She was desperate. She couldn't go to the law. The law had already made up its mind, and not in her favor. From what she knew of the law in Texas, the local level couldn't be bothered with her and the Rangers didn't have time for her. That's why she'd trusted in her reply from Harmon Bass. Three words. *I'll be there.* So she'd left everything behind to make the tiring trip to Texas, counting on one man to set her world aright.

But she didn't have to trust him.

"Perhaps you'd like to get yourself a meal and—and clean up." She pushed a ten-dollar gold piece toward him. "I have a room here in the hotel. Come up when you're ready and we'll discuss terms." Suddenly, she was very anxious to escape this room where the bloodstains were drying not five feet from her.

He palmed the coin and rose without a word. No, he wasn't tall. He was compact and wiry, as tough and lean as the Texas mustangs she'd seen corralled by the train station. Maybe a sleek, leggy thoroughbred wasn't what she needed now. Perhaps she needed someone like this man, who looked to be built for endurance rather than for speed. He was right about one thing. It was his ability to track, not his proficiency with a gun, that interested her. If he could find her brother, she didn't care what name he used. He could call himself Harmon Bass. As long as he could find Randolph Duncan and the fortune in jewels that had disappeared with him.

It was nearly dark. A surprisingly cool breeze wafted in off the baked Texas plain into the town of Fort Davis. The price of enjoying that refreshing air was enduring the brunt of noise from saloons situated on either side of the hotel. Even before it had begun to cool, staying in this small, hot little room was better than suffering the hard scrutiny of the men below. In her earlier excitement, she hadn't noticed it. But when she asked for her key at the desk, there was no mistaking the interest she stirred in the hard cases loitering nearby. No self-respecting man in the east would regard a woman as if she were bereft of clothes and decency. It made her wonder if everything she'd read about the "land of material plenty and human bliss" was all a lie.

Restlessness played upon Amanda's nerves like unskilled fingers on the tinny pianos below. She paced, uneasy with her decision but too stubborn to reconsider it. It wasn't as though she had any alternatives. She couldn't forget everything and go home. She had nothing to go back to. Randolph Duncan was the only thing of value in her life, he and the considerable estate their parents' death had divided between them. Of the two, Randy was the more important. For him, she would sacrifice every cent of her extensive trust fund. For him, she had journeyed almost two thousand miles on her own to place their fates in the hands of a perfect stranger. Because there was no one else she could trust.

She almost didn't hear the light tap on her door over the pulse of Fort Davis's nightlife as it gathered steam. When she leaned close and asked who it was, the quiet reply came: "Harmon Bass." She closed her eyes and sighed. Oh, how she wished it were that Texas legacy come to rescue her from despair. But she would settle for a lowly little cowboy who claimed he knew how to track. She had no other option.

He slipped inside the moment she opened the door and secured it behind him. Then he waited, appearing slightly uncomfortable in the presence of her partially unpacked female paraphernalia. He looked much more presentable than at their first meeting, having cleaned up quite nicely. His plain blue shirt had a just-off-the-shelf crispness. It was tucked into a pair of faded denims, and she noted his lean hips were still bare of any sidearms. He had no hat in a country where no man went bareheaded. He was freshly shaven in a time when no man went barefaced. Even scrubbed and newly laundered, there was something about this Harmon Bass that took one step outside the ordinary and acceptable.

Breed, the man downstairs had sneered at him. Could that be true? He didn't look Indian or Mexican, but then she had never seen a real Indian or Mexican to offer the comparison. He wore his hair collar-length and finger-raked to one side. It was straight and dark enough to make her wonder, and so was his deeply bronzed skin. His face was broad through the cheekbones, but his features were finely cut; eyes heavy-lidded against the perpetual glare of sun off hard-packed ground, nose thin and straight, mouth disinclined to move from its noncommittal line. Without the dirt, he looked even younger. Without a gun, he looked vulnerable. Was she wrong to trust this man?

She had no time to argue it. The first thing he asked was, "Tell me about your brother."

Tears quickened in an instant. She had to blink rapidly to hold them at bay. Amanda had promised herself she wouldn't cry over Randy, not without reason. And she staunchly refused to believe she had reason. She began to pace again. Harmon Bass stood by the door, watching her agitated movements.

"Randy left New York three weeks ago carrying one hundred fifty thousand dollars worth of jewelry to a Judge McAllister in Perdition, Texas. The judge's men were waiting for him to get off the stage but he never met up with them. They checked with the other passengers, and it seems my brother and another man got off and disappeared."

"With the jewels?"

She nodded.

"What kind of place was your brother working for?"

"My uncle got him a position with a very prestigious jeweler. He'd been doing courier work for about a year."

"Did he ever carry such a large amount such a distance before?"

"I don't think so. Most of the deliveries were right on the East Coast. Why? Why do you ask?" Her voice sharpened, just as her suspicions sharpened. "If you're asking if he caved in to temptation and ran off with a fortune in stones, the answer is no."

Harmon Bass stared at her inscrutably. "Why should I believe that?"

"For one thing, Randy didn't have to steal. We're both quite well off financially. And for another, I love my brother, but Randy would never have conceived of doing something like that. He simply doesn't have the imagination. He's honorable, but he's not terribly clever or ambitious. He's no thief. Something happened to my brother and I can't convince the authorities that he's not involved as a guilty party. I want you to find Randy. I want to know what happened to him and the jewelry. I want his name cleared of any wrongdoing. I want to take my brother home with me."

If he had any other doubts or judgments, he kept them to himself.

"When do I get started?"

She tried to contain her relief. "Is the morning too soon?"

"No, ma'am." He studied the toes of his boots for a moment, building up to something. "About the money?"

"We agreed on one thousand dollars. I'll have it for you when I see my brother again."

He looked up. Blue, she noticed with some surprise. His eyes were blue. Not a fierce black, but a blue as searingly clear and intense as the midday West Texas sky, a startling contrast to the darkness of his complexion.

"I was hoping to get it up front."

Amanda smiled. She was not that young. She may not have had a great deal of worldly experience, but money was one thing she understood very well. She'd been handling it all her life. "Mr. Bass, I don't know you from Adam. If I handed you a thousand dollars, I'd have no guarantee of ever seeing you again."

"You have my word on it."

"I'm sorry. It's not enough."

Not so much as a muscle twitched in his impassive face, but she sensed that his expression had suddenly turned to granite. "How do I know you'll pay me once the job's done? Especially if the news I bring back isn't good?"

"I guess you'll just have to trust me."

"I'm sorry, Miss Duncan. I'm not that trusting, either."

"Well, it seems we're at a standoff unless you'll agree to another proposition."

"I'm listening." And he was suddenly very wary. She could feel his tension as he waited and watched her.

"I'll give you five hundred dollars now for a horse,

20

supplies, and all expenses. And I'll pay you the full thousand dollars when the job's done."

"I already have a horse."

"But I don't. I'll be going with you."

Chapter Two

He was crazy. That was the only explanation.

Harmon Bass was still scourging himself for letting the little lady get the better of him. When he was running a trail, he worked it alone. Even when he was on the Ranger payroll he made sure they stayed far back and out of his way. He didn't like to be crowded and he didn't like to worry over anyone's mistakes but his own. The Big Bend of Texas was mighty unforgiving when it came to mistakes. And he had the feeling he was making a dandy.

If he was the kind of man who was affected by such things, he'd vow she'd bedazzled him with her fresh-faced beauty and all that honey-blond hair. Most men would find her more than passably pretty. He thought she was. He held a very clear picture of how she'd looked sitting in the hotel bar, a delicate dew-kissed cactus flower amid scorched wasteland. And like that blossom she would be quick to fade. She'd been sweltering in all those silly eastern wrappings, yet they had brought a becoming flush to her lightly freckled cheeks. And those eyes. Huge, seeking brown eyes in which a man could lose his soul. Eyes that pleaded without words and fired with the promise of spirit.

I'll be going with you.

Why hadn't he laughed? Why hadn't he turned and walked away?

Because when she'd said it, so clear and bold, her chin had angled up just a notch and those big, soul-snatching eyes had sparked with courage.

And he needed the money.

Fifteen hundred dollars. He could tolerate anything for that amount. It would not only pay for the necessities, it would also bring a coveted windmill from Chicago to feed the parched land. He couldn't walk away from it, and Amanda Duncan wouldn't part with it on less than her impossible terms. So he'd done the foolish and unforgivable, and he'd agreed. How long could it take to track down one eastern tenderfoot who thought to blend into the harshness of West Texas with a fortune in stolen stones? It would be easy money.

She was waiting for him in the hotel lobby. Her eyes brightened with anticipation when she saw him. So young! He was crazy. The years that separated their ages might well have been a hundred. He was taking an innocent out into a land that showed no mercy. What had he been thinking? It wasn't too late to back out.

"Are we ready, Mr. Bass?" How expectant she sounded, as if they were about to embark on a delightful adventure.

He was blunt. "Miss Duncan, where I'm going, every insect has a sting, every bush a thorn, every snake a fang. The sun is hot, the water's scarce, and the ride is hard. Most sane men would refuse to make the trip."

"I'm not most men, Mr. Bass."

She was standing now and his gaze swept her from head to toe. No, she was no man. She'd traded her fancy society clothes for a sensible split skirt and white cotton shirtwaist. Glossy boots replaced kid shoes. The glorious

23

twists of her hair had been braided back from the milky softness of her face and topped with a flat-brimmed hat. Even so, she looked no less feminine, no less fragile. She would wilt within the hour and be begging for mercy by nightfall. And then he'd have to lose precious time bringing her back. He tried a different approach.

"You know a lot about men, do you, Miss Duncan?"

The low purr of his voice woke a sudden wariness in her eyes. Good. He took a step closer. In her boot heels, they were almost eye to eye. She was tall for a woman, built like a supple reed. Easily bent, but not easily broken.

"How do you know I won't take you out there where there's nothing but nothing and slit your throat?" He let that sink in before adding with a whisper of menace, "Or worse."

She didn't even blink. "I guess I'll just have to trust you, Mr. Bass." When he drew a surprised and exasperated breath, she smiled wryly at him. "Besides, if that was what you were planning, you'd hardly warn me of it ahead of time, would you?"

She was right about that, he conceded reluctantly.

"And then," she added with a bit more tartness, "you'd be losing out on the thousand dollars. I hardly think a man would be willing to sacrifice that for me. We're wasting time, Mr. Bass." And she walked toward the door.

His critical gaze lingered over the coltish way her stride moved her hips. He was thinking about the courageous fire in her eyes. He was thinking she could be wrong. He was thinking too much. He strode after her.

Amanda was at the porch rail where he'd tied off their two horses. She turned to him with a bright eagerness that kicked him back on his heels.

"Which one is mine?" She was talking about the horses.

"The paint."

"Oh, he's beautiful," she cooed, reaching up to rub the soft muzzle with both hands. Watching those caressing touches brought an odd tightness to Harm's chest. "What's his name?"

"Name?" He stared at her blankly.

"I'm going to call him Fandango."

He was looking at her as if she were loony. "I don't care if he don't care."

Amanda glanced at his mount, a shaggy lean-limbed gray, and she seemed perplexed. "I thought you rode a black horse." She recalled it quite clearly. Harmon Bass and his fiery steed, a large stallion as black as coal who answered to the name of Midnight.

Harm was smiling to himself as he went around the gray to check its girth. She was confusing fact and fiction again. "Seem to remember a black horse once. Tough as boot leather."

"What happened to him?" Amanda asked innocently.

"I ate him."

"You . . . what?"

"I rode him till he dropped, I had a good hot meal, and I got me another horse. Miss Duncan, out here a horse is a faster way to get from here to there, nothing more. We don't name them, we don't coddle them, and we don't make pets out of them. Understand?" He looked at her from over the smooth curve of his saddle and he could see she didn't. She was pale enough to shame him for his graphic words. Her eyes formed huge dark circles. But she didn't say anything, and suddenly he was angry. "If you're going, get on board," he told her gruffly as he swung up and gathered the reins. He watched as she awkwardly grasped the saddle horn and fit her boot in the stirrup iron. She came straight up, then hung there at a loss for momentum while the horse shifted nervously.

"Try it again," he suggested, adding apprehensively, "You ever been on a horse before?"

Amanda stepped down, blushing in her chagrin. "Actually," she began as she hauled herself up a second time, this time swinging her leg over in the same motion, "no, I haven't." She clutched the horn with both hands and looked at him in triumph. "Until now." She lifted the reins uncertainly and the horse started backing. She dropped them and grabbed for the security of the horn. The horse stopped. She smiled shakily and bravely loosened one hand to pat the animal's neck.

Harm moaned softly under his breath.

Amanda straightened and gave a confident "Let's go."

Rolling his eyes heavenward, Harm brushed the reins along the left side of the gray's neck. Amanda mimicked the motion. But her fiery steed Fandango made a right turn instead, starting back for the livery and the shade of its stall.

"Mr. Bass," she called weakly, hanging on to the horn for dear life.

Without a trace of expression to betray his thoughts, Harm reached out to snag the limp reins and pulled the paint in a wide circle. Amanda didn't look up at him. They were off to a great start.

Didn't the woman ever pause to draw a breath?

For five hours, they'd been riding. For five hours, she hadn't shut her mouth for longer than the time it took to swallow.

She'd started in with questions; about where they were

going, about what he hoped to find, about how he knew what to look for, about how long he thought it would take. At first he'd been civil, but one answer seemed to lead into three more questions. Not a man used to being so free with his conversation, Harm tired of it after a short while and began responding with noncommittal syllables and sounds. If he'd thought to discourage her non-stop chattering, he was wrong. She simply shifted from talking *with* him to talking *at* him.

She rambled. In no time at all, her sharply clipped New York accent became abrasive next to his own lazy West Texas tones. She described every detail of her trip from New York. He knew what she dined on each evening and the particulars of every passenger seated near her. In the third hour, he learned more than he cared to know about her schooling in the east. She was in her last year at an exclusive young ladies' academy and went on in excruciating detail about her lessons, her fellow students, and her teachers, even elaborating upon what one wore to attend the prestigious school functions. From there, she moved on to her brother. His finer points supplied a good two hours worth of tender dissertations. Harmon didn't want to know as much about any man's life as he was force-fed on Randolph Duncan's. And listening to Amanda Duncan yammer, he wasn't at all surprised that the unfortunate fellow had headed west. It was probably to escape his prattling sister.

Harm tried pretending her words were like the wind . . . an incessant whining that one grew used to after a time. He'd just succeed in dulling his mind to her continual monologue when she'd call him back to full attention with a pertinent question. It was enough to snag onto his attention, preventing him from finding that numbing bliss he craved. It was enough to drive a man to a desperate act. Abruptly, he kicked back his heels and his horse surged into a brisk trot. Behind him, he heard Amanda's little gasp of surprise and he felt guilty enough to cant a glance back at her. She was clinging to the saddle horn as her bottom met saddle leather with jarring slaps. She'd lost her stirrups. The irons dangled as uselessly as her feet. But she was quiet. Her jaws were gripped to keep her teeth from rattling. A most effective muzzle. He smiled to himself and enjoyed the silence. After a time, he began feeling sorry for her jouncing loosely in the saddle and Harmon slowed back into a walk. It started up almost at once.

"Mr. Bass, are there any Indians around here? I read that—"

He nudged his heels to pick up the pace and Amanda's sentence was clipped short. When he slackened to a walk again, she was ready.

"Mr. Bass, we won't run into any outlaws, will we? With you being unarmed, couldn't we be in some trouble?"

"I can take care of us, Miss Duncan," he assured her with a quiet confidence. But that wouldn't satisfy her.

"But wouldn't it be smarter to carry—" Her teeth snapped together as the paint took up the bone-shaking stride of Harmon Bass's horse. Finally, she got the idea. He was no more interested in her conversation than he was in her discomfort.

The sun was at its zenith when her call came rather weakly from behind him.

"Mr. Bass, could we please stop for a minute?"

She sounded genuinely miserable, and when he reined in to glance around, he was somewhat dismayed by her appearance. Her hat had fallen back, and wisps of honey-blond hair clung damply to her flushed face and neck. Her shoulders sagged with fatigue. She looked ready to

28

drop. Her color climbed even higher as she cast an uncertain look about them.

"Where can I . . . I need to . . ."

Harm didn't smile at her embarrassment. He swung down and caught her reins, holding Fandango steady while she crawled down from the saddle. He gestured broadly toward the low, ground-hugging shrubs and murmured, "Wherever you like. I'll cool down the horses. Just don't wander too far."

He loosened the saddles and moved them along the horses' sweaty backs to get their circulation moving. When they were watered and tethered, he found himself a piece of shade and began to wait. She was gone long enough for him to become concerned, but not long enough for him to go looking.

"Miss Duncan?"

"Right here, Mr. Bass."

She was so close, she surprised him. He wasn't used to being taken unaware. He'd been thinking about her out there in the greasewood and mesquite, and his thoughts had dulled his senses. That made him irritable.

"Sit down. The horses need some time to blow."

She gave him a wry smile. "No, thank you. I'll stand, if you don't mind. I've done quite enough sitting."

"Suit yourself." He jabbed the blade of his knife into the tin can he'd taken from his supplies and expertly peeled back the lid. Using the tip, he speared a section of fruit and sucked it down greedily, savoring the sweet taste and moisture. When he was almost to the bottom of the can, he thought of Amanda. "Want a peach?"

She stared at the slice impaled on his knife blade and wet her dry lips. It looked inviting when she took it in her fingers, but after she put it in her mouth, the syrupy thickness nearly made her gag. Amanda managed to swallow. Feeling suddenly woozy and overheated, she reached for her canteen. But the refreshing cascade of water over her parched features was short-lived. He was on his feet in a second, snatching the container from her hands.

"Don't waste it." He didn't raise his voice, but the words cracked with censure. Before she could recoil, his tone soothed patiently. "Like this."

He poured a small amount of water into his bandana and blotted the wet square along the delicate contours of her face, wiping away the salty perspiration with its cool chill. Her eyes closed in a rapture of relief, and at once his hand stilled. He drew back with a gruff "You get the idea."

"Yes, thank you." She took the cloth from him and continued to dab it over hot, sun-pinked skin. Her head tipped back as she cooled the graceful bow of her throat. When she opened the first few buttons of her shirtwaist, Harm gulped down the remaining peach juice from the can in a hurry and went to cinch up the saddles. By the time he was finished, she was knotting the damp bandana around her neck, letting its loose ends trail down into the valley of her blouse. He should have said something to her, that she should button her shirt back up or risk a nasty sunburn, but he couldn't form the words. His tongue seemed cemented to the roof of his mouth by heavy peach syrup.

"Are we ready, Mr. Bass?"

He had to admire her determination. With an awkward scramble, she was back in the saddle and looking to him to lead on. He turned away so she wouldn't see his bemused smile.

"How much farther will we travel today?" she asked, grabbing for the saddle horn as Fandango started forward.

"As far as the light holds out. Should reach Persimmon Gap. That'd put us about halfway out from the Bend."

"The Bend?"

"The Rio Grande's gift to Texas. It cuts down into Mexico like an elbow. The Indians say when the Great Creator completed the earth and placed stars in the sky, fish in the sea, and birds in the air, He had a heap of stony rubble left over that He hurled down into the Trans-Pecos. It landed in a pile and became the Big Bend."

"You sound like quite the romantic, Mr. Bass."

Her soft voice gave him an odd quiver. He sounded like a fool. "I didn't make it up, Miss Duncan. It's an old Apache legend."

She wasn't deterred. "It's beautiful country. No wonder it stirs more than an occasional poetic thought."

He waited for her to say more but she didn't. The silence got him waxing sentimental. It was beautiful country. Harsh, inhospitable, and sometimes deadly, but to him always beautiful. He was surprised that an eastern girl would view it the same way. He'd expected her to see only desert and desolation. Instead of complaining over the broad monotony of drab gray-green, she never failed to exclaim in delight at the occasional splash of blooming color tucked amid arid wilderness. She made awed sounds that touched him to the quick, as if she were praising something he held as a special secret close to the heart. He was filled with a desire to share the wonders of the land around them, but the strangeness of that want was enough to hold him silent. She was doing funny things to his thinking. He didn't like it.

"How do you know my brother came this way, Mr. Bass?" There was just enough challenge in her voice to rub his mood in a surly direction.

"That's what you're paying me to know, Miss Duncan."

"But how can you be sure——"

He cut her off curtly. "They left Fort Davis heading

31

south. There's not a whole lot of choice in the matter. They don't have a slew of garden spots to pick from out here. If they're smart, they'll stick to the Comanche Trail, just like we are."

"And if they're not?"

"They're probably out there getting their bones bleached."

Amanda had no reply. She started praying that Randy's companion wasn't a fool.

They were about forty miles out of Fort Davis. Amanda had grown used to the feeling of interminable distance spread out in all directions. For a time, she was puzzled by what seemed to be a glittering expanse of water up ahead of them, but when she asked her guide about it, he smiled thinly and told her the only water close by was in their canteens. As he said it, the rippling mirage obligingly receded and disappeared into a wide, smooth carpet of buffalo grass. On the edge of that flatness, mountains rose dark and jagged against the shining sky . . . a sky as bright and transparently blue as Harmon Bass's eyes. Mountains had been a surprise. Amanda hadn't expected Texas to have such rugged terrain and had wondered over the ranges draped in a fiery opalescence by the quivery up-drafts of dusty desert air as they approached. They'd ridden for the better part of a day and still those cool peaks seemed no closer. Perhaps the impression of distance was just as illusive as the shimmering lake of buffalo grass. Suddenly, she felt very vulnerable out in this vast stretch of sameness.

"How do you know you're going the right way, Mr. Bass?"

He must not have heard the slight catch of apprehension in her tone because his reply was caustic. "Kinda' hard to miss running into the mountains, ma'am. If we fall into the Rio Grande, we've missed our turn."

She studied the straight set of his shoulders and the arrogant way he rode without effort. Even with the sun broiling down on his bared head, he seemed not to mind the heat. When she mentioned it, he remarked offhandedly, "You get used to it."

"I don't know if I ever could." She risked letting go with one hand long enough to wipe her brow on her shirtsleeve. The cloth came away wet. Maybe if she ignored the continual trickle matting her clothing to her body, she could forget the oppressive temperature. Amanda untied the bandana. It was warm and damp. Think of something else, she told herself as she gazed ahead at the mountains. "Don't you ever get lost, Mr. Bass?"

"Don't you ever worry about your tongue getting sunburned?"

The quiet sarcasm drew her up with a shock of hurt. She was thoughtful for a moment, staring at the inflexible line of his shoulders, then she told him point-blank, "There's no need to whip up your horse. I'll save on them and my own posterior by keeping my comments to myself." Then she immediately contradicted herself by saying, "You are very rude, Mr. Bass."

"Another one of my many *short*comings, I'm sure, Miss Duncan," he drawled, not bothering to look back to face her indignant expression.

"A lack of manners is just one, I assure you. You're not what I expected."

"But I'm all you've got."

"Cold comfort, Mr. Bass. I suppose everything they wrote about you was a lie."

"A good portion of it, I'm sure. Real life makes for pretty dull reading."

"You probably never even tracked for the Rangers."

"That, I do."

She scowled, feeling hot and petulant in her misery. "You probably never killed your first man when you were twelve years old."

"No, I didn't."

She sniffed disdainfully. "All lies, just like I—"

"I was ten."

Something in the cold snap of his answer put an effective end to all conversation.

"We'll camp here."

Amanda glanced up and blinked dully. She must have been nodding off in the saddle, because the ground was angled and the air was surprisingly cool. When had they reached the mountains? And where was "here"? She saw nothing that even remotely suggested shelter, just a few scrubby junipers and more of the gnarled Texas brush. But Harmon Bass was off his horse, so she obligingly climbed down, too. And continued down when her knees failed to hold her. Only her grip on sweat-dampened saddle leather kept her from sinking to the hard-baked ground in a puddle of misery. All her bones seemed to have dissolved.

"Where are our accommodations, Mr. Bass?" Her words sounded as thick as the daze slowing her thoughts.

"Right behind your saddle, ma'am. Take any room you like."

She smiled with a vague uncertainty. Was he serious? All day in the saddle and only hard ground to look forward to? Apparently, he was. She unlashed the unpromisingly thin roll of blankets and spread them out on the closest flat spot. Her muscles protested the move. Her head was swimming with weariness and heat exhaustion. An unpleasant film of exertion clung to her, especially where her split skirt was stiff and damp from rubbing saddle leather. She could only imagine what she must smell like. It prompted her to ask the impossible.

"Is there someplace to wash up, Mr. Bass?"

"No, ma'am. We won't come to any water until tomorrow."

"Oh." It didn't matter. She was too tired to manage the effort of bathing, anyway. She started to ease herself down upon the blankets, not bothering with the removal of boots or hat. Why had she worried that the ground would be hard? It felt wonderful to be stretched out on something that didn't move. She uttered an involuntary sigh.

Hearing it, Harm went still. Then he quickly continued with the building of his fire. "I'll have us something to eat as soon as I see to the horses."

She muttered that she wasn't hungry and rolled away, releasing another of those gut-prodding sighs. Then she was motionless, falling asleep as instantly as a babe.

Harm let her sleep as he saw to the details of securing their camp for the night. At least, she was quiet. The silence allowed him to relax the tension that had mounted over each progressive mile. He didn't have a name for that collecting discomfort. He only knew it had to do with Amanda Duncan. He had no experience being in the company of a woman, and certainly not one such as the refined and overly talkative Miss Duncan. She overwhelmed him. She battered the barriers of his inbred shyness. Her aggressive manner made him squirm. Yet, when he would try to hold to his annoyance, he found he couldn't. He admired her; for her courage, for her endurance. She hadn't complained, not beyond those submissive little moans that had his flesh tightening over rigid muscle. For a tenderfoot, she'd done well.

He waited until the rabbit he'd snared was hot and

browned before waking her. There was no response when he called her name, so he went to crouch down beside her. Then there was a moment's awkwardness as he wondered over what part of her to shake. Harm settled for her shoulder. Beneath his hand, she felt alarmingly fragile, all small bones and soft woman. His throat seized up.

"Ma'am, food's ready," he croaked, giving her a brusque rattle. When he felt her jerk in startlement, he quickly backed away. "You'd best be eating something. We've got a long day ahead of us tomorrow."

"Smells divine," she murmured as she hauled herself into a sitting position. Her hand pressed to the small of her back as she tried to suppress the steady ache. He brought her a chunk of the slightly greasy meat, and the roar of her own appetite surprised her. The desire for rest was overruled by the need for sustenance. She took a bite and blew rapidly to cool her mouth.

"Careful. It's hot."

She frowned at his late warning, then approached the meat with the appropriate caution. He hunkered down on the other side of the fire to eat his share with a single-minded urgency. She watched him, bemused. Harmon Bass. The idea still fit awkwardly. Killed his first man when he was ten. She thought of the dapper gunman in the hotel staring sightlessly through glassy eyes and she shivered. Taking a life sounded heroic on the printed page but in real life death was ugly. How had he accomplished the grisly feat when just a boy? she wondered with a perverse horror. With that big knife he'd used to eat his peaches? Crouched there in the warm bronze glow of firelight he didn't look dangerous, yet she'd heard the lethal edge in his voice and she'd been afraid. Perhaps appearances were deceiving, just as her beloved novels had been deceiving.

"I'm sorry if I've been a trial to you, Mr. Bass."

He looked straight across the fire at her, pausing in the midst of chewing. The blue of his eyes seemed to take on its own hot fire. Then he looked down and continued wordlessly with his meal.

"It's just that I tend to talk too much when I'm upset. Randy is the only family I have. If something were to happen to him . . .".

"It's late, Miss Duncan," he interrupted sharply. "Morning comes early." He threw the remains of his dinner into the fire and wiped his fingers along the taut denim covering his thighs. Without so much as a look or a polite good night, he lay back on his bedroll, closing his eyes, arms folded across his chest, dismissing her and her troubles with a severing abruptness.

Amanda set aside the rest of her rabbit, her appetite suddenly gone. Some hero. She glowered at him. Just when she thought she might get to like him. *Her* Harmon Bass would never be so intentionally rude. *Her* Harmon Bass wouldn't be slumbering without the slightest care for her comfort. But then, her Harmon Bass didn't exist beyond the worn pages of her dime novel. This improbable little cowboy was all she had. And as she'd said, that knowledge was cold comfort.

But cold comfort was better than none, she discovered the moment she tried to close her eyes. Unfamiliar night sounds crowded close, threading the cool evening air with the eerie threat of the unknown. The wail of a distant coyote, the shuffling of the horses, the whisper of furtive movements just outside the small circle of light their fire cast against an enveloping blackness. She curled into her covers, tense and watchful, fighting down the weariness that would lessen her guard. How could he sleep so unconcerned? She cast a resentful glance at Harmon Bass and her gaze lingered upon the inviting stretch of flat ground beside his bedroll.

What importance had pride when in desperate need of sleep?

And cold comfort was better than none.

Chapter Three

A soft whisper of breath along his cheek and a quiet sigh.

Harmon was instantly awake, his every sense tingling in alarm. Without moving so much as a muscle, he eased his eyes open. He wasn't a sound sleeper, so finding himself nose to nose with Amanda Duncan was a severe shock to his overly cautious system.

He wasn't sure when or how she'd come to tuck herself up beside him like a friendly dog on a cold night, but there she was, and for a moment he feared his heart would never recover. It tripled into an anxious beat as he beheld features softened to an indescribable loveliness in sleep. All the skin appearing above the rough nap of her blanket was burned to a rosy blush. Her lashes made dark golden crescents along the curve of sun-warmed cheeks. But it was the trusting part of her lips that gave him panicked pause. Because they were sweet and near and offered more temptation than he'd ever experienced in his entire life. Every grain of his hard-earned discipline fought against the unexpected yearning to explore the mystery of kissing upon those beckoning lips. Only when he heard how raw and labored his breathing had become was he able to jerk himself free from the spell of her nearness.

He started to ease back, but at the same time she

muttered a groggy complaint and rolled up flush against him. Her arm shifted, sliding across his neck to curve up behind the back of his head. Her face nuzzled into the vee of his shirtfront beneath his chin. Then she was still, while Harm was petrified like ancient wood.

For a long while, he didn't even breathe, afraid he'd wake her, afraid he'd wake himself from the sudden sensual stupor. He could feel every warm contour through the thin blanket, the way her breasts flattened to his chest and her hips nestled against his own. Nice. Before he could stop himself, he bent to draw in the scent of her hair. Texas dust and fragrant soap. And soft, so soft. Not at all like the greasy tangle of the Mexican whore he'd been with so many years ago. That one's most knowledgeable touch hadn't roused a fraction of what he felt stirring now, sensations as intoxicating as *tiswin* and as dangerous to his control as that mild Apache beer.

This was dangerous, what he was thinking, what he was feeling. These deceivingly tender sentiments curling about his insides were linked to the violent pleasure he'd sworn by his own blood and pain to avoid. He had no right testing the parameters of that long-ago vow all cozied up in Amanda Duncan's arms.

Carefully, Harm reached around for her lax wrist and slowly unwrapped her embrace.

Coffee. Hot, strong enough to pluck at her senses like a good hard shake.

Amanda opened her eyes to a cool, misty morning and the sight of Harmon Bass kneeling at the fire. He glanced up when she stirred and for a long second held her gaze without any betraying expression on his browned face. Then he began to fill a tin with the steaming brew. Amanda darted a quick look beside her but all evidence

40

of his bedroll was gone. If he had any comment about discovering her bunking next to him, he kept it to himself behind that impassive stare.

"Best get a move on. We want to make time while it's still cool."

But getting a move on was easier for him to say than for her to do. If there was a muscle in her entire body that didn't pulse with agony, she didn't know where it might be. Sitting up brought a clamor of protest from the majority of them. Her back, her thighs, and her bottom seemed fused stiffly into one giant ache. He was watching her inscrutably, probably waiting for her to start moaning and carrying on so he could vent his righteous contempt. Well, she vowed stubbornly, he could wait. If only she could move. Amanda floundered like a newly foaled calf, and to her chagrin, Harmon came wordlessly to offer her a hand. She took it with an embarrassed gratitude, allowing him to haul her up on uncertain legs. She was forced to grip onto his forearm until the trembling in her limbs quieted. It was then Amanda noticed how hard he felt beneath her hand. All spare, tough Texan. The instant she released him, he stepped back to an impersonal distance.

"Here." He bent to snap off the fleshy leaf of a nearby plant. By squeezing it, a creamy liquid oozed into his palm. He dabbed it with his fingertips and reached out to touch the end of her sun-ravaged nose. The burning tightness of her sensitive skin vanished almost at once. "Spread some of this on your face and on your—wherever else you might need it." A deeper color seeped up beneath his tan as his gaze lowered, then abruptly shifted away. "I'll make up some biscuits."

Thinking how young and unexpectedly shy he appeared with that blush warming his cheeks, Amanda took the medicinal leaf off into the underbrush to see to herself. As she rubbed the soothing ointment into the tender misery of her backside, she blessed Harmon Bass for his silent understanding. The only thing that could possibly make her feel any better was a good long soak in a hot tub, but she would settle for what she had.

Hobbling gingerly back into camp, Amanda took a moment to survey their surroundings. She'd been too exhausted to notice much the night before. As she came up to the fire, she stopped and stared beyond, mesmerized by a sight so fantastic, she disbelieved what she was seeing.

"Ma'am? Are you all right?" Harm rose, alerted by the strangeness of her expression.

"Oh . . . my! Oh, Mr. Bass, what is that?"

He pivoted on his heel to follow her rapt gaze, then relaxed, empathizing with her awe. "Those are the Chisos, the Phantom Mountains."

A fitting name. The whole range seemed to float mysteriously on cushions of rose-colored mist against the morning's iridescent sky, its high peaks like castles built upon the clouds.

Amanda felt him at her side when he came to look upon the fantasy of nature from her perspective. They didn't touch, but the low pitch of his voice moved over her like a whispering caress.

"The Apache believe it is a refuge of ghosts and spirits. The place where rainbows go to wait for the rain. Where the big river is kept in a stone box, and water runs uphill, and the mountains float in the air except at night when they go away to play with the other mountains."

Amanda smiled. "There's that poetic soul again, Mr. Bass. One would almost think you're part Indian." She spoke without thought, and questions of consequence came too late.

"I am." The fierce way he said it startled her almost as much as the truth. "My mother was half Apache." The muscles of his face tightened as he observed her confusion of dismay. He turned away from her and stalked back to the fire. "Eat," came his hard command. "I'll saddle the horses."

Amanda crouched before the fire, blowing on her seared fingers as she pulled the biscuits apart. As she chewed thoughtfully, she watched him. Half-breed. She recalled the contemptuous way the man at the hotel had spoken it. She considered the portrait painted in the books she'd read, of a mixed-blood villain possessing the worst passions of both races without any of the virtues, without the pride of belonging to either side. A renegade loyal only to his own embittered greed and moved by dark lusts of the flesh. A quiver of panic shot through her, then was immediately stilled. A fearsome renegade who blushed at the mention of female anatomy?

"Ready?" he called flatly as he turned and caught her staring. The stiffness was back, bringing a taut rigidity to his features. "Unless you'd rather I take you back to Fort Davis."

No pride, her books had said. Why, Harmon Bass fairly seethed with it as his narrowed gaze pierced hers. A man's pride, not that of a single nationality. He waited, coiled tight, anger roiling beneath the steady surface. Expecting her disgust.

"Why on earth would I want to do that, Mr. Bass?" She tossed back the contents of her coffee cup with a casual air, grimacing at the strength of the unfamiliar drink. It collided in her stomach like a plummeting brick. She'd get used to the taste just as she'd get used to the facts surrounding Harmon's parentage. Amanda stood and made an impatient gesture. "I'm paying you to take me to my brother and I trust you'll do just that. I'm perfectly satisfied with our arrangement." She walked past him, refusing any degree of uneasiness. "Unless, of course, you can't bear the thought of another day of my conversation."

She looked over her shoulder in time to see his quicksilver smile.

"I've survived worse, Miss Duncan," he assured her with a touch of quiet humor. She liked him at that moment . . . very much.

"Well, Mr. Bass, the morning's wasting. Could you give me a boost up? I'm afraid my legs won't bend."

"Yes, ma'am."

Gritting her teeth, Amanda wrestled her foot up far enough to fit the stirrup. Then his hands were on her waist, careful in their grip, strong in their upward lift. She dragged her leg over Fandango's haunches and settled cautiously upon contoured leather. Her breath expelled in a hiss and she managed to smile as she took up the reins. One of his hands lingered at the curve of her lower back, the other resting upon her thigh. She didn't think he was aware of it, for suddenly, he jerked both away and strode to his own mount, swinging up with an enviable grace.

"Lead on, Mr. Bass."

Wordlessly, he did.

By late morning, they'd passed through Dagger Flats, where a forest of giant yuccas transformed the desert with their whitish flowers and cactus bloomed in sequence, painting streaks of pink, yellow, purple, red, and white across the seared land. There wasn't much time for talk as the wild beauty of the countryside and the treacherous nature of the trail vied for Amanda's attention. The horses picked their way along badly eroded gullies, and she was content to trust her guide and her mount while she clung to the precariously tipping saddle. The rugged walls of mountain rose with a majesty the expanding New York skyline couldn't rival. Here the colors were brilliant; the rocks a vivid red shading to mauve, the weathered scrubs of brushwood deeply and unexpectedly green. And there ahead was the taunting illusion of the Chisos, where clouds developed a depth of highlight and shadow, changing hue and form like patterns in a kaleidoscope. Unlike the flatlands she'd passed through, here the scenery was never tiresome and always a surprise. And it was cool. The spirit-sapping lethargy of the day before was gone, and Amanda found herself once again eager in her quest.

She had no doubt that Harmon would find her brother, and once that was accomplished, there would be an easy way to explain away the problem of his guilt. Then . . . what? Return to New York and her stuffy boarding school? To the endless parade of relatives who endured her because the conditions of her trust fund rewarded them well to give her a room but no real home or welcome? Perhaps that was something she and Randy could discuss when they were reunited. The fact that she made this trip should be enough to prove to him that she didn't need to be in the cosseting care of strangers. Strangers who had to be paid to show her kindness. They didn't need outsiders to make a family. They were a family, just the two of them, and she made a vow to allow no further separation once they were together again.

Where water runs uphill. The memory distracted her from thoughts of her brother.

It had made no sense when Harm said it, but she was learning that nothing in the Bend was quite what it seemed. Beneath her, Fandango began to wheeze and labor, as if struggling to climb while the ground appeared to be a gentle downward slope. She puzzled over it until she saw the stream and watched, amazed, as the current did, indeed, seem to run backward. Amanda reined in to study the odd phenomenon. Her own breathing was strained and her head felt light.

"What is this place, Mr. Bass?"

He pulled in his mount and smiled at her with a mysterious glint of humor. "Tornillo Creek. Look behind you."

Amanda did and she gasped, grabbing for the saddle horn as she was struck by sudden vertigo. Looking back was like looking down into a bottomless hole. The trail plunged downward.

"We've climbed over twenty-five hundred feet in the last half mile," Harm told her. She stared at him blankly.

"How can that be? I thought we were going downhill."

"It's an illusion. Look at the brush along the trail. None of it grows straight up and down."

Amanda did and was, again, amazed. The tough Texas shrubs grew at an angle, reinforcing the optical trick that the trail was flat when it was actually steep as a staircase.

"Let the horses catch their wind for a minute, then we'll get moving." As he spoke, Harm turned easily in the saddle, looping one leg over the horn to dangle casually while he reached for his water. Amanda did the same, savoring the tinny taste from her canteen as she studied him; Harmon Bass, as much an illusion as this deceiving trail. She wondered if the mild manners and soft drawl, his slight stature and unarmed stance, lulled the observer into believing something that was not real. He caught onto her scrutiny and was quick to settle back into his saddle, lifting up the reins. His narrowed stare was almost unfriendly, as if warning her to keep her distance. Amanda gave up trying to figure his subtle shifts of mood as she urged Fandango to follow.

By the waning hours of afternoon, they were climbing into the foothills of the ghostly Chisos. Stone that shone bright yellow at midday began the return shift to resplendent reds with the lowering of the sun. They'd scared up a few lean fan-tailed deer, but the sudden unmistakable sound of cattle lowing took Amanda by surprise.

In the sparsely wooded Basin area where grasses grew deep and thick, hundreds of head of Texas cattle grazed and cropped on drooping juniper branches. Sighting several mounted cowboys, Amanda started forward, only to have Harm snag Fandango's bridle.

"You can't go down there."

"Why?" she demanded. "They might have seen Randy."

"I'll ask. You stay here, out of sight."

"But—"

But he was already headed down the rocky path and out into the open, where he was spotted almost at once by the herd's outriders. Several men straightened from a small camp fire and turned his way, their expressions guarded, their eyes touching on his lack of armament and the quality of his horse. And then their gazes left him altogether to fix with lean intensity. Harm twisted in his saddle but he knew what he'd see: Amanda Duncan riding after him in careless disregard to his command. His jaw clenched as she drew up beside him and smiled, actually smiled, as if quite pleased with her defiance. He wanted to beat her with a good stout stick but instead turned an amiable face toward the cowboys.

" 'Afternoon. Mind if we ride into camp?"

"Ride ahead," one of them called back in response to that bit of range courtesy. "Can't offer much in the way of grub. Down to 'bout our last turn of coffee." He was smiling, but his hand was close to his sidearm and his eyes were making free with the damp contours of Amanda's shirtwaist.

"Got some extra if you'd like to trade for a little talk."

The men stiffened to a one. Then the speaker drawled, "That all you willing to trade?"

Harm's smile never faltered from its mild bend, but he angled his horse closer to Amanda's. He chose to ignore the comment, and for that, she shot him a challenging stare. "See," he said calmly, "me and my wife's looking for her brother. Passed this way, oh, 'bout a week ago, I'd say, him and another man riding with him."

"He's tall, blond, wears a thin moustache, an easterner, like me," Amanda supplied helpfully. Then, she gave a start as one of the cowboys eased up on her right to put his gloved hand on her knee. She jerked away, causing Fandango to shy and bump Harm's gray.

"What's a pretty little thing like you doing shacked up to a breed?" the man with the bold hand asked. He reached for her reins and her gaze cut over to Harm's, insisting that he take some action. His soft-spoken words weren't what she had in mind.

"Now, boys, we don't want no trouble here. We were just looking for those two fellers, but I can see you haven't seen them, so we'll be on our way."

Amanda's dark eyes flashed fire. She was appalled by his meek attitude. As she pulled her rein from the grinning cowhand, she snapped, "Perhaps you don't know who you're dealing with."

"And who's that, ma'am?"

Ignoring the warning shake of Harm's head, she blustered, *The* Harmon Bass. Why, any man with half a grain of education knows who he is and would know enough not to mess with him."

The cowboys frowned warily, then exchanged smirky looks as they studied the compact little half-breed Texas nobody sitting with his hip bare. And they weren't half as impressed by her words as they were by the fit of her clothes.

"Harmon Bass," the first spokesman rolled out leisurely. "Hear that, boys? A real dangerous man. A legend, hear-tell. Guess we wouldn't want no part a' tanglin' with the likes a' him. Sorry if we was outta line there, mister. Didn't recognize you."

"No problem." Harm cut loose his ration of coffee beans and tossed them down. "Thanks, anyway. Enjoy the coffee."

"Oh, we aim to."

Amanda was still stewing when Harm grabbed her reins and jerked Fandango around. He didn't release the lead until they'd climbed up out of the Basin into the anonymity of the thick scrub trees. Then he turned on her like the cold snap of a blue norther.

"When I tell you to do something, you do it. I'm not talking just because I like the sound of my voice."

"I don't know why you're so mad at me," she declared angrily. "I'm the one who should be mad. Here I'm paying you good money and you back down at the first sign of trouble. Some hero. *The* Harmon Bass. They were laughing at you. Don't you care? What does it take to get you to fight?"

"I fight when I can win," he told her with a curious quiet. "And I don't let pride make me foolish when I have to watch out for a little girl who doesn't know how to follow directions."

"They didn't tell us anything."

"And they weren't likely to, either. Not when they were running stolen cattle down into Mexico." He goaded his horse forward with the thump of his heels. His thoughts were hot with fury. Because she'd disobeyed him. Because she'd placed them in terrible jeopardy. Not from cattle thieves, but from men who were hungry for the sight of a woman like Amanda.

And because part of him wanted to play Harmon Bass the Hero in her dreamy eyes.

Daylight melted into night. Harm had wanted to put a

few more miles between them and the cow camp, but he couldn't risk working a dark trail with an inexperienced rider following. Amanda was angry with him. She climbed down off her horse and began stalking toward the privacy of the underbrush without a word. Her silence said more than a spew of criticism.

"Don't go too far."

She didn't even slow at his quiet warning.

He'd built a small fire and almost at once began to feel the loss of the coffee. It was a weakness in his mixed blood that made him crave the harsh white man's brew. He would do without it, just as he'd do without sleep tonight, and both deprivations had him grumpy when Amanda finally returned to sit on the far side of the fire. She wouldn't look at him or speak to him. He should have considered it a blessing.

"Here."

She caught the withered strip he tossed her and handled it gingerly. "What is this?"

"Dinner."

Amanda eyed the jerked meat suspiciously but hunger overcame doubt. She bit hard and wrestled a chunk loose, then began an aggressive chewing. Not one to keep her annoyance contained for any length of time, she found herself glowering at her guide. His stoic manner was an irritant. Had he no sense of shame? Didn't he mind her thinking him a coward? If he didn't already feel those things, she was determined to provoke them.

"Not much in the way of a meal, Mr. Bass. I thought I paid you well to buy provisions."

He glanced up, unperturbed by her nettling. "I like to travel light, Miss Duncan. I hunt up my own chuck. You won't starve."

"I'd rather starve than eat any more of this." Petulantly, she flung the jerky into the fire. His black brows lowered a notch. So did his voice.

"Am I supposed to offer to ride the eighty miles back into Fort Davis to fetch you a hot evening meal? Is that what *The* Harmon Bass would do?"

"I wouldn't want to inconvenience you."

"Who let you loose?"

His abrupt question set her back. "What do you mean?"

"How'd you get down here? Who's supposed to be watching out for you? Do folks in New York City allow little girls like you to just roam free?"

"I'm not a little girl, Mr. Bass," she corrected tautly. "I've been watching out for myself and my brother since our parents died when I was seven. The rest of my family doesn't care what I do as long as they have access to my money."

Her bitterness shocked him and the loneliness of it touched a chord of understanding clear down to his soul. His annoyance quieted to a gentle sympathy, but he wouldn't let her see it.

"What about your fancy school? They just let you pack up and head to Texas all by yourself?"

She smiled. It was a small, tight gesture, one befitting somebody much older. "I doubt that they would have approved had I asked their permission."

"Just snuck off, did you?" He marveled at the thought and at the courage it must have taken for a sheltered city girl of seventeen to embark on such a journey.

"*Escaped* is a more apt description. I gathered up all the money I could get without arousing suspicions, packed a few things, and jumped on the first train west the minute I got your reply."

Her words made him feel suddenly guilty, as if he'd somehow encouraged her impetuous act. And he didn't

51

want to feel responsible for her. "Doesn't anyone know where you are, Miss Duncan?"

She met his curious gaze directly. There was a weary candor to her reply. "I think they're probably glad that I'm gone." The wry smile returned. "At least until they find out that I left instructions with my solicitor that all my monies go to charity if something happens to me."

When he spoke, Harm's tone was neutral. "I wouldn't have figured you for such a hard piece of work, Miss Duncan."

"And I wouldn't have figured you for a coward, Mr. Bass."

He drew his large-bladed knife from its sheath behind his back. A deft movement reversed it in his hand and a quick flick of his wrist sent to flying toward her. She gasped as it whizzed by, embedding itself in the darkness behind her. Harm uncoiled his feet and stood, circling the fire as she stared up through wide, uncertain eyes. He strode past her, into the shadows, and reached down to retrieve his knife. As he straightened, she saw something long and thick hanging down from the heavy blade, extending from shoulder height all the way to the ground.

With a squeal of alarm, she was on her feet, scrambling to a safe distance.

"Want me to cook this up for your dinner, Miss Amanda?"

"Mr. Bass, please tell me that isn't a snake!"

"Diamondback. Nice one, too. Skin ought to fetch a pretty price over in El Paso. Always a fool looking to buy a good length of pattern to wrap around his hat." When he started toward her, she scuttled back even farther, but he paid her no mind as he carried the monstrous thing over to the spread of his blankets. Amanda shuddered. The rattler was as big around as the calf of her leg. Harm stretched it out in front of him and began to slit it open.

She watched with a morbid fascination, standing, arms wrapped tightly about herself as if to hold the shivers in.

"You afraid of snakes, ma'am?" He glanced up at the casual delivery of that question, watching her features pucker.

"I loathe them, Mr. Bass."

"I wouldn't worry on it. There's only five varieties of rattler in these parts, not to mention the copperheads."

Her gaze began a panicked scanning of the shadowed ground. Every stick was suddenly suspect. "Are there any more of them nearby?"

"Could be he had some big brothers or sisters. Most of the time they're obliging enough to let you know they're in the neighborhood. But not always. They start waking up about now to go out looking for dinner. Best shake out your blankets before you go to bed."

He laid aside the freshly scraped skin and began skewering the meat on a thin branch.

"Surely you're not going to eat that."

"Why, yes, ma'am, I am. Out here, you eat anything that doesn't eat you first."

"Is that civilized people or just you, Mr. Bass?"

"That's anyone who wants to survive, Miss Duncan. Texas land promises less and gives more than any other. It's all in taking what she gives you. Turn horses loose and they'll get fat as hogs on bunch grass. A hungry man can live off the land like a king if he knows what to look for."

"I'd—"

"Sooner starve," he finished for her. "You'd be of a different mind right quick if you knew what real hunger was, ma'am. And I'm not talking about that delicate little rumbling you get when the cook is a tad slow bringing your platters to the table."

"What do you know about it, Mr. Bass?"

In that soft, chill voice, the same one he'd used when

telling her about the first man he'd killed, he said, "Ma'am, I know everything there is to know."

And she believed him.

She stood, nervously surveying the thicket around them. His sudden words startled her.

"Want to try some of this?"

He was extending the kebob of snake. Her expression pinched and paled.

"No, thank you."

He shrugged and pulled off a piece for himself, chewing with considerable relish. Amanda swallowed hard.

It was very black outside the circle of their camp fire. She was bone-weary and anxious for rest. Her toe prodded the limp covers. Nothing moved.

"Could we have a bigger fire, Mr. Bass?"

"Thinking about them snakes, ma'am?" he drawled. He wasn't polite enough to try to conceal his amusement.

"No," she snapped. "It's cold and my blankets are thin."

"You can come on over here and nudge in next to me if you want." He said it easily, as if lying down with a man who was nearly a stranger weren't the least bit improper. And because he was so nonchalant about it, Amanda got irrationally angry.

"Thank you, Mr. Bass, but I'll make do with the blankets."

"Suit yourself." He finished the last of the rattler and added the stick to the fire. Then he watched her ease down atop her bedroll, as wary as a man angling his head into a lion's mouth. He didn't feel guilty about scaring her half to death. He was looking for a way to get her close at hand for the night without having to explain himself. The truth was much scarier than her imagined night prowlers. He searched for an excuse to lure her to his side of the fire where he could protect her better.

"Another thing, ma'am," he added as an afterthought. "Don't be alarmed if you hear rustling during the night."

There was a long pause, then a faint, "What kind of rustling, Mr. Bass?"

"The kind bats make. These caves in the Chisos host the world's only yellow bats."

"Bats?"

She was up and dragging her bedroll around the fire. Wordlessly, Amanda spread it out beside him and bundled down inside it. She had her back to him. It was as stiff as a mountain range. Slowly, as fatigue wore down the sharp edges of tension, she sighed and wiggled and finally, scooted back until her cocooned shape was fitted along his ribs and thigh.

"G'night, Miss Amanda," he said softly.

"Good night, Harmon," she mumbled back.

Chapter Four

Rough, masculine fingers clamped down over her mouth.

Her scream effectively smothered, Amanda tried to rise up but a man's hard frame angled atop her, pinning her helplessly to the ground.

"Shhh!"

She went still. Her eyes opened. It was minutes before dawn. Everything was in sleepy shadow. Everything but the brilliant blue of Harmon's intense stare, only inches above hers.

"Quiet."

She nodded, and his hand gentled and finally lifted. "What is it?" she whispered. Danger was telegraphed by the tautness of his body pressed over hers. He didn't answer, not exactly.

"Stay down and stay quiet. I'll take care of it."

"Take care of wh—?"

But he rolled off her and was gone, a shadow himself amongst the thick morning mist.

Amanda lay motionless, her heart pounding, her senses alert for any movement. She was aware of the cold now that Harm's covering warmth was absent and she shivered, partly from chill, partly from fright. She bit her lips, forcing down the need to call out to him, to ask what was going on. Then she heard them and she knew.

"Ain't that a pretty sight."

Low, coarse laughter. Her eyes squeezed tightly together.

"Shh. Doan wake her up. Not yet."

"You boys track down the little feller whilst I comfort his widow."

Harm had left her! He'd run off and left her to these men!

Her eyes flew open and widened in recognition. It was the cowboy who'd mocked her bold speech. He wasn't laughing now. There was something altogether different darkening his expression.

" 'Morning, ma'am. Don't bother to get up. You're fine right where you are."

She couldn't move.

"Where's your husband?"

She tried to speak but the words came out like a whimper.

"Doan you worry none. We'll bring him back. For burying."

"What do you want?" It was a hoarse whisper.

His chuckle was ugly. "Now, what does any man want when he gets an eyeful of a woman like you. Doan fret. We aim to be real nice."

We.

Amanda started screaming.

The cowboy's lustful grin froze into a grimace. He glanced down in surprise at the hilt of Harm's knife protruding from his chest. Amanda recognized the glaze of death when it came over his eyes, and she was quick to scramble up and away as he began to fall.

"Harmon!" She ran, wildly searching the brush for a sign of him.

"Amanda, get down!"

She saw him as he stepped into full view. There was a disquieting calm to his features, almost a void of emotion as he pumped up the lever-action carbine he held in his hands. She didn't heed his warning. Instead, she raced toward him. By then, the others saw him, too and his carbine boomed in answer to their fire. Just as she hurled herself into the open circle of his left arm, Amanda felt a numbing smack to her backside, as if someone had struck her with a length of timber. She cried out and then his arm was firm about her, hugging her close, pushing her behind him. He worked the lever-action single-handedly, sweeping the sawed-off barrel across the clearing of their campsite as regularly paced explosions rocked through Amanda's ears. She clung to him, face buried against his shoulder, eyes screwed up tight, quaking with each volley of sound. Until all was quiet and her mewling cries could be heard.

"It's all right."

His soft assurance fractured the last of her control. Her arms cinched up around his neck as her slender body shivered against his. She could feel his cheek pushing hard into the spill of her hair and the frantic rush of his breathing as it stirred the loose tendrils.

"Harmon?"

"Shhh. It's all right."

"I thought you'd left me."

That weak little admission brought both of his arms around her in a crushing band. "I would never let them hurt you. I'd sooner die than let them hurt you. You know that, Becky. I'd never let them touch you. Never."

Becky?

It was then she realized he was shaking worse than she was.

"Harm?" She pried away, rubbing the wetness from

58

her eyes. His were closed up tight, seeping dampness, too. That shocked her into forgetting her fears. "Are you all right, Mr. Bass?"

He inhaled sharply, as if someone had shaken him awake, and his eyes blinked open. He looked at her for a moment with such confusion. Then it was gone. His voice was a gruff growl.

"I thought I told you to stay down."

He put her away from him and began stuffing shells back into the hot chamber of his rifle as he strode toward the sprawl of dead men. The blankness was back in his face as he went from man to man, nudging them with his toe. Until one of them moaned.

He'd been shot in the stomach, a great gaping wound that gave no chance of survival and a promise of terrible pain. His dazed eyes flickered and fixed on the somber grimness of Harm's.

"Help me, friend. I'm in a bad way."

"I'm not your friend, and if you want me to see to you, you'd best be coming up with some answers."

"A doctor. I need a doctor."

"I'll see you get what you need. Talk."

The cowboy's head tossed restlessly. "I ain't telling you nothing, you sonuvabitch. You shot my insides all to hell."

Harm knelt down, his knee pressing on the man's torn abdomen. The injured man shrieked.

"A blond man riding with another feller. An easterner. Hard to miss. Talk to me."

"Yeah, we seen him. God . . . I need a doctor!"

"When? Where were they headed?"

Amanda came closer, her breath suspended. She tried not to see the gore. Randy. This man had seen her brother.

The cowboy was coughing up blood. Harm waited

patiently for his reply. "Couple a' days ago. They was headed for Terlingua."

Amanda crouched down awkwardly. The numbness hadn't left her. It seemed to be creeping down her leg. She had no time to think about it. "The man with my brother . . . what did he look like? Did you know him?"

"Seen him around. Hard case. Doan know his name." The dying man started to wheeze. A horrible gurgling sound. Amanda stood. The man might be a cattle thief and a killer, but she couldn't bear the thought of any of God's creatures in so much agony.

"The doctor," the cowboy was pleading faintly. "That's all I know. You promised to see to me." His bloody fingers clutched at Harm's sleeve.

"Yes, I did."

As Harm straightened, Amanda began walking toward the horses. The report from his carbine jerked her to a standstill. For the longest time she stood, trembling, unable to look around to see for herself the helpless man Harmon Bass had just slain in cold blood.

"Get your gear together," Harm told her as he went to roll his rifle up into his bedroll. He yanked his knife free and wiped its blade on the shirt of the man he'd killed with it. "Get a move on. We don't want to be here when their pards come looking for 'em."

Amanda was in shock. Even prepared for it, the sight of the cowboy with his face blown away by Harm's bullet sent her into spasms of shaking. "You killed him."

Harm looked up as if surprised that she'd make such a big deal of it. "He came looking to kill me and do worse to you. Don't figure I owed him any favors. He was dead, anyway."

"You gave him your word." Her dulled mind kept repeating the catechisms from her western dime novel bibles: A hero was noble in his treatment of friend and

60

fallen foe, a true champion of good. What she'd witnessed wasn't noble, it was . . . savage.

"And I kept it. Told him I'd see to him and I did. Kinder to plant him here than to drag him through a day of hell just to have him up and die someplace else."

Amanda didn't move. She just kept getting paler and paler. Harm got impatient.

"What did you expect me to do? Grow up, little girl. Pity and mercy are luxuries you can't afford out here. Unless you want to be as dead as he is and never see your brother again, you'd best be moving."

He saddled the horses with a brisk efficiency. When Amanda went to gather her bedroll, she discovered it caked with the blood of her attacker. She knew right then she'd freeze before she'd wrap herself up in it. She'd leave it for his burial shroud.

Harm was already mounted and waiting for her. She hesitated, and the dark look of annoyance returned to his features.

"Aren't you going to bury them?" A decent, Christian man always paused in the midst of the most desperate circumstances to provide that final service for the souls of the slain. But not Harmon Bass.

"Let their own kind bury them." He jerked his reins and started off down the trail, never glancing back at the carnage he'd wrought or to see if she followed.

They rode hard. Harm didn't say so, but she guessed he was worried about the dead men's friends. Disoriented and slightly dizzy, Amanda gripped the saddle horn and trusted Fandango to keep up the pace. Her own discomfort had grown steadily over the past miles but she was at a loss as to how to approach her guide with her predicament. She thought she could endure it stoically until they reached Terlingua, but every jounce, every jostle, was pure agony.

"Could we stop for a while, Mr. Bass?"

"I'd rather we made Blue Creek first. It's not far."
Then he nudged his horse on and it was too late to say
anything more. Amanda gritted her teeth and followed.

Blue Creek ran on the western slope of the Chisos
below the tree line, where bunch grass was thick and
greasewood threatened to take over. Harm reined in. He
was fairly certain they weren't being trailed by the thieves
out for evens. He'd been careful to leave little or no path
for them to follow. He was tired, though he could easily
go on, but the horses couldn't and Amanda looked ready
to topple. It was a good place to set up a temporary camp.
He rolled down from the saddle, planning to get Amanda
settled in before he went in search of fresh game. She
deserved a good hot meal after the morning she'd been
through.

When she stayed atop Fandango, he cast a curious
glance. Then he looked more closely and began to frown.
Her features were flushed and wet with perspiration. She
sat the leather in a lopsided slump. Something was wrong.

"Miss Duncan, climb on down. We'll be here for a
time. You can wash up in the creek."

"Mr. Bass . . . Mr. Bass, I don't think I can move."

Thinking she was crippled from three hard days of
riding, he went to offer up his hands and a slight smile of
sympathy. No more than that. He hadn't asked her to
come along and wasn't responsible for the tender state of
her posterior. She put her hands on his shoulders and
leaned toward him, letting him catch her at the waist to
ease her down. Her fingers tightened, digging deep. That
pinching grip was the only thing that kept her on her feet.
She sagged into him, hanging on, holding in the need to
weep.

"Miss Amanda? What—?"

Then he was looking at the damp crimson smeared on

his fingertips. He pushed her back, turning her so he could see for himself where buckshot had torn a pattern of small oozing holes in the seat of her split skirt.

"You've been shot!"

"I know that, Mr. Bass," she sniffled with an attempt at bravery.

"Why didn't you say something? Why didn't you tell me?"

It was no use. The tears let go in a flood, racing down cheeks so hot with humiliation and hurt she was surprised they didn't evaporate on the spot.

"What was I supposed to say? I didn't listen to you. I did something stupid and I got my pride peppered with buckshot. If I'd just listened, none of this would have happened. Those m—men would all still be alive."

"Amanda." He said her name quietly but couldn't think of any other words that would give comfort. Instead, he put an awkward hand to her shoulder, then flinched when she threw herself upon his chest with great wailing sobs. He encircled her quaking form with caution. He couldn't tell her she wasn't to blame. She was. She knew it. Such sentiments would be empty. So he held her, gingerly at first, then with increasing care. Again, he was taken by the delicate feel of her, by the softness, the vulnerability, as foreign to him as the tender curls of emotion stirring at the thought of her pain. He wanted to hold her longer, tighter, but there was no wisdom in those desires.

"Amanda, we'd best see to those bullets."

She rubbed her face against his shirtfront, muttering, "I'm so embarrassed, I could just die."

He smiled faintly. "I don't think they're fatal. But they probably hurt like the very devil."

She continued to lean into him, her arms lax about his middle, her forehead touching his shoulder. He allowed it. "I thought I could make it to Terlingua where a doctor could—"

"There's no doctor in Terlingua."

She looked up at him, wide-eyed in dismay. "What?"

"Buried a couple of months ago. Haven't replaced him that I know of."

"Then what am I—"

"I'll see to you."

She stared at him, then pulled back. Discomfort flamed in her face and darkened her gaze. "Like you took care of that cowboy? No thank you, Mr. Bass." She planned to stalk pridefully away. The best she could manage was a catching limp that did, indeed, hurt like the very devil.

Harm approached the situation reasonably. "We've got a day's ride to town. If you're not full of blood poisoning by then, maybe you could find someone to tend you. You gonna waltz on into the first saloon and ask if anyone has the know-how to take a load of shot out of your rump?" His cool gaze swept her form appraisingly. "Bet you'd get a lot of volunteers."

"I am glad you find this all so vastly amusing, Mr. Bass." She turned to glare at him.

It hurt to keep the muscles of his face sober.

Amanda continued her hobbling. Her eyes watered. She knew there was no way other than belly down in the saddle that she'd make the ride into Terlingua. But the alternative . . .

"Have you done this sort of thing before?" she challenged abruptly.

"Lots of times." That was true. Sort of. He'd taken bullets from the arms and legs of the Rangers, from several badmen, and even from his own thigh. But that wasn't quite the same thing as extracting shot from Amanda Duncan's backside.

She glowered at him, trying to discern his mood. He

looked properly somber. She couldn't read what danced behind those squinted eyelids. "I suppose I don't have much choice."

"No, ma'am."

"Let's get it done, then."

"Yes, ma'am."

He built a fire and tucked the blade of his wicked knife up against the flames. Amanda tried to concentrate on the pain instead of the awkward circumstance. She watched him wash up in the clear waters of the creek. His expression was bland, betraying no sign that he was taking an unholy enjoyment in her situation. She would just have to trust him. She wondered if there'd be more dignity in throwing herself into the creek to drown.

He'd put the knife aside to cool, then sat cross-legged upon the hard-packed Texas ground. "I'm ready."

She wasn't. If there were a way she could have jumped in the saddle and ridden hell-bent-for-leather in any direction, she would have. She was mortified. He was waiting, unsmiling, with a capable patience. She swore under her breath and came to him.

"Where do you want me, Mr. Bass?"

"Right here." He patted his denim-clad thighs. "Stretch on out."

The fact that it hurt so much to lower herself into the humbling position helped her not to dwell upon it. Carrying her weight upon her toes, her forearms, and on Harm's lap was, without a doubt, the most dreadful moment of her life. Until he said quietly, "Peel down them drawers so I can see what I'm doing."

"I think I'd rather have you shoot me, Mr. Bass." However, she undid the band of her skirt and shimmied it over the throbbing curve of her bottom. Exposed to the open air and his blue-eyed stare, Amanda hid her face in her folded arms.

"Five pellets," Harm announced calmly enough. He surveyed the pale contour of her seat, trying to remember to breathe normally. "Nice tight pattern."

"Get on with it, Mr. Bass," she gritted out. "And don't put your hands any place they're not supposed to be."

He pulled his palms back from making contact with her white skin.

Agitated by the delay, she snapped, "Is there a problem?"

"No, ma'am." He couldn't very well tell her that his hands were suddenly sweat-soaked and shaky. "Just trying to decide how best to proceed."

"Just hurry. It's not like you've never seen a woman's bare backside before."

He smiled at that. The truth might surprise her. Or scare her half to death.

"Hang on. I can't promise it won't hurt."

Amanda held her breath. His hand settled warm and firm upon the top of her thigh to anchor her down. Her gasp became a yelp.

"Easy. Easy now. Don't jump around. It'll just take a second. There. There's one."

A round pellet dropped in front of her face. Her breath gushed out shakily.

"Going for two," he warned, and she sucked in air. "There's two. Doing fine, Amanda. Just hang on for me."

As if she had something to hang on to. Her fingers cramped around clumps of grass and her toes dug furrows in the dirt. It took all her concentration not to squirm upon his knees. As if she could. His grip was like iron, holding her steady. He was quick and expert with the knife. The third pellet rolled in the grass.

"All right. Here's number four. That's a lucky number."

"Not for me," she groaned.

He chuckled as he probed for it. He felt her tense and tremble, but she didn't cry out. Gutsy female, Harm thought proudly. Most men wouldn't endure so heroically. "There's four. Last one. How you doing?"

"As well as can be expected, Mr. Bass."

"Good girl. Just think on what story you're going to tell on your wedding night when your husband asks about these scars."

She'd started to laugh when he inserted the blade in search of the last bit of lead. Her jaw gripped hard. She fought down the whimpers of pain but they escaped in a wavery moan.

"This one's a little bit deeper than the others. I'll have to go again. Don't move now."

"Harmon . . . ahhh!"

"There! All done. Got 'em all."

She sagged across his lap, panting softly. Now that his focus wasn't trained on the tiny sites of entry, Harm noticed the placement of his hand wedged, innocent in intention, up against the heat of her, with his thumb riding the soft curve of her buttock. He didn't move. So close to all the moist secrets of the female form. It was a curiosity he'd never succumbed to, had never felt quite so keenly as at this moment. He wanted to . . . to touch her. He suddenly wanted to know all the forbidden things from which he held himself apart. He wanted to learn them from her, from the strong-headed, strong-hearted Amanda. Realization brought a hot heaviness to his groin, and rather than alarm her with the obvious direction of his thoughts, he carefully moved his hand and gave Amanda a push.

"Go soak in the creek. It'll take the pain away."

The moment her knees hit the ground, she was tugging up her clothing, wincing as she did. She couldn't look at him as she mumbled, "Thank you, Mr. Bass, but I don't—"

"There's nobody within miles, ma'am, and I promise to keep my eyes to myself."

She glanced toward the water, watching it shimmer in enticing little ripples. She'd never felt quite so dirty in all her life or quite so miserable. Amanda sighed. "I'd give a hundred dollars for a nice bar of soap about now."

"Just have to know where to look."

She followed him with a perplexed gaze as he searched among the underbrush for the plant he sought. She remembered the soothing balm he'd gotten from the leaves, but he was digging, unearthing roots. Those he placed on a flat rock, dicing them into pieces with his sharp blade, then grinding the bits beneath another stone until mashed. He scooped the pulp into his hands and started for the creek.

"C'mon."

She limped after him.

At the stream's end, he knelt and mixed water with a portion of the pulp. Rubbing the pulp between his palms created a surprising amount of lather. He raised his hand so she could smell it. The scent was mild and not at all unpleasant.

"Not very fancy, but it cleans just as good."

"I owe you a hundred dollars, Mr. Bass."

"Just tack it onto my fee."

He smiled then, and she found herself responding with her own as if they were old and dear friends. An odd thought considering she didn't know what it was like to have friends other than her brother and the few acquaintances at school. She'd never been in one place long enough to cultivate them or to decide if they liked her for herself or for her wealth. None of those short-term associations touched upon the companionable warmth she shared with this unlikely man.

Still smiling, she said, "Go away, Mr. Bass. I should like to take a bath and rid myself of about two inches of Texas dust."

"Yes, ma'am. I'll see to the horses." He rose then, leaving the plant pulp in her palms, and strode back toward their crude camp.

Amanda waited, suspiciously eyeing the underbrush while the teasing sound of running water lapped away at her inhibitions. Finally, it didn't matter if he was peeping at her through the bushes. Let him look! She couldn't resist the thought of cleanliness another second.

The water felt delicious against her sun-baked skin. She sank to her knees, where the level came just below her shoulders, and knew of moment of pure heaven before she began the task of scrubbing up a lather. Grime and sweat rinsed off in sheets and was swept away on the current, leaving her wonderfully refreshed. She took down her hair and soaped it generously, letting it float on the surface behind her in a dark, silky ripple. And as Harm promised, the pain eased. If it were possible, she would have stretched out naked to be baked dry in the sun, but even though she didn't see him when she glanced toward shore, she knew Harmon was up there somewhere and he'd seen quite enough of her for one day.

It was then she noticed something else.

"Mr. Bass?" she called out furiously. "Where are my clothes?"

"I was just rinsing them clean along with my things."

His voice came from behind her. She spun, sinking deeper into the water. He was downstream, kneeling on the edge of the creek bed as he soaped what could only be her chemise. And she thought she'd experienced the depths of embarrassment before. Here was a man handling her intimate attire! And . . . and what a man!

Harm had stripped to the waist. Black hair was slicked back and plastered wetly against his skull. Sleek bronze skin gleamed as sunlight refracted off droplets of moisture that remained after his hurried washing. She had guessed at his strength of compact body but here it was, displayed in the powerful evidence of bunching muscle and taut corded sinew. It took her a moment to recover from an odd breathlessness and remember her complaint.

"I appreciate the thought, but please be so kind as to return them immediately."

He didn't look up. "If you want to get out, wrap yourself in that blanket. It'll only take a few minutes for things to dry once I spread 'em out in full sun."

Amanda frowned. She did like the idea of clean clothes. She'd been naive not to pack more than her single set. She'd assumed they would be traveling between points of civilization where she could replenish her wardrobe, not guessing those points to be days apart. She didn't like the thought of creeping out of the stream in her altogether to where he'd left the blanket folded. Amanda started easing toward the shallows. Harm didn't glance in her direction. Boldly, she darted as rapidly as her sore behind would allow to snatch the coarse blanket around her. Shivering despite the heat of the day, she began walking toward camp.

"Watch where you step."

She shot him a look, but he was still busy with the wash. Maybe he was more gentleman than savage after all.

Sitting down was out of the question, so with blanket tucked about her, Amanda stretched out on her belly to watch Harmon Bass. She'd never seen so much bare man before. The sight intrigued her. With his dark coloring and his hard build, he looked like something wild and dangerous. She knew he was. The way he'd killed those men. The way he'd looked while doing it; so cold, so passionless. A shiver passed through her. She wasn't exactly afraid of him. He'd been too gentle with her for her to think he'd do her injury. But he wasn't the docile little cowboy she'd first believed him, either. So what was he?

Then it occurred to her. He was *The* Harmon Bass. Her novels may have exaggerated in description but not in deed. He'd reacted with a swift, ruthless justice when it was unavoidable. He was a man of courage and honor, with an independent pride and a fierceness of spirit few would recognize at first glance. She hadn't. She'd been too disappointed in the lack of physical flash and social polish to note the true merit of the man. She must have been blind.

He came up from the creek, his arms draped with wet things, and something in the way she looked at him stopped him in his tracks. Suddenly wary, he began to spread their clothing over the low brush to dry. She tried not to blush at the sight of her perforated drawers hanging between his shirt and socks.

"If you want a hot meal, I'm going to have to leave you alone for a little while. Do you know anything about guns, Miss Duncan?"

"I know they kill people, Mr. Bass."

"Could you, if you had to?"

She stared up at him and answered with unswerving candor. "I don't know that I could."

"Let's hope you don't have to find out." He strode to his gear and jerked his carbine free. When he straightened, she saw that his feet were bare and that his denims clung damply to his sturdy thighs. They must have been washed while he was still in them. He had a strong, graceful stride, and she wondered how much he resembled his Apache relatives. She supposed he must have

71

inherited the animal fluidity along with his swarthy looks. When he knelt down beside her, she bundled the blanket tight and sat up, careful to keep her weight to one side. "Here."

She took the rifle with a dainty distaste. "I didn't think you owned a gun."

"I don't like them. Wouldn't have a hand piece. But when I want to stop a man, I intend to see he stays stopped, and this will do it."

"So I recall."

For some reason, the acid drip of her disdain riled him. He wasn't one to go explaining himself. In fact, Amanda had hauled more words out of him than he'd spoken in a lifetime. But suddenly, there was a need to make her understand. To erase that haunted shadow of disgust from her big brown eyes.

"I'm a tracker, not a killer. I get paid to find folks, not gun them down."

"I see. Tell that to those five men back there."

"Happen I think more of my life than theirs, and I'm not such a fool as to let them shoot me down. You were the one spoiling for a fight, little girl, and I but obliged you. Don't go blaming me if you lost your taste for it. I could have spared the bloodshed by hying outta there and leaving you for them. They might not have killed you. Not right off, anyway."

His words brought back the memory of hard lust in the cowboy's stare. She clutched at the carbine. No, she admitted to herself. She didn't value the stranger's life over what he had planned for her. Her gaze sobered. "I thank you for what you did, for what you saved me from. But I can't like it."

"I'm not asking you to like it. Now, pay attention whilst I show you how this works."

She watched him guide her through the motions of

72

firing the carbine, trying not to wonder if she could actually use it, if she would have used it had she been holding it when the cowboy came at her.

"Keep that with you and keep a watch on the horses. Shoot at anything you hear approaching the camp."

"But what if it's you?"

"You won't hear me." He went back to his gear and slipped his bare feet into a pair of hard-soled moccasins.

"Aren't you going to take your horse?"

"I'm going hunting, not on a trip to the mercantile."

On foot, bare-chested, with just a knife. She stared at him in awe. "Be careful." The soft warning just slipped out. He stared back, an odd expression on his face. It might have been a smile but she didn't think so. "And bring back something that has four legs and no rattles."

"Yes, ma'am." White teeth flashed against bronze skin. Then he was serious once more. "You be careful. Stay alert and don't let anything into camp."

"I promise, Mr. Bass. I'll keep my eyes open."

But she didn't.

Chapter Five

She was asleep.

Curled up in his blankets, her honey-blond hair loose, one long slender leg bent at the knee and bared nearly to the hip. Beneath one lax hand was his carbine.

He stood for a long time staring down at her with the carcass of the deer he'd slain and gutted still draped along his shoulders. Fierce emotions shook through him, so powerful they were almost unrecognizable. Fury was the first to separate itself as he stared down at her, she so carelessly unaware in slumber. Then came fear, rising in terrible black waves. He thought of what he might have come back to find and sickness overwhelmed him. Then there was the guilt; remembered guilt and dreadful blame, echoing up from his past.

I should have been there. I should have kept it from happening. I should have been able to do something.

Those were harsh, soul-torturing emotions, but with them was something else, something unfamiliar.

He felt it stir when he compared the spill of her golden hair to the warming splendor of the midday sun. He felt it seethe when he followed the turn of her shapely leg from ankle to calf to creamy thigh, remembering how butter soft she'd felt to the touch. Slowly, it was that hot, desperate desire that controlled him, even though he didn't know it as such. He only knew how much he would like to lie down with her, to put his hands upon the places hidden within the blanket, to move himself over her, inside her.

But that would make him just like the men he'd killed that morning.

No better than the men he hunted even now.

The rage returned, and with it, his sense of balance. He shrugged off the deer and bent down to jerk the carbine out from under Amanda's hand. The movement woke her and she looked up with a gasp. Then she smiled in welcome, oblivious to her danger and his dark mood. The naiveté of it lanced his heart.

"Oh, Mr. Bass, there you are. Is that our dinner?" Then she felt the piercing chill of his stare and she frowned in uncertainty. "What's wrong?"

"Wrong?" he drawled with a fearsome quiet. "I could have been anyone. I could have been after anything."

Then she understood.

"Why can't you listen? I tell you to be on your guard, and I find you slumbering like a baby in its mother's arms."

"I'm sorry. I didn't mean to. It was so warm and I was—"

"You could have been dead. The horses could have been stolen. Do you know what it would mean to be on foot out here?"

Her wide eyes flashed to where the animals were grazing contentedly, then back to the lean, angry pull of Harm's features. "Nothing happened."

"But it could have. You weren't ready for it. Out here, you always have to be ready for it. You never should have come. You don't understand, Amanda. You just don't understand."

His hands curled into tight fists upon the hard swell of his thighs, as if he were struggling with the need to shake her. Terrible things, frightening things, worked the muscles of his face. He could see that he was scaring her. That was good. He wanted her afraid. He wanted her to recognize the dangerous consequence of one careless mistake so she wouldn't make another. But there was fear of him in those dark pooling eyes and that, he hadn't wanted. He hadn't wanted her to be scared of him.

Impulsively, he reached out to capture her face between his palms. His senses registered the soft silken heat of her skin even as his mind refused to let him dwell upon it. His grip wasn't kind. "You have to listen to me. You have to do as I tell you. Amanda, I don't want to bury you."

He was hurting her. He was terrorizing her with guilt and fright. Again, she had disappointed him and brought him to this point of hard, desperate anger. She felt tears build in her eyes and apology swell in her throat. But as wrong as she'd been, she would not give in to it, either.

"How comforting to know that you wouldn't leave me lying out here to have my bones bleached. Don't worry, Mr. Bass, I intend to live long enough to pay you. As soon as I find my brother, I'm putting this violent, godforsaken place behind me so I won't have to be bullied and yelled at by hateful men like you."

Oh, she had fire, such fine, fierce fire.

For a moment, their stares battled and their breaths raced. Then Harm's grip gentled. Rough palms scraped along the stubborn line of her jaw. His fingers spread wide, threading through the golden tumble of her hair, pulling ever so slightly as they bunched up into fists. Amanda felt it, that change of mood between them from hard to hot, and she quivered with excitement. She thought he was going to kiss her. The devouring look in

76

his eyes told her he was thinking about it and hers began to close obligingly.

Then he was shoving away, stumbling to his feet with a growl of, "Get dressed."

Amanda blinked, suddenly adrift as her sensory daze snapped into one of confusion. She watched him grab up the deer to drag it to the other side of the fire, where he put his back to her and began hacking through meat and bone with his knife. Stiffly, she made herself stand. With dried garments in hand, she cast a cautious look at him but she knew he wouldn't turn around. He had too much honor for that. She pulled on her clothes.

The tiny wounds had stopped bleeding but the throb was incessant. Amanda settled gingerly upon one hip to give the other ease. She wouldn't complain and she would try not to groan, at least not loud enough for him to hear it. Harm continued to dress out the deer, ignoring her, but she could tell by the jerkiness of his movements that he was well aware of her presence.

However unpleasant he was acting toward her, she liked watching him. He hadn't put his shirt back on, probably because this was the state he was most comfortable in. The sleek darkness of his back bore witness to constant exposure to the sun. The shirt, the boots; those were civilized trappings to make him appear more acceptable. But this was the man he was, half-naked, half-Indian, half-wild. She was intrigued by the way muscle moved the coppery flesh that covered it; strong, smooth poetry, and she wondered how that same pull and ebb would feel beneath her hands.

She'd wanted him to kiss her. Even thinking of it now brought back the inner shiver of expectation. She wondered if the hard line of his mouth could be made to soften the way it did with his infrequent smile. She wondered how passion would taste on a man like Harmon Bass.

As she watched him, she came aware of inconsistencies in the deep brown of his back, of small white lines drawn against the even darkness, of patches of scarring, some slight, some raised and thick, all faded by time. What would cause such a variety of marks? Such cruel reminders?

Then he was rising, turning toward her, and she was quick to mask the questioning sympathy in her gaze.

"Will we be traveling on today, Mr. Bass?"

"No." His reply was curt. As if he'd felt her stare and her curiosity, he strode to the brush to fetch his shirt, shrugging it on but leaving it loose and untucked. "We wouldn't make Terlingua by dark. This is a good place to camp, lots of water, time for you to heal up. We'll eat well and rest, then ride in tomorrow."

"I can make it . . ." she began to protest, not wanting to slow him down. His stare was hard when it touched on hers with a dismissing brevity.

"That would be foolish." End of discussion.

But wasn't everything she'd done since getting off the train foolish? Hadn't she rubbed him with a constant irritation since demanding she go with him? She was paying him well to put up with her reckless folly, but he wasn't about to pretend he liked it. Nor could she blame him. Leaning her head upon one bent knee, she closed her eyes and let misery overcome her. She hurt both in pride and person. She shouldn't have forced him to babysit her in this dangerous land. She should have let him do his job while she waited, out of the way. But she'd been caught up in the spirit of adventure, in the want to have a hand in rescuing her brother from whatever he was embroiled in. She wanted to taste just a degree of excitement before returning to the loneliness of her proper life. But all she'd managed was to nearly get them killed and to make Harmon hate her for her frivolousness. She hoped upon hope that tomorrow she'd be with Randy and that together they could leave this savage place to men like Harmon Bass.

The press of his hand against her cheek brought her eyes open with surprise.

"You've got a touch of fever." He said that too emotionlessly to imply any concern. "I'll make something up for you."

"Don't go to any trouble, Mr. Bass. If it gets any worse, you can always shoot me."

"Then I'd have to go to all the trouble of digging a hole and I wouldn't get paid, Miss Duncan." His mouth pulled into that narrow smile.

She had no retort. That was enough to convince him that she was unwell.

"Drink," he told her after several minutes had passed, and she swallowed obediently from the cup he held. When it was empty, he went back to the fire to spit and cook the slabs of venison. The scent of roasting meat, the warmth of the sun, a feeling of well-being, all began to swell, dulling the pain and the unhappiness. She wanted very much to lie down and did so with a soft contented sigh. An odd lethargy pulled at her senses, confusing her to the point of asking, "What was that you gave me?"

"Peyote."

She'd never heard of it and said so.

"It's a small, thornless cactus. The Mexicans use it ground in water to combat fever. The Indians use the fruit to—for religious purposes. Are you feeling better?"

"Mmmm. Yes. Much better. Tired." Her eyes drifted shut and she found she couldn't open them again. When at last she could, the sun had set, casting their camp in soft firelight and Harm in shadow. She'd never taken alcohol but she'd seen the effects of overindulgence upon her brother. She guessed this was how he felt in its thrall. She dragged herself upright with a quiet moan. The pain of her injury was far removed, but her head ached and her thoughts were sluggish.

"I saved you some meat. Think you could eat something?"

She was ravenous. He brought her thick slices of venison and she had no qualms about digging in with her fingers. She'd never eaten deer. It was tender as beef but the taste was wilder. As she chewed, Harm touched the back of his hand to her brow and was apparently satisfied, for he returned to his side of the fire and to his silence. He was withdrawn and she wondered if he was still angry with her. But until her hunger was appeased, it really didn't matter.

Darkness brought the night chill. Amanda trembled with it before remembering she had no blankets. A dead man was wrapped in them. Harm had his spread close to the fire and was stretched out atop them. She hugged her arms about the thin material of her shirtwaist and wondered if it was possible to freeze to death over a spring night in Texas.

"Are you cold?"

The flat inquiry made her colder. "I'm f—fine, Mr. Bass."

Apparently, he was satisfied to let it go at that, for he tugged the blankets over himself and seemed to forget her. Her teeth started chattering and her backside ached. She slid closer to the fire but it didn't help. She was overcooked on one side and turning blue on the other.

"Amanda, come over here."

He said it quietly. She hesitated until he lifted the corner of the blanket. Deciding it would, indeed, be foolish to freeze for the sake of false modesty, she went to join him in his bedroll. The enveloping warmth was immediate and enough to make her burrow into his side without the slightest reservation. For a moment, he lay stiff as stone while she cuddled close with a grateful sigh.

"You smell good," she murmured sleepily.

"It's the yucca."

"Mmmm. Nice."

She was quiet for a moment, then began a restless wiggling, shifting against him, fidgeting as she sought a comfortable fit. The motion was disturbing. He tried to ignore it. He couldn't. The swell of her breasts pushed against his arm. Her knee nudged innocently between his thighs. His body rumbled with awareness of her, each sinew tensing in unbidden response.

"Lie still," he growled direly, but she only muttered, "Sorry," and continued her seductive twitching. He was going crazy.

"Here. Is that better?" He put out his arm so she could rest her head upon his shoulder. He'd thought in doing so, he could trap her motionless in the bend of his elbow. He hadn't counted upon the soft stroke of her breath against his throat or the push of her palm across his chest. By the time she settled in, he was wound tighter than a cheap pocket watch.

Amanda's thoughts were floating. The remnants of whatever he'd given her in that drink, she was sure. She couldn't remember ever feeling this safe, this warm, this content. Discomfort was brushed aside by that pleasant numbness. Who would have imagined she'd be sleeping in Harmon Bass's arms? Certainly not the girl who slipped from New York all full of romantic notions. She would have expected her dime novel hero to behave with sensible restraint and decorum. That shining prince of the Texas plains would never have plucked buckshot from her bare bottom or washed out her unmentionables in a cold stream. Nor would he compromise her with the comfort of his embrace. What a silly girl she'd been to think that was the kind of man she'd prefer.

"Harmon?"

A questioning noise vibrated beneath her cheek.

"You've been very good to me. I know I've been a terrible bother."

"Go to sleep."

Clouds of weariness thickened about her mind but there was one more thing she wanted to say to him. "Harmon?"

"What?"

"I like you very much. I'm sorry that you think me foolish."

He was quite still for a long moment, then she felt his knuckles graze along the curve of her cheek. "I don't think you're foolish. I think you're very brave. And I think you talk too much. Go to sleep."

She smiled into the fresh-scented folds of his shirt. Brave. She'd never thought of herself as particularly brave. Strong-willed and wrong-headed was what her relatives called her. She liked brave better. And she liked Harmon Bass. She nuzzled more deeply into the cove of his shoulder and the sense of security enfolded her. Thoughts and emotions quieted until one surpassed all others, a feeling that was old yet startlingly new. One she'd held for her brother yet was not quite the same when applied to this man. She considered speaking it aloud, but then she thought perhaps she should keep it to herself. Like a secret. She smiled again.

I think I love you, Harmon Bass.

Just before sleep overtook her, Amanda thought she felt his fingertips sketching along her jaw, weaving through her hair. But she wasn't sure. She could be dreaming it.

Just like she could be dreaming the words he said, so low and forceful, just as she slipped away.

"I won't hurt you. I won't ever hurt you."

As the sun rose, they traveled down out of the Chisos through some of the most explosively beautiful country Amanda had ever seen. They looked out over a vast domain of basins, rolling plains, isolated mesas, distant mountains, and the blue thread of the Rio Grande. And there were colors, so breathtakingly pure: bright primary reds; unnatural blues; violent yellows along the far crests, with streaks of vivid cerise on the white walls behind them. But the closer they got to Terlingua, the more the desert sameness settled in, along with its searing heat. And the more miserable Amanda became.

There was no comfortable way to sit the saddle. Riding hurt. The constant smack of her aggrieved behind to unyielding horse had her eyes swimming and her jaw aching from the force of grinding back her groans of complaint. She would be brave. If she had to grind her teeth all the way to the cheekbones, she wouldn't betray how much that trip from the foothills to the dusty adobe-lined streets of Terlingua cost her.

She couldn't imagine a more desolate town. There wasn't a blade of grass within sun-baked miles. The heat made it hard to breathe and harder to move. Despite those things, Amanda was alive with anticipation. Perhaps Randy was somewhere close by, in one of the daub buildings. Her anxious gaze swept over them as they rode past. And the people of Terlingua stared back. They were a motley mix of Texan, Mexican, and Indian, all rolled up into one uncaring race, hardened by Border life. There was no sense of curiosity in the eyes that watched them, just an indifferent or greedy evaluation of livestock and the possible pocket worth of the riders. As the rough lot of men eyed her, so did the blowsy Mexican harlots take an active interest in her companion. Several of them called out to him, wagging their shoulders so that pendulous breasts swung within their loose white blouses. He smiled, calling back something in Spanish that made them laugh. And a sharp foreign pang shot through Amanda.

Harm steered his mount in at one of the few two-story frame buildings and rolled to the ground. Without a word, he came around to put up his hands toward her— only to be greeted with a glare so venomous, he recoiled in momentary surprise. Amanda fit her palms to his shoulders and let him guide her from the saddle. She settled on the dusty ground toe to toe with him. When she didn't move her hands or step back, he sidled away with the same evasive caution he'd applied to her since she'd awakened to find him saddled and ready to ride. As if he'd prefer her at arm's length. For heaven's sake, she'd only said she liked him, not that she meant to marry him!

Then that thought sank in deep as she watched him stride across the sand-polished boardwalk. Marry Harmon Bass? What a ridiculous notion. She followed him more slowly, hampered by her injury and by what should have been a clearly preposterous thought.

It was a hotel, probably the most shabby excuse for one that she'd ever seen. Dust lay inches deep upon the floor. Harm's boots left tracks in it all the way to the makeshift front desk.

"You like room, *senor?*"

"Two, please," she said as she stepped up beside him. "And a bath."

"One room," Harm corrected, and she looked to him with brows raised. Did he mean for them to share accommodations? Then he explained, "I won't be staying here."

"But it's all right. I have the money. I promised expenses."

"One room," he told the desk clerk again, repeating it in Spanish. He glanced at Amanda, then away. "I'm putting up somewhere else."

It struck her all at once and she flushed hot. He was a man. He'd want to be somewhere that provided sweaty male companionship, cards and drink, and cheap female distraction. Amanda thought of the smirking Mexican tarts and her face grew warmer as her temper grew shorter. And the pang in her chest twisted.

"I see. That is, of course, your choice."

Harm saw that she'd misunderstood him. He could have corrected her but he didn't. Better she think him in the arms of some Border whore. Better she not think of him at all.

The desk clerk spoke rapidly and Harm supplied the meaning. "He says there's a public bath at the barber shop down the street."

"No," she stated firmly. "I want a hot bath in my room. I'll pay extra for the inconvenience. I don't care what it costs. Ask if he can see to it."

The big Mexican looked perplexed and Harm translated her words. He smiled broadly and nodded, gesturing toward the stairs. Amanda started to follow his bulky frame, then paused when Harm hung back.

"I'm going to check around and see if anyone's seen your brother. Stay in your room. You'll be safe there. I'll come up later."

She nodded, suddenly terrified at the thought of being separated from him in this rough town. She also saw beyond her own danger. Forgetting what he'd done to her would-be attackers, she saw him again as a man of slight stature with no gun and questionable heritage. And the

85

sentiment slipped out again with no less feeling, "Harmon, be careful."

"I'm always careful, ma'am. Lock your door. Don't open it to anyone but me."

He might as well have confined her to an airless prison. Her room was tiny, as dusty as everything seemed to be in Terlingua, and its small window let in the heat off the street. There was a narrow bed with a sagging rope suspension and sheets she didn't want to inspect too closely because she knew she'd have to sleep on them that night. A chipped basin on a rickety stool was the only other piece of furniture. Since she had nothing to store, it was enough. All her belongings had been left behind in Fort Davis. Amanda had no need for an afternoon ensemble or a promenade costume in the likes of West Texas. From her little window, she saw Harm cross the wide street and disappear with the swing of batwing doors. She felt that hurtful stirring again and again, it puzzled her.

She was tired and sore. That's what made her out of sorts. She'd be able to think better once she'd had her hot bath. She'd soak and think of what she and Randy would do once they found one another. Yes, that's what she'd do. She *wouldn't* think about Harmon and the sloe-eyed sluts who'd beckoned to him in their husky foreign tongue. What did she care if he chose to bed one or a dozen of them . . . with her money? It was the heat and the nagging throb of her backside that tormented her mind to such a confused degree.

Finally, the tub arrived. It was a dented, rusty-looking affair made for a child if size were any measure. A wilted whisper of a girl trudged in with pails of water and sloshed them in. She laid the dingy towels and a cake of soap upon the bed, saying in broken English that the bath was ten American dollars. Amanda didn't quibble over the exorbitant price. She felt a twinge of pity at the gush of gratitude from the girl as she gave her an extra coin for her trouble.

Stripping down to bare skin, Amanda approached the tub with anticipation. No steam rose from it. She paused, frowning, and dipped in her finger. Tepid. Cooler than dishwater. Suspiciously, she studied the water itself. It was gray. From the horse trough or the public baths? Amanda wondered in distress. She decided she would rather bathe after horses than after the men she'd seen in Terlingua. Hoping she would contract no diseases, Amanda stepped over the metal lip and sank down in a twist of limbs. She soaped the cloth and rubbed it over her arm. It stung! The soap was as harsh as a corrosive against her fair skin. It would strip the varnish off Harmon's coffee.

Disgruntled, she climbed out and dried herself with the scratchy towel. She dressed, trying to pretend it didn't feel as if someone were jabbing knives into her rump. The poor excuse for a bath was obviously not the answer. There was no doctor in Terlingua, but that didn't mean there were no medicines. She needed something, anything, to dull the gnawing edge of complaint.

The desk tender smiled up at her.

"How was the bath, *senorita?*"

"It was fine, thank you. You can have someone take it away." When he frowned, she gestured toward the upstairs and made a shooing motion. He grinned toothlessly and nodded.

"You wish something more?"

"Yes. There is no doctor?"

"No. No doctor."

"How about medicines? A pharmacy? Apothecary?"

He shook his head. She wasn't sure whether he meant no or that he didn't understand. Frustrated, she tried again.

"Something for pain. Do you understand? Pain? For comfort?"

"Ahhh! *Si*. I get for you. Bring your room."

"Yes. Thank you." She smiled. She'd done just fine on her own. Let Harm desert her in favor of his soiled doves. She could take care of herself.

When Amanda didn't respond to his first tap on the door, Harm grew worried.

"Amanda? Are you in there? Are you all right?"

He pressed his palms against the door frame. It wouldn't take much to kick it in.

"Mr. Bass? Is that you? Just a minute. I can't seem to manage the lock. Oh." Giggles. "There."

She sounded very strange. Wondering if she'd become ill, his chest seized up with guilt. Then she opened the door and the odor struck him forcefully.

"Do come in. It isn't much, I must say, but I don't seem to mind it so terribly anymore."

Harm stepped in cautiously as she swayed across the room. All she was wearing were the thin drawers and lacy chemise. And a fog of liquor.

"Amanda, where are your clothes?" He wasn't sure if he should close the door, and then she turned toward him. He slammed it shut. He didn't want anyone else to see her. The fabric of her undergarments was near to transparent. He jerked his stare upward, but not before the image of dark-centered breasts and the taunting shadow of her thighs was burned into it.

"It was so hot, I just took them off. Who would know or care down here? You don't mind, do you, Mr. Bass? After all, you've seen me in less." Again, the silly giggles.

"What have you been doing?" he asked gently, as if to a naughty child.

"Nothing. Whatever is there to do, Mr. Bass? For a lady, I mean. You men seem to have all the entertainments sewn up." She frowned at that and at him. But her sullenness was of short duration. She smiled smugly. "I have done just fine without you, Mr. Bass. You needn't have worried."

"What have you been drinking?"

"The nice man downstairs found me some medicine. I was not feeling at all well."

"What did he bring you?"

"I can't recall the name of it."

He stepped to the bed, where an earthen jug sat on the floor. One sniff snapped his head back. "*Mezcal.* How much of this did you drink?"

"He told me to take enough to kill the pain. I don't feel any pain, so I guess I've had enough."

"I think so, too."

"I feel ever so much better."

"Just wait until tomorrow," Harm muttered prophetically as he recorked the jug. "I came up to talk to you, but I guess it will have to wait until morning when you have a clearer head about you."

"You can talk to me now," she purred thickly. Her weaving steps had carried her all the way around the room, until she was facing him once more. The backs of his knees bumped into the bed frame. His mind full of the way she looked in the fragile underthings, Harm kept his eyes locked on hers. They were dark liquid pools of affection. Suddenly, his blood felt thick and hot, his senses warning of danger.

"The morning would be better. You need to rest. And no more medicine." He started to move around her, but a subtle shift of her body blocked him.

"Don't go, Harmon."

She touched him. Where her fingertips pressed to the

fabric of his shirt, a paralyzing tautness spread outward. He should duck around her and flee the room. He really should. She was quite tipsy—no, that was too delicate a word. Amanda was roaring drunk on the colorless, fiery potion the Mexicans brewed. How she'd ever swallowed it down he couldn't imagine, but he knew it held a kick more volcanic than a quart of Scotch whiskey. She couldn't know what she was doing or what she was asking, weaving there before him in the dainty underclothes that had taunted his thinking since he'd handled them at the stream and imagined what she'd feel like inside them. He should go quickly. But he couldn't force action into the odd heaviness of his limbs.

"Ma'am, I should be go—"

Before he could get out the rest of his reluctant speech, she had her arms locked about his neck and her mouth adhered to his.

Chapter Six

He was so shocked, he didn't try to push her away.

Finally, she stepped back, surprised to find him wide-eyed and staring. "You're supposed to close your eyes, Mr. Bass."

"What?" The sound croaked from him.

"Close your eyes and open your mouth, not the other way around. Don't you like kissing?"

"No."

"I thought all men liked kissing. I think it's very nice. I think you're very nice. Have I told you how much I like you?"

"Yes, ma'am. You told me. You don't need to show me." He was trying to disentangle her arms but she was proving quite determined. And surprisingly strong. She swayed into him and that was worse, feeling her softness, the supple invitation of it. She was watching his face, and suddenly she was struck with insight.

"Is it the kissing you don't like or is it me?"

"I like you fine," he answered stupidly, and her lips were fastened once more over his. Harm stood planted, unable to breathe, the discipline of a lifetime fracturing.

When he didn't respond, Amanda gazed up at him with an endearing hopefulness. "You'd like if you tried," she coaxed. "Harmon, you act as though no one has ever kissed you before."

He had quicksilver images of his mother, of Becky, of the tender, treasured brushes of affection against his unwilling cheek. But that wasn't like this . . . nothing like this. This was not chaste. It was dark, hot temptation, calling with wicked seduction to the violent passions of his soul. And he wanted to answer. She was stroking his shoulders, stoking fires inside.

Angrily, he remembered himself. He reached for her arms but they evaded him. Instead, he found his hands at her breasts. He froze, startled by the swelling ripeness, by the perfection of fit within his palms. She made a wondering little sound that scalded his senses. *Stop.* But he couldn't. He was mesmerized by the feel of her, by the way softness yielded up such hard points of desire in reaction to his touch. He wasn't going to hurt her. He just wanted to know just a little of what it could be like with a woman like Amanda. Sweet. He guessed it would be sweet. He wished he didn't know different.

"Amanda." His voice was thick, unrecognizable. Like the forceful hammering of his blood.

She pushed against him, moving against his thigh in innocent suggestion. She couldn't know, she couldn't suspect what that did to him. He tried to move back, but the bed was there and he started to fall, she with him, stealing his balance. His head hit the wall, hard, and for a moment there was swimming blackness, then the lustful blackness stirred by Amanda's eager little mouth upon his neck and ear. There was darkness in his heart, a fierce, driving darkness that made him grab her wrists, made him compel her with one wrench of his body onto her back beneath him. She didn't object. She didn't struggle because she didn't know, as he did, what it would mean if he didn't stop. If he couldn't stop.

Control crumpled beneath governing impulse. He was breathing too fast, too hard for reason to take hold. He didn't want reason. He fought it. He wanted the darkness and the consuming fire that accompanied it. His fingers tightened around delicate bone, grinding, pushing her wrists down into the lumpy mattress, as his hips ground over her, pushing his hard arousal along the groove between her thighs. His body felt unfamiliar to him, all tensile strength and powerful. Too powerful to be checked by such things as conscience or promises. Or by any weak resistance she could offer.

I won't hurt you.

But wasn't that what he was doing? His grip was bruising her. His weight was crushing her. The pounding heaviness in his loins demanded he do worse, much worse. Yet she was looking up at him through great trusting eyes. Because she didn't know. She didn't understand the violent nature controlling him.

But she would.

What was he doing? What was he thinking? She was the one who had the excuse of liquor clouding her senses, not him. And he was using her momentary compliance to assuage his most contemptible lusts. She would hate him. He hated himself. He released her wrists, then pushed her arms away when they would reach up to hold him. So innocent of what she wanted to embrace. The need to protect her overcame all else and the darkness receded with an ugly whisper.

"I'm sorry, *shijü*. I would not hurt you for the world."

Confusion was evident in her gaze. Better that than fear.

"Harmon?" A soft, fragile sound snagging on his heart.

He wanted to show her some tenderness, some expression of regret and apology. Such things were unknowns to him. He couldn't speak to her of these things, not through

93

all the mixed emotions crowding his throat. He wasn't a man of demonstration or sentiment, and he felt that lack in himself, for that was what was needed now. Some token to ease the awkwardness of his retreat. He rubbed compressed lips across her cheek. It was all he could think to do. He'd never before kissed a woman. He supposed he did all right, because she made a cooing little noise and put her hand to his face in a manner that made his insides shake apart. The *mezcal* had full rein, sucking her down into a sleepy oblivion. Yet she found the presence of mind to quiet him with a gentle touch. How could she be so kind after what he had thought to do to her?

With an agile roll, he was off the bed and free of her dangerous proximity, if not her essence. Not so easy to run from the scent of her lingering in his clothing or the feel of her impressed upon his body or the taste of her branded upon his mouth. But those were his torments to bear, and at least he would have the pleasure of knowing her safe in her besotted slumber.

"Sleep well, *shijii*," Harmon murmured as he slipped silently out the door.

It was cold and the ground was hard, but he didn't notice either discomfort as he watched the hotel. He'd found a shadowed alleyway to serve his purpose, and Harmon sat cross-legged upon the ground with his carbine cradled in the bend of his arms. He had an unobstructed view of the hotel entrance and of Amanda's darkened window. He didn't mind the loneliness of his watch. He wasn't tired. He wouldn't have been able to sleep, anyway.

Because of what he'd done.

Because of what he hadn't told her.

That very probably her brother was dead.

He was surprised that he could still feel compassion so strongly. He'd thought the capacity had been wrung out of him long ago, leaving only dry indifference. He didn't concern himself with the value of life. In typical Border-bred thinking, he knew every man was important only to himself and a corpse to no one. He was so numbed to violence, it no longer affected him. But he knew—he *knew*—he would feel all the pain of it again through Amanda Duncan. And he wasn't ready. Despite all the tough conditioning to make it otherwise, he was still weak inside.

How was he going to tell her?

As soon as they'd arrived, he'd headed for the local law office, only to find the sheriff was out of town. From there, he went to the nearest saloon, knowing that anything worth knowing could be discovered around the tables of chance and tongue-loosening drink. He went to the bar, ordering up a beer and a whiskey. The beer was for him, just one. He liked the way it cut the Texas dust. The hard liquor he wouldn't drink. He paid for it with one of Amanda's ten-dollar pieces. The barkeep's eyes grew round when he told the man to keep the change for his trouble. And he nodded his thanks as Harm pushed the shot glass toward him.

"Man oughtn't drink with the likes a him."

Harm didn't look toward the speaker. He knew what he'd see . . . the same thing he saw in any saloon. The faces were different but the attitude was engraved in stone. *We don't want your kind in here.* A white-skinned man could travel anywhere without question and was always accepted, a dark-skinned one not at all. He was only one-quarter Apache, but discerning eyes could spot it easily in his coloring, in the flare of his cheekbones, and in the slippery grace of his movements. He usually ignored the stench of their dumb-animal bigotry. He'd

95

learned as a child that he couldn't change men's minds through brute force or by superior reasoning. It didn't matter that they hated him for something beyond his control. It wasn't personal. Precious little was. So he pretended he didn't hear while all his senses sharpened.

He smiled blandly at the barkeeper. "I'm looking for a man. Blond feller, moustache, easterner. Would have come through here a couple of days ago riding with another man, hard case."

The barkeep leaned on his elbows, fingering the gold piece. "Well, could be I recall—"

"Who wants to know?" the rough voice at his shoulder growled again.

Harm ignored him. No man had the right to demand he give his name. It was a dangerous breach of Texas etiquette. What a man hailed by was his own business and no one else's. Harm continued his conversation with the man behind the bar.

"Don't mean the man any trouble. Looking for him for his sister. Could be a taste of reward money in it for you if—"

"Hey!" A stiffened finger jabbed him in the temple. "You deaf? I'm talkin' to you, breed. What's your business here? And who'd you murder and rob to get that kind of money?"

Harm tensed by degrees. Slowly, he turned his head to fix the loudmouth with his stare. He kept all signs of irritation from his face. "Don't believe I owe you any explanations."

"That's where you're wrong, friend." The bully was grinning, egged on by the trio of dirty *compadres* who thought it might be fun pushing an unarmed little half-breed around.

Harm let his eyes open a bit wider so the aggressor

could read the glitter of warning there. "I'm not your friend."

The tough was taken aback by the unexpectedly lethal glare but couldn't back down from the icy challenge of his words. "Then jus' who the hell are you?"

Harm's hand eased around so that his fingers could close on the hilt of his knife. He didn't want trouble. He wanted some answers. But if one came before the other, he'd have to accept that.

Then a hard hand clapped over his.

"Don't do it, son."

The quartet of saddle bums immediately backed off from their truculent stances.

"Howdy, Sheriff. We was jus' having us a friendly drink and this here breed starts makin'—"

"It won't wash, Baker. I heard all I needed to hear. You boys finish up your drinks and get on outta here."

"Whadabout him?" one of them complained.

"I'm going to buy Mr. Bass a drink. Howdy, Harm."

Harm had relaxed the moment he recognized the authoritative voice. "Calvin. Was looking for you."

"Jus' got in." The lawman glared at the cowboys. "What you-all starin' at? I said skedaddle."

"Harmon Bass," came a shaky whisper from one of them. "Kee-rist, Jed, heard tell that little feller gutted ole Sandy Corbel from neck to navel and cooked up his chestnut gelding for dinner. You're lucky you ain't kilt!"

"Shaddup," Jed Baker hissed as he slid nervously away from the bar. *Harmon Bass!* His entrails shriveled at the thought of what he'd almost provoked. A man looking to stay alive didn't prod the likes of Bass when within striking range.

The sheriff released Harm's wrist and they both turned to the bar, putting their backs to the foursome as if their threat was insignificant. It was. Harm could scent their fear. Better that than the spill of their blood.

"How's Will?" Calvin Lowe signaled for another round as the hard cases behind them slunk out the door.

"Fine last I saw him." Harm put his hand over his glass and shook his head at the barman.

"What can I do for you, Harm?"

"Looking for a feller name a' Randolph Duncan." He ran down the description and watched for signs of recognition.

"He wanted?"

"No bounty that I know of. Just a job."

"Well, sounds kinda like the two what rode through here day afore yesterday, doan it, Hobby?"

"Jus' what I was a-thinkin', Sheriff," the barman nodded as he brought Lowe his drink. Then he glanced at Harm. He saw all kinds come through but he wouldn't have pegged this one as dangerous. "Missed him by half a day—the other one, that is. He came back through jus' this morning to trade for a new horse. Seems his up and went lame on him."

"And Duncan?" Harm felt his belly contract.

"Doan know about him. The other one came back through alone."

So where was Randolph Duncan?

Harm sat in the darkness, afraid he knew but knowing that at first light he'd have to ride out to see for himself.

The first thing she did when she awoke was to touch her lips. Had she really kissed him? Had it really been . . . wonderful? Or was that just a part of a dream that lingered? She ran her tongue along her lower lip and tasted something totally unpleasant. The medicine. Now she recalled. My goodness, hadn't it been potent stuff! Even now she felt no pain.

Until she tried to open her eyes.

"Oh . . . goodness!"

She closed them quickly, praying the hot points of light couldn't penetrate her eyelids. It took a moment for the wooziness to go away, and with it, the searing brightness that burnt her eyeballs. Blindly, she fumbled for the tattered draperies and yanked them across the window. Only then did she try to face the day.

It was hot. Already the air stifled energy in thick, nearly visible waves. That meant it was noon or better. She'd slept past noon? Never could she remember doing such a thing. If it was so late, where was Harmon?

Harmon!

"Oh, goodness," she moaned again, falling back upon the bed in despair, then wincing at the consequence. She shifted to one side. Harmon. He'd come to her door. He'd said something about needing to talk to her. Then she'd kissed him. And he hadn't liked it. Of all the vague gaps in her memory, that was painfully clear. She'd shocked him with her boldness. He'd not responded, not at all, and it wasn't because she didn't know how to kiss.

Oh, she'd made a terrible fool of herself! Again.

So why hadn't he liked her kiss?

It was the one thing she could do well. She had a mouth made for it, her handsome cousin Roger had told her when he taught her all there was to know. She'd been a mischievous fifteen and he a dashing seventeen, about to go off to college. It had started as a forfeit in some silly parlor game but the excitement of it led to further experimentation: behind the stairs; in her uncle's leather-scented study; during outings when they'd pretend to get lost, then lose themselves to the passion of the moment. Oh, she had liked it very much, kissing handsome cousin

99

Roger, because he told her things silly girls of fifteen longed to hear: that she was beautiful; that he cared for her; that as distant cousins they could one day wed. All lies, of course, but she'd wanted to believe them. Wanted to share the closeness, the intimacy of shared secrets, and the hurried rush of shared breaths with someone. She'd been so lonely with just her brother to care for her. For an entire summer, they'd arranged rendezvous to steal those breathless kisses. At the end, there'd been some touching, too, but she hadn't liked that as much and he stopped when she told him to. She'd like it when she was older, he'd confided huskily.

And then her aunt had caught them. She could remember the words she'd used: strumpet, easy piece, loose-moraled, fast. And she'd cringed, wondering why Roger didn't say anything in her defense. Why he'd been willing to let her take all the abuse. She found out later, when she heard mother and son together. Roger had been blatant about his reasons. The money. Cousin Amanda was filthy with it. Why shouldn't he want to attach himself to that future fortune before anyone else got a chance at it? Weren't they doing the same thing by putting her up in their house as if she meant something to them beyond a bother?

Amanda shouldn't have been surprised, but she was. Randy was away at school and she begged to be allowed to attend a girl's seminary, unable to stand their forced charity another moment. They hedged at first, citing the cost, which was high, but considering it was all her money, finally they agreed and off she went. She'd learned about more than kissing that summer. She learned about the price attached to affection, and it was too high.

Apparently, she wasn't paying Mr. Bass enough for him to endure her unwanted advances.

Why wasn't he interested? Because he saw her as a little

girl who talked too much? Well, she wasn't a child and she didn't . . . well, actually, she did tend to run on forever once gravity got a hold of her tongue. But she wasn't unattractive. Then she put her hand to her peeling nose. Or was she? After three nights in the most impossible places, she probably looked worse than the desk clerk below.

What if her behavior had scared him off?

Where was he?

His horse was still there, snoozing contentedly in the rickety stall next to Fandango. Amanda breathed a sigh of relief. She spent some minutes petting her loyal mount, liking him better from the ground than in the saddle.

"Miss Duncan?"

She whirled at the low, unfamiliar voice. The first thing she saw was a lawman's star and the second a kindly smile. "Yes?"

"Ma'am, I'm Sheriff Lowe, and Harm asked me to keep a lookout over you. You really shouldn't be wandering these streets by yourself, even when they seem all sleepy like."

She felt herself blush. This man must be a friend of Harmon's. What could she tell him? That she'd run to the stables to make sure he hadn't abandoned her?

"Do you know where I could find Mr. Bass?" Amanda asked with all the dignity she could muster.

"No. Not exactly. Up in them hills somewheres, I would guess."

"Without his horse?"

"Ma'am, Harm Bass can dogtrot more miles through them hills than the fastest horse. He said he'd be back by nightfall and you wasn't to worry. Said to tell you he'd be careful." The lawman smiled knowingly, as if those words implied some tenderness lay between she and Harm. She didn't refute his assumption.

"Did he have word about my brother, Sheriff?"

"Well, miss, you'll have to ask him when he gets back. Now you'd be well advised to return to your room till then."

The thought of the hot stewpot of a room wasn't at all appealing. "But I need to purchase some things, some clothes . . . things." She trailed off vaguely and he didn't blush. A married man, she concluded rightly.

"Tell you what. I'll take you on home with me and my wife, Elena can see to whatever you might be wanting and a good hot meal to boot."

"Sheriff, that's very kind but—"

"But nothing, missy. I owe Harm Bass and I owe him deep. He says for me to take care a' you and it will be my pleasure. You c'mon home with me. I'll drop you off and leave word at the hotel where Harm can find you. Not that he'd have any trouble tracking you down." He grinned and Amanda smiled, willing to trust this man who was a friend to the solitary Harmon Bass.

Elena Lowe was a quiet, dark fragile flower of a woman who was more than delighted with the company. Her English wasn't very good, but she managed to convey what was on her mind with fluttery gestures and a gentle smile. Amanda found herself tucked like a queen in a spare bedroom with a wealth of colorful tiered skirts and white Mexican blouses to choose from. When she caught a glimpse of herself in the mirror, she stopped in shock. It was no wonder Harmon had taken to the hills at a run! Her hair was a matted tangle, her face blotched with freckles and patches of bright pink skin where the leathery burn had peeled away. Elena smiled and provided hair brushes and a soothing face cream, then bewildered her with a gentle hug and a murmur of something about "Harmon's woman."

Calvin Lowe returned for supper and made her blush by declaring how pretty she looked in his wife's red skirt and dainty white peasant blouse. She felt pretty, and as the hours eased into darkness, Amanda felt an accompanying anticipation of Harm's return. Would he think so, too? What would she say to him about the night before? About the way she'd cast herself upon him? That she was sorry? Well, she wasn't. She was only sorry he hadn't liked it.

Then she heard him on the front porch, speaking to Calvin in a low voice. Her heart had taken on a peculiar tempo as she hurried down the hallway toward the door. She could see him silhouetted against the night and the lights of Terlingua, could hear Elena's happy greeting as she went up on her toes to hug him tight and kiss his cheek. He murmured low to his friend's wife in Spanish and she stroked his face. Then he looked up and saw her.

Amanda stopped. She felt breathless and slightly giddy as he came inside. He looked so tired, so worn. She wanted to go to him like Elena had, to welcome him with a warm embrace. But something in his expression held her motionless. He didn't notice her lively clothes or the way she'd braided her hair into a thick golden tail or the gladness in her eyes. He couldn't force himself to look at her at all.

"Amanda." His voice broke.

"Harmon, what is it?" she asked with a desperate quiet. But she knew. Even before he raised his tragic, solemn eyes, she knew. Even before he held out a dirty gold pocket watch, she knew.

The watch was Randy's. She'd given it to him for luck just before he'd gotten on the train to go west. It held her likeness.

Her brother was dead.

She reached out for the watch and Harm let the chain trickle down into her palm. She couldn't speak. The shock was immeasurable, the blow too sudden, too horrible for her to absorb. So she stood there, staring at the watch, waiting for Harm to tell her the worst.

"I followed their tracks up into the hills, the other one following your brother, riding hard," he began flatly. "My guess is, he was chasing him. There was gunfire. Your brother fell off his horse and managed to crawl up into the rocks. Looks like he bled to death before the other man found him."

Amanda made a soft, moaning sound, then managed a hoarse, "Why? Why was he killed?" The image of the watch blurred in her hand as her eyes filled up with tears.

"They must have had a falling-out over the jewelry. He didn't have any of it on him."

Amanda lifted her head slowly to look at him. His expression was a careful void. "A falling-out? You mean, as in thieves?"

"Yes, ma'am."

An awful wail tore from her throat. She slapped him. Her palm connected with a loud, ringing crack, but he never so much as blinked.

"How dare you? How dare you suggest that to me! I'm not paying you to defame my brother to me. Keep your lies and your lowly opinions to yourself, Mr. Bass. And don't you worry. I'll wire for your money in the morning."

With that, she fled into the lonely sanctuary of her borrowed room, away from where Harmon stood in the hall, his face stinging from her slap, his soul dissolving from her scorn.

* * *

Numbness, blessed numbness, stayed with her through the evening hours. Elena came and went in her room like a gentle breeze, bringing her a delicate lawn sleep dress to wear, dragging in a big copper tub, and seeing it filled with steaming water. Amanda soaked until the fragrant bath turned cool, but still, the tension wouldn't leave her. Emotion clogged inside her, hard and nondescript. It wasn't until she'd donned the soft nightdress and tried to sleep that she knew what it was she was feeling. It wasn't grief. It was fear.

She'd never been afraid before. When their parents died, she had to be strong for Randy's sake. He was older but she was the strong one. Just a child, she'd stepped in as surrogate mother, fussing over him, caring for him, loving him because they were all each other had. No one else cared about two orphaned children except for the money that came with them. Amanda had blunted herself to that terrible aloneness because she had Randy and he was all she needed. He needed her, he loved her, and nothing else mattered. Not until she went to boarding school did she allow herself to be frivolous and dream, and she took to it with a passion after years of wearing somber adulthood upon her child's shoulders. She could be carefree and even foolish for the first time in her life. Coming west to rescue her brother had seemed such a great adventure. Everyone loved kind, tenderhearted Randy Duncan. Surely nothing could happen to Randy.

But something had. And now she was truly alone.

And she was terrified.

Unable to rest, she wandered out onto the veranda, where a wide inviting swing had been bolted into the sturdy roof beams. It was quiet and cool. The noise from the Terlingua saloons seemed very far away. As far away as her pain.

"You had no call to do that."

She looked up at Calvin Lowe. "I'm sorry?"

"To wade into Harm like that."

She sighed and closed her eyes, resting her head on the back of the swing. "I'm paying Mr. Bass very well to suffer my character flaws. I'm sure he'll be quite happy to be rid of me." Why did that notion hurt so much?

"That what you think?"

"That's what I know, Sheriff. Once my money crosses his palm, I won't be seeing Mr. Bass again."

He chuckled softly, sadly, she thought, then he said the strangest thing. "You don't know Harm at all, do you?"

She had no reply.

"Let me tell you something about Harm Bass." He walked to the steps and stared up toward town. "Met him when I was Ranging. I had me this pretty little Mexican girl and I was trying to save up enough to ask her daddy to let me marry her. Apaches hit her village, slaughtered every man and half-growed boy, and took the women with them. I was crazy with grief, not thinking I'd ever see her again. Then my captain, he says he knows a man who might get my woman back for me. When I saw Harm, I didn't hold no hope at all. He was just a boy back then, coming from who knows where. Hell, from the looks of him. He was wild as any Apache and so wolf-cautious he made you nervous watching him. Told him all I had in the world was fifty dollars and he said fair enough. Came back three days later with my Elena, him all cut the hell up. Asked him how he'd come to get her away from the Apache and all he'd say was, 'Don't ask.' Wouldn't even let me thank him."

"So he didn't take the money?"

"Oh, no. He took the fifty dollars."

She began to frown and the sheriff just shook his head.

"Missy, the money ain't for him. Harm don't need nothing to live off of. He's got all that out there." He gestured wide toward the open desert. Amanda understood without further explanation. "Hell, what he did was worth six times what I could pay him. He did it because my captain asked him. There ain't nothing he wouldn't do for them he cares about."

"Then why does the money matter so much?"

"It's for Becky."

Becky.

I won't let them hurt you, Becky.

"Harm told me to watch out for you because you meant something to him and you kicked him away hard. Can't say I care for that. He don't take to most folks, so there must be something special about you, a reason for him to be over at the saloon crying in his beer."

"He's what?"

"Just an expression, ma'am." He smiled wryly. "One I doan think he'd like me using. Best be saying good night to you. You can stay on as long as you like. Tomorrow morning I'll send some men out to see to your brother."

"I'd appreciate that, Sheriff."

"Doing it for Harm, ma'am. Like I said, I owe him."

And Amanda sat rocking, staring up toward the lights of Terlingua, wishing she could believe that Harmon Bass cared—just a little.

Chapter Seven

He wasn't responsible for Amanda Duncan.

Harm told himself that as he tossed back his beer. It went down as smoothly as the first, so he ordered another and stared sulkily into the golden brew. Gold like her hair. Gold like the coins she thought to toss his way in angry parting. Hang it; he didn't ask to be the hero in her sheltered little dream. He wasn't anything like the legend she adored. Not one bit. She'd know that if she could read his thoughts for just an instant. She'd run back to New York screaming.

He didn't owe her anything else. Once she paid up, there was no reason for him to stick around, no reason for him to care one way or another what she did. Let her pretend her brother was some saint who couldn't be tempted by the greed that was a part of every man's soul. That wasn't his problem. It wasn't up to him to help her grow up. The man was dead. Now she could go home and get on with her fancy life and brush him off like the dust of Texas.

So why couldn't he shake off her look of desolation?

Because he knew all about being lonely and alone, and he couldn't bear the thought of Amanda being adrift like that. There were so few people who could touch upon what little softness was left inside him. Somehow, the silly little eastern girl had become one of them. He'd seen the look in her eyes back at the stream, that look that promised heart and soul, and it quite plainly had scared him to death. He couldn't come close to giving her what she wanted from him. He had nothing left to give. He'd turned from those things fourteen years ago, forging his future with sweat and pain in the way of the Apache. He'd been taught that a display of gentleness was unmanly, that to hunger for a woman showed a lack of self-discipline, which was a despised flaw. A man went with men and did not crave the company of a female. The way he craved Amanda's.

She was a strange one, so bold with her emotions. She didn't seem to mind the big things that bothered most folks, like his Indian blood. She whined over the unimportant; silly things like manners and proper clothes and useless romantic notions. He took an odd comfort in her ramblings, because when she talked enough for both of them, he didn't need to think of something to say. She got sentimental over a horse and burying those who were beneath her contempt. She worried about him. *Harmon, be careful.* As if it really mattered to her. She puzzled him. She terrified him. Because around her, he had trouble remembering things. Things like why he couldn't let her grow to care about him.

He hadn't thought it possible for a woman to hurt him with mere words, yet she had.

Harm looked at the beer, no longer wanting it, wanting, instead, something he knew he couldn't have.

Suddenly, he was there.

Amanda had been looking toward Terlingua yet she'd never seen him come down the street. He just appeared

109

on the porch steps like that vision of water out on the West Texas plain, so near yet impossible to reach.

She'd been thinking of what she would say to him when he came for the money. The words hadn't come. And they weren't there now as she stared up from the swing into the blue of his eyes. Wolf-cautious, Calvin had said of him. How apt a description. He paused on the steps and she could feel the quiver of his uncertainty. A movement could tempt him forward or send him shying back into the night shadows. So she didn't move.

He'd hoped she would say something but she was silent. She looked small and so very vulnerable curled upon the porch swing, with her knees drawn up and her bare toes peeping from the hem of her borrowed white gown. Her big dark eyes were asking for answers he didn't have. He didn't know why he'd come back. He just couldn't stay away.

The moment stretched out between them.

It was one tear that started the flood. That single drop of misery rimmed her lower lashes before collecting at one corner. A fluttery blink sent it coursing down her cheek, gathering momentum, prodding Harm from his wary stance as he watched it shiver at the curve of her cheek.

"I'm sorry, Amanda."

It was said gracelessly but obviously from the heart. She made a sound, a wounded little noise that brought him across the porch and down upon the swing beside her. There was no place to go except into his arms. Anguish broke like a summer storm, shaking through her shoulders, soaking his shirtfront, necessarily violent yet quick to extinguish. Harm said nothing. He'd thought to just hold her but his hands refused to be still. They rubbed up and down her back, massaged the quaking line of her shoulders, stroked the silken weave of her hair, calming her. And surprisingly, himself as well.

Amanda felt foolish when the tears were all cried out. She'd made his shirt soggy and had it crumpled in the tiny balls of her fists. He hadn't complained. Small things crept into her awareness: the rhythm of his breathing, the steady pulse of his blood, the scent of his weariness and that of beer. And she was no longer afraid.

"I can't believe he's gone," she whispered, her voice low with the rough aftermath of weeping.

"I'm sorry," Harm said again, unable to think of anything that would offer more comfort. Speaking of the dead touched off the Apache uneasiness in him but he suppressed it, sensing she needed to unburden her breaking heart.

"Harmon, he was all I had." So much aching loneliness in that admission.

"Is there no one else who would care for you?"

She began to shake her head. It was then she felt the gentleness of the hands that stroked and petted her. His movements were instinctive. She didn't think he was conscious of doing it.

"Will you go home now, back to your city?" His hands stilled as he awaited her answer.

"Home? My home was with Randy. It wasn't in a building. I don't have anything to go back to."

"What of your school? Your family?"

A sudden strength came into her voice. "The only thing I have is my brother's honor." She sat back to look up into the inscrutable blue eyes. His arms stayed about her. "Harmon, I know he didn't steal those jewels. I don't care if you don't believe that. I know it. I know it in my heart."

His hand rose to cup the side of her face. His thumb rubbed away the trace of her tears. "Then we'll have to find them, won't we?"

She stared at him, almost afraid to hope.

"That's part of what you hired me to do. I can't take your money until that job is done."

"Harmon . . ."

"Tomorrow I'll start after the other man. When I find him, you will have your truth."

"When *we* find him," she corrected.

Harm's mouth curved up slightly. "We can talk of that in the morning."

She felt like crying again, this time from something much more complicated than simple sorrow.

"Amanda . . ." She stilled at his hesitant tone. "Amanda, what if he's guilty?"

She looked him straight in the eye and said, with enough confidence to convince an entire country to follow her into battle, "He's not."

Oh, sweet Amanda, I don't want to prove you wrong.

She said nothing more. He knew she couldn't read the doubt in his face. Nothing would betray itself there unless he wished it. She looked so full of despair, so exhausted in body and spirit. Tenderness swelled inside him but he was afraid to act upon it. Instead, he stated softly, "You should go to bed now."

Amanda thought of being alone and of all the torments that would return, and she boldly leaned her head upon his shoulder. "I'd rather sit with you for a while longer . . . unless there's someplace you'd rather be."

He smiled to himself. She posed that with all the bluntness of his knife's edge. He really should get up. He was tired. She needed rest. But he didn't move. Instead, he answered, "I'm not going anywhere."

"Good." Her hand rose and began an absent rubbing of his other shoulder. It was pleasant, yet disquieting, too. He'd ask her to stop. . . . soon. She shifted and so did he. He brought his legs up onto the seat of the swing and she placed her knees over one of them, then settled into the vee of his thighs with her weight against his chest. He leaned back on the rolled arm of the wicker swing, absorbing the feel of her stretched out over him. He should get up and send her off to her own bed. He would. In a minute. His eyes closed. When they opened, it was dawn. And he was alone.

Calvin never exactly commented while the four of them were seated at breakfast, but there was a certain smirk to his expression that rankled Harm. Over Elena's buttery biscuits, he finally growled, "Something on your mind, Calvin?"

"Not a thing, Harm."

But Calvin was grinning like a coyote and drawing a connecting gaze between him and Amanda. He'd seen them curled up together on the swing. What good would it do to tell his friend it meant nothing? Let him grin like a fool. But Elena was looking at him, too, her smile soft and well-pleased. He felt as if her biscuits were swelling up in his throat. Amanda was no help, not when her features took on a particular glow every time he glanced in her direction. She looked very pretty in one of Elena's off-the-shoulder blouses. It showed a fair amount of gold skin and a teasing splatter of freckles. The sun became her, giving her a healthy, tawny sheen, like a supple mountain cat. He realized he was staring at her and all three of them were grinning at him. How was he supposed to swallow down his coffee? It was enough to make a man look for a hole to pull in after him.

"I'm going for supplies," he announced gruffly as he pushed out of his chair.

"I'll have your horses ready for you, Harmon."

Calvin said that innocently enough, but Harm scowled just the same. "Much obliged, Cal."

"No problem, Harm." And he was smiling as if he was already planning to help the two of them build a cozy house to share next door. Harmon stomped out to suck in some sensible air. What was wrong with all of them, anyway? He was just doing a job and getting paid darn well for it, too. That was all. It wasn't as if Amanda was any of his business once that was done. Maybe it was a good thing she was riding out with him. A few more days under the Lowes' roof and they'd have her picking out wedding china! He stormed up the dusty street in full-blown male outrage and yet, for all his indignant bluster, there was a warmth inside him that wouldn't go away. Which, of course, made him all the angrier.

Harm was still scowling sourly as he loaded his arms up with coffee beans, canned peaches, and ammunition. Even with his mind distracted, the sound of a man's gritty laughter caught him like an unexpected punch to the spleen. He reacted from years of harsh training, protecting himself from notice. Quickly, he faded back behind a stack of farm implements, his eyes closed, his heart hammering. Then, with a fierce draw of breath, he was calm all over. Carefully, he peered out to see if he could be mistaken, knowing he wasn't.

As if he could forget.

The man in question was standing at the counter buying a pouch of Bull Durham. He didn't look like anyone out of the ordinary, just a shabby cowboy who happened to tote a fine pair of matched pistols. Harm was panting softly. His eyes took on a metallic glitter as they followed the cowboy's arrogant swagger toward the door.

"Can I help you with those things?"

Harm never heard the question. He started for the door as if in a trance.

"Hey, boy. You got to pay for them things!"

Without any awareness of it, he put down the goods he held and slipped outside. In front of the saloon across the street, the cowboy stepped up onto a big bay and wheeled it away from the rail with a rough hand. Harm waited until man and horse reached the edge of town before he left the store. Running.

"Harmon, I thought you went to—"

Amanda broke off in alarm. He didn't hear her. He didn't even spare her a glance. He went from mid-stride up over the rump of his horse and into the saddle. In the same movement, he jerked the reins free and slashed back with his heels.

"Harmon? Where—"

Amanda choked on his dust. Wherever he was going, it was in a flat-out hurry. Leaving her behind.

Panic was a powerful motivation. She didn't think. She tossed Fandango's reins over his head and clambered up onto his back, with skirts bunched awkwardly and heart racing. Hanging on tight, she kicked the paint and, with a neck-snapping jolt, headed out after Harm.

She was no tracker but she knew the direction he'd taken. She wasn't much of a rider so she had no chance of catching him. But she kept on, stubbornly, ignoring the discomfort, running on raw fear. Because of the look she'd seen on his face. The same look that had accompanied the killing of the cowboys. If she'd taken a second to think, she'd have realized that staying put would be the best thing she could do for him. But it wasn't logic that drove her so madly, it was emotion. Something terrible was behind Harm's flight from town and she had to know what it was.

She wouldn't lose him to the cruel countryside the way she'd lost Randy.

After countless hard miles passed, every shrub and stony gully looked the same, and if there was a way to follow tracks on the hard-packed ground, she didn't know it. She slowed her horse and gave a minute to thought. She could still find her way back, but if she went on, there were no guarantees that she wouldn't become more than bleached bones. It would be foolish to try to find him, and hadn't she already done enough foolish things? But what if his haste had something to do with Randy? What if he needed some kind of help? Not that there was anything she could do, Amanda realized with a depriciating frown. If anything, she was more hindrance than help.

What if he never came back?

She nudged Fandango ahead. Just a little ways. She'd keep an eye on the mountains. And if she fell into the Rio Grande, she'd know she made the wrong turn. She was learning from him already, she thought with a wry smile. Where could he have disappeared to in all this nothingness? She kept on for what must have been thirty minutes but seemed liked three hours. She wasn't sure. Randy's watch was broken. No sign that human life had ever existed out here between the thorny lechuguilla and prickly pear flats encouraged her. It was time to turn around. She'd run out of excuses to continue.

Then she heard the first scream.

It was so horrible she thought it must be some animal in terrible agony. Surely a man couldn't be made to produce such a sound. She found she was trembling. Dear God, it couldn't be Harmon.

But if it was, what could she do about it? Amanda moaned at her own helplessness. What if he'd run across the rest of those cowboys? Should she run back to Terlingua for Sheriff Lowe? And return, too late? If she had to bury both Harm and Randy, what would that leave her? She kicked Fandango up, steering toward the sound at a reckless canter.

More screams, more horrid than the first, if that were possible. And a man's hoarse pleading. Her relief was overwhelming. Not Harmon. She slid down off the saddle, cautious now because if it wasn't Harmon, she could well be intruding into someone else's trouble. The last few days had hardened her. *Every man for himself.* She could hear him speaking that cold, hard code of the West. She didn't want to think it applied to her. If someone was hurting that badly, she couldn't, in good conscience, allow it. Amanda started forward on foot. The voice became clear. It was frantic.

"Why you doing this? What do you want? I don't got nothing! Take the horse, my guns! Anything!"

"There's only one thing I want from you."

Amanda drew up short. That was Harm. Only he sounded . . . different.

"Anything! Tell me!"

"I want to watch you die."

He said it quietly, almost in a reverent whisper. The blood chilled in Amanda's veins. Nothing could be worse than the soft horror of that voice and what it suggested. Until she saw what it was Harm was doing.

Her mind refused to accept it. For a moment, all she could do was stare while shock and hot gorge built inside her. Never . . . never had she imagined . . .

Harmon Bass sat cross-legged and calm, watching the uncontrolled jackknifing of the man he'd hung suspended, head down, over a small fire, his brain slowly roasting.

"Cut me down! You can't do this! Please!"

Harm's voice drawled with contempt. "You weep and wail like a woman with your fear. In the hours to come, you'll have reason for your screams."

"Please, friend! Please!"

"It does please me. And I'm not your friend."

"Harmon."

He hadn't heard her approach. He'd been too caught up in the rapture of his revenge. Harm stiffened, bracing for her reaction. He wouldn't consider what this would look like to her. Her opinion didn't matter. He couldn't let it matter. Not now. Not when his blood ran thick and hot in the way of the Apache. Not when his head was full of the sound of past screams and pleas for a mercy that never came. His heart was dark, beating with the full force of his rage and unquenchable hatred, driving it through his veins in a hard, primal rhythm. It was a current too strong to be curbed by the horror he saw in her face when he looked up.

"Get back to town, Amanda. This doesn't concern you."

The tight, controlled tone, the silvery glitter in his eyes; this wasn't the man she knew. But she'd seen him before as he held a rifle on a helpless man. As he'd pulled the trigger without an instant of remorse. It was the face of a man who could kill without care. And she was terrified of him.

"Harmon." Her voice wavered in uncertainty.

Seeing her, the cowboy began to twist and wriggle like a trout on the end of his rope. He turned all his pleading attentions upon Amanda. "Please, ma'am. I didn't do nothing. Cut me loose. Cut me down afore he kills me."

Amanda was not a woman of the West. She came from a gentle society, where human life was lauded, where one did not act upon violent impulse, where such atrocities would not be borne. Her stomach was in nauseous knots. Her mind reeled. "Harmon, cut him down." It was a soft request, one she hoped would touch upon the heart of the man she knew. She was wrong.

"Don't interfere," Harm warned her coldly. "Get away from here. You've no part in this."

"Harmon, what are you doing? Why are you torturing that man?"

"I'm seeing justice done," he corrected fiercely. "You would not understand."

"I don't. I don't see how you can do this. Stop it. Stop it at once. Cut him down."

"No." That was a rumbling growl. He looked away from her expression of taut confusion. Her anguish was playing havoc with the softness of his white soul. So he wouldn't look and he wouldn't listen. She wouldn't deprive him of this savage satisfaction. He closed his eyes, bringing back the awful images to sear across them, returning his strength of purpose, his capacity to enact this vicious retribution. His calm settled. His eyes opened to behold his writhing prey. The darkness returned inside him. Nothing he could do would be vile enough, cruel enough, for adequate compensation. But he would try his best. He knew thousands of ways and he would implement them with meticulous care. Because he was honor-bound to see it done. Amanda was no longer a distraction. She didn't exist in the hot, blood-scented world he'd slipped back into, where scars ran deep enough to sever heart from soul. Nothing could touch him there. It was like madness.

Amanda knew she'd lost him. She watched the impassive mask cloak his features, hardening them to a one. The victim of his torment was bucking, choking on the thickening smoke of the fire. He didn't speak or beg. He was making moaning, guttural sounds. Amanda couldn't take it.

"Harmon, please." She knelt beside him on the ground. He ignored her. Her hands pressed his forearms. They were like rock. "It's indecent. It's inhuman."

Inhuman? He almost laughed. His lips twisted with the irony of it. Inhuman wasn't what he was doing, it was what had been done to him. This . . . this was purification of that pain. It was his right, his duty. He couldn't explain

119

that to someone outside his blood, to someone who didn't *know*.

"Amanda, go away."

She grabbed him hard, trying to shake him. He wouldn't budge, not in body, not in conviction. "Stop this! You're behaving like an animal!"

"An animal?" He looked at her then, staring through eyes white hot in misery and ferociousness. He pointed at the twitching cowboy. "That is an animal. That is something that needs killing. Would you step on the scorpion that stings your hand? Would you crush the insect that sucks your blood? Would you strike out in righteous fury against something that rips and mutilates the foundations of your life until all you can see is ugliness and pain and death and despair?"

His eyes blazed. He was gripping her, too, his hands cuffing her upper arms in constricting circles. Her face was pale, wet with tears of fright and distress. Small gasping sobs snagged at her throat. Yet he wouldn't bend. He pushed her away, sending her sprawling in the dust.

"Go back to town. Wait for me there. Go now."

"No," she returned with a surprising strength. "I'll not leave you to this—this horror."

"Pleeese. Help me." The low moaning began again.

Amanda shuddered. How could Harm sit so stoic? How could he not respond to the horrendous suffering of another man? She felt sickened to the core of her being. Her words reflected her inner agony.

"Harmon, if you proceed with this, I will never forgive you. I will never be able to look upon you as anything but a despicable murderer."

His reply was inflexible. "It doesn't matter."

It didn't matter. She didn't matter. Her mind was stunned by the truth. Continuing this brutality was all that mattered to the half-breed Harmon Bass. If he didn't care about decency and he didn't care about her, what else was there? She grabbed for an idea with a desperate panic.

"Cut him down or I'll never pay you one cent of what I owe you. I mean it, Mr. Bass! I'm paying you to help me, not to butcher some poor creature and enjoy doing it."

"Don't pay me. The money's not important."

"What is?"

He didn't respond.

She struck at him with her ineffective fists, until he grew annoyed and gripped her wrists to hold her away. She looked nearly as wild as he did, with her face contorted and her eyes swimming wetly. "What will make you stop?"

"Nothing. You don't understand. I hope to God you never understand." He gave her a shove. She was back at him with a tenacity that under other circumstances would have impressed the hell out of him. Then he saw she had his knife. He froze. "Are you going to use that on me?" His drawl was icy.

She was up in a flash, the blade sawing on the taut rope. He caught her wrist, caught her about the waist to halt her struggling. He could feel her convulse with weeping.

"Harmon, please. Please cut him down."

In one quick arc, Harm parted the rope with his knife. The groaning cowboy fell onto the fire, where his clothing began to smolder and smoke. Harm kicked him off it. Amanda sagged, her tears rolling in relief. And the cowboy began a weepy mumble.

"Thank you. Thank you. I don't know who you are, mister, or what your beef be with me, but I thank you for sparing me that. Cut loose my hands and we can forget the whole thing. Musta been a mistake." His bound wrists lifted in weak supplication.

"No mistake."

Harm bent. The knife made an efficient move. Blood

121

gushed in a spurt from where he opened the man's throat from ear to ear with one ruthless pull of the blade. With a gurgle and a few jerks, it was done. Harm was crouched over him. He rested his forehead atop arms crossed over bent knees. The blade in his hand began to shimmer as sunlight glanced off it in unsteady flashes. For a moment he was motionless, then the shaking of his hands spread to encompass the rest of his body. After several seconds of hard, fitful shivering, he was still again. A long sigh escaped him. A sound of unburdening fulfillment. Then he wiped his knife on the dead man's shirt and stood.

Amanda was staring at him with a fixed horror. He fought not to retreat from it. A toughness of expression settled into lines of hard challenge. He waited for her to condemn him for what he was: a killer, a savage, a madman.

"You killed him." It was spoken more in confusion than in accusation.

"You wanted him cut down and I did. Keeping him alive was never part of it. Let's go."

Chapter Eight

Amanda collapsed without a sound. Everything was whirling in great dizzying swoops. She managed to roll over onto her hands and knees just in time to retch up all of Elena Lowe's tasty breakfast. Then, with her insides quivering weakly, she crawled a few feet and dropped into the sand.

His hands were on her, stroking her shoulders, carefully lifting her. His gentleness was now an obscene parody. She couldn't endure it.

"Don't touch me!"

Harm jerked back as if she'd hit him. He balanced on the balls of his feet like a cat and watched her. He felt concern now that his soul was freed of vengeance and it shone in his pale gaze. But there was no guilt over what he'd done, no shame or regret. He put it behind him as if the vicious act was no more than a gaffe in proper behavior. As if she could forgive what she'd witnessed or forget what she'd seen shimmering in his crazed stare.

"Amanda." He reached toward her again with bandana in hand, meaning to wipe the perspiration from her brow.

"No! Stay back." She was trembling all over.

"I'm not going to hurt you," he said softly. "I'd never hurt you."

Her eyes were wide, filmed over with grief. "How could I ever believe that after what you just did?"

"That has nothing to do with you," he argued fiercely.

"But it has everything to do with you, Mr. Bass. A rational man would have stopped. A compassionate man would never have conceived of such a thing."

He sounded annoyed. "You just don't un—"

"Understand? That's become quite the excuse." Her voice rose shrilly. "How could a respectable person understand? How could a sane person condone such—such—" Words failed her but her meaning was very clear. Harm stood. His features were stony.

"Get on your horse. I still have to get supplies before we—"

"I'm not going with you."

He paused and frowned for a moment. Then he nodded. "It's probably best you don't. You can stay with the Lowes."

"I'm not going anywhere with you. I'm going back to New York. This place has taken enough from me already. I refuse to surrender up my decency or my humanity."

He stared at her, then gave a snort of irritation. "Oh, please, Miss Duncan. Now is not the time to indulge in playing out one of your dramatic novellas. Get on your horse."

"No! You are not going to push me around. I have been taking care of myself and my brother for ten years. I may not have the wherewithal to hold my own out here, but it's not because I'm weak or stupid, Mr. Bass. I am not a child and you will not treat me like one. I don't need you to tell me what to do."

"And look how well you've done for yourself so far. Your brother's dead and you're stranded in the middle of a desert with a half-breed murderer. No, I can see you're doing just fine."

Instantly, he regretted the words. Even before her tender lips began to quiver, he cringed beneath his own cruelty. She had him twisted inside out. He couldn't think. He couldn't see beyond her tear-stained face, and it had him acting like a fool.

"Amanda, I'm—"

"No, Mr. Bass. You are quite right. I have made a terrible mess of things. I've made some awful mistakes; in allowing Randy to come out here, in following, in trusting you. I just can't afford to make any more of them." Amanda climbed to her feet with a painful awkwardness, but then stood with such dignity that he felt reduced.

"I'll take you back, ma'am," he offered quietly.

"First, you bury him."

Harm went rigid. "No."

"Bury him. You inflicted an indecent death upon him, now, by God, you'll see him buried decently!"

He squared off in outrage. "I won't! Let him boil under the sun to get used to the temperature in Hell. Let the buzzards and the coyotes tear the flesh off his bones. He doesn't deserve more than that. Not from me!"

"Then I'll do it."

If he had any doubt that she meant her firm declaration, it was soon quashed. She hobbled stubbornly about in search of a place to dig. Dropping down on her knees with the dusty skirt belling out around her legs, she started scraping with her hands in the arid Texas dirt. After an inch or two of surface sand was scooped aside, Amanda came to a layer of hard, sun-baked soil. In less than a minute, her hands were raw. It was like burrowing through stone.

"Amanda, stop." Harm's tolerance was gone the instant he saw she was bleeding. He grabbed her elbow but she twisted away. "Enough. You've proved your point. You are a fine Christian woman and I am a damnable villain. Now let's go."

The exertion winded her in the searing mid-morning heat. She wished for a shovel but feared she'd need dynamite to cut through the impenetrable ground. But she wouldn't give up. She tottered to her feet and bristled when Harm had the nerve to smile as if he'd won some small victory. She set him straight quick enough. "Not until he's buried," she wheezed. "If I can't dig a hole and put him in it, I'll just have to build a grave up over him."

Harm made a noise. It sounded like a word, probably an Apache curse.

Amanda hesitated. "Will you help?" She refused to plead with him. She'd seen how far that got the last few who depended upon his mercy.

"No," he stated again.

She flung back her shoulders and glared at him. "Fine. Just stand there and watch, then."

"I always enjoy watching someone make a fool of themselves." He was angry; at her for her unreasonable demands and at himself because he couldn't compromise his honor to help her. She was already sweating buckets.

Casting about for a likely spot to inter the deceased, Amanda spotted a small gully clogged with gnarled scrub. If she pulled out the bushes and rolled the man in, half her job would be done. "What's his name, so I can cut some kind of mark over him."

"I don't know," Harm growled.

She looked at him, long and hard. "You don't know? You knew him well enough to torture but not to get a name?"

"We were never formally introduced. Like I said, he wasn't my friend."

"Maybe he has something in his pockets that might

identify him. Would you look, please?" She didn't want to touch him any sooner than she had to with that horrid second smile beneath his chin.

"No." It wasn't said with belligerence, it was said with uneasiness.

"I don't think he's going to mind."

"I don't care to have anything to do with corpses."

"You just like getting them to that state, is that it?"

Somberly, he announced, "There are bad spirits with the dead. Ghosts—"

"Ghosts?" She laughed brittlely. "Now who sounds like the fool? Ghosts and spirits, indeed. How conveniently you turn Apache when it suits your purpose, Mr. Bass."

She knelt on the edge of the shallow ravine, where it was choked with brush, and grasped a stiff greasewood branch. The moment she gave a hard yank, she heard an odd sound.

"Amanda!"

At the same time she heard Harm's anxious cry, she felt a sharp pain just above her wrist. When she jerked back, she lost her balance and tumbled headfirst into the gully. Right on top of a ball of rattlesnakes.

They'd been curled up together out of the intensity of the sun and weren't at all pleased by the intrusion. Amanda could feel their long, thick bodies writhing beneath her. She thrashed frantically, but one foot was twisted under her and the bank kept crumbling away. Whirring and buzzing sounded all around her, making the horses snort and rear and finally bolt. Something struck her in the same arm just below her elbow. Pain scissored along her cheekbone as she got a close-up glimpse of diamond-designed skin. She was screaming by then.

"Ammy, grab on!"

She looked up wildly to see Harm. Her arms flung

upward, waving, winding tightly about his neck. He tried to lift her up and slid, one foot furrowing down the slope on top of the seething mass. He felt one, then two strikes deflected off his boot, then a stab in the calf of his leg. By then, he'd twisted and hauled and finally rolled the both of them clear of the gully. He tore out of her arms, scrambling for the spot where he'd laid his carbine. He emptied it into the nest of serpents with a methodical haste, until there weren't enough pieces left for even half a hatband. Then he let the rifle drop and turned to Amanda.

She was huddled where he left her, her big eyes blank with shock. Though his system was jerking with the delay of fright she'd given him, Harm forced cool, survivalist thoughts. Their situation was grave and every second was precious. He knew what he had to do as he drew his knife. After pushing the blade into the ashy remains of his fire, he went to Amanda, sinking down on his knees before her, calling her name. When she didn't respond, he frowned slightly and rubbed his thumb along the cut in her cheek. It was one mark and it was too soon to tell if it was a dangerous one. She leaned instinctively toward the warmth of his palm.

"Harmon." A whisper as fragile as his control. Then she was in his arms, her face pressed up against the bare heat of his neck, clinging with desperate tremors.

"Shhh, *shijii*. It's all right. It's all right. Hush. Don't be frightened."

She calmed at the sound of his voice, settling into a faint trembling. "Oh, Harmon, I hate snakes."

"I know you do, little girl. I made stew out of 'em for you."

He felt her smile and then what could only be the brush of her lips over the rapid pulse in his throat. His eyes squeezed shut. *Yusn*, he loved her more than his own life!

Realization struck him hard, and the knowledge was more potent than the venom coursing through his veins. He was in love with her and probably had been since the first time she'd told him, *Be careful, Harmon*. But now was not the time to wonder what he was going to do about it. He took her by the forearms and held her back. He lost a long minute just looking at her. She was beautiful even with the redness of weeping around her eyes, the two-tones of burn and peel upon her freckled nose, and the scratch from a rattler's fang across her cheek.

Mistaking the reason for his intense stare, Amanda asked with a hushed sobriety, "Harmon, am I going to die?"

His smile was faint. "No, *shijii*, but before the poison runs its course, you may wish it. Show me where you were bitten."

When she pointed out the two sets of puncture marks, he wrapped his bandana around her elbow and knotted it tightly, checking to make sure a pulse remained below his hasty tourniquet. Then he looked at the bites. There was no marked bleeding, just an oozing of clear yellowish fluid. He reached for his knife and she tensed. He took up her hand so that the back of it was nestled in his palm and his thumb was lightly stroking in the basin of hers.

"Ammy, I want you to listen and not to be afraid."

She nodded.

"I'm going to make a cut over each mark and suck the venom out. You stay as quiet as you can so it won't go pumping through you any faster than it has to. Can you do that for me?"

"Yes."

He picked up the sterilized knife to open small gashes over the puncture wounds, lining them up along the length of her arm and making quick slices, careful not to go so deep as to damage muscle or tendons. Then he put

129

his mouth to the first site and began to draw out the poison. She closed her eyes and tried to do as he asked and relax. It wasn't easy, knowing that every beat of her heart carried the toxin throughout her system. Still, he had said she wouldn't die.

"Have you ever been bitten by a rattlesnake before?"

He glanced up. "When I was little. I almost—" He'd been ready to say *died*. Then he smiled. "That's when I learned to eat snake and like it." He went on to the second wound.

"I thought snakebites killed people."

"You read too much." He drew and spat another mouthful. "Half the time, they don't sink enough venom in for you to notice."

"And the other half?"

"It can get bad."

She frowned at that generalization. "By bad, meaning what?"

"Bad. Hush now and let me finish."

Bad. She swallowed hard, trying to keep her imagination from running wild over that one. Then she glanced around and cried out in dismay. "Harmon, the horses are gone!"

"I know."

"What are we—"

"Shush! Let me finish!"

It was harder to stay calm. No horses and the threat of "bad" hanging over her. "I've really done it this time," she muttered.

Harm looked up. Instead of agreeing, he gave her a puzzled look. "Why did you come after me?"

She flushed uncomfortably. "You'll laugh."

"No, I won't."

"I—I thought you might need me," she answered lamely.

He didn't laugh. He didn't even smile. An intensity came over his features that altered her circulation more efficiently than his tourniquet. Then it was gone. "I do." He sat beside her and used the tip of his knife to rip an opening in the leg of his denims. She gasped when she saw the twin puncture marks, already swelling and beginning to discolor.

"Oh, God. You've been bitten, too."

He was busy tearing one of the sleeves from his shirt to knot securely about his calf. With a steady hand, he scored the wounds, then he looked up. "I need you to draw the poison out. I can't reach it."

She nodded quickly and he was proud of that lack of hesitation. "What do I do?"

"Just what I did. Make sure you spit, don't swallow."

He lay back on the hot ground when she began. He had to think. The horses were gone. They had no supplies. Amanda had been bitten twice, and he knew from the way numbness gave way to pain that his own bite was a severe one. The best way to combat snakebite was to stay quiet but that wasn't going to be possible. If he got sick, he wouldn't be able to take care of Amanda. They'd both die, not from the poisons but at the mercy of the elements. They couldn't stay here. He had to get them both to aid. He wasn't about to let Amanda Duncan die.

He touched the back of her head. "That's enough."

She watched silently while he got up and tested the strength of his leg. He didn't favor it but she could see the muscles of his face pull taut. Then he did the unexpected. He went to the dead man and dragged him over to the ravine, slinging him in on top of the snakes.

"Fitting grave," he muttered. "That all right with you?"

She nodded.

He rounded up stones and dumped several armloads

over the stiffening corpse. In the excitement, she'd forgotten all about the cause of their troubles. Her horror and disgust had faded with the gentleness of his touch. It no longer seemed important to her and she wondered why it suddenly was to him. He worked without comment and Amanda felt the sting of tears. She blinked them away. He was doing it for her, by way of an apology, the only one he could make within the stiff boundaries of his pride. Even if he didn't care about the poor soul he'd sent to hell, he cared enough about her peace of mind to go contrary to his convictions. He couldn't have made a grander gesture to show how much she'd come to mean to him.

When he was done, he tore the other arm from his sweat-soaked shirt and tied it about his forehead to keep the dampness from his eyes. Standing there, surveying their surroundings, he looked every inch the Apache. Then he began to move about with crisp, unwasteful actions, using part of the severed rope to make a sling for his carbine; checking the rounds in the dead man's pistols before tucking one in the waistband of his jeans, next to his knife sheath in the back, and handing one to Amanda.

"Let's go." He put down his hand and she took it. She didn't ask but the questions were clear in her eyes. So he told her. "We're going to have to walk out, Amanda. No one's coming to look for us."

"All right, Harm." Said trustingly, without hesitation.

"Put your arms around my neck."

That she did without pause, hugging him tight. He felt her surprise when he swept her up off her feet, bunching her dusty skirt behind her knees as he did.

"What are you doing, Mr. Bass?"

"I'll make better time toting you than I will waiting for you. Let your arm hang down lower than the rest of you. Good." He wouldn't tell her that motion hastened the sickness and that by keeping her still he was saving her from the worst of it. He wouldn't think about it, just about what had to be done. He started off in an easy lope. Immediately, she was protesting.

"Harmon, Terlingua is the other way!"

"I know. This way is faster." He was heading toward the foothills of the Chisos.

"Where are we going?"

"For help. Now lay your head down and be quiet."

Obediently, she leaned her head upon his shoulder and let her eyes close.

For the next hour, his shambling gait never altered. He said nothing and showed no sign that she was a difficult burden. Wrapped in his arms, rocked by the jogging movement, Amanda started to feel bad. Her arm hurt, progressing from a tingle to a steady throb. She was dizzy and so nauseous she grew afraid to open her eyes. And it was hot, so hot. Harm's shirt was unpleasantly sticky and her own clothes clung disagreeably. She wanted to strip them off. She wanted cool air and cold water. She wanted to lie down and rest without the constant joggling. She wondered if dying would be more merciful.

Harm stumbled. He caught himself and continued, but his pace was broken. Within minutes, he was limping badly, weaving in his path and finally close to staggering.

"Harmon, stop. Put me down. You have to rest."

"Can't. Have to go on. Can't stop now." His words were slurred together. Despite what he claimed, he slowed and sank down to his knees. When he didn't release her right away, Amanda wiggled out of his embrace. He went down on hands and knees, gasping shallowly for breath.

"Let me see your leg," she demanded. He obeyed the authority in her voice and toppled onto his side. The swelling had grown and spread upward. "I don't think this is good."

He blinked hard to focus; his pupils were pin dots in a sea of hot blue. He fumbled with the band around his calf, unable to coordinate the movements.

"What do you want me to do?"

Harm lay back, closing his eyes, panting softly. "Tie that off higher, up above my knee. It needs to be cut and drawn again."

"I'll do it. You rest."

It was hard to move. She fought against a dragging lassitude. The poisons, no doubt. She knotted the make-shift tourniquet and checked to assure some circulation was getting through. Harm hadn't moved. Amanda looked at the angry swelling and swallowed uneasily. She reached for his knife.

"Do you want me to do this?" she asked faintly.

He heard the fright in her tone and struggled up. "I'll take care of it." But when he took the knife from her, his hand was wildly unsteady. Amanda stilled it with her own. He looked up. There was no focus in his gaze.

"I'll see to it, Harm. It's all right. You lie back."

He flopped down with a soft moan and was unmoving except for his irregular breaths. Taking a deep one of her own, Amanda cut into the purplish swelling. Harm's leg jerked and trembled, but he made no outcry. She set the knife aside and began a steady suction. When that was done, he made an effort to gather his strength. He rolled onto his belly and tried to tuck his knees up under him. It was a weak and futile gesture. He couldn't get up.

Watching him worriedly, Amanda stalled for time; time he needed to rest. "I could sure use a drink of something cold. I read somewhere that cactus pulp holds in fluid. Is that fact or fiction, Mr. Bass?"

He turned onto his side and blinked slowly. "Fact."

She picked up his big blade. "I'd like to see for myself. Which one of these would be the tastiest."

"Try that one there and watch the spines. Don't put anything with a milky sap in your mouth."

"Goodness. I don't think I have to worry about it killing me at this point in time, do I?"

He smiled faintly. "Jus' do what I tell you."

Every plant in the Big Bend was a porcupine. Nature armed to the teeth, Amanda thought as she gingerly sliced into a thick-bodied cactus. It yielded a surprisingly moist center and she hurriedly trimmed away the outer skin so she could cut it into sections. Sucking on one, she brought a handful back to Harm.

"Chew it," he mumbled. "Don't swallow it." He stuffed a piece into his mouth and began crushing it for the precious juices. Amanda did the same. She looked a mess; all sticky from the heat, with her hair in wet strings. Her inappropriate clothing was damp and the tender skin of her shoulders an angry red from burning. But she looked beautiful to Harm. Wild and beautiful, like the countryside, sucking on cactus like an Apache squaw, dressed like a Mexican gypsy. She was a pain. She talked too much. She rushed headlong into trouble, dragging him behind her. But at that moment, there was no place he'd rather be than half-dead of snakebite in a desert with Amanda Duncan.

When all of the cactus pulp was gone, Harm dragged himself up into a sitting position and glanced about. "We're not far. Just a couple of miles. If we can keep a steady pace, we should be able to—" He broke off and doubled over with a low groan. A terrible roiling began in his belly. Sweat beaded upon his face.

"Harmon?"

Waving her back, he crawled several feet and was violently ill. When he rolled to his back, his knees tucked up tight against a weakly spastic stomach, Amanda knelt down beside him, blotting the dampness from his face with the hem of her skirt. He felt embarrassed and wretched beyond belief.

"I'm sorry."

"Oh, I know exactly how you feel," she soothed with words, with her touch. "I've been fighting to keep things down for the last hour. This is what you meant by 'bad', isn't it?"

He nodded jerkily and closed his eyes. Then he told her the worst of it. "I can't get up."

Her palm was gentle upon his cheek. "I know. It's all right."

"You can make it, Ammy. It's not far. Then you can send back help. I'll be all right here."

No, he wouldn't. He was completely helpless, too sick to stand or even move to defend himself if he had to, too weak to help himself to the necessities he had to have in order to survive the heat.

"I couldn't make it alone," she lied quietly. She couldn't leave him. She wouldn't even consider it. "I'd be afraid out there all by myself. I'll just sit with you until you're stronger."

He was too far gone to see through her pretense. "Okay."

She angled herself around, drawing his head and shoulders into her lap while shading him with her body. His eyes didn't open again. She stroked his face anxiously.

"Don't you die on me, Harmon. I'd never forgive you. And you'd never get paid."

The corners of his mouth curved slightly. "I'm not planning to, ma'am."

She smiled and had to swallow down an enormous wad of emotion. "Just rest easy, Mr. Bass. Let me take care of you this time."

"I'll be better soon," he muttered.

I hope so. God, I hope so.

Instead of admitting that wish, she brushed back the sticky dampness of his hair and crooned, "Of course you will."

Despite her determination to stay alert, Amanda drifted as the poison pushed through her. She came awake with a start, finding herself bent double over Harm with her forehead resting atop his. The first thing she did was check for his pulse. It was weak and fast, like his breathing. He didn't stir. Slowly, she forced her back to stiffen so she could sit upright. The dizziness came up in sickening waves. She sat quiet for a moment until it receded. Then she heard again what had awakened her, a rustling in the underbrush nearby.

Panic leapt within her sluggish mind. Indians. Outlaws. Wild animals. Danger. "Harmon?" she whispered anxiously. His head shifted on her knees. His eyes didn't open. He was no help. He couldn't defend her. He couldn't defend himself. That's when it sank in deep. She would have to keep them both safe. Her arm curved over Harm's chest protectively as she drew the heavy .45. A stillness settled inside her, along with a certainty that if any man or beast threatened, she would blow a hole right through them. The movement sounded again, closer. Amanda used her thumb to cock the pistol.

Harm exploded at that gentle click. He lunged off her lap, rolling to one side and up into a crouch with such fierce grace, she knew it was instinct rather than conscious thought directing him. He had his knife in one hand, the second pistol in the other. His gaze darted for a sign of attack.

And then it came. A low nickering sound and the jingle of reins as Fandango pushed through the mesquite, looking for care and companionship. The taut readiness drained from Harm. He sagged to his knees, weapons dropping to the sandy ground. When Amanda made a glad noise and started up, the horse snorted warily and Harm grabbed her arm.

"Don't scare him. You go chasing after him and he'll run."

She stared at him levelly. "No, he won't. He'll come when I call. He's my horse."

Harm gave a soft bark of laughter. "Ammy, that's fiction. We're talking about a dumb animal, not some trained pet. Ease up to him slow and grab for the reins. Do what I tell you."

Amanda ignored him as she slowly stood on unsteady legs. Making soft smooching sounds and calling him by name, she extended her hand and waited. Fandango whinnied and walked right to her. Grasping the reins, she smiled down at Harm with a smug I-told-you-so attitude. He shrugged, happy to be proven wrong. Hell, he'd have come running, too, if she'd called him like that.

Within minutes, they were both mounted, Amanda in front holding the reins and Harm leaning into her back.

"Which way, Mr. Bass?"

He lifted his head. It took a tremendous effort. With vision rapidly dimming, he had to rely upon memory. "See that break in the rocks up ahead?" He felt her nod. "Steer for that."

It was close to dusk when Amanda made out the shape of buildings. A ranch with adobe house and scattered outbuildings. Relief flooded through her. She knew she couldn't have held out much longer.

"Harmon, is this the place?"

He made a low sound but didn't stir. His head was heavy upon her shoulder.

Seeing nothing else on either horizon, she headed for the ranch. When Fandango shuffled up into the dusty yard, a woman appeared on the porch of the house, a shotgun in capable hands. Two black-haired children clung to her skirts.

"Get back inside," she hissed down at them, and they scampered away soundlessly.

Amanda tried to speak. Her tongue felt thick and the result was garbled. "Water, please. Snakebite. Can you help us, please?" Blackness fogged her vision, but she saw quite clearly that the woman was setting her gun aside and advancing rapidly.

"Oh, my God," she was crying. "Harmon!"

Amanda felt him straighten behind her at the sound of the woman's voice. "Becky?" he slurred, then began to slide. Right off the saddle into the woman's arms.

"Oh, Harmon. It's all right. You're home now. You're home."

And that was the last thing Amanda remembered. That and falling.

Chapter Nine

Whispers. Soft giggles. Children. A quiet, firm dismissing word. Amanda drifted, unable to make sense of it. She was surrounded by softness. Something cool was pressed to her forehead and that brought everything into focus. She opened her eyes.

"Good morning. I hope the children didn't wake you. They don't get a lot of company, so I'm afraid they're hard to shoo away. I'm Rebecca."

Amanda tried to form the words. "Becky," she murmured. Isn't that what Harm had said?

"Yes. Rebecca Bass. You're at my husband's ranch. You're going to be fine."

Amanda might have believed it right up until that moment.

Rebecca Bass. Her husband. The little black-haired children. Harmon was married to this woman. This was his family, his home.

She closed her eyes and moaned softly, not from a pain that was physical. He was married. That news was almost too much to bear atop all else. Her Harmon Bass. She'd never guessed, she'd never thought . . . Was this the reason he disliked her kisses? Because he had a wife and children? Dear Lord, was she in love with another woman's husband? She whispered his name forlornly.

"Shhh." Rebecca Bass leaned over her, applying the cool cloth once more. "Harmon's right here. Don't wake him. I just convinced him to get some sleep. I hope you don't mind the close quarters. He wouldn't leave you."

Amanda didn't understand until she turned her head and saw Harm asleep beside her. In the same bed. With his wife in attendance. She grew terribly upset at the thought of it. Because she'd begun to think very seriously about how much she'd like to share a bed with Harmon Bass. But of course that was quite impossible now.

"I'm sorry," she stammered in agitation. "I didn't mean to take your bed, Mrs. Bass." She was edging away from Harm, trembling with a confusion of distress. "I can rest elsewhere."

"What? My bed?" The woman was looking at her peculiarly, then she glanced to Harm and back. And smiled. "Oh! I see. No, you're fine, my dear. Just rest. Maybe I should have introduced myself better. I'm Rebecca, Harmon's sister. This is my children's room."

"Sister," she echoed in a near stupor of relief. *Oh, thank goodness.*

"I've made some soup. Do you think you'd be up to eating something?"

Amanda smiled with a foolish gratitude. "Oh, yes. That sounds wonderful. Soup." *Sister.* Oh, yes. It sounded wonderful.

When Rebecca left the room, Amanda turned toward the sleeping figure stretched out next to her upon the narrow bed. His features were lean, pale, and very still. She put a hand to his cheek and rubbed gently. She moved it from there to the side of his neck, feeling for his pulse and pleased to find it slow and strong. It was then she noticed his shirt was gone. He wore only the torn denims. For a long moment, she watched the regular rise and fall of his bronze chest before timidly moving her hand over its smooth, hard contours. And she was immediately lost to the sensation. So warm, so spare, so manly. When her fingertips trailed down to the flat plane of his abdomen, she glanced lower, skipping quickly over more interesting contours, to where his pant leg was ripped away from his neatly bandaged calf. It was then she remembered her own injuries.

She tried to lift her arm and found she couldn't. Perplexed, she shifted slightly so she could see it. And she smiled. She couldn't move her hand because Harm's fingers were wound tightly through hers.

"Here you go."

Rebecca came back through the doorway carrying a tray. Amanda was quick to jerk her palm off Harm's bare middle, then more carefully unthreaded their fingers. She was blushing fiercely by the time she sat up. How perfectly awkward, she thought, not only cozied up in bed with him but to have his sister catch her adoring his bared skin with her touch. But Rebecca displayed no discomfort. In fact, she continued to smile as she plumped some extra pillows behind Amanda's back.

"So, you're Ammy. Is that right?" At her nod, Rebecca smiled wider. "I wasn't sure. Harmon wasn't making much sense last night."

Ammy. Her mother had called her by that endearment and no one since. No one until Harm. "It's Amanda. Amanda Duncan."

"And you are Harmon's? . . ." She lifted her brow, waiting for the clarification.

"Employer," Amanda murmured quickly.

"Oh. I see."

Amanda thought she was seeing way too much but didn't comment.

"I'll let you eat your soup. We can talk later, when you're stronger." She rose and went around the bed. A gentle hand touched her brother's brow, checking efficiently for fever. Then she brushed back his hair in a gesture both tender and affectionate. Amanda was slightly surprised. From what she knew of Harm, she hadn't expected him to come from a loving family. But that was evident. Rebecca smiled at her again and went back into the other room.

Though she could have used a bath, some clean clothes, and a week's worth of sleep, the soup was good for starters. It was delicious. With its filling nourishment came a satisfied weariness. Amanda set the tray upon the floor and lay back into the indescribable comfort of a decent bed, the first she'd enjoyed since leaving New York. Quite naturally, she turned toward Harm, nuzzling her cheek against the warmth of his shoulder and banding his chest with the casual drape of her arm. She'd been sleeping beside him for a week and was too familiar with his closeness to think it out of the ordinary. Her eyes shut and her breath escaped in a contented sigh.

When Rebecca returned for the tray, they were twined together like companionable lovers. Her brow rose in momentary surprise as she observed the way the young woman's hand curved along her brother's ribs. Employer? She smiled indulgently. Perhaps. But that wouldn't explain the way Harm became irrational at the thought of being separated from her side. Of course, he had been clearly out of his head at the time. Nor would it explain the way the pretty female's expression fell to pieces at the thought of her being other than Harm's sister. Rebecca could be totally wrong in her assumption. But she hoped she wasn't.

"Good for you, Harmon," she said softly. "It's about

time." Then she turned to chase her curious brood away.

It had been a long time since he'd gone to sleep under a roof in a real bed. He knew exactly how long. Fourteen years. It took being half-dead from snakebite and Amanda Duncan to place him there now. And he wasn't inclined to move.

Someone—no, he was sure it was Rebecca—had opened the shutters to let light and warm air in. Brightness streamed across the bed, playing with molten intensity upon the highlights of Amanda's hair. He opened his fingers to draw in several strands, rubbing them, enjoying the feel even though it was far from its usual silken texture. It was late afternoon. The children would be off about their chores, which was why it was so quiet in the house. Harmon let the peaceful lethargy of the moment seep into his soul and he sighed in response to the powerful stirring inside him. Then he frowned, taken off guard by that sensation. He hardly recognized it. It had been so long since he'd known . . . happiness. It was a vague concept, one tucked away in childhood when he still held a naive sense of well-being. Happiness. He mused over it, turning it over and over like an odd puzzle. But he had to admit to the truth: He was happy to be home, with his family, with this woman; he was happy to be alive.

He shifted his knee cautiously, testing and tensing in readiness for the pain. A mild ache remained. The nausea had eased to just plain weariness. Most of the venom must have been worked out overnight or during that hellish trip to the Bass ranch. He had vague recollections: of Amanda cutting capably into the swelling on his leg; of her hunching down over him like a protective lioness when she thought danger threatened; of her feeding him the cactus.

He wouldn't have made it without her. That surprised him. She was always surprising him.

He eased up onto his side to watch her sleep. He must have been weaker than he thought, because his typical guardedness refused to surface. Instead, there was a welling tenderness and, beneath that, a simmer of desire. He was in love with her. The idea wasn't quite such a shock anymore, but he was no less afraid of it. As he was afraid of her and her ability to confuse the relationship between his heart and mind. She made them war with one another. As they were warring now. His mind told him to get up, to stay away, to protect himself and her. But his heart whispered of warmer things, seductive things.

Her face was turned toward him, serene in sleep yet wan from the effects of illness and fatigue. Looking at her with her delicate features burned cruelly by the sun, one wouldn't guess at her resilience or at the sheer grit she'd shown out on the plain. She looked so soft, so fragile with her pink lips gently parted in healing slumber. How would it feel to lean over and touch his mouth against hers? Her kisses in the hotel at Terlingua had thrown him so hard, he'd had no time to distinguish pleasure from panic. She'd promised that he would like it. He wondered if that was the truth.

"Amanda?"

He whispered it. She didn't move. He swallowed hard and lowered himself a resistant inch at a time until he could feel the warmth of her breath upon his face. He could imagine her voice.

You're supposed to close your eyes, Mr. Bass.

Very slowly, he did. Even slower, he lowered the remaining fraction that kept their lips apart. Soft. Her mouth was so soft, cushioning the cautious press of his. He made a sound, a low, wondering sound, and he felt her

145

stir to awareness. At the same instant, there was a tap on the door.

"Harmon, are you awake?"

He was off the bed in a roll, stumbling to his feet, banging into the washstand, and sending the graniteware bowl and pitcher to the floor with a deafening clatter after first deflecting off his bare toes. He was hopping on one foot, cursing in heated Apache, when the door opened to the inquisitive stares of his whole family. And on the bed, Amanda sat up, her big eyes open wide and fixed upon him. His heart was gone in an instant. He couldn't look away. The pain in his foot was forgotten. The presence of his sister and her four children was forgotten. All he saw was Amanda.

She smiled up at him and he melted right down to the bone.

"Are you all right?"

That was his sister. He glanced at her and all the warmth froze up inside him. What had he been thinking? He stared at Rebecca Bass as a deluge of guilt swept over him, cutting all other emotion out from under him like a flood along a soft bank. How could he have been thinking such things—*in his sister's house?*

"Harmon, are you all right?" she asked again, worriedly, because he was standing there on one foot, his features stark with desolation.

He took a slow breath. "I guess I'm not as steady as I thought." He forced an apologetic smile that hurt all the muscles in his face. Then he said very quietly, with a dozen different shades of meaning, "I'm sorry."

Rebecca was all tender sympathy. "I was going to see if you and Miss Duncan wanted to join us for dinner."

His glance slid to Amanda. She was gazing up at him, awaiting his response. Dinner. He didn't want dinner. He wanted to curl back up into that comfortable bed with

Amanda cuddled close. He wanted to sleep with her for a week. Then he saw the dampness on her mouth and recognized the threat.

"That'd be fine," he muttered gruffly. "Be out in a minute."

"I can't sit at a table like this!" Amanda exclaimed, plucking at her soiled clothing in horror.

Rebecca waved off her dismay. "No one is going to mind, Amanda. Eat first, then we'll find you something to wear." She looked between her brother and the woman on the bed, feeling the tension gathering there like a cloudburst ready to unload. And she smiled. "The food's hot, so don't take too long." Then she backed out, shoving the rest of the family behind her so she could close the door.

On the bed they'd shared, Amanda waited for him to say something, for him to look at her again. Cautiously, her tongue crept out to touch her lower lip. She could have sworn she'd woken with the feel of his kiss. That seemed unlikely, until she remembered the tight lock of his fingers through hers and the way he'd looked at her just minutes ago with his defenses stripped bare. For just an instant, she'd seen heart and soul in that look.

Or was she mistaken?

Harm was sidling around the foot of the bed, glancing at her with a sidelong wariness. As if she presented some kind of subtle danger.

"How are you feeling?" His question was stiffly posed as he picked up a fresh shirt his sister had laid out and shrugged into it. The politeness felt funny between them.

"Still a little queasy and my arm hurts, but much better than yesterday. You?"

"Fine." He looked toward the closed door as if measuring the time it would take to sprint the distance.

"Harmon?"

He slid her a look.

"Come here."

She could almost picture the quick turnings of his mind. He didn't move.

"Come here," she said again, and he advanced with a coiled-spring tension. "Sit." She pointed to the edge of the mattress. He eyeballed the spot for an uncertain second, then sat down. She wrapped her arms around him before he could draw a protesting breath, encircling his shoulders, her warm cheek mashed against his, her breasts flattened to the hard wall of his chest. He couldn't move. He didn't want to. Then, awkwardly, his hands came up, touching her slender waist, along the supple ridge of her back, unsure of where to settle. His eyes slid closed when he felt her lips buss the tender spot on his neck just below his ear.

"We made it, Harmon." Her breath tickled maddeningly. He struggled to contain a shiver of response. Thankfully, she leaned back just then, but there was no relief because she stopped so that their gazes were inches apart. He absolutely could not look away.

"Yes, we did," he said with an equal hush. "Thanks to you."

She smiled at that and he let out his suspended breath, sure the danger of the moment was gone. Until she leaned forward to quickly touch her lips to the corner of his mouth. It was brief pressure, but it shot through him like the force of a point-blank blast from his .40-.44 carbine.

"Introduce me to your family," Amanda was saying as she eased away from him.

In a wild rush, he wanted to say to hell with his family and drop her down upon the bed. But he didn't. Harmon smiled thinly, with a taut-wire control, and put out his hand. "C'mon." Hers crossed it. The first thing he noticed was that the softness of a week ago was gone from her skin. The second thing was how good the possessive curl of her fingers felt, clasping with a strength forged from hardships unknown to the pampered schoolgirl she'd been when she arrived. Toughness looked good on Amanda Duncan. Too damned good.

The moment they left the room, they were under siege.

"Uncle Harmon! Uncle Harmon!"

Harm met the barrage without flinching. In fact, he surrendered himself quite willingly to it, kneeling down so even the youngest of Rebecca's children could hug him about the neck. Apart from the exuberant welcome, Amanda watched as Harm's features softened into a genuine smile. The sweetness of that expression stunned her with tenderness. He loved these children. That was evident as he returned each hug, each noisy kiss, with like intensity. With the three smaller ones still hanging on him, he straightened to smile at the oldest boy.

"Howdy, Jack. Guess you're too old for all this now."

"Yessir." The boy put out his hand in a grown-up fashion. Harm gripped it firmly, using it to pull the somber child into a hard embrace, which the boy returned just as fiercely. Finally, Harm shook all of them off and they began peeping at Amanda with interest.

"Ammy, this rowdy lot are my niece and nephews." His tone was steeped with pride as he began with the tallest and worked his way down. "That there is Jack. He's fourteen going on forty. And Sidney, he's eight. Sarah is seven and Jeffrey—Jeffrey how old are you now? Five?"

"Six!"

Harm grinned to prove that he'd known it all along. With his hand on the youngest's head, he lifted his gaze to Amanda's. "Kids, this is Miss Duncan."

"She's awful pretty, Uncle Harmon," the little girl, Sarah, spoke up. "Is she your lady friend?"

"Sarah!" Jack growled in outrage, and the girl scowled

at him as if she'd done nothing to earn such censure. After all, they'd all been wondering the same thing. He shouldn't shout at her because she was the first to ask.

"I work for Miss Duncan," Harm clarified firmly.

Smiling to overcome the hurt of that brusque summary, Amanda's warm gaze swept the row of handsome faces. "Pleased to meet all of you. But you must call me Amanda. Miss Duncan sounds like a schoolteacher, and I'm not so very old as that."

The younger ones giggled. They were all dark-haired and dark-eyed duplicates. Jack surveyed her with a directness belonging to a lad of greater years. He shared some of the family features, but his hair was a dark auburn and his eyes a piercing ice-blue.

Rebecca spoke up, drawing her attention from the row of animated children. "Are you feeling up to this, Amanda? Our table's small and this bunch has no manners. I could bring you a tray."

Amanda smiled at Harm's sister. The resemblance was strong—the slightness of build, the Indian heritage—but her warm stare was dark and deep. "Oh, no, I like the noise." She almost added that she'd grown used to Harm's lack of etiquette. "Don't go to any trouble for me."

"No trouble, ma'am. Guess I'll have to introduce myself. I'm Will Bass."

For the first time, she noticed another figure in the room. He was standing back from the initial surge of welcome, regarding all the fuss with a reserved smile. He was tall, with thinning dark hair and a strong body supported by crutches under either arm. Amanda went to him, steps slightly wobbly as she skirted the cluster of children to offer her hand. His grip was gentle but not lacking strength. She was confused by the name Bass, wondering over the relationship to the rest of the family.

150

Rebecca answered it by saying, "Will's my husband," but that still didn't explain why he and Harm shared the same last name. She let the question pass because just then, she got a whiff of dinner.

It was a noisy affair with the seven of them crammed elbow to rib at the trestle table. But to someone like Amanda, who had never been surrounded by the fond clamor of family, it was wonderful. All the children talked at once, vying by volume for their uncle's attention. Harm sat at the end of the table, opposite Will, and took the adoration in stride. They wanted to know all the details of their arrival: why they were on one horse; how'd they'd both been snake bitten; what kind of job he was doing for the pretty Miss Duncan . . . everything. He answered them easily, one at a time, with infinite patience, especially those posed by Jack, who she could tell was his favorite. With the four of them chattering, he scarcely had time to grab a mouthful until Rebecca scolded them for being such pests. Harm looked to her and, with all the sincerity in the world, told her he didn't mind one bit. He could eat anytime, but it was rare when he got to fill up on his family.

And from his end of the table, Will Bass stared soberly at Harm with an expression Amanda couldn't begin to decipher. It wasn't fondness, but it wasn't exactly dislike, either. Worry was the closest description to what she saw in the silent man's face.

Rebecca set the children off to their after-dinner chores and fulfilled her promise to see Amanda comfortably cared for. While Amanda bathed in a big copper tub, rinsing away the worst of the day out on the desert, Rebecca found her some fresh underthings and a simple cotton dress to replace her tatters, as well as a soothing ointment for her sore shoulders and nose. Hesitantly, she mentioned the cream worked very well for other types of

151

injuries, and by her evasive glance, Amanda knew Harm had told her about her dappled backside. She thanked his sister for her generosity with only the most meager of blushes.

When she emerged from the bedroom, cleanly scrubbed and hair tied back with a ribbon, Amanda was met with Harm's sister's scrutiny. It was kind but no less keen. Wondering what she saw, she waited awkwardly for some sign of direction. She felt very much the intruder in the Bass home. Rebecca must have sensed her discomfort, for she was quick to smile and suggest their guest enjoy the cool evening air. She nodded her dark head toward the front porch and Amanda could see Harm standing out on it, staring up into the mountains. Suddenly, fresh air sounded very inviting.

"I like them."

Harm smiled at her as she came up beside him. "Me, too." Then he looked away again, and she could feel a restlessness settling over him. It was a sharp contrast to his easiness at dinner.

"Don't you get home very often?"

"When I can. Not as often as Becky and the kids would like."

"Often enough to bring them money?"

His glance was quick. She could see him wondering who'd told her, followed by the conclusion that it didn't matter that she knew. "Yeah. About that often."

"What happened to Will?"

He was used to her many questions and showed no signs of annoyance. "Shot from ambush. Took a bullet near the spine. Doctors said he would never get outta bed but they didn't know Will. Takes more than a coward's bullet to keep a Ranger down." He gave a taut smile of admiration. "He does the best he can, but he can't sit a horse or do a lot a' things that need doing. I help out when I'm around but I'm no rancher. I give what I can to see he has the hands he needs and I try to stay outta his way."

"What do you mean?" she asked, puzzled by that last tight phrase.

"Sits hard on a man with pride to see another taking care of his family. I don't take it personal." That was said very softly. And she could see he did. Harm took a cleansing breath. "The boys'll be doing a man's share soon, then they won't have to depend on me." And she could see, as well, how that notion bothered him. As if when they became self-sufficient, they'd have no reason to want him. The poignancy of his expression nearly broke her heart.

"They love you, Harmon." *I love you, Harmon* was what she wanted to say.

"What? Oh, yeah. Sure."

"So, what happened to the man who shot Will? Did they catch him?"

She knew before he answered. His features hardened into that inscrutable mask, with only the glitter of his pale eyes to betray him.

"I did," he told her matter-of-factly. "I tracked him down and I killed him."

And Amanda could see him ripping the blade of his knife across the helpless cowboy's throat. Suddenly, the night was too cool. She shivered. Harm couldn't help noticing. He grew even more remote without physically moving an inch. She regretted ever bringing it up between them, but now that she had, how to force the memories away?

"How is it that you and Will have the same name? Rebecca's your sister, isn't she?"

"She's my half sister. Her father was a farmer named

153

Peterson, married to my mother until he died when Becky was still a baby. After my mother died, Will and his wife—his first wife—took us in. When Mrs. Bass died, Will married Becky." He fidgeted uncomfortably. He didn't like speaking of the dead. He didn't like speaking of the past. But he figured it would be easier to answer her outright, because Amanda wasn't likely to let the subject drop until she was satisfied.

"So you and Will aren't—"

"We aren't anything to each other," he concluded for her. "His name is Bass, not mine. It was something folks started calling me 'cause they thought I belonged to him."

"So what's your real name?"

She knew that without hearing it, too. She could tell by the angry tension that fused his every muscle together.

"Damned if I know."

"Uncle Harmon!"

Immediately, three little bodies were pressing close, all grabbing for a hand or a sleeve, and his dark mood melted away.

"We want a story, Uncle Harmon," Jeffrey demanded.

"Well, I don't know. Your chores all done?"

A chorus of yeses. Grinning, Harm allowed them to drag him to the steps, where they pounced upon him until he sat on the top one. He had a nephew on each knee and Sarah's arms about his neck. And he looked ready to burst from the pleasure of it. Too old for such fussing, Jack sauntered up and sat cross-legged at the foot of the steps.

"Read to us," Sarah pleaded, kissing his ear until she had him squirming. Amanda leaned against the porch post, smiling. He didn't look like such a hard case with his lap full of kids and his face wreathed in smiles.

Not at all like a cold-blooded killer.

"All right. All right! What do you want me to read?"

"This!"

154

Sidney thrust a raggedy novel at him and Amanda recognized the cover at once: *Harmon Bass and the Texas Rangers; or, The Mexican Stand-off.*

"It's my favorite," the boy exclaimed.

It was her favorite, too.

Harm took one look at it and snorted. "I told you I'd tell you a story, not a bunch of lies."

"Pleeese, Uncle Harm!"

Sidney's plea started a harmony of precocious begging until he was worn down.

"Oh, all right. I'll read it. But don't you go believing a word of it, you hear?"

"If it's all lies, why would they print it?" That was soberly put by Jack.

" 'Cause the folks back east need something cheaper than whiskey to dull their minds on. Only a fool would believe what's printed up in this here moralistic garbage." Then he caught himself. He couldn't bring himself to look up at Amanda, nor could he lower himself to apologize for the truth. He amended the harshness of his statement with a quiet, "Folks read 'em because they like to pretend that there's something out there better than what they have."

"Is there?" Jack asked.

"I don't think so, Jack. What you got is usually the best you're gonna get." He heard the sound of Amanda's footsteps as she went into the house and he sighed to himself. "Still want me to read this?"

"Yes!"

He opened the cover and began.

"How long is he going to stay?"

"Will, he just got here."

"Ask him."

"I won't. He needs time to rest up. He needs time with his family."

"With my family, you mean. Becca, you know how I feel."

"Will, he's my brother."

"He's crazy."

"Will!"

"You know he is! And he's dangerous. He's a stick of dynamite with a smoldering fuse and I don't want him going off under my roof!"

The words came to an abrupt end. Man and wife stared, Rebecca flushing, Will seething and searching for control.

And Amanda, who'd come to a dead stop in the doorway, didn't know what to do or say.

Chapter Ten

"Oh, Amanda. I'm sorry. I didn't hear you come in. Was there something you needed?"

Rebecca Bass was all sweet smiles, as if the conversation Amanda had overheard had never taken place. As if she hadn't heard her husband calling her brother dangerously insane. Amanda smiled back, somewhat stiffly. This wasn't her business, she reminded herself. She had no right to intrude.

"I was just going to say good night and to thank you for dinner."

"I'll turn down the bed for you."

"Oh, you don't need to—"

But Rebecca was already hurrying from the kitchen, where her husband leaned against the table with a pint of bourbon at his elbow.

"I don't want to inconvenience your family, Mrs. Bass. I can sleep—"

"You'll sleep right in here," Rebecca declared with a no-nonsense authority as she swept into the room Amanda and Harm had shared the night before. "The children will think it a great adventure to all bunk together under the eaves. But be warned. They'll probably keep you up half the night with their whispering."

"I don't think a tornado could keep me awake tonight."

She stood watching as Rebecca bustled around the room, making it inviting for her. Pillows were fluffed, the spread turned back, and a dainty calico nightgown was already draped across the footboard.

"If you need anything, I'll be right across the hall." She paused in her cheery rambling and looked Amanda in the eye. Suddenly, she was as intense as her brother. "Miss Duncan, please don't let what you overheard upset you. Harmon is a very good man."

"I know he is, Mrs. Bass."

"There are reasons for the way he is. Please be patient, even if you don't understand."

Then she was gone.

Of course, she didn't understand. No one ever told her anything but vague, misleading half-truths. Harmon Bass was not who or what he seemed to be. He was a man without a name, and as to what he was, she hadn't a clue. She only knew that she was in love with him. Perhaps that was more foolish than believing in fiction. And if what Will Bass suggested was true, much more dangerous.

"Amanda, are you awake?"

He was silhouetted against the light in the main room.

"What is it, Harmon?"

"I want to check your arm. It'll just take a minute. Come on out here."

"I'm in my nightclothes. You come in here."

Silence. He didn't move. "Turn up the light." There was an unmistakable tension in that command.

Only when the darkness was dispelled did he advance into the small room, closing the door to give them privacy. Then, he crossed first to the window, pushing open the shutters to suck a deep draw of night air. He looked nervous, and she wondered if it was because they were alone and she was in her nightdress. Was he afraid she was going to kiss him again? Amanda sat with the covers tented over her knees, scowling at the idea that dread of her kisses should have him shaking in his boots.

"I'm quite tired, Mr. Bass. Could you get on with it, please. Believe me, I'm just fine."

"I'll feel better when I look for myself."

And he did seem better, at that. He came to sit on the edge of the bed without hesitation and took up her injured arm. His touch was very gentle as he unwrapped the wounds. Both were still bruised in appearance but the swelling was gone. They continued to ache dully and she said so when he asked about it. Then he retied the dressings expertly and, without looking up said, "I should probably check on the others, too."

Her eyes squinted. She was not going to drop her drawers for Harmon Bass. At least, not for medicinal purposes. "I don't think so, Mr. Bass."

"How would you know if any infection set in?" He was trying hard to sound detached.

"I'm sure it would make itself known. If I have any doubts, your sister can check for me."

He scowled as if greatly insulted that she should question the purity of his motives. In truth, she had every right to. His hands began to sweat just thinking of her soft, white bottom. He wasn't sure if he was relieved or remorseful as he got to his feet. "I'll let you get some sleep."

"Harmon?" Suddenly, she was reluctant to let him go. "What?"

"I . . . it . . . good night."

"G'night, Ammy."

"Where will you be?"

"Close by. I'll hear you if you sing out."

She glanced at the space beside her and almost asked

him, then was shamed to the soul because of it. Had her standards so deteriorated since coming west that she would invite a man to share her sheets right under his family's roof? Not that she was planning anything immoral. Or so she told herself. They weren't out on the dangerous plains now. There was no excuse to have him that close. But that didn't stop her from wanting him there. She wondered how she was going to get to sleep without the soothing sound of Harm's breathing next to her.

"Good night, Mr. Bass," she said again, more forcefully.

Harm smiled slightly, reading all the torments in her mind and feeling the need to be cautious. That spot beside her did, indeed, look inviting, but impossible as his resting place. For reasons she would never guess.

"G'night, ma'am."

Then before he gave way to temptation or she thought of something else that would provoke unwanted desires, he stepped out, closing the door, turning. Into complete darkness. Nothing. No shadows. No light. Blackness. Sense of time and place evaporated into that depthless void.

Harm froze. Every coherent thought shut down in an instant. His breath pulled in raggedly. There was no air in the strangling panic that followed and he made small choking sounds as he struggled for it. He knew Amanda's door was right behind him, its knob within reach, with the comfort of light and her presence readily at hand, but the knowledge couldn't connect with movement. He knew he was standing in his sister's cheery great room, but somehow, that failed to make an impression through the cold anxiety crushing his chest. He was sinking in time, into terror, and there was nothing to grab onto to save him.

"Harmon?"

"Becky . . ."

The hoarse quality of his voice spurred her into action. "Don't move, Harmon. It's all right. I'll get the light. Just hang on. Just hold on."

Then brightness flooded around him, obliterating shadow. He dropped to his knees, gasping, as if the darkness had suddenly released its clutching hold about his throat. And Becky was there, holding him close, rocking him against her as if he were one of her children.

"It's all right, Harmon. It's all right. Breathe deep."

"Mama?"

"No, *silah*, it's Becky."

For a long while, he was too weak and cold inside to do more than cling to the folds of her robe. She continued to speak to him, quietly, firmly, until finally he heard the words over the terrible drumming in his ears.

"Becky?" He sounded confused, as if waking from a terrible dream.

"Shhh. It's all right, Harmon."

Slowly, he eased back on his heels and wiped at the sweat on his face.

"Better?"

He nodded, feeling absurdly grateful and close to weeping. Then all traces of vulnerability were gone. He looked up at her through solemn eyes.

"I found another one of them."

Becky was motionless for a moment, then she asked, "Did you kill him?"

"Yes."

"Did he die horribly?"

"As bad as I could make it."

"Good." That sentiment was short and savagely spoken. Then her palm stroked her brother's cheek with an infinite tenderness. "I love you, Harmon."

His eyes closed. He said nothing.

"Four more. Then it will be over."

Harm nodded, suddenly so weary he could hardly move. It was an effort to stand, an agony to hug his sister close and share the tremors of her distress. Then she released him and he was able to stumble outside to suck in the renewing freshness of the night.

Rebecca turned down the light, sending everything back into blackness. When she started for her room, she came up short. Will was standing in the doorway, watching impassively. She didn't want to hear what he had to say.

"He's crazy, Becca. You're making it worse."

Wordlessly, she pushed by him into their shared bedroom.

"I want him out of here. What's it going to take? Him coming after me with a knife again?"

She faced him with a deep, vibrating steadfastness. "He's my brother and he will always be welcome in my home. I owe him, Will. You know that. I won't let it happen again."

"How are you going to stop him? He won't even know who you are." She said nothing, going white with upset. Because it was true. He saw tears in her eyes and let one crutch drop so he could open his arm to her. She was curled into him in an instant. Her weeping tore through him with guilt and despair. Then he sighed heavily and said, "I don't like what you become when he's here."

She went still. "What I am is not Harmon's fault. No matter what he believes, it's not his fault."

"Good morning."

Rebecca paused in the hanging of her clothes to greet Amanda with a smile. "There's coffee on the stove. You'd

162

better not touch the pie until Harmon gets back. It's peach, his favorite."

"Harmon's gone?" A terrible emptiness settled inside her. "Where?"

"Up there." Rebecca gestured toward the foothills of the Chisos.

The panic lessened, allowing Amanda to take a normal breath. "Is he hunting?"

"No. Running." She picked up the emptied basket as the wash moved languidly in the dusty morning breeze.

"Running?"

Rebecca smiled at her confusion. "Sometimes I think my brother is more Indian than most full-blooded Apaches." Amanda followed her into the house, to where the scent of fresh ground coffee flavored the air. "When the Apache are boys, they're toughened by swimming and running every morning before dawn. One of the more pleasant cruelties they put their bodies through to become warriors. He still does it once in a while when he's feeling a weakness inside himself."

Amanda glanced out the window toward the imposing Chisos. She was thinking weakness of the body from the snakebite. Rebecca knew it was a weakness of the soul but she said nothing to her brother's companion.

Amanda took a cup of the dark, bracing brew gratefully and seated herself on a high stool. The kitchen was warm and the opportunity ripe to find out more about Harmon Bass.

"Was Harm raised with the Apache?"

"What has he told you?" Rebecca asked politely, but there was no mistaking the edge of protective caution.

"Very little," Amanda confessed. "When he talks, it's not about himself."

Rebecca chuckled softly. She liked this eastern woman who spoke the truth without pause. So perhaps she was strong enough to hear it spoken. It was doubtful that she'd ever hear it from Harm. At least, not all of it. She began running the next batch of clothes through the wringer. "Our mother's mother was Mescalero. To the Apache, family is traced on the mother's side, so they consider Harmon Indian, not white. There was no man in our house, so his great-grandfather and Apache uncles saw it as their duty to see Harmon learned to be a man." She smiled somewhat wryly and added, "An Apache man, of course. And there is no rock or man-made metal on this earth harder than an Apache male. They're raised and bred for one thing, and that's killing—killing animals for food or men for revenge. And that's what the Apache made of my brother."

Amanda said nothing. She didn't know what to say to this calm revelation. But she began to understand.

"Oh, Harmon didn't live with them. He was considered the man of our house and we were his responsibility, but he'd go off, just disappear for days without a word, then reappear without any apology or explanation. It used to make our mother furious." She leaned her elbows on the washtub and smiled wistfully. "I remember the day Mama told him to shell peas. He was about six, and he gave her this indignant look and drawled out, 'Apache men don't do women's work.' She told him this one would if he wanted to eat. But he wouldn't budge. She whaled the daylights out of him and he still wouldn't budge. And to this day, he won't eat peas. The next day, Mama tells him to pick beans."

Amanda was grinning, full of the image of a haughty young Harmon. "And what did he do?"

"He picked them. He couldn't sit down after the business with the peas, but as long as he didn't make any grand declarations about what he wouldn't do, it was just his appetite and not his honor in the balance. So he kept

164

his mouth shut and picked. That was when he learned about humility and to closely guard his tongue."

"How old were you when your mother died?"

Rebecca didn't pause in her work. Her tone was neutral. "I was almost sixteen. Harmon was ten."

Ten. He'd been ten when he killed his first man. She had to wonder if the two incidents were related. But she didn't ask. Instead, she shared some of her own sadness.

"My parents died when I was seven. They drowned in a boating accident. My brother was killed a week ago. Harmon's tracking down his murderer for me."

Rebecca gave her a long, somber look. There was a deep knowledge of suffering and loss in that look. But no pity, and that lent Amanda strength. "Harmon will take care of it for you. That's what he does best."

But Amanda was no longer listening. She was staring out the window with an expression so still and strained, Rebecca took an immediate fright. She leaned forward to follow the glassy stare, past Harmon at the rain barrel and up into the hills for signs of possible threat. There was nothing out of the ordinary to cause such alarm in the woman beside her. Then Rebecca looked again. The focus of Amanda's stare was *Harm*. And it was the hungriest look Rebecca had ever seen. She smiled slowly.

"Amanda, I'm right in the middle of this. Could you be a dear and tell Harmon to round up any clothes he wants me to wash or mend? I'm not about to go crawling around in his saddle blankets looking for them. I don't do that for my husband and I'm certainly not going to do it for my brother."

"Of course." And Amanda was off the stool, grateful for the excuse.

She had to remind herself to walk, to breathe, to even close her mouth, which had begun to sag as she crossed the yard. The nearer she got, the harder it was to remember those simple things. Because the sight of Harmon Bass next to naked stunned the stuffings out of her. Her heart was flopping around inside her chest so wildly, she felt as though she was continually swallowing it down. When she finally stopped, it was to stand and stare, devouring more sleek brown flesh and tautly corded muscle than her virginal fantasies could contain.

For his tough predawn training in the hostile hill country, Harm had turned out in pure Apache fashion. His feet were encased in the leathery moccasins, and just about every other inch of him was bare except for the strip of cloth looped between his legs, with trailing ends tucked up into his belt so as not to entangle in his stride. Everything but the most basic male features was uncovered: the compact strength of his upper body; his hard, lean hips, the strong clean line of his legs; all of him bronzed, all of him glistening, each muscle swelled and defined with the hot blood of exertion. Beautiful. Awareness throbbed through Amanda in hurried little beats. She was afraid to move, afraid he'd hear her and grab up something to conceal the perfection of what she feasted upon with a visual abandon. She wasn't ready to surrender up the sight, not yet.

Harm hadn't heard her approach over the rawness of his breathing. His thoughts were preoccupied. He'd hoped the exercise would purify them as it had when he was a boy, when he'd made the run with his mouth full of water to discipline himself to breathe through the nostrils and build up lung capacity. He'd pushed himself ruthlessly then, just as he was now, to gain tight control over his body. He'd learned by treating himself more harshly than his cruelest enemy might. He'd been trained to hunt, to ride, to run, to climb. He'd plunged into creeks with the ice yet glazing them, then denied himself the warmth of a fire. He'd wrestled and fought with other

Apache youths until bleeding. He could travel for two days cross-country, on foot, without food, without stopping, living off the land while others perished of hunger, thirst, and sunstroke. The moccasins on his feet weren't as tough and resistant to abuse as he was in physical form. He could take pride in that. It was the other that disturbed him. Emotionally, he was an open wound.

There was no sense of oneness inside him. No purity of Apache blood. No wholeness of his spirit with *Yusn*, the Creator of All. No calm of purpose. The division held him helpless, keeping him from true harmony. He could run the hills until sweat broke and muscles cramped and breath labored, but he couldn't run from what he was. Or from what he was not. And he never felt that more acutely as when he was here, the place he called home without really belonging.

To purge his thoughts, he dunked his head into the catch barrel. It had been cold the night before and the water was a deliciously icy shock. He came up dripping, gasping, then shook himself like a wet dog, slinging water everywhere. That's when he heard her small cry of dismay.

Shoving drenched hair from his face, Harm turned to Amanda. Even his exhaustion couldn't prevent the sudden burst of inner energy. Pulse beats that had just begun to slow lurched back into a speeding tempo. It was the way she was looking at him, with a daze of unashamed desire. His first instinct was to duck behind the rain barrel like a bashful boy as her gaze trailed slowly down the hard-packed terrain of his chest to the scant covering of his loincloth. He could feel himself stirring, responding to the immodesty of her stare, just as she was responding to the evidence of his arousal with shallow little pants for breath. Suddenly, he didn't want to hide himself from her curious admiration. He stood, letting her look, liking the

167

detailing attentiveness of her eyes, feeling powerfully male and proud of it.

" 'Morning, ma'am. Was there something you wanted?"

He'd meant to prod her with that silky question, to force her to back down behind her blushes. But she didn't. Her dark eyes smoldered, caressing over him so slowly, so thoroughly, there could be no doubt at all as to what she wanted. His taunting play on words came back to hit him hard. She wasn't even inclined to be ladylike about it.

It wasn't until her lingering gaze lifted to his that she remembered herself. Yes, there was something she was supposed to tell him. What, she hadn't the slightest recall. When she looked perplexed, he began to smile lazily.

"Why, Miss Amanda, I can't believe you're at a loss for words."

"Oh, I'm not, Mr. Bass. I was just fumbling for the right ones."

"What might those be?" he coaxed with a huskiness of voice.

Amanda drew a tight breath. Her gaze swept over him once more. She plunged on recklessly. "That you are the most exquisitely gorgeous thing I have ever seen in my life, Mr. Bass. And I suggest you put something on before I'm tempted to forget myself."

He couldn't resist. Her adoration heated him up to a steady boil. His words were provokingly soft. "Just what might you be tempted to do, Miss Duncan?"

She touched him, first with fingertips, then with palms, sliding over the flatness of his belly in slow appreciation. He tightened like a green hide in the hot sun, until tension became an exciting torture. He knew he should stop it. They were standing in the middle of the front yard, where any of the four Bass children could come upon them at any second. That only made the moment tauter.

She took a step closer. Her hands moved up the hot slickness of his chest, fingers pausing over flat male nipples until they, too, stiffened with arousal. Unbearable sensation shivered through him. He reached up, catching her hands, pulling them down. She swayed against him, her cotton blouse adhering to sticky flesh. He felt her mouth press to his shoulder and the startling rasp of her tongue on salty skin. He forgot about breathing through his nose and began a rough panting as he speared the fingers of one hand into her golden hair, clenching, twisting without gentleness to pull her head back. Her eyes were mere slits through which passion glimmered. His other hand fit over the top of hers, directing it down to the hard contour of his bared flank, rubbing it in restless circles, then up and down his thigh. He moved against her, just a subtle shift of his hips, but enough for her to feel the massive thrust of him pushing at her skirt.

"Oooo." Her eyes opened wide, then fluttered shut. "Oh . . . Harmon. Ahhh . . . I had no idea."

No, she had no idea.

Abruptly, he shoved her away and was snagging a damp shirt off the clothesline. "Guess that answered my question. I'd better put something on."

The brusque rejection, his colorless voice; Amanda was spinning with confusion. She'd been completely lost to sensual pleasure, to the feel of his sleek skin and hard body, to the hot taste of him, to the firm promise of him. It would have taken nothing at all for her to have fallen right down into the dirt with him into a fornicating frenzy. The uncontrolled power of it should have scared her to death. Should have, but didn't. Next to the roaring in her blood, the mild nag of conscience was a whisper. She watched Harm shrug into his brother-in-law's bulky shirt and wondered a bit wildly if anything could break through the daze of her desire.

"I'm leaving tomorrow morning."

Amanda blinked. "What?"

"I want you to stay here. Becky will look out for you and she'd like the company."

"Harmon—"

He shied away from the hand groping for his arm.

"I don't want to stay behind."

"I'm not giving you a choice."

"Is it because of—of this?" She had no other way to describe the throbbing sexual tension.

"No." *Yes.*

Stubbornness gained rapidly on anxiety. She planted herself in front of him. "But we agreed—"

His hands cuffed her upper arms, painful in intensity. "Dammit, Ammy! Either you trust me or you get yourself someone else!"

She stared up into the angry blue of his eyes. Her words were quiet. "I trust you, Harm."

That soft agreement neatly undercut his fury. His grip eased, becoming an agitated kneading. "You'll be safe here while you get your strength back. I'll only be gone a few days. I have to ask some questions in places you don't even want to know exist."

"All right, Harmon."

Then he went striding up toward the house, angry because her submission worked upon him in a way her combativeness never would. Because he didn't want to leave her, not for a minute.

All day, Harm worked around the ranch house. Dressed in boots, jeans, chambray shirt, and an old Stetson, he looked every inch the cowboy he claimed not to be. He repaired the corrals, cleaned the trickling irrigation ditch of sand, fixed what needed fixing, and painted what needed painting, all without a directing word. His motions were tireless, slowing only so Jack could keep up in the tasks needing his assistance. And Jack loved assisting his uncle. Not to be excluded, Sidney appointed himself fetch-it, bringing tools, the wrong ones often as not, and generally getting in the way. Sarah skipped around his feet, running for dippers of water and carrying down lunch while little Jeffrey was a plain nuisance, asking a never-ending slew of whys and managing to put his foot into a full bucket of whitewash. And for a fellow of such unbending independence, Harmon accepted each overture with a grateful smile and infinite patience, aware that Will Bass watched from his chair on the porch, his expression hard and his coffee bourbon-laced. And that Amanda followed his every move with a lusting gaze. What he didn't know was that his sister had to turn away from the window where she'd looked down over him and his little helpful brood, unable to watch any more through the tears in her eyes.

Over a dinner Rebecca and Amanda prepared companionably between them, Harmon talked in earnest about the windmill from Chicago. So far they'd been lucky to tap into a spring, bringing water nearly eight miles down from the hills to feed the parched land. But the spring was sanding in, Harm warned. It was time to prepare for the day when the source was dried up completely. With a windmill, they could sink one hundred to two hundred feet of pipe and pump the needed water up into float-controlled metallic tanks. He'd read all about it and was excited to try it out.

"You're forgetting one thing," Will drawled after he was done. "How we gonna afford such a luxury contraption? The water from that there spring is free."

Harm's gaze slid briefly to Amanda, then back to his plate. "I'll see to it, Will."

"Why, that's right generous of you, Harmon. But no thanks."

Harm's gaze flew up, wide and blue. "The ranch needs a windmill. Less you're willing to tote the buckets down by hand." He broke off, eyes touching uncomfortably upon the older man's crutches. "I just think it'd be a good idea."

Rebecca's stare darted between husband and brother. She tried to smile. "Will, if Harmon wants to do it—"

"This ain't about what Harmon wants, is it? This is still my ranch, even though he pays to keep it going. I say we stick with what we got. Are you saying different?" He stared at his wife until she relented quietly.

"No, Will."

"No windmill." He went back to his meal with a fierce concentration.

The bowl of peas nudged Harm's elbow. He took it and passed it to Amanda without a glance. Rebelliously, she leaned over to scoop a big helping onto his plate. He blinked down at them and began to frown.

"I don't like peas."

"Eat them. They're good for you," Amanda insisted, ladling more for good measure. Then she waited, feeling Rebecca's bemused stare, until he picked up his fork and began accumulating them on the tines with swift stabbing motions. Then, wordlessly, he ate them. Smiling, Amanda passed the bowl to Rebecca.

After pie was cut and served and Will's drink was refilled, Harm announced his intention to leave the next day. Will looked grateful. The children moaned. Rebecca was quick to assure him that Amanda would be welcomed to stay and he smiled his thanks.

"Can I ride with you, Uncle Harm?"

Harm looked up at Jack's eager face, expression cautious. Reading his refusal in it, the boy hurried on with his appeal.

"Uncle Harm, you promised to show me how to track.

172

And what with all we did today, I won't be missed for a while. Please. I'd really like to come along."

Harm studied him, then his features eased, softening in a way that warmed through Amanda's heart. And Rebecca's. "I guess you wouldn't be no bother to me. And the company'd be nice."

Jack lit up like a candy store window.

"No."

They looked to a somber-faced Will for a reason, one he was quick to supply.

"I need the boy here."

"No you don't, Papa. I won't be gone but for a few days. Uncle Harm will look out for me."

"I said no."

"Will, the boy's old enough to decide such things—"

Will cut Harm off cold. "Not until I say he is. This is my family, Harmon."

Harm said very softly, very coolly, "Seems the boy is more kin to me than he is to you."

Rebecca's chair screeched back as she rose. "Children, you've got chores to tend. Get a move on. Now!" At her prodding, they scuffled off, mumbling while Will and Harm locked stares across the tabletop. All but Jack.

"Papa, I'd like to go with him. Why can't you trust me? He's gonna teach me—"

"Anything you need to be taught, you can learn from me," Will interrupted. His tone was cold and final. When Jack's expression remained mulish, he put it even plainer. "The only thing your uncle can teach you is how to kill mean and ugly. That what you want to learn? How to sneak up on a man whilst he's asleep, like a goddamn ghost, and cut the heart outta him while it's still beating?"

"Will!" Rebecca stood, white and trembling. Harm sat his chair, not a muscle twitching.

"Is it, boy? Don't you think I got enough to worry

about with the bad blood you inherited from your daddy, without your Uncle Harmon sharing his madness with you, too?"

Jack made a small sound in the back of his throat and raced outside with a slam of the door behind him.

"There was no call for that, Will." Harm's drawl was deadly quiet. "It's not the boy's fault."

"Whose fault is it, Harm? It sure the hell ain't mine." He reached for the bottle and Rebecca intercepted it.

"You've had enough, Will," she said with the same steely tone as her brother. "Maybe you ought to go lie down."

"Don't you treat me like a baby, woman," he snarled. "I may not be able to walk, but everything else works just fine."

Amanda stared down at her plate, horrified and uncertain if she should be witness to the escalating family tension. She could feel it quivering through Harm as he sat immobile beside her. When Will Bass jerked the bottle from his wife's hand and sloshed more in his glass, she pushed carefully away from the table, planning to steal away to her room.

"Will, no more."

When her husband's hand closed over hers, Rebecca gave a soft gasp of hurt. And Harmon was across the table in a heartbeat. He had Will by the throat.

"Let her go!"

Rebecca stumbled back as she was released. She was instantly trying to force herself between the two men. "Will! Harmon! Stop it!"

"Don't you ever hurt her!" Harm was seething.

Will had levered his palm beneath Harm's chin and was prying him backward. "C'mon, you savage little sonuvabitch! Prove me right!"

Harm's free hand flung outward, scrabbling over the

174

tabletop until his fingertips brushed across the cutlery. He seized one of the place knives and whipped it up over his head to the top of a killing arc.

"Harmon, no!"

Rebecca wrapped herself around his arm, angling across her husband. Harm froze, breathing hard, blinking slowly.

"He didn't hurt me. Harmon, please. It's all right. It's all right."

His arm began to shake. The knife clattered to the table, and Harm backed down. He never once looked at Will. His gaze was locked in his sister's.

"I'm sorry, Becky."

"Harmon—"

But he'd pulled away and was striding for the door.

"Harmon!"

"Let him go," Will growled, rubbing his raw throat reflexively.

Rebecca turned frightened, teary eyes upon him. "What if he doesn't come back?"

Amanda stared at the door in a panic as Will Bass pronounced coldly, "I'd say good riddance."

Chapter Eleven

Heat settled in for the night with an uncomfortable stickiness, foretelling of the long summer to come. Amanda sat on the porch, listening to the now-familiar night sounds. She was busy working her way through a big pail of dried peas, splitting and scooping them with her thumbs while she watched the shadowy hills. She was waiting for Harm.

Silence reigned in the house behind her. The children had been put to bed and quickly shushed when they asked for their uncle. No lights burned inside. But the moon shone bright and full overhead, and Amanda was too restless to think about sleep.

What if he didn't come back?

" 'Evenin'."

She gave a start. "I wish you wouldn't do that!"

"What?"

"Pop up at my elbow like a gho—" Those were Will's words, weren't they? She looked back into the bowl of pea pods.

"Sorry. Habit. You looked to be thinking so hard, I probably could have rode in on a herd of longhorns and you wouldn't have heard me."

She gave a faint smile.

"What are you doing?"

"Helping Rebecca out."

"You don't have to do that. You're a guest here, not a hired hand."

"I don't mind. I'm enjoying it, actually. I've never had a chance to be useful before." Amanda looked up to catch his mystified expression. She set the bowl on the step next to her. "Make yourself useful."

He was incredulous, then wary. "You want me to shell peas?"

She smiled innocently. "Do you mind?"

"No." He dropped down beside her and picked up a handful. One couldn't tell from watching him that he hadn't had much experience. He shucked his way through those on his lap, silently, efficiently. Then he held one of the pods up, frowning. "What's with all these peas all of a sudden?"

Amanda grinned down into her bowl.

"A lesson in humility, Mr. Bass."

His chuckle was low and warm. It stirred all the right things inside Amanda Duncan. With a careless flip, he tossed the last pod into her pot and sat for a moment, staring out into the night with his empty hands dangling between his knees. His smile faded gradually into a look so bittersweet, it bruised her heart. He stood and paced restlessly to the edge of the step, leaning there against the support post.

"I'm sorry about dinner."

Up until this very second, she wasn't sure how she felt about it. She'd been shaken by the explosive violence. It was a side of him that would frighten her half to death if she had enough sense to see around the thrall of attraction he held for her. She wasn't afraid. It worried her more than anything. Harm would kill without conscience but she couldn't believe he'd do so without cause. She

177

couldn't excuse it but she wouldn't allow it to push her away, either.

"That's all right. It's not the first family fight I've ever been wedged in the middle of."

"Your family usually go at each other with table knives, do they?"

"No, Mr. Bass. They go after one another with words that cut more sharply."

He said nothing for a time, thinking of her casual reply. Then it just came out. "I love my family, Amanda. I don't want to hurt them. Every time I come here, things get all ripped open again. If it wasn't for Jack needing somebody so bad . . ." He let that trail off, but Amanda was quick to pick up the thread of his thoughts.

"Will isn't his father."

Harm cast a fleeting glance her way. "No." He didn't offer more details and this time she didn't pry, sensing the matter was too private for casual discussion. When the threat of her questions waned, Harm sighed and looked back toward the hills. "He doesn't mean to treat Jack any different. I know that. I know it's got to be damned hard for a man, especially . . . He tries not to blame the boy, to care for him like his own. It's not fair, is all."

He fell silent and Amanda wondered if he was thinking of his own lack of a last name. And she wondered who had fathered Jack Bass. Then Harm's next words disrupted her thoughts.

"I'm thinking maybe I shouldn't come back."

"What?"

"When I'm here, I'm always coming between Will and Jack and Becky. I try to keep out of it but . . . I just can't stand to see them hurting."

She put aside the pail and went to stand next to him. Her fingertips grazed his elbow. Just that. Nothing more. "Then you would be hurting them. And yourself." She

178

was remembering the shiny little faces looking up at him with such unabashed adoration. He was their hero, their Uncle Harmon, a legend who could do no wrong. And if she wasn't careful, she'd be looking at him the same way all over again; only this time at the man, not at the empty engraving on a dime novel cover. They wouldn't understand if he turned away from them, just as she wouldn't understand if he disappointed her. "Don't do that, Harmon."

He sighed again. Someplace inside him, a terrible weight let go. He'd been roaming the hills for hours, fighting between head and heart, trying to decide the right thing to do, and here it was. Here she was. The answer was in Amanda Duncan. Within his family, emotions were so deep, so complex, it was hard not to get swept away by the current. But Amanda was young and unsullied by experience. Her thoughts were pure, her logic crisp. Hers was the voice of quiet reason long denied him. That was the charm she held for him. Her simplicity. What she loved, she loved. What she loathed, she loathed. No complicated shadings in between. She calmed him in soul even as she chafed his desires. It was a nice friction. If only it could stay simple.

But it couldn't.

Her fingers began to stroke the back of his arm. Lightly, absently. He wasn't sure she knew she was doing it, but he notched tighter with every movement.

"You kissed me the other day."

He didn't answer. He didn't deny it.

"Why?"

"I wanted to see what it would be like."

She peered up at him curiously but he continued to stare stoically ahead. "You hadn't ever been kissed before, had you?"

179

"Apaches don't kiss," he growled haughtily. "It's considered too personal."

"So is women's work, but you were doing pretty well with those peas."

He scowled at her but she could tell he wasn't annoyed. He was in an unusually receptive mood and it was time to take advantage of it.

"What do they do?"

"Who?"

"The Apache. How do they express . . . affection?"

"By embracing."

"Like hugging? Well, that doesn't sound very personal." No wonder the hills and plains of West Texas weren't crowded with them anymore. Nothing sounded less intimate than a passionless hug.

"You'd like it if you tried." He smiled to remind her of her own bold words in a dingy Terlingua hotel room. She was quick to call him on it with a purr so low and rough, it sent shivers to his very soul.

"I'd like to try."

For a moment, he didn't move. She didn't, either. She waited, encouraging him with a smile of sassy challenge and a look of pure promise. Finally, he came away from the porch post in an easy ripple of strength and turned toe to toe with her. One arm curved around her waist so that his palm opened wide along her spine. He pulled her into him, then used his other hand against the back of her head to anchor her. That was all. No mashing, no fondling, just a complete enveloping of him around her. Her face was pressed into his shoulder, her legs trapped between the slight straddle of his, and everything in between was fused tight. She could feel the hard contours of his body, the steady rock of his breathing. She couldn't move an inch if she wanted to.

It wasn't passion that stirred with that melding of one

into the other. Passion was just a fraction of it. There was a stunning power to the simple hold, a controlling discipline that bottled emotions to the point of fierce compression. The longer he contained her with his surrounding strength, the weaker she felt, the more she lost herself to him. She'd been wrong. They couldn't have been more intimate if she crawled inside him. And it was very personal.

Amanda was trembling. His arms were the only things holding her together. There was nothing impulsive about the desire thickening through her. The heat, the closeness, the wanting; it was all a part of the same thing. It seemed only right to build and expand upon them. His head lowered and his cheek rubbed hers. When her lips touched to his jaw, he started to flinch back, but her hand rose quickly to cup the other side of his face, holding him still. He was motionless as her kisses eased from ear to chin, to the warmth of his throat where she could feel his hurried swallowing. He tasted good—hot, salty; and he smelled like Texas, all sun and sage and soothing yucca.

"Did you like it?" she murmured against the pulse of his neck.

"What?"

"Kissing me?"

He was silent, then came a barely audible "Yes."

"It's even better when I'm kissing back." It was a whisper of indescribable temptation. One he couldn't resist. His fingers sank into her hair, curling into a fist so that when he pulled down, her face tipped up and her neck curved into a taut arch.

"Show me."

When his fingers opened, she came up against him, moving her mouth over the hard, thin line of his. She did her best but it was like trying to provoke granite. Her gaze canted up and she found him staring intently at her. He looked unconvinced, as if she were trying to force something unpleasant and medicinal down his throat under the pretext of saying 'It's good for you.' How to get him to lower his guard? Amanda thought for a moment, stroking his taut bronze cheek with her thumb as she did. Then she remembered what her mother would do when she'd refuse to take tonic.

"Harmon, how old are you?"

"What?"

"How old are you?"

His brow puckered in a moment of distraction before he replied, "I'm twenty-fo—"

And she was kissing him, taking full advantage of his soft, unsuspecting mouth. He went tense all over but it was too late. She was already feasting on his lips, shaping them with her own, drawing them even farther apart with the downward pull of her thumb on his chin. To remove the last of his objection, she let her tongue slip along that unwilling part, moistening the way, erasing his stiffness like a blast of steam on a starched shirt. Resistance wilted. Victorious, Amanda pushed inside his mouth and, with an inquisitive sweep, conquered him completely.

Harm relaxed. He went as pliant as a pool of hot butter. He allowed her full access, full reign, and she overtook him by storm. She sketched his lips with quick, hungry nibbles, then delved deep to suck his breath away. He felt her smiling.

"Harmon, close your eyes."

"Why? Then I can't see you."

She had no logical answer so she explained with a tender patience, "Because that's how it's done."

"Oh." And obligingly, his eyes slid closed.

He realized why almost at once. It was like falling down into a deep hole, like drowning, like being swallowed whole. External things ceased to exist. They were no

182

longer standing on his sister's front porch locked in each other's arms beneath the moonlight. She was leading him through a world of hot, detached sensation, so much sharper because it was all he had to cling to. So he clung, tightly, fiercely, as her kisses grew wet and persistent. The tip of her tongue teased along the contour of his mouth so he opened it wider, wanting her to come inside, not knowing how to ask. He moaned restlessly, with a low desperation. Still, she stayed poised on the brink, drawing damp figure eights with maddening little flickers. Finally, he went after her, and the instant he crossed over the separation between them, he was gone.

He plunged, circled, stroked, losing himself within her welcoming warmth. She encouraged him on with a flirting banter of her tongue against his. And then he knew why the Apache didn't approve of kissing. His control shattered. He spun her roughly so her back was smashed against the porch post. He filled his palms with her up-turned face, holding her for the aggressive assault of his mouth upon hers. All sense of play was gone. Intensity rose so fast and hot, there was no way to prepare for it. Need shuddered through him and the kissing only seemed to whet it; kerosene upon a smoldering fire. And then he realized she was making small, squeaking noises of protest as her hands pushed against the pinning crush of his shoulders. He broke from the succulent paradise he'd found. His first thought was that he'd hurt her with his forcefulness and his gaze searched hers worriedly for the truth.

Amanda was sagging against the post, her flushed face framed by his hands, her hair spilling down over the backs of them in a tangled splendor. She was panting unevenly. But she didn't look upset. When she met his eyes, she smiled faintly.

"There's one thing about kissing you need to learn, Harmon," she gasped.

"What?"

"You have to come up for air sometime."

Then he noticed the achiness in his own chest and breathed deep. It hadn't seemed important moments before. They stood, leaning into each other, breathing in each other's ragged breaths until the push of urgency eased. His hands had fallen to the caps of her shoulders, where they rubbed in tight little circles.

"You were wrong about one thing," he told her at last.

"What?"

"It's better than nice. Is it always like that?"

She looked up at him, into the sincerity of his blue eyes. Was he asking her to compare what had just happened to the immature samplings she'd shared with a boy beneath the stairs? It was like matching a tornado to a spring breeze. Harmon Bass had torn her loose from the foundation of reason. Her insides were still shaking.

"No, Harmon," she said with a touch of honest awe. "Not like that. It's different with you."

He looked arrogantly pleased by her answer.

When she lifted her arms, curling them behind his neck, it took very little persuasion to coax him into continuing. He sank into her kiss with fullmouthed anticipation. Yet even knowing what to expect didn't soften the shock of longing started by the wet tangle of their tongues. Kissing wasn't going to be enough, just as the companionable friendship of minutes before hadn't been enough. It brought the need to press and move against one another, as hearts hammered an anxious rhythm. Kisses grew rugged and pulsing in counterpoint to the rocking of their bodies. Mating kisses fostered dusky desires, those that would require the shedding of clothes as well as inhibitions, and when Amanda's hands nudged up the bottom of his shirt, Harm decided to put a limit to their desire.

"No."

Amanda felt as though he'd knocked her feet out from under her. So much urgent momentum had gathered, it was no easy task to rein it in. She wanted to strip him down to bare skin. Her fingers clenched in the fabric of his shirt. It was hang on or be carried away by the need to touch him. She hung on. But she couldn't break from the surprising luxury of his lips that easily. Nor did Harm want to, despite his cautious protestations. The recklessness of their kisses quieted into slow, lapping exploration, then became feathering touches. Finally, when only their breaths mingled, Amanda asked, "Oh, Harm, what are we going to do about this?"

He didn't want to think of an answer. "What is it you want to do?" Her hips were moving against his, rubbing where sensation was raw and throbbing. He'd been crazy to let things go so far, but God, how could he say he hadn't loved it?

With a touch of coyness, Amanda toyed with his shirt collar. "I want more of what we started in the yard this morning."

What she wanted was much too much. Kissing was one thing, with its hot, mutual pleasures. If they went any further, he wasn't sure he could stop. Even if she begged him to. Better not to tempt or trust the darker forces.

He stroked her cheek with the back of his hand and she read "good night" in his lambent gaze. "I have to leave in the morning," he told her quietly.

"So?"

"So, I'm going to bed."

Her lids slid to half-mast in a gesture so seductive it startled him. Her soft, well-kissed lips parted as if to ask the impossible. "Harmon—"

185

"Good night, Amanda."

He was leaving! Amanda's eyes flew open wide in protest. He couldn't just walk away! She was a mass of quivering expectations. He couldn't tease her to a distracted bliss, then just say good night. She felt as if she were hanging in midair, all her hopes, all her wants, suspended. It didn't matter that he was right to end things now. They were pushing toward an intimacy she shouldn't pursue. But oh, how she wanted it, wanted him. She wasn't thinking of what that would mean . . . of all it would mean. She just didn't want to let him go, not after he'd lit her up like the Fourth of July.

"Harm, I don't want you to go."

"Ammy—"

"Not tonight. Not in the morning."

He smiled as if she were being young and silly and making absolutely no sense in her demands. And maybe that was true. But there was nothing silly about the emotions ripening beneath that Texas moon.

"Harmon—"

"You talk too much."

Then he quieted her most effectively. When his mouth lifted off hers, she was reduced to a dazed silence, one he took advantage of. By the time her thoughts were stirring out of their sensual sluggishness, he was halfway across the yard.

"Harmon?"

He paused, looking back. She couldn't see his expression. He was standing just outside the wash of the moon, where shadows waited to embrace him.

"Don't leave without saying goodbye."

She thought she saw the white flash of his teeth. "I won't." Then he was gone.

Amanda sank to the porch steps on strengthless legs. Her heart was beating like crazy. Her emotions were all wrought up into a coil of damp disappointment. Closing her eyes, she leaned her head back against the porch post, reliving the feel of his kiss.

Oh, Harmon, what have we started?

Fandango was saddled and ready in the yard. The younger Bass children ran circles around their uncle as he came up from the barn toting his bedroll and supplies. Jack Bass stood silently at the edge of the porch, trying to keep the look of longing from his eyes. So did Amanda.

She gave a start and flushed with awkward pleasure as Rebecca slipped her arm through hers. This was what Harm would remember, her standing on his porch, linked with his family. Amanda hoped it was an image that would burn deep and long. She was glad for Rebecca's support. She didn't want to make any foolish declarations as Harm readied to ride away. Her insides were a jumble of panic and anguished need. She wanted to grab on to him and hold hard. She wanted him to kiss her yet was afraid if he did, she'd be dragging on him like a ball and chain. She didn't want to overwhelm him with the heavy shackles of her affection. Not just yet.

"I'm all set," he announced, ambling up to the base of the steps. "Shouldn't be gone more than a couple of days." He said that to his sister, but his gaze couldn't stay away from the anxious woman at her side.

Rebecca came down to hug him close. He tensed in the embrace and tried to shy away from her kiss, but she pursued his cheek determinedly to press one upon it. "Take care, Harmon."

"I will, Becky," he muttered as he sidled from her grasp. She let him go. She knew she could never hold onto him for very long. It was that shy Apache reserve between male and female relatives that made him balk, and she wouldn't push beyond his personal comfort. As long as he knew she cared. She never failed to weep for days after he'd ride away. And this time, she sensed she would not be alone in her misery.

He was looking up at Amanda, controlling his features with an obvious effort. She smiled down at him, the effect just as strained.

"Have you plenty of supplies, Mr. Bass? I would hate for you to come back carrying my saddle with my horse sticking to your ribs."

"I'll try not to be tempted, ma'am." Oh, he could try, but tempted he was; by the blush of regret on her cheeks, by the way her hands gripped at her skirts to keep them from reaching for him, by the way her eyes kept detailing the curve of his mouth. It was getting hard to breathe.

The thump of Will's crutches broke his concentration. Harm backed from the porch as his brother-in-law came out of the house, and he went to recheck all his saddle ties.

Will's gaze went from Harm's avoidance to Jack's unhappy failure to meet his eyes. Daylight brought a lot more to focus than just the pulsing ache of excess. He heard again the cruelty of his words. He felt again the dampness of his wife's silent tears as she lay beside him in the night. He remembered the fondness he'd had for Rebecca's brother when he'd thought of him like a son. And he knew he was being small-minded and unfair. Harmon always put him on edge. It was no one's fault, not really. So much more was at stake here beyond his own bruised pride.

"Jack," the big man called to the sulking boy. "Rig up the black if you're meaning to go with your uncle. Don't keep him waiting."

Jack stood for a moment, paralyzed with surprise. Then he vaulted over the porch rail and ran for the barn.

Smiling warmly, Rebecca went to her husband's side

and let him hold her close. Harm looked away from that expression of care, his own tightening.

"Watch out for the boy, Harm."

"You can count on it, Will."

The big ex-Ranger watched the smaller man swing up into his saddle. They exchanged a wordless look, one of grudging apology and wariness. Then Jack came tearing up on his black mare, all smiles. He slid off and hugged both parents excitedly.

"Thanks, Papa."

"Get some things together, son," Will told him quietly.

"And make sure you take something warm," his mother added.

Harm sat Fandango as they waited for the boy to stuff a few belongings into a bag. Amanda's mount danced restlessly, feeling his rider's want to be gone. Then Jack burst from the house and scrambled up into the saddle.

"Behave yourself, Jack," Rebecca cautioned. "Don't make your uncle sorry he agreed to take you."

"I won't, Mama."

Then the two of them were wheeling away, heading out west toward the wide plains without looking back at those they left behind.

In two days, Amanda made a place for herself in the Bass household. For half her lifetime, she'd been forced to adapt, going from home to home, relative to relative, trying to fit in as best she could so as not to become burdensome. But she'd never been made to feel as welcome by her own family as she was within Harm's.

Rebecca was endlessly patient. She taught Amanda the rudiments of western life, mainly, if something needed to be done, you had to do it yourself. There were no servants, no conveniences that she'd been spoiled with in

189

New York. Laundry couldn't be sent out and returned all folded and pressed. Baked goods came from hours of toil, not from the woman who came in on Mondays to make them. Amusements weren't readily available. There were no theaters, no parks, no boardwalks. No nothing. Just long, hot hours filled with work and family.

As far as conversation went, Rebecca was as stingy as her brother. Unless she was responding to a question, she was mostly silent and industrious. She never volunteered details of her own life or offered her opinions. Like Harm, she watched, she listened, and she kept to herself. There was never a lack for noise as long as the children were in the house. Sitting with them in the evenings on the wide front porch was Amanda's reward for a day of hard work. They renewed her with their laughter and endless energy. And it was easy to love them; Sidney for his somber curiosity, Sarah for her flirtatious smiles, and Jeffrey for his boisterous affection. They were crazy about their Uncle Harmon and envious of Jack for getting to accompany him on an adventure. In two days, she read them all five Dime Press issues of the Harmon Bass series, enjoying each one every bit as much as they did.

Surprisingly, it was Will Bass who supplied her with the most talk. From his porch chair, he spun stories of his Ranger and lawman days with an amazing lack of bitterness. To Amanda's thinking, that took a tremendous amount of personal courage. He loved what he'd done for a living and he loved his family. Philosophically, he told her that crutches were a small price to pay for the privilege of being with them. Most men he knew would have preferred death rather than the confining life he was forced into. He thought they were fools. She agreed with him.

Surprising, too, was the great respect Will had for Harm. Despite all the hostility when Harm was under his roof, in his absence, Will had only good to say about his wife's brother.

"I'd never seen the likes a' him," he told her as they enjoyed the quiet hours after the children were put to bed. "He can look at a crushed imprint in the grass and tell everything about the man that made it, right down to the color of his eyes, whether he was walking at day or night, whether he had a pack animal or a ridden horse, if he was herding animals or letting them graze. Told me he could tell how much time had passed by the discoloration of the print and by the amount of juices left in the crushed grass. Can you believe that? I've seen him follow tracks over desert sands and floors of solid rock even after the trail had been crossed by hundreds of cattle. He can see things visible to no white man's eyes. Would have made one helluva Ranger."

"Why didn't he?"

" 'Cause he's Harmon. He'd trail for us but he'd never ride with us. He'd hunt down any Mexican or outlaw or other tribe of Indian but not his own, and seeing as how they were the ones causing the most grief, he couldn't carry no Ranger badge in good conscience. Never faulted him for that. The Apache always been good to him and he's been able to talk around trouble with them more than once. Like the time they took Calvin Lowe's little lady."

Rebecca slipped out of the house carrying empty cups and a pot of hot coffee. After they were filled, she settled on the arm of her husband's chair, putting her own arm around his neck. The look they shared was warm enough to start kindling. And to start a pining for the absent Harmon Bass within Amanda's heart. What Will and Rebecca Bass had was what she'd longed for all her life: family, love, security—home. To forestall that wistful ache, she asked, "How did Harmon get to be a dime novel hero?"

Will chuckled. "That was Cal Lowe's doing. Some fancy New York writer came down looking to do a story on the Rangers for his eastern paper. Cal started going on about how Harm'd saved Elena from the Apache, and pretty soon we got us a wire from one of them publishers wanting to know if they could send someone down to interview him. Said they'd pay fifty dollars for every story they ran."

"And Harm talked to them?"

"Hell, no. You ever know him to put together more than three words when it comes to boasting? He ran for the hills. Told us to take the money and tell 'em whatever they wanted to hear. Kept that writer feller busy for two days taking notes. 'Course, what came out in his books weren't nothing like fact. They couldn't get their readers to believe a little feller like Harmon, who don't carry guns, is more dangerous than any ten men."

Amanda knew he was. But the girl she'd been in New York City wouldn't have.

"So they made him into a strapping six-foot-four legend with pistols blazing."

"That's about it." Will smiled ruefully. "No eastern audience wants to read about a heathen half-breed who skins and eats the horse he's riding. That'd be a little too blunt for their tender sensibilities. They want their action violent and exciting, but they want to watch it through misty eyes. Eyes that see good as good and bad as bad. They don't want to be confused and Harmon would confuse them plenty."

Oh, yes. How she well she knew it. In the East, they liked sensation not realism. How would they view a Harmon Bass who toasted his victims over an open fire? Not fondly, she suspected. Better the more palatable version created through the exaggerated pen of their writers.

Would she have come all this way if she'd known the truth?

No.

But even more difficult was the question of how she was ever going to leave now that she did know.

Chapter Twelve

She was going to marry Harmon Bass.

Amanda knew right from the outset that it wasn't going to be easy. The biggest obstacle was Harm himself. She was sure he had no interest in the wedded state. It would be up to her to convince him otherwise.

She came to her decision the second night Harm was gone, when the house filled up with emptiness around her. Bold little Sarah got her thinking about it over dinner when she asked, out of nowhere, if Amanda was going to be their aunt. Amanda had been terribly embarrassed as Rebecca shushed her daughter, but then the other woman regarded her with a dark-eyed directness, as if restating the question herself. As if asking just what her intentions were toward her only brother.

She was in love with him and she wanted to make love with him. In Amanda's mind that spelled marriage. It was the only solution to both things. She wanted a man to curl up with at night. She wanted children to care for and love. She wanted a home of her own where she wasn't living on someone else's reluctant charity. And she wanted Harm to give her those things. He was all she had. Randy was gone. There was nothing for her in New York. The thought of returning there was worse than living with the snakes in a West Texas desert.

She was no fool. She knew her relatives probably had detectives looking for her even now, to snatch her back under their control. Not so much from worry or to protect her, but to protect their interest in her fortune. They wouldn't have learned about Randy yet. And when they discovered that Amanda was the sole heir, she could imagine the pressure. Her dear cousin Roger would become quite enchanted with her kisses again. And she would be ever on her guard against runaway carriages knocking her down in the street or sly shoves to the middle of her back when she was at the top of steep stairs. That wasn't how she wanted to live, but she would have to for nearly four more years until her trust was released at twenty-one. Or until she married.

If she was married, she could do as she pleased, and it pleased her to think of doing it with Harmon Bass.

Of course, the idea should be his. That was the proper way of handling such things. But, given the circumstances and Harm's probable aversion to the whole plan, Amanda was not above taking matters into her own hands. All she had to do was get him to believe he couldn't exist without her. Which wasn't going to be easy, because he was the most self-sufficient person she'd ever known. He seemed to have no need for creature comforts or companionship, and while he loved his family, she sensed a restlessness about him when he was beneath their roof. He didn't seem to need anyone.

She knew he cared about her. She also knew he considered her a tolerable nuisance. There seemed to be nothing she could do for him that he couldn't do better on his own. All but one thing, and he'd liked that well enough. He desired her. She was young and inexperienced, but she'd learned from example how powerfully a woman

195

could control a man upon the leash of his lust. For two years, she'd watched her roommate at school make manipulation into an art. Rose was vivacious and lovely, and she could turn a boy inside out with the hint of her cherry-ripe smile. When she'd decided upon the one she would have, she confided to a wide-eyed Amanda just how she meant to go about getting him. Her parents didn't approve of the match and the boy was resistant, but Rose was "in love" and determined to have her Steven. She boasted of how she'd arranged it so they "had to get married." It was all quite scandalous but ingenious, too, Amanda had to admit. Rose teased the poor fellow into a panting frenzy, and when the deed was a *fait accompli*, she broke the news tearfully to her shocked family about how she was now ruined. The wedding was scheduled as soon as tastefully possible, with both sides grim and Rose positively beaming.

Harmon didn't love her. That was the only factor that gave her pause. She didn't wish to push him into anything he'd find intolerable. Amanda knew love entered into few arrangements until after vows were said and years had passed. She was young enough to want love as the motivating force in her marriage yet wise enough to realize it might have to wait. Surely once she and Harm had consummated their passion, love would follow. Just as marriage would follow. And once Harmon loved her, he wouldn't leave her. She wouldn't be forced to return to the cold, emotionless clime of New York. She would stay here in the warm Texas sun and learn to be a good wife. Which was all she wanted in the world. That, and clearing her brother's name.

She would become Mrs. Harmon Bass. She would see his family lacked for nothing. She would apply herself to making sure he never regretted answering her letter. She would refocus all the considerable love in her heart on making him happy, and all she would ask in return was that he give her a home. And children. And, eventually, love.

Wasn't that all any woman wanted?

"Uncle Harmon! Uncle Harmon!"

Amanda had to stop herself from racing out into the yard, just as wild with glee as the children, when the two riders came in just in time for supper. Looking tired and dirty but grinning from ear to ear, Jack Bass shinnied off his horse, surrendering himself up to his mother's hugs and kisses. She looked up at her brother.

"Did he give you any trouble?"

"The boy held his own, Becky. Be proud to have him ride with me anytime."

Harm's praising drawl set Jack's place in his siblings's eyes. They crowded around their big brother, leaving Harm to climb down by himself. Rebecca had a hug for him, too, and he sagged into it easily this time.

"You look all in, Harmon. Wash up. Dinner's ready."

He hung back slightly, hesitating. He glanced up at the house, not seeing Amanda there in the shadows. His look was carefully masked. "Maybe I'd better not. Don't want to wear out my welcome. I can fend for myself, Becky. I'll go out and see to my own chuck after I grain and water the horses. . . ."

"Harmon Bass, you will do no such thing. You set your rump down at my table before I start chewing on it. Sidney can see to the horses. Now move!"

"Yes, ma'am," he muttered, but he was smiling faintly as she turned to precede him up to the porch. He followed more slowly, thumping the dust from the thighs of his denims as he walked. He was on the second step when he drew up short, sensing rather than seeing her.

"Hello, Harmon."

"Amanda."

She came out of the cool recesses of the porch into the light and he looked his fill without betraying any expression. She was disappointed. He gave no sign that he'd missed her at all. Or that it was a trial to refrain from grabbing her up in a hard embrace. Those were the things she was hoping for. What she got was a penetrating stare that seemed to see everything without giving anything away. Could he tell that she'd spent hours getting ready to greet him in the hope that he'd return today? Could he tell she was practically shivering with excitement? If he could, he didn't care, because all he said was a curt, "I'll talk to you after supper." Then he went inside to his surrounding family. All Amanda could do was follow.

Jack spent most of the meal regaling them with details of the trip. Harm stayed quiet unless he was asked to explain or agree with one of Jack's statements. Dinner went by peacefully. When Rebecca asked if her brother cared for coffee, he said he'd make time for a cup before he headed out again.

Headed out.

Amanda seized on that in a panic. Surely he couldn't mean to ride off after just an hour with his family. With her. She held her tongue and tried to contain her anxiety. He'd said they would talk after the meal. Perhaps he would then elaborate on what he meant by "head out." She wondered if she was going to like hearing it.

She didn't.

He didn't stop at the porch. He carried his cup of coffee down to the corral, where Jack was busy finishing the grooming of their horses. After nodding to the boy, he leaned on the rail and waited for Amanda to come up beside him.

"I found him, the man your brother was with."

Immediately, all her thoughts of slighted romance were forgotten. "Where?"

"Just missed meeting up with him in Lajitas. Seems some of Judge McAllister's men caught up with him there and gave him an escort to Perdition."

"McAllister. He was the one Randy was taking the jewels to."

"Appears he wants 'em back."

"Who is this man?"

"Goes by the name of Dave Dexter. Small-time robber. Never did much of nothing until he got sentenced to six months in prison in New York for stepping outta line up there. He got his release a month ago. Must have met up with your brother on the train ride back to Texas."

"And decided Randy would be an easy mark," Amanda concluded bitterly. Oh, yes. He would be. Innocent, trusting Randolph Duncan. "When do we head to Perdition?"

"I aim to saddle up in a few minutes."

His meaning was crystal clear. Amanda froze.

Harm didn't look at her. He could feel her glacial stare. "Things might get . . . complicated in Perdition," he began. "See, McAllister pretty much owns the town and the law there according to Calvin. He's got himself a rich spread and he means to get richer any way he can. One of the ways is by ordering up expensive things in the East and taking out big insurance policies on them. Then his merchandise disappears along the way—in a train robbery, in a holdup at the station, on the buggy ride to his ranch. Then McAllister collects his insurance money, and funny, a couple of months later he has the exact same thing that was stolen out at his ranch."

"You think he hires someone to steal his own belongings?"

"Why not? When he can have his fancy art pieces and jewelry and the money, too? Who's gonna stop him?"

"If he had something to do with Randy's death, I am."

Which was exactly why Harm couldn't take her with him. She was looking up at him with that obstinate glow of righteous anger, never realizing how easily a man like McAllister could crush her.

"I think you'd best forget about McAllister and just concentrate on clearing your brother."

"And how are we going to do that, Mr. Bass?"

She kept saying "we," but for now he ignored it. "By snatching Dexter out of Perdition before McAllister can tuck him away in Mexico. Once I get him, I can probably persuade him to tell me the truth of it."

Amanda shivered. He probably could. She could picture all too vividly Dave Dexter hanging by his heels.

"Why don't you just turn him into the law?"

"What law? McAllister's law? It's not likely that they'll prosecute the feller what pays 'em. The Rangers don't tangle up in such doings and it's out of Calvin's jurisdiction. Now if I can get ahold of Dexter and take him to Terlingua and get him to spill it to Cal, we'll have him."

"Then that's what we'll do."

"That's what I'll do," he corrected softly. "You'll stay here where I won't have to worry over you getting in my way."

"I won't get—"

"No, you won't because you'll be staying here. I'm gonna be riding hard and fast. Once I get to Perdition, I'll be lucky to get out with my own hide intact. This is what you hired me to do and I'm doing it my way. You stay clear of it or I don't go."

She glared up at him, seething, searching for some argument, but she knew he wouldn't listen. Then one fact from all that he said settled deep: he was riding into terrible danger. Alone. He was leaving her behind. He might never come back. She could be sending him to his death.

"I don't want you to go, Harmon."

He stared at her. "What?"

"I don't want you to get hurt."

"I'm not going to get hurt. This is what I do, my job. I don't plan to announce my intentions and let them blast away at me. Give me a little credit, Amanda. And once it's done, just think, won't it make one helluva story for you to tell to your New Yorker friends? Besides, like I said, I need the money and what you're offering is just about right."

He was making fun of her, and in light of her distress, it hurt. She could feel the tears wanting to well up and she fought them.

"Jack, saddle me up a good fast horse."

"Yessir, Uncle Harm."

"I'll give you the money."

He turned to glare at her, suddenly furious. "I earn my way, Miss Duncan. Nobody buys me. I agreed to a job and I'll do it. Now if you want to back out, I can't stop you. I thought your brother's reputation meant something to you."

She firmed her lips into a narrow line to keep them from trembling. "It does," she told him shortly. "I guess it's all that does matter to me anymore. Do your job, Mr. Bass. It's what you get paid for." Then she turned and stalked up to the house.

From inside the darkness of her room, she heard him saying his goodbyes to his family. Choking up on her tears and her angry pride, she refused to answer his light tap on her door.

"Amanda?"

The knock came again.

"Ammy, I'm heading out."

"Goodbye, Mr. Bass. Good hunting."

"I'll be back."

He hesitated for a long moment, then she heard the clack of his boot heels on his sister's puncheon floorboards. And the slam of the front door.

Please come back, Harmon. Please come back to me.

It was the sound of hoofbeats leaving the yard that spurred her from her brooding. She shot up off the bed and out the door, calling, "Jack, saddle up my horse."

Jack gave her a startled look. "He's winded, ma'am."

"He'll just have to make do. Hurry now."

"Amanda," Rebecca began cautiously.

"Thank you for your hospitality, Rebecca."

"Harmon said you were to stay here."

"Harmon works for me, not the other way around." With that haughty claim, she strode out after Jack.

"She's gonna get your brother killed," Will predicted solemnly.

But Rebecca was smiling. "I don't think so. I think she just might be giving him something to live for."

It was foolish to start out so late. He only made a dozen or so miles before having to stop for the night, but he'd had to leave the ranch and leave fast. While he could.

Bunking down in front of his lonesome fire, Harm closed his eyes and tried to ignore the facts. He was running from Amanda and the desire he couldn't check.

He didn't want to hurt her or himself in the process. The way things were snowballing between them, soon the question of stopping would be out of their control. He couldn't let it get that far. The only solution was to stay the hell away from her until he collected his pay. Then she'd be gone back east and he could breathe easy again.

He'd lost his perspective beneath her hot kisses. He'd forgotten what he was: her hired man. He was being paid to work for her, not woo her. Amanda was just a confused little girl who'd lost the only family she had, and she was looking for some comforting affection in the arms of a legend.

She was using him. She was making him the anchor in her reeling world, but once she was steady, she wouldn't need him anymore. And where would that leave him? As a fool, that's where. She wasn't interested in him. She wasn't looking beyond the gilded pages of her precious books. She saw him as some grand noble knight of the plains even when presented point-blank with the truth: that he was a man with no name, a half-breed, a wanderer; a man driven by a violence he couldn't contain and secrets he wouldn't share. How could she be so blind?

Angry and anguished, he tossed on his saddle blanket but could take no comfort from the hard Texas earth. That's what he was, just like this ground: hard, unyielding, unwilling to give or take. She'd get tired of the dust and the heat and the desolation of the life he led and she'd leave. He wasn't what Amanda wanted and could never be. The problem was, she was everything he wanted and that was making him crazy. Because he knew he couldn't have her.

Eventually, he slept. It was a hard, dreamless slumber, unusual for him when he was out on the trail where he was alert to every noise. The pastels of daybreak were just teasing over the far mountains when awareness drifted back and, along with it, a sense of seeping contentment. He shifted slightly and the warm figure curled around him shifted, too. He adjusted his arm to accommodate her and she answered with a sleepy sigh, burrowing closer into him. Nice. Warm.

Amanda.

He was instantly awake, jerking with the force of his surprise. How had she gotten into his camp without him hearing her? What was she doing all cozied up to him in his blankets as if she belonged there? She stirred and lifted her head, meeting his startled gaze with a well-satisfied smile.

"Good morning, Harmon."

His shock lasted only a second. Then fury settled in. "What the hell are you doing here? I thought I told you—"

She silenced him with a kiss. It was deep and desire-drenched, stunning him into an immediate stupor. When she finally came up for air, he was staring up at her somewhat dull-wittedly. And she smiled, again. And he was angry, again.

"You were supposed to stay at my sister's."

"I wanted to be here with you."

"Amanda, you can't just—"

Her mouth was on his again. Coherent thought collapsed. Starving for the taste of her after three nights of uneasy dreams, he gave in without a struggle. She was here and he didn't care about the whys and wherefores.

"I missed you." She was whispering against his lips. "I missed this last night when you said goodbye."

How could he pretend not to agree, when he was grabbing for her kisses with an urgent hunger?

Amanda came up over him, lying across his chest as she eagerly sought his mouth, his cheeks, his chin; any part of his face she could reach with that hot, damp scattering. His hands came up, awkward at first, then clasping her straining rib cage. She felt so fragile, so damned exciting. She lifted up and his hands slid, curving beneath the swell of her breasts, filling with their soft spill. She found his mouth again and moaned against it, as his thumbs provoked a hardness through the fabric of her bodice. The

204

sensations were dizzying, encouraging a recklessness of need; a need to feel him closer. She reached down for his hands, grabbing them, guiding them, shoving them up under the shirtwaist she wore, beneath the cottony chemise, right to bare skin. She arched and rubbed against the roughness of his palms, going wild at the rasp of them upon untested flesh.

"Harmon . . . oh, Harmon, I want you to make love to me. Show me how good it can be."

Amanda knew the exact instant her words hit home. He went rigid as a porch post beneath her. His hands, his mouth, even his breathing stilled. And his eyes opened. She expected to see passion burning there but there was none. Just a terrible stark dismay. Enough to convince her that she'd made an awful mistake by blurting out the truth.

His hands tore out from under her clothes. With an abrupt movement, he dumped her onto her rump, making her wince, and was up on his feet, moving to saddle the horses as if she'd never spoken. He might pretend it but the erratic chug of his breathing betrayed him. Amanda swallowed down her own disappointment as best she could and sat up to watch him.

"You shouldn't have come after me," he growled without looking at her.

"But I did."

"Then you'll go back."

"No, I won't." It was a quiet challenge but there was nothing flexible about it.

He jerked the cinch strap tight and Fandango gave an unfriendly snort of displeasure. Dropping the stirrups down, he turned to face her. His expression was taut, as were his words.

"Are you so anxious to get yourself into trouble again?"

The belligerence was gone from her expression. Instead, she met him with a look as gritty as the Texas landscape. "It's my right to be there when you bring my brother's murderer to justice. Isn't that what you believe in, Mr. Bass? In a man—or woman's—right to retribution?"

He stared down at her, breathing hard, thinking hard, but he couldn't argue that one fine point of fact. Yes, revenge he understood. The right to it was unquestionable. Who was he to stand in the way of her satisfaction? He was her hired tracker, not her protector, not her conscience.

"You'll do just what I tell you."

She responded to his flat command with a beaming smile.

"I mean it, Amanda. No questions, no arguments."

"All right, Harm. I promise."

"Yeah, sure," he grumbled, turning back to saddle his horse, cursing them both under his breath. Her for her stubbornness, him for his weakness. "How did you find me?"

Amanda was busy rebraiding her mane of golden hair. Harm didn't dare watch the way the soft wisps of it flicked through efficient fingers. He was having enough trouble regulating his breathing as it was.

"It wasn't easy. I think I rode in circles for half the night. Fandango finally led me here. I think he got tired and figured this was a good place to put in for the night."

She said it so nonchalantly, as if oblivious to the dangers of traveling by night. She might have tumbled into a ravine. She might have been thrown and left to die. Any number of four- or two-legged predators could have come upon her. It was the stupidest move he'd ever heard of. And one of the gutsiest. That's why he could never get truly furious with her: Whatever foolishness she attempted was heralded by such tremendous bravery. He hated that about her. And loved it just as fiercely.

"If you're going with me, get a move on."

She wanted to complain that she'd been in the saddle all night and was ready to drop from exhaustion. She wanted to beg a hot breakfast and a cup of his fortifying coffee. She wanted to receive just a hint of kindness from him to prove she hadn't destroyed whatever chance they had together. But she did none of those things. She got up and climbed into the saddle. Whining wouldn't earn her the killer of her brother or the respect of Harmon Bass. She'd keep her complaints to herself.

Perdition was the harshest West Texas town east of El Paso. The proximity of the border brought in the worst sorts: gunmen, grifters, pimps, and parasites, who changed the Big Bend's rough amusements into hardened vices. It sat smack-dab in the middle of desert country, where just a man's survival was proof positive of his virility and fortitude. The finest buildings were the saloons, while the shabbiest were those of the town's populace—ugly little adobes huddled together like oversized dirt dauber wasp's nests. It was not a place a man chose to go if he had his wits about him. And it was not the kind of place to which a man brought his woman, unless he didn't give a damn about her.

Amanda felt the nastiest kind of stares crawling all over her as they rode down the wide center street. Harm looked neither right nor left, but she wasn't fooled by his apparent ease. The butt of his carbine brushed against one lean hip in immediate access to his fingers. She stared at the back of his dark head, trying not to shiver with foreboding. She never should have followed him. He'd been right to try to keep her away from here. But she hadn't listened. She vowed on the tinny taste of terror in her mouth that she would listen scrupulously from this point on.

They came to a stop in front of a run-down hotel. Across the street was a large, fine-looking building, obviously the best lodgings in town. She glanced at it with longing, knowing they could afford it, but she didn't argue Harm's choice. She'd promised to be agreeable. Until he grabbed her by the arm and jerked her from the saddle.

His grip hurt. When she looked up at him in a daze of surprise, he snarled, "Ain't got all day. You walk with me and you walk fast." With another jerk, he pulled her up onto the sand-scoured boardwalk and into the hotel. Several heads turned to see the little cowboy towing his pretty lady across the lobby. Harm glared at them with enough ferociousness to send their stares scuttling elsewhere. He stomped to the desk.

"A room, *por favor.*"

"Yes, sir."

"One where we won't be bothered."

"Of course, sir."

Amanda had been glancing about their shabby surroundings. Several hard cases who'd seen them ride in drifted inside to stare at her with undisguised interest. One of them was a tall man with lots of facial hair and a toothy smile. It widened when Amanda's gaze touched upon him. And suddenly, the flat of Harm's hand smacked across her cheek.

"You lookin' at him?" he growled.

"W—what?" she stammered, her hand rising to the fiery mark on her face and her huge eyes demanding a reason for such abrupt cruelty.

"I said, you lookin' at him?"

"N—no."

"See you don't. You don't belong to him. You belong to me. Don't go forgetting that."

She was speechless as he turned back to the desk, dismissing her. Her cheek ached and her eyes sparkled with tears of surprise and shock. The men at the door eased in farther to watch.

Harm signed the desk registry, then glanced up to catch the clerk eyeing Amanda. His hand shot out, gripping the man's throat until his Adam's apple bobbed frantically above the squeeze of his fingers.

"You lookin' at my woman?"

"No, sir," he wheezed.

"You wantin' a taste of what's mine?"

"No, sir."

Harm's big knife flashed out, lining up beneath the frightened man's chin. "You see you don't go gettin' hungry whilst I'm gone. And if you're a real smart man, you'll watch them stairs for me to make sure whoever climbs 'em has business up there. 'Cause if I find out someone's been pestering her, I'm gonna come down and I'm gonna peel you like a grape. *Comprende?*"

"Yes, sir. I understand."

The knife lowered and Harm placed a ten-dollar gold piece on the counter. The clerk scooped it up beneath trembling fingers.

"Quit draggin' yer feet." Harm's grip snarled in Amanda's braid, pulling down hard to make her cry out. "I ain't had me a real bed for a long time and I aim for it to be a good while afore I'm ready to do any sleepin'. If you ain't there spread and waitin' when I get back, I'll hunt you down and kill you quick. Understand?"

She nodded weakly, then stumbled beside him as he stalked toward the stairs, never lessening his hold on her hair. She scrambled into the room he'd rented for them, backing into a defensive position as he crossed to the doors on the far end. They opened onto a balcony shared with the length of the second floor. He checked the latch, then turned back toward Amanda. He sounded himself again.

"I'm sorry if I frightened you. I meant to scare those fellas downstairs into thinking twice about coming up here the minute I walk out. They respect a man who marks his territory. Might be they'll stay clear."

"Why didn't you warn me?"

"I wanted it to look convincing."

Oh, it did. She was convinced into fearful tremors that knocked her knees together when he started toward her. Amanda took a wobbly step back. And he frowned.

"Ammy?" He stretched out his hand and she flinched involuntarily, tensing as his palm caressed over the red imprint on her cheek. She could see that same hand jerking his knife blade across a man's throat. "You know I'd never hurt you." She thought she did, but her face was throbbing dully. He leaned close and she felt his mouth move tenderly upon bruised flesh. A small sound escaped her and she was instantly in his arms.

He held her tight.

"That was just playacting down there. I want you safe, and that seemed the best way to guarantee it."

"Will it, do you think?" she asked weakly, not bothering to pretend bravery any longer. He could feel her shaking right down to the bone.

"Just might. Remember those whores in Terlingua?" She stiffened in his embrace. Of course, she did. "I told them you cut the nose off the last woman who looked at me. Now they might not have believed that, but not a one of 'em came within ten feet of me. Folks tend to heed might over right out here in West Texas."

She'd quieted in his arms. He could feel her fingers teasing through the hair at his nape. His scalp tightened.

His groin tightened. He couldn't stay in this little room with her any longer.

"I've got to go. You take this big gun and blast the innards outta anyone who tries to come through that door other than me."

She was silent, and that worried him.

"You gonna be all right, Ammy?"

"I'm sorry, Harmon. I should have listened to you. I shouldn't be here. I'm putting you in greater danger, aren't I?"

He was noble enough to overlook the truth of that. "Shhh. It's all right, *shijii*. I can take care of you. I won't let anyone hurt you. I'd die to protect you." That last statement rumbled with sincerity.

"Oh, please, Mr. Bass, don't go to such great lengths. Then you'd be dead and I'd be alone." She pulled back, trying to lighten things with a smile and failing miserably. His look was intense. Hers sobered. "Harmon, don't leave me here alone for very long."

"I won't." His fingertips sketched along her cheek, sealing his promise with a gentle touch.

"Harmon?"

"What?"

She kissed him, softly, stirringly, until he was intoxicated by her sweetness. And as she hugged him about the neck, he could hear her words against his rising panic. *I want you to make love to me. Show me how good it can be.*

Only he knew it wouldn't be good. All he could show her was pain.

Chapter Thirteen

"Beer."

He dropped his coin on the bar and surveyed the room behind him in the wavy mirror. Typical saloon crowd beneath the heavy wreath of smoke and stench of sweat. Harm downed his first beer and ordered up another. He was in a dangerous place and it wasn't smart to take the edge off his alertness, but he needed something to calm the agitation Amanda quickened inside him. He wasn't used to being tied in knots over a woman. Usually, he never thought about them one way or another. Between his Apache reserve and the pain of his past, he generally steered a wide berth to avoid confrontation of any kind. Desire was as new to him as a baby's cutting teeth and just as achy.

Though he'd been forced to a knowledge of the ways of men and women at an early age, he'd no desire to experience them. He'd never been tempted. Women were scarce out in the scorch of sun amid the sage and mesquite, but in towns there were always some willing to make his acquaintance in an intimate fashion. He valued his money over their counterfeit affections and dark promises. He didn't want to recognize that such carnal violence existed inside himself, but he knew it did. His one occasion in lust's embrace had ravaged him with shame and guilt and a depthless disgust. Only Becky could come close to understanding and help him make sense of it, but how could he approach her with his weakness and disgrace? How could he tell her he'd failed in his vow to her?

Thinking to reward him for work well done, the Rangers had bought him a night with a Mexican whore. He'd been nineteen and modestly chaste. They'd gotten him drunk on tequila, another first for him, and had his will not been so wobbly, he'd never have succumbed. But their ribald laughter encouraged and the potent liquor weakened. And he wanted to know. He wanted to know. He learned everything in less than two minutes, then spent two hours on his knees in a dirty back alley retching from the sicknesses of stomach and spirit. That cured him of curiosity. Until Amanda Duncan's kiss surprised him. Until then, he'd no idea a woman's touch could evoke a gentleness within him. Until then, he'd no notion that passion existed. He'd been learning since the day he'd met her, and now it was becoming hell not to act upon the knowledge flooding through his heart and soul.

Oh, Harmon, what are we going to do about this?

He didn't know what to do. He'd never held any female except his sister in his arms. He'd never kissed or been kissed. He'd never woken to find a soft, beguiling form wrapped cozily around him. He'd never considered what it might be like to be in love or to want to share his thoughts with another living being. Or his future with one special individual. He was thinking about it too much now. They were impossible thoughts. Futile dreams.

Amanda wanted him because of what she thought she saw in him and because of what she'd been fooled in her silly books to believe loving a man would mean. He'd seen the way she'd looked at him when he'd shot those cowboys, when she'd come across him toasting that scum over his fire, even minutes ago when he'd turned toward her in their squalid little room and she'd been terrified. He'd seen horror in her big, beautiful eyes. A horror at what he was doing, at what he was. And it reduced him to nothingness. Rightfully so. And if she found those isolated acts of violence reprehensible, what would she think if she knew the whole truth? Would she want his kisses then? Would she want to curl close to him at night? He smiled wryly into the last of his beer. Not likely.

"Harm Bass."

He let his attention shift slowly to the man at his elbow, but his senses were tensed and ready. He glanced up at a rail-thin man with a lush drooping moustache and a deputy badge.

"I thought so. Ain't seen you since you was just a runt of a kid running with your nose to the ground trailing a passel of thieving Comanches, but I remember you." He signaled the bartender. "Bring my pard here a shot of dust cutter. Harm Bass," he mused. "I'll be damned. You don't recall me, do you?"

The face was beginning to look familiar. "I remember a corporal's uniform, but no name. Sorry."

He looked pleased that he'd made that much of an impression. "Pager. Lon Pager. I'm deputy here in Perdition now."

Harm smiled blandly and accepted the small glass of gut twister. He tossed it down and clenched his throat against the harsh sear. It couldn't hurt to get friendly with the law, such as it was.

"So, whatcha doing down our way? Lookin' for somebody?" A cautious edge crept into the smiling man's tone and Harm knew instinctively that this man was not his friend. Or a friend of the law.

"Passing through. Picking up some supplies. On my way to Terlingua to see Calvin Lowe."

"He still sheriff?" More caution seeped into his words.

"Yeah, but me and him go back to his Ranger days. Got right fond of his wife's cooking and can't pass it up when I'm this close by."

Pager relaxed, his smile growing genuine as suspicions eased. Then he looked beyond Harm and signaled. "Hey, Ty. C'mon over here. Someone you should meet. Harm Bass, this is Perdition's sheriff, Tyrell Cates."

Harm turned, and the fires of hell engulfed him.

"I know you by reputation, Mr. Bass. Pleased to meet you."

A hand extended and hung there, unmet for a long second. Then Harm placed his within it, shaking it hard and firm.

"Sheriff," he drawled softly. There was a benign smile on his face. Behind it, Harm was taut as steel, right down to the bone. Heat flared in his chest, rushing up like a wind-teased blaze to scorch his mind. Breathing in and out was like pushing flame through his nostrils. He could feel his molars crack from the grinding pressure it took to maintain that smile. Veiled behind the droop of his lashes, blue eyes burnt like coals.

Tyrell Cates hesitated. He studied the wiry little Texas half-breed through a thoughtfully slitted stare. "Have we met before, Mr. Bass?"

"I don't recall us ever being formally introduced. I would have remembered the name."

He remembered everything else: the deceivingly easy grin; the incredible chill of his laughter; the acrid scent of his cigarillo; the icy brilliance of his pale eyes; even the thin line that crisscrossed his cheek from the corner of his mouth to the outer edge of his eye. Harm remembered everything.

215

"Buy you another drink so's we can get acquainted."

Cates's hand fell upon Harm's shoulder. He endured the man's touch. He took the man's drink. He listened to the man's talk and answered his questions with an amiable manner, never saying much of anything. Tyrell Cates. That was his name. Every nerve beat hot for vengeance. Every breath he watched the man take was the worst sort of obscenity. He found his stare fixed upon the side of the sheriff's throat, measuring the steady pulse throbbing there, wondering how long it would continue once he was eviscerated. And he was smiling as he gulped his drink.

Two hours later, he reeled down the sidewalk. He was wildly intoxicated; on the liquor, on the anticipated scent of blood. Only one thing kept him from crouching in the nearest alleyway, lying in wait with his blade drawn. The same thing that kept him from launching himself with a raw war cry for the murderer's jugular right in the middle of the saloon. Nothing else could have controlled him at that moment when Cates asked if they'd met before. No one else could have intruded into a mind so clogged with savagery. So he went to her instead of seeking his swift satisfaction. Because the promises he'd made to her held him hard. His love for her wouldn't allow him to abandon her. As he staggered down the walk, he cursed her for her interference. He cursed himself for hesitating. Darkness rose within, seething, churning, poisoning like venom, bringing blackness all around him.

"Ahagahe!"

There was no translation for that roaring Apache cry. It was a centuries-old expression of personal rage warning of an attack to come. It tore up from the heart of him as his fist slashed out, bursting through his own image in a haberdashers's window. Plate glass exploded, and he stood staring stupidly at the destruction and at the gashes in his hand. Pain swelled in immense waves, not from the outer cuts but from those within that would never heal. His head dropped back and he wailed up at the moon in soundless despair.

Save me, Amanda! Please save me!

Amanda knew it was him because she never heard anything before his soft knock.

For hours, she'd sat tense and alert upon the bed with the big pistol in the hollow of her crossed legs. Every heavy footstep on the warped hall floorboards had her thumbs dragging back on the hammer. Every time they receded, she let out her breath and eased the pistol off full cock. Her underclothes were damp from the stifling air and endless anxiety. Harm had made her promise to keep the balcony doors latched and the room was like a refractory oven. She'd shed her outerwear long ago. Tomorrow, she would demand new clothes. Her skin would be crawling if she had to wear the ones she had another day. Just because they'd reached the bowels of the earth, they didn't have to surrender up civilized ways. Harm would laugh at her but she vowed not to care. Fresh garments were necessary for a fresh outlook, and at this point, things were looking very grim.

"Ammy, it's Harmon."

With a cry of relief, she was off the bed, racing for the door. He didn't have a chance to step in from the hall before she was wrapped around him, snug as his wet denims at Blue Creek. He closed the door, bolting it, then peeled her off so he could stride to the far doors, pushing them open to let in the night breeze. He stood there with his palms braced outward on either jamb, sagging as if it were an effort to remain on his feet. She noticed the crude bandaging of his left hand and the tension shifting through the muscles of his shoulders beneath the taut fit of his cotton shirt.

"Harmon?"

No response.

She went to him without caution, because she could feel something was not right with him. Then she smelled alcohol. Still, she wasn't afraid.

"What did you find out?"

"These things take time, Amanda," he snapped back at her. "I can't just go up to any stranger and blurt out my business."

"No, of course not. I was just——"

"Let me do my job!"

He shoved away from the door frame and stalked restlessly into the heavy heat of the room. Unwisely, she followed. Her palm rubbed over the hard swell of his arm and he winced away.

"Harmon, what's wrong?"

"Wrong?" He turned and she could see his features. They were as harsh as the wind-tortured buttes, all cut by deep scoring lines. "Everything. This world, this place, fate, me, you. Where do you want me to start?"

She ignored his gruff mockery and restated firmly, "Harmon, what's wrong?"

He looked at her as if really seeing her for the first time. His gaze took in the scantiness of her attire, the way it clung revealingly to slender limb and soft contour, adhering close to the damp heat of her skin. Her feet were bare and that acted upon him strangely. How small they were, with their delicate arches and dainty little toes. His stare came up with the forcefulness of a steam train, boring into the compassionate pools of concern.

"This is wrong," he told her as his hand clamped behind her neck to compel her up against him with a bruising strength. His mouth was hard and almost cruel

218

upon hers, but she was quick to open under its ruthless slant, inviting his possession, asking eloquently for his love. He made a raw sound and let his tongue plunge inside. It was like sinking into madness.

Amanda hadn't the experience to know passion from danger. She didn't know she should step away from him while controlling darkness roiled inside. All she knew was the wild excitement of his rough embrace, every bit as fiery as the taste of liquor seasoning his kiss. And she knew if she pressed him now, he wouldn't stop with a few tentative caresses.

His mouth twisted away. His breath burnt along the curve of her cheek in short, savage bursts. She could feel him beginning to think, to reason, and she rubbed herself against him to keep him from distraction. He was so hard—in body, in soul—so tense, she could feel the taut coil vibrating through him. Her hands pushed up and down his chest, then clasped either side of his lean hips to tug him suggestively into the receptive softness of her own form. For a moment, he moved with her, rocking in instinctive rhythm. Then he caught her hands and drew them up, pinning them against his chest.

"What do you want from me?"

"I want you, Harmon."

"You want what you see, and you're so blind, Amanda. So blind."

"Then open my eyes," she pleaded huskily, arching up in offering as she did.

"No." He pushed her away but she was back in an instant, her arms winding about his neck, her hot little mouth pressing kisses there until his pulse was beating so hard and fast, he felt as though the pressure might blow the top of his head off.

"I want it to be with you," she was whispering along the line of his quivering jaw. "Harmon, make love to me.

All I know is what I've read and what I've heard. Show me that it's wonderful."

His hands cut into her upper arms, hurting, shaking her loose. "It's not wonderful," he told her hoarsely. "I'm not wonderful. When are you going to understand that? Ammy, I'm not one of your paper heroes. I'm not perfect or honorable. Life is not like those fairy tales you read. It's hard and it's ugly and it hurts. Bad. There is nothing romantic about what a man and woman do together. Ask my sister if you don't believe me. I won't do this. Don't make me hurt you."

His words confused, but there was no mistaking the male definition throbbing against the thin fabric of her drawers. A maiden's shock and a woman's desire chafed her emotions. Amanda thought perhaps she should pull away. But she leaned in closer. She was shaken by a rushing thrill. And suddenly she knew there was no going back, not for either of them. This was what she wanted. He was what she wanted.

"Harmon."

She was looking up at him through great dark wells of desire. Her lips, still parted with the speaking of his name, were too lush to ignore. His crushed down over them.

Wet heat was everywhere, hanging heavy in the air around them, flowing thickly to the womanly places she'd never been so aware of as at this moment. It became unbearable. Her body flamed. It was wonderful. It was everything her roommate's tantalizing descriptions had led her to believe. Amanda couldn't wait to experience it all. With Harm.

It was only a few subtle steps back until they were at the bed. She sank down and he followed, the momentum of his weight carrying her to the mattress. And that's when it stopped being wonderful.

She expected tender, courting kisses, but his mouth was bruising. She'd wanted sweet words, not just the harsh rasp of his breathing. She waited for him to touch her adoringly, to awaken her to a blissful yearning. He grabbed the fragile cotton of her drawers and yanked them down. Then his jean-clad knee was shoving between hers. He was still dressed, right down to his boots. This wasn't what she'd wanted. She'd wanted to relish the pleasurable friction of his bare skin upon hers, not the impersonal abrasion of denim and the bite of his belt buckle against her belly. She wanted time to acquaint herself with the differences of his man's body before being forced to recognize them. But he wouldn't slow and he wouldn't wait, and then he was pushing, hard and thick between her spread thighs, settling there so she couldn't close them in protest of his haste. His weight was smothering and she felt uncomfortably helpless.

"Wait," she cried out in alarm. "Harm, I'm not ready."

Not ready. He didn't understand. She'd practically dragged him down to this point of madness, and he was so far beyond ready, he was aware of nothing else. Not her sudden reluctance. Not her virginal panic. All he felt was the silken heat of her, that dangerous beckoning heat, and he couldn't resist. Not tonight. Not when he needed the savage release passion would bring him. He didn't understand slow or sweet. He didn't understand what it was she expected from the romantic notions held in her sheltered mind. He didn't know anything about giving, just taking, and tonight he couldn't say "no" or "wait" or "stop" to the rampaging wants she fired inside him. He didn't want to try.

He caught the hands that braced against his shoulders, trapping them above her head with one of his, reaching down between their bodies with his other. Then Amanda felt his foreign heat as he tugged the front of his jeans open, and she went stiff all over. His intensity confused her. His fiercely controlled power frightened her. Why wasn't he gentle?

He went through the delicate barrier of her innocence like a battering ram, driving full length until he was wedged all the way to her womb. The shock made her gasp, the pain made her slender body arch and tighten in panic. She heard his breath suck in, then expel violently. And he began to move. Perhaps if he'd just stayed still long enough for her to adjust to the scalding invasion, but he was drawing and plunging again, streaking her insides with that same glassy fire. She began to struggle. He overruled her with his strength and forceful purpose. Her soft cry of appeal was swallowed up by the noise of his labored breathing. With a half dozen of those hard, punishing thrusts tearing her asunder, he uttered a ragged moan that was as much regret as it was relief.

For a long second, he held himself suspended on trembling forearms, panting against the side of her neck. He lifted his head to look down at her, and his features screwed up into an agony of remorse when he saw the tears seeping from the corners of her eyes. Then he grew unexpectedly angry. He tore from her as brutally as he'd entered and Amanda cried out, not so much from pain this time as from the hurt of disillusionment. He didn't know the difference.

"There," he growled tautly. "Now you know. Now I've shattered all your myths about men and life and love. Now maybe you'll stop believing everything you read. Now maybe you'll leave me the hell alone."

He was sitting just outside her room with his carbine cradled in his arms. He hadn't moved in the last hour and probably wouldn't for the remainder of the night. He was Apache. Endurance was inbred. She could see him through the open balcony doors, from where she shifted restlessly upon the damp, stained sheets. Her tears were dried. She'd stopped crying long ago and now she simply watched him. He looked like one of the stone sentinels from the Texas mountains, straight, rugged, unyielding, with a strength only time could wear away.

She wanted to get up, to wash away the stickiness on her thighs and the grit of perspiration from her body, but she was afraid she'd draw his attention. She had no idea what they would say to one another now that they'd been . . . intimate.

Amanda almost laughed. Intimate. Was that what they'd been? What a lie. There'd been nothing personal in his rough possession of her. And afterwards, he'd chided her for all her tender fantasies. Well, he'd woken her from them, hadn't he? He'd been right to think her a fool. Only a fool would make a hero of someone like Harmon Bass. Her great plan to seduce him for the sake of security was in tatters. Imagine asking him if he meant to marry her now that he'd lain with her! He'd laugh himself sick over that bit of female folly. What would prompt him to do the decent thing when she was no longer certain he was even a decent man? What kind of threat could she hold over him? His reputation? Hers? She had no family to demand he do right by her. He would probably look her in the eye and say she'd asked for it and he'd given it to her. What reason did she have for complaint?

The achiness of ready tears rose again and she swallowed it down. Her throat was already raw from weeping, and what good had it done her? It couldn't restore her blissful naiveté. Harm had torn that from her at her own insistence.

223

He hadn't even cared enough for her to take his time, to make it nice.

She tossed onto her side, putting her back to him. Unbidden, the tears came again.

Out in the cool night air, Harm closed his eyes, his guilt redoubling at the soft sound of her distress. He was cruelly sober now. The fire and fury had flickered out in his soul, leaving an emptiness so vast, so deep, it was like dying.

He had lost something so precious to him, he had no way to estimate the value. He hadn't wanted to care for Amanda Duncan. He'd been totally unprepared. He knew how to read sign, how to find water, how to snatch a living from the greedy fist of West Texas. What he knew best was how to protect himself. He'd made a vow to never be caught with his wits unguarded, to never display any vulnerability. And in a few short weeks, an eastern schoolgirl had him flat on his back with his throat bared in submission. She'd pursued him so diligently, with such determination, he'd been secretly flattered. He'd liked kissing her. She'd liked it as well. And the first rumblings of passion . . . they'd been good, too. He'd started to think, to hope that what Becky told him long ago was true. That it didn't have to be awful. That such things weren't only done in violence or out of duty. It wounded him to think she'd lied to him about that.

He hadn't wanted to hurt Amanda. She'd never believe that now. He'd frightened her. He'd made her cry. She'd feared him and now she would hate him, too. And the tender blades of hope that had been pushing up through the arid soil around his heart would wither on the stem. Squeezing his eyes tight, he could see the caring in her face as she called, *Be careful, Harmon.* He could feel the shiver of satisfaction clear down to his toes when she'd told him she'd missed him. Then there was the night she'd sat out on his sister's porch with the bowl of peas. It had been a long, long time since someone had waited anxiously upon his return. Those were quiet memories, poignant ones to a man who had known so little peace.

Then there was the way she'd felt sheathing him in hot liquid fire. The intensity of sensation had been so exquisite he'd lost all control. As a young man, he'd taken the sacred peyote buttons to chart his life's path. Coupling with Amanda had been like that; everything so bright and sharp and vividly alive. Yet even as the final surge of pleasure sent him soaring and for a brief eternity held him suspended, it was followed by a fall that nearly killed him. That fall into disgrace. Because by weakening, he was every bit as bad as those he hunted.

He could hear the shrieks. He could see the sights no boy of ten was ever meant to see. The horror of it massed inside him until he wanted to scream. But he didn't now, as he hadn't then. And finally the images faded beneath the toughness of his Apache training. Faded but were never forgotten.

Amanda glared at the motionless figure guarding her door. She wondered resentfully if he was tired, if he was sore. He hadn't altered his vigil and now the warm morning sun was edging across his knees, glinting on his rifle barrel. Why should she care as long as he was doing his job? As long as he was protecting her. But in lieu of last night, that was ironic. She'd needed more protection from him than from the nameless brutes downstairs.

Amanda dressed quickly and quietly. She went without undergarments. Hers were ruined. As she was ruined. She approached him cautiously and without a word of good morning.

"I want a hot breakfast and I need new clothes."

"All right." He rose with a fluid movement. She hated that she still enjoyed watching him. "Let's go."

"You don't need to accompany me, Mr. Bass."

"Yes, I do." He came inside, closing the doors behind him and bolting them. His gaze touched upon the rumpled bed and the blotchy evidence of her lost virtue without pause. And she was so angry, she could have cheerfully gutted him with his own knife.

"You needn't watchdog me," she drawled out searingly. "I've nothing of value left for anyone to steal."

His gaze was opaque. "Don't be stupid."

She laughed. "A little late for that warning, don't you think?" Angry with him for his indifference, angry with herself for sounding so peevish, she reached down to snatch up her boots. The chafing misery caught her by surprise and she moaned.

"Are you all right?"

How dare he sound so concerned? He hadn't cared when he was pummeling her until she felt like the insides of a butter churn. "I'm fine, Mr. Bass. And if you offer up any of your old Apache remedies, I will slap your face so hard, you'll be picking your teeth out of the door."

"Yes, ma'am."

Amanda glared at him, but his expression was carefully neutral. If he was amused or annoyed by her temper, he had the good sense not to show it. She jerked on her footgear and stomped to the door. He followed without comment.

She was being stupid. Amanda knew it and was too upset to care. How was she supposed to act? She'd thrown herself at a man who saw her as an silly irritation. She was in love with a man who took her virginity as casually as he'd claim his fee. And then he'd shouted at her afterwards, rubbing her face in her own foolishness. She'd been hurt and humiliated on what should have been the most rapturous night of her life. So she would try to match him for indifference, only it was so very difficult when all she wanted to do was cry her heart out. Worst of all, she wanted him to hold her while she did it, because she had no one else to comfort her. She was a seventeen-year old city-bred girl with ideals straight from the exaggerated pages of her beloved books. She was angry because they'd been shown to be a lie. She was frightened because now she didn't know what to believe. She stormed from the hotel and out onto the street, too preoccupied with her own pain to notice anything else.

Then she saw her reflection in a storefront window and her mood plummeted even farther into despair. Her hair was sloppily braided and listing to one side. Her face was nearly as dark as some of the Mexicans she'd seen. Her clothing was a mess and her mouth was as bruised as an overripe peach. She looked like a whore.

Harmon Bass's whore.

Harm saw her stop but he couldn't guess what she was staring at so fixedly within the feed and grain store. She was behaving strangely and it kept him on his toes. He'd expected her to be in a fragile state, all weepy, regretful, and full of blame. This gruff belligerence made him edgy. He'd believed what she said about his teeth. It made it hard for him to think of a way to apologize and still keep the evenness of his smile. Warily, he kept himself beyond arm's length, safe from her temper, safe from the temptation of touching her. And he wanted to touch her . . . badly. A tender echo deep inside told him to breach her thorny manner and hold her close. Colder common sense told him to do no such thing. She wouldn't want him to. Not now. She didn't trust him now.

"Clothes first," she said in a tight little voice that bit like barbed wire.

He followed her down the walk. In his conscience, he felt as though he should be slinking at her heels, groveling for forgiveness, but he was too aware of other things. Like the appraising stares that noted them with interest. He kept the strutting swagger in his walk and his sawed-off carbine swinging easily at his side. As his gaze covertly studied both sides of the street, he moved up closer to Amanda and placed a governing hand at the curve of her waist. She almost jumped out of her boots at that unexpected contact.

"Just walk," he told her with his lethally quiet purr. She did so, but he could feel her trembling. Had he frightened her that badly? His features tensed into a formidable scowl. Only a fool looking for a taste of lead would have stepped into his path.

Perdition's fashion offerings were severely limited to a rack of ready-mades in the mercantile. While Amanda fingered the rough, practical fabrics expressionlessly, the proprietor approached them.

"Can I help you folks with something?"

"My woman needs outfitting down to the skin. Get her whatever she wants. I'll see to it."

Amanda lifted a cool gaze to him. Her tone was even icier. "You don't need to do that, Mr. Bass."

"Yes, I do. Figure I owe it to you."

He'd meant it as an apology, because he'd ruined her things and he felt damned bad about it. But he could see in an instant that she misinterpreted his gesture. Her face drained of color. Her big brown eyes welled up with an awful anguish. Then she swallowed hard and the glimpse of vulnerability was gone. She glared at him and he could almost feel his teeth flying.

"I suppose they could be considered as part of your expenses, Mr. Bass." She turned her back on him and he wished she would hit him. Maybe then, he'd feel better.

Chapter Fourteen

Breakfast was a solemn affair in the elegant hotel across the street from theirs. Amanda attacked her food and Harm stared into his coffee. He was watching her through the fringe of his lashes and at the same time keeping an alert vigil on the room around them.

In her fresh garb, with her hair neatly arranged, she didn't look like a ravaged virgin. Nor did she look like a little schoolgirl, Harm realized with some surprise. She was beautiful and composed. There was a strength to the set of her shoulders within the white cotton shirtwaist, a determination to the way she kept her soft lips unsmiling. West Texas had toughened her. Experience had jaded her. Silently, he mourned for the innocent she'd been while admiring the woman she was becoming. Amanda Duncan was a survivor. He wouldn't have believed it a few weeks ago. He wouldn't have given her a spit-in-the-wind chance those first days out on the trail. She'd proven him wrong. She'd drawn snake venom from his leg, had held him in her lap ready to defend him with an unwavering Colt. She'd come after him, once in a misguided notion that she could somehow help him, then again to exact a vengeance for her loved one. With all the handicaps she'd arrived with, Amanda was shaping up to be a fine Western woman.

Suddenly, Harm was aware of a powerful stirring. Desire thickened into a hot, insistent coil. The memory of how she'd felt around him brought a fever to his mind. She glanced up just then and he met that guarded look impassively. If she had any idea how much he wanted her right then and there, she wouldn't have bravely returned his stare. But he was "Mr. Bass" again, not "Harmon," and he was to keep his distance. He knew it without her telling him. And that ached as badly as the cuts on his hand, as miserably as the throb of excess in his head, as fiercely as the pulse of longing that made it uncomfortable for him to sit still beneath her cool challenge.

"There you are, Mr. Dexter. What'll it be? Just coffee?"

Harm jerked from his mooning reverie, instantly all taut attention. Amanda stiffened across from him. She'd heard the name, too, and was looking to him for direction. He canted a casual look toward the next table. Dave Dexter. He recognized him from the description he'd been given in Terlingua. Then he felt a chill of awareness crawl over his skin, bristling the hairs on his arms into a wary tingle. He brought his gaze up slowly, steeling his gut as he did. His toes were curling for purchase within the confines of his boots, digging in instinctively.

" 'Morning, Mr. Bass."

"Sheriff."

Amanda glanced up. The subtle frost edging Harm's tone was enough to alert her to danger. Her gaze touched upon a tall man with glacial blue eyes and a wicked scar. He was wearing a lawman's badge. Then she dropped her stare back to her companion in question. Harm was smiling; that bland baring of teeth. He looked relaxed, even affable—if one didn't know him. His right hand was no longer on the table. His left was holding his coffee cup in a convulsive grip. Amanda was shocked to see fresh blood trickling from beneath the crude wrapping over his knuckles as his fingers tightened. Something about this man, the sheriff of Perdition, pulled Harmon Bass as taut as fencing wire, and she sensed it wouldn't take much for him to snap into deadly coil.

The sheriff was smiling down at her. He was familiar, somehow, but she didn't know why he should be. She wouldn't have forgotten someone as intimidating.

"Can I beg an introduction to your pretty lady friend?" he crooned in a sensuous slide of syllables. Amanda's flesh shivered uncomfortably. She felt the same way she had when that diamond-patterned skin had flashed in front of her face. She wanted to draw back in fright, but she held herself still and offered a tentative smile.

"Ammy, this is Tyrell Cates. Sheriff, Amanda Bass. My wife."

"Ma'am."

She held carefully to her surprise and to her revulsion as he took up her hand and pressed unpleasantly warm lips to it.

"Pleased to meet you, Sheriff. Are you a friend of my husband's?" She glanced between the two men, trying to guess at the relationship. She knew it wasn't one of camaraderie.

"I know him by reputation only, Mrs. Bass, and them's mighty impressive credentials. Might you be going to Terlingua with him?"

She didn't hesitate to spin a little fiction of her own. "Yes. We're going to visit my cousin. Perhaps you know him. Cal Lowe. He's the sheriff there."

"Why, I didn't know Calvin had such a fine-looking cousin. You're a lucky man, Mr. Bass, catching yourself a pretty little lady like this."

"I always get what I go after, Sheriff."

"I've heard that about you."

They exchanged gauging looks and Cates tipped his hat respectfully. He eased into a chair at Dave Dexter's table. Though Harm never looked at the two of them, Amanda could feel his energies focused tautly on the men at the adjoining table. She could feel something else, too. The dark eddies of violence were there, lapping just beneath his surface calm. He'd had that same chiseled set to his expression while he watched an unfortunate soul twist over his smoldering fire. Surely, he wasn't planning to tangle with Perdition's sheriff. At least, not before he finished what she'd hired him to do. She wasn't about to let him kill or be killed.

"Harmon?"

No response. His eyelids were narrowed into concealing slits. Behind them, his gaze glittered like a knife blade, hard and sharp. Lethal.

Gingerly, she reached out until her fingertips brushed his hand. His fingers snapped around hers, curling them into his palm with a desperate strength. Clinging as if she were some sort of lifeline. His intensity alarmed her, but it was his silent plea for support she reacted to. Her thumb rubbed below the taped ridge of his knuckles, absorbing the tension of his grip the way a soothing ointment would ease the sting of the wounds above it. She knew exactly when he broke from his dangerous concentration. She heard him strain a shaky breath through gritted teeth and expel it in a cleansing rush. Then his awareness of her returned. His grip on her hand loosened. However, he made no move to let her go. The glaze was gone from his eyes as he used them to gesture to the pair at the next table. That was when she started to pay attention to their low exchange of words.

"I don't want to hang around here," Dave Dexter was whining. "What if somebody comes nosing around?"

"I'll take care of that," Sheriff Cates assured with a cold impatience. "You'd be better off at the ranch."

"No sir. I'm safer here till my dealings are done. I ain't gonna turn my back on you."

Cates smiled thinly. "It's not in my best interest to do you harm. As long as you cooperate."

"When's he getting back? I want to get this over and done."

"Tomorrow morning. Till then, you jus' relax. Why don't you go and treat yourself to a hot bath and a shave? Getting so a man can smell the fear on you a mile away."

Cates sent a coin spinning across the table and Dexter slapped his palm over it. When he stood, Cates's stare rose with him, all traces of amiability gone from the icy depths.

"Don't wander off," he warned quietly.

Dexter gave a nervous smile and carefully sidled around him before making for the door. Cates watched him run, then turned his attention toward the big breakfast delivered up in front of him.

Harm slid out of his chair and bent to scoop Amanda up in a tight embrace before she could utter a gasp of protest. The warm feel of his breath against her neck was enough to efficiently subdue her. This was the closeness she'd wanted from him last night, this firm, enveloping clasp of possession. She'd just begun to turn to liquid in his arms when he whispered very unlover-like, "Keep the sheriff here. Do what you have to, but don't leave this room with him. You promise me that, Ammy. Don't you leave with him."

His words were taut and fierce, not with jealousy but with a hard edge of concern. She understood. Tyrell Cates was dangerous and Harm was worried about her.

Her nod created a pleasant friction between her cheek and his, and somehow, her hand had come up to cup the back of his head, her fingers threading through the black hair at its nape.

"Where are you going?" she whispered back, enjoying the excuse to nuzzle close in a frustration of longing.

"I need a bath and a shave." His mouth grazed the tender spot below her ear in a seemingly unintentional caress. Her fingers clenched. "Stay here, Amanda. I'll be back for you."

Then he straightened and was striding, not toward the front door as Dexter had, but out through the hotel lobby and to the front desk.

"A back door?" he asked the clerk. "Tell me, don't show me."

"Down the hall to my right, at the very end."

Harm nodded and made a casual turn in that direction. He didn't break into a trot until he was beyond the vision of those in the hotel's dining room.

Amanda let out a shaky breath, then glanced cautiously at the man at the next table. She wasn't particularly excited over the task of keeping him occupied, not when she'd much rather be with Harm as he wrangled Dexter's confession. Not when the sheriff of Perdition made her think of a reptile curled around a warm rock. Just because he was lazy now didn't mean he couldn't strike without warning. Harm wouldn't have given her the chore if he didn't think she'd be safe in the midst of the town's citizenry. And there was no way she was going off alone anywhere with Tyrell Cates. She took a deep breath, fortified by the knowledge that Harm was counting on her.

"Excuse me, Sheriff," she cooed, coming to stand at his table. "I hope I'm not intruding."

"No, ma'am." His grin was quick and anything but comforting.

"I wonder if I might impose upon you." She gave a helpless little simper. "I find myself temporarily abandoned. Harmon thinks I'm dreadfully silly to worry over such things, but I do get quite distressed when left alone in . . ." She broke off, letting her gaze survey the room, touching on several unsavory-looking characters before concluding, "In such rough surroundings. Might I join you at your table until he returns?"

"Why, I'd be honored by the company, Mrs. Bass."

She sank into the opposite chair, smiling with a foolish simplicity. Harm had entrusted her to something she could do well. When she was nervous, she could rattle on for hours nonstop. "Why, Sheriff Cates, you must tell me all about yourself. I've read some marvelous stories about the West, and you must enlighten me. My cousin Calvin thinks me so naive. Why, he won't share any of his exciting adventures with me. And Harmon . . . he won't talk about himself at all. So modest, you know. I would love to hear some authentic stories from an honest to goodness western hero." She opened her big brown eyes wide and Tyrell Cates fell right into the enchantment of her stare.

After nearly thirty minutes, she could see the charm had worn off. His initial politeness had become a glaze of boredom. If she hadn't thought to unbutton the top two buttons of her shirtwaist under the pretext of rising humidity, she would have lost him after the first ten minutes. Every time she sensed he was about to get up, she would lean forward to touch his arm encouragingly or bend to pick up something she'd carelessly dropped upon the floor. Basic ploys she'd learned watching Rose, her roommate, but astonishingly successful. Once his pale gaze dipped down her blouse, it was lost in the visual plundering of that tempting valley. She endured the ogling only because she knew it wouldn't be followed by any groping, not here in front of half of Perdition. So she teased him and kept him waylaid, so Harm would have time to do what he had to.

"Sheriff." Lon Pager was momentarily stunned into silence by the sight of glistening bare skin where Amanda's cotton blouse gapped open.

"What is it, Lon?" Cates grabbed at the distraction. Amanda Bass was a fetching creature, but she could talk the ears off a deaf man.

"I got to talk to you. Business."

"Mrs. Bass, if you'll excuse me." He was rising and Amanda knew she couldn't stop him, so she stood as well.

"That's all right, Sheriff. Harmon's probably back at our room by now. I'll just go meet him there. Thank you so much for keeping me company."

She waited until the two Perdition lawmen had left the dining room. She promised Harm she wouldn't leave with Cates. He hadn't said anything about leaving after him.

Dave Dexter took a long pull on his Cuban cigar and sighed a smoke ring toward the dingy ceiling of the bathhouse. He'd been tense for days, ever since Cates and his men had caught up with him. He'd be meeting with McAllister in the morning, and if everything went well, he'd be a free man by afternoon. He'd worked for the old judge before he did his stay in upstate New York and he knew the shrewd feller appreciated ambition. They would come to terms, he was sure of it. What he'd done hadn't been the smartest thing and the way it had turned out was a plain and simple disaster, but it could be salvaged. If he talked fast and was plenty humble, he could be living high in Mexico within the week.

The curtain affording him privacy gave a jingle and

pulled away from the foot of the big metal tub. He glared up at the compact little nobody who interrupted his musings. Dexter's gaze measured him for a threat and found none. No fancy gunbelt, no truculent expression, no menacing stance; just an insignificant cowhand of mild demeanor and the dark complexion that marked him as some Indian's by-blow.

"Wait yer turn, boy. I paid my two bits and I aim to enjoy a good long soak."

"Oh, I don't want you to get up. You're fine right there. Just thought we might talk a minute."

"You thought wrong. Get gone afore I'm motivated to teach you some manners."

"Dave Dexter?"

"That's right," he growled in response to the soft-spoken inquiry. "Who the hell want's to know?"

"The name's Bass. Harmon Bass."

His eyes narrowed. Harmon Bass. He knew the name. Dog-eared dime novels were a mainstay of entertainment in prison. He looked the small man up and down and had a good, long laugh. "Sure. And I'm Sam Houston." When the swarthy features remained impassive, Dexter's humor darkened. "Fun's over. Get on with you 'fore I get riled."

Dexter froze as the stoic half-breed lifted a sawed-off carbine. A feed sack hung from the barrel by a loosely tied knot. The burlap was moving suspiciously. The bag extended until it dangled over the tub. Dexter frowned as the coarse weave undulated.

"What you got in there, boy?"

"You don't need to know unless you refuse to talk to me."

"I ain't fallin' for no trick. You plannin' to shoot me?"

"I don't do things that way."

The carbine bounced a couple of times and the knot

slipped. From inside the sack came a very perturbed rattling. Dexter nearly created a tidal wave in his haste to scramble back against the curved metal side of the tub. "How many of them things you got in there?"

"Only takes one if he's good and mad." Harm jostled the sack again. The knot gave another fraction and the snake gave another warning.

"You wouldn't."

Harm smiled flatly. "You ever seen a man die of snakebite? Figure I'll just sit back and watch the poison swell you up until the skin pops. You can talk to me now, or we can wait until you're begging me to tie a tourniquet on you."

Dexter cursed. "What the hell do you want to know?"

"Tell me about Randolph Duncan."

"Duncan? You mean that prissy eastern kid? Met up with him on the train from New York."

"Got to be good friends, did you?"

"It's a long trip. He liked to talk and I listened, that's all. I swear to you."

The bag rocked. The snake buzzed. And Dexter began to run with sweat.

"All right! All right! The boy was green as grass. He was toting some sparklers for Judge McAllister. Used to work for the judge, so it was easy to convince him that I was the man sent to escort him to Perdition. I just got out from doing hard time and was lookin' for a way to get back on my feet."

"And back-shooting some dumb kid from the East seemed a pretty good way to do it, is that what you figured?"

"Didn't mean for that to happen. Hell, I ain't no murderer."

"Then why'd you shoot him?"

"Got wise to me. Don't know how. He took off like a

bat outta hell right out in the middle of nowhere. Couldn't believe it! Where'd the fool think he was gonna go? He got up into the hills and I was afraid I was going to lose him, so I fired off a couple just to scare him. His horse had started to climb and he took one. He was dead by the time I found him."

"And the jewelry?"

"Didn't have it. Honest to God!" he shrieked when the sack came perilously close to slipping off the barrel into his bath-water. "Careful there! He didn't have it. I was stupid enough to let him hang on to the jewels. Never thought he'd try anything. He musta buried it someplace afore he died. I went to town to pick up some supplies, meaning to spend a week or so digging all around where I trailed him, but McAllister's men picked me up."

"Then why aren't you dead?"

" 'Cause I told Cates I could lead them to where the jewelry was buried but that I'd only give the information to the judge hisself. Figured I'd live a sight longer that way."

"Maybe. Least until they find the jewels. Then I wouldn't give odds on you having much of a future."

"So," Dexter growled nervously, "now that you know, whatcha meaning to do? Go after the jewels yourself? You ain't got no idea where to look."

"I found Duncan."

Dexter paled. "Dang my bad luck. You are Bass, ain't-cha?"

"But I'm not interested in the gems. I'm interested in you telling the truth of it to Cal Lowe over in Terlingua."

Dexter gaped at him. "What? No! No way! I'd be dead for sure. McAllister's men would be using me for target practice if they thought I was skipping out on them."

A cold voice intruded. "You'll be dead right now unless you do."

Harm didn't spare her a glance. "I told you to stay put."

"You told me to keep an eye on Cates," Amanda corrected. Her pistol was leveled on a very agitated Dave Dexter. "He left with his deputy. Thought you might want to know."

"So you've told me. Now go on and get back to the room."

"Not without him. He killed my brother and he's going to Terlingua to stand trial for murder. He's going to clear Randy's name. Harmon, what's in that sack?" She stared at it for a moment, fascinated by the waves of motion.

"Don't ask. Just go. Amanda, let me take care of it."

"No. Get out of that tub, Dexter."

"Ma'am, I ain't got nothing on. At least toss me that there towel."

"Amanda!"

Harm's warning cracked, curt and clear. And too late. She'd already pitched the towel to Dexter. The instant he caught it, he sent it flying in Harm's face, momentarily blocking his vision. As Harm flung it aside, the sack fell from the muzzle of his carbine and burst open on the floor. At the sight of the five-foot rattler, Amanda screamed and lunged back. Dexter surged up out of the water without a hint of his earlier modesty and grabbed for her pistol. He pulled forward and the gun discharged with a deafening roar.

Amanda stood stunned as Dexter slumped back into the tub. The choppy water was quick to color a bright red. The pistol dropped from her numbed fingers as her hands flew up to cover her mouth. The snake, forgotten, slithered under the tub and down a hole in the floorboards, to freedom.

"He's dead."

"A bullet in the heart usually does the trick," Harm

snapped as his gaze swept the back room for other possible exits. There was only one, the way they'd come in, and it was filled with the curious.

"I killed him," she mumbled in disbelief. Then her thinking started up, seizing on unpleasant truths. "Oh, Harmon, what are we going to do? Now who's going to tell the truth about what happened with Randy?"

"You should have wondered that before you put a piece of lead in him!"

"In here, Sheriff," came a cry from the outer room of the barber shop.

Amanda whirled to face this new threat. She glanced expectantly toward Harm, waiting for him to barge through the crowd and shoot their way to a quick escape. Instead, he stood his ground and calmly held his carbine out away from his body, while the other hand reached above his head.

"What are you—?"

"Mr. Bass, you've had one busy morning," Tyrell Cates exclaimed mildly as he took the rifle from him.

If Amanda was surprised by his lack of resistance, she was totally unprepared for what came next.

"I didn't shoot him, Sheriff. Check my barrels."

"Now, am I to believe your pretty little wife plugged him?"

"She's not my wife. She hired me to find Dexter. I didn't know she was fixing to blow him to hell or I wouldn't have agreed to take her money. I'm a tracker, not a killer."

When he concluded that incredible statement with a look so impersonally cool she felt herself a stranger, Amanda's composure shattered.

"You liar! You stinking, cowardly liar! How could you say that? First you roll over and play dead instead of

242

trying to save our skins, then you try to pretend you had nothing to do with anything."

He met her glare with an unwavering control, until hers crumbled bit by bit. She was furious yet tears were quick to burn for release.

Cates surveyed the scene, his expression tightening at the sight of the dead man bobbing in the tub. "Now, ma'am, are you trying to say you didn't shoot this here feller?" he asked reasonably.

"No. Well, yes, I did, but it was an accident. He grabbed the barrel of my gun and there was this big snake and—"

"I don't see no snake, ma'am. Alls I see is one very dead man and a lot a big questions."

She shut her mouth tight and blinked fiercely to contain the need to cry. She couldn't believe Harm would betray her to save himself. Then she remembered his stoic Apache philosophy: *I only fight when I know I can win.* Apparently, her fate was now considered a no-win situation; a fate now in the hands of the cold-eyed Tyrell Cates.

"Are you taking me to jail, Sheriff?" Amanda asked with all the shaky bravado she could muster. She wouldn't let them all see how weak her knees had suddenly become and she *would not* grab on to Harmon Bass for support. Her mind was spinning wildly in its ignorance of western law and how it would apply to her. Her money couldn't buy her a fancy trial lawyer to plead her case of self-defense, not here in this barren wilderness. Would they even bother with a trial, or did the Big Bend of Texas discourage violence with the swift dispensation of frontier justice? Try as she might, she couldn't block the image of a hangman's noose from her frantic thoughts.

Sheriff Cates smiled grimly. "I don't think so, ma'am, considerin'. We'll be taking you and Mr. Bass out to the

243

judge's ranch. I'm sure he'll want to handle this particular matter personally when he gets back."

"What do you need me for?" Harm objected. "I already told you I didn't shoot him."

Cates studied him for a moment, no longer misled by the slight stature and mild expression. "I don't think I can afford to have you running around loose, Mr. Bass. So, if you all would just come along real quiet like, I can have my deputy clean up the mess."

They reached McAllister's ranch by late morning. Amanda was learning that nothing was minutes away in West Texas. By the time they came to the sprawling stucco house, heat was broiling down upon them in shimmery waves. Between the temperature and her inner trepidation, Amanda feared she would swoon from the saddle. Only the presence of a seemingly impervious Harmon Bass kept her going. She would not collapse until she had the opportunity to tell him exactly what she thought of him and his honor.

From the outside, McAllister's dwelling was more featureless adobe fortress than home. The compound was surrounded by a wall meant to be manned against armed attack. The only break in it was set with big wrought iron gates and guarded by well-equipped sentries. As they passed through, single file, she could see the house. It was built with all the swagger and stark utility of Texas, yet tempered with appealing hints of Mexican romance and mystery. There were fountains where clear water splashed invitingly and shaded patios hung with baskets trailing bright floral streamers, to cast welcoming shade across the tiles and arbored seating. But that wasn't where they were led. After being jerked out of the saddle by Cates's men, the sheriff approached them with a pensive frown, apparently trying to decide what best to do with them.

"What happens now?" Amanda demanded with a brusque belligerence.

Cates smiled at her. "You're in a good deal of trouble, and you, Mr. Bass, I haven't quite decided what you are yet. Guess I'll leave it up to the judge. Lock 'em up in the tack room in the barn," he snapped to his seconds, then he strode to the house without a backward glance.

Amanda had to be towed forcibly by one of the hands, but Harm walked on his own between his guards. Until he saw the small, windowless room that would be their prison. He set his heels.

"I'm not going in there."

His escort was in no mood to argue the point. The quick smack of a rifle butt between his shoulder blades applied enough convincing power to spill him headlong into the tack room. Amanda was shoved in behind him, and before he could recover himself, the door was secured from the outside. Harm was instantly up against it, palms pressed to the solid wood frame in hopes of finding a weakness. There was none. His hands curled slowly into fists and his breath expelled noisily. Finally, he turned to confront Amanda. She was waiting and ready. The flat of her hand cracked with numbing strength along the side of his face, followed by the return slap of her fierce words.

"You cowardly son of a bitch!"

And her hand drew back, eager to deal out more.

Chapter Fifteen

Harm caught her wrist before she could strike again.

"Stop it."

Amanda tried to pull away, twisting within his grasp until the pain of her struggles, not the compression of his fingers, made her quit. Then she stood her ground and glared at him. "You liar," she spat.

He never so much as blinked while the imprint of her palm inflamed darkly against his brown skin. His voice was pitched low with dead-sure reasoning. "And I told you to let me handle it. I told you to stay put until I came for you. You're the one who can't seem to remember how to keep a promise. Now get over there, shut your mouth, and let me think."

Sullenly, she retreated to a far corner. Knowing he was right didn't soothe her temper one bit. They were where they were because of her inability to follow his directions. She'd cursed him, and the unfamiliar use of profanity shocked her more than it had him, proof she was too angry and upset to act like herself. Feeling the desperation of their circumstances, she hugged her arms about herself and asked, "Are they going to kill us?"

"If they don't, I just might wring your neck. *Yusn!* If you couldn't do what I asked, at least you could have trusted me. If you hadn't opened your mouth, I would have been out there where I could help you. Now, we're both in here and I don't hold a missionary's chance in hell of anyone letting us go." He began to pace the perimeter of the tiny room, his gaze restless and searching in its sweep of the wall.

"You would have let them take me," came her wounded accusation. That surpassed the rest of what he was saying.

"What did you want me to do? Shoot our way out through a half-dozen innocent people? You think Cates would have kept us breathing if I came out shooting? I'm no bulletproof pulp fiction hero. They'd have killed me. And I wouldn't have been able to do you a helluva lot of good then, would I?"

She paled beneath his hard, probing stare. "I—I never thought—"

"No, you never did. You never do."

Softer still. "I'm sorry."

"If you spent half the time thinking that you do apologizing for the lack of it, we wouldn't . . . oh, never mind." He continued to stalk around the edges of the room, pushing against the boards at irregular intervals. She watched him, fighting down the panic and awful anguish welling up inside.

"I'm scared, Harmon."

His gaze cut to her dispassionately. "Well, you deserve to be." Then he stopped his pacing to take a deep breath. His tone gentled. "But you don't deserve to die from it. I'm not going to let anything happen to you, Amanda."

She nearly strangled on a sob. For a moment, Harm looked as if he was going to come to her, to let her seek comfort in his embrace and reassurance from his strength, but he didn't. He began the restless traveling from corner to corner to corner again, careful to see his wanderings didn't bring him within arm's length of her as he checked the hanging harnesses and hardware for any possible means of escape. He left her alone to garner courage from within herself. And after several minutes of battling tears and fright, she didn't disappoint him.

"What can I do?"

He paused to give her a long, thoughtful look. "Trust me. Listen to me. Do what I tell you the second I tell you, without any questions, without looking back. Can you do that?"

"Yes."

He gave a curt nod, as if he wasn't convinced but supposed he had no choice but to accept her answer. He dropped one of the saddles to the floor. "Have a seat. Get some rest. It's going to be a long night."

And something in his dire prediction brought an ominous shiver through her.

It was close to dusk. Amanda had been alternately dozing and watching Harm's anxious roving. She guessed he must have walked at least ten miles as he circled their dark little prison like something caged and fretful. He didn't speak and she honestly didn't think he was aware of her. His eyes were constantly moving, covering every inch of the surrounding walls. He turned toward the door when it opened, his movement so swift and urgent, the guard's rifle jerked up at ready.

"Stand back. I brung you dinner and when you finish, I'll be taking you out one at a time to wash up and see to yourselves. Doan try nothin'."

Harm backed up and the guard bent to cautiously place a tray on the floor of the tack room. He gave it a push with the toe of his boot, then closed and relatched the door.

Having had nothing to eat since a light breakfast that morning, Amanda scooted eagerly to see what they had. Her brow wrinkled up in uncertainty as Harm knelt down to look for himself. He didn't hesitate. Since they had no cutlery, he dipped his fingers into the colorless glop provided in a bowl, spreading it on one of the tortillas and rolling it up the way he would a cigarette. Then he made quick work of it and reached for another. He glanced up at Amanda. Since she showed no interest in preparing her own, he fixed up two more, handing her one and devouring the other. Amanda took a bite, chewed once, and looked for a place to tactfully spit.

"What is this?" she mumbled without swallowing.

"Beans. Eat up. Probably be all you get."

She forced the mouthful down. The tortilla was soggy. The beans were cold and bland. "Ugh! It's disgusting."

"If you'd rather starve, I'll eat your share."

When he reached for her small stack of tortillas, she pushed his hand away. It may have been disgusting, but she was hungry enough to overlook it. Gingerly, she spread her own thick paste of beans and rolled it up the way he had. She finished her portion and helped him swab out the bowl with her last tortilla. He was smiling faintly at her.

"You're learning, Miss Duncan."

The guard returned and motioned Amanda out with the muzzle of his Winchester. She glanced at Harm uneasily. She didn't like the idea of being separated from him. Neither did he, because his voice was grim.

"Go with him, Amanda. And don't worry. If he touches you, I'll see he pays for it, real slow." He met the guard's eyes to convey that promise. A threat from a small, unarmed man shouldn't have concerned the cowboy. He should have laughed. But he didn't smile or find it amusing. He swallowed hard.

"C'mon, gal. Get a move on. Ain't nobody gonna touch nobody. Leastwise not until the judge says different." She went out and the door locked again.

Harm waited, pacing, forcing himself to breathe deep and regular. It was worse, being alone. He could feel the unreasonable terror swelling, until the room seemed even more cramped and confining. He walked faster. He breathed faster. And he began to talk to himself in low Apache gutturals.

"Oh, God. Dear God. Don't let me start screaming. I'm all right. I'm going to be all right. The door's going to open. Any minute now. Any minute. Just hang on. Keep breathing. Plenty of air. Plenty of room."

And then the door did open and Amanda came back in. A quick look told him she'd suffered no abuse. He was shaking with the relief of her return, feeling so weak inside that he nearly snatched her up in a wild burst of gratitude. But he didn't. She would have thought him crazy. He wiped wet palms on his jeans.

"C'mon, Bass. Ain't got all night. Lessen the Injun in you don't care if you sleep in your own filth."

The jibe cut through Harm's failings. Dignity starched him. "An Apache would walk two miles from camp to see to matters of the body in private. It was the white man who introduced them to filth."

The guard just snorted and gestured with his gun. "Move, and don't make any quick ones. I won't kill you, but I'll make you hurt plenty."

Harm walked past him and out into the stale-smelling barn, then into the cool, fragrant night. He sucked in the scents greedily, letting the freedom fill his lungs to bursting before letting it back out in a sigh. He stood for a long while just pulling in that sweet, fresh air, letting it dry the sweat of fear upon his face and neck. Then he was prodded.

"Over there by the wall. Hurry up and take care of whatever you need to."

Harm went to the appointed spot, then waited for the guard to look away. When he wouldn't, he scowled.

"What the hell's the matter with you?" the cowboy growled.

"It's not something a man does for the eyes of another," he said indignantly. "I will not disgrace myself."

"Damned odd Injuns," the man grumbled, but he angled away. The muzzle of his rifle touched to the back of Harm's skull. "I hear anything out of the ordinary, pard, and you'll have nothing but shoulders."

When he was finished, Harm made for one of the fancy fountains. He put cupped hands under one of the streams and drank deeply from their basin. Then he tilted his head under the cool jet of water so it ran down his face and the front of his shirt, turning to wet down the dust in his hair.

"I ain't gonna wait whilst you take no bath. Get on back to the barn so's I can put you away for the night."

Back to the little room. Harm tensed. Everything inside him knotted up in rebellion. He couldn't do it. He couldn't go back there. Panic raced through him just thinking about it.

His gaze flashed about him, looking for escape, measuring the distance to the surrounding wall. A long sprint through a wide open courtyard. He'd be shot down within the first twenty yards. If he made it to the wall, he'd be on foot and without weapons. He could overpower the guard, take his rifle. He could make a run for the far wall where shadows lay deep. Maybe he could make it. If he didn't, did it matter? Wouldn't a bullet in the back be more welcomed than the madness awaiting him in the airless prison? Anything was better than that slow suffocation of the senses. He took a step back and began to balance on the balls of his feet, readying for a fight and a flight to freedom.

"C'mon, Bass. Don't keep your little gal waiting."

Amanda.

He went flat-footed in surprise. He'd forgotten about Amanda. If he left her behind, what would happen? Maybe everything. Some calm seeped back into the fever of his thoughts. He couldn't leave Amanda and he couldn't escape with her.

And then his chance to run was gone. Two more of McAllister's pistoleers came out of the night, smoking cigarillos and laughing together over some crude joke. They paused to look Harm over, perplexed because even though he was their prisoner, they were afraid of him. Everyone knew Harmon Bass was someone you didn't mess with.

"Move."

The rifle barrel jabbed him in the kidney, driving him forward with a shock of pain. He walked easily, as if he wasn't surrendering himself up at the gates of hell. Damned if he was going to let these men know he was already screaming on the inside. He'd endured countless tortures of the body without a betraying sound. But this was an agony of the mind, harder to control, more difficult to ignore. But he would. He had to.

The look of thanksgiving etched upon Amanda's face was his reward for stepping through the door. But she didn't come to him and he didn't go to her. There was still a restraining tension between them. Then the door shut, sealing out much of the light like the sealing of a tomb. The sound of the bolt shooting home sent a paralyzing terror through him. It shook him in crippling waves. So he started walking, briskly, trying to outdistance the fear. Knowing he couldn't.

He could feel Amanda's curious gaze upon him, tracking his restless travels from side to side. He glanced her way, to find her frowning slightly. That look was invitation enough for her to ask, "Are you all right?"

He swallowed down a gurgle of laughter, because it wouldn't be a sound of amusement if it escaped. It would ring with hysteria. He didn't want to scare her. He didn't want to lose his tenuous grip on sanity. "Fine," he gritted out. "I just don't like being closed in." Incredible understatement, but it satisfied her for the moment.

Harm continued to pace. Every pore was oozing cold sweat. His palms scrubbed up and down on his Levi's but couldn't rid themselves of the clammy dampness. He reached up to tug at his shirt collar. It was choking him. "It's hot in here," he mumbled. Then he was yanking at the fabric, popping buttons, ripping the shirt off his back and over his head with frantic movements. He balled it up in his hands, wadding it convulsively as he continued to retrace his steps. Amanda sat stiff and silent, watching him. He paced and wrapped his shirt around and around the fist of his right hand.

How fast could a man's heart beat before it gave out under the strain? Blood roared in his ears. He could hear nothing over that loud thrumming pulse. He tried to block it out.

"Amanda, talk to me."

"What?"

"Talk to me."

"About what?" She was wary now. Harm had no fondness for her ramblings, she knew. Something was very wrong with him.

"Anything. Talk about anything." He was wiping his face. It was wet and very white. Then he veered toward one of the walls and struck it hard with his padded fist. Again. As if he could splinter the solid wood. "I've got to get out of here! I can't breathe in here!" He hit the wall again and there was a brittle snapping. Certain it was the sound of breaking bones instead of weakening wood, Amanda rushed to stop him. She hung on his arm, dragging it back.

"Harmon, don't! You're going to hurt yourself. What is wrong with you?"

He shook her off and reeled away, staggering like a drunk. He was panting hard. The gaze flying about the room was more than a little crazed. "I've got to get out. I can't breathe. There's no air in here."

"Of course there's air."

Unable to hear her voice over the fierce drumming in his head, Harm went to lean against the door, his cheek pressed to the wood, his eyes screwed tightly shut. Anxiety flooded his mind, crowding out all trace of reason, crushing his chest until the pressure was unbearable. He pushed on the barrier with his palms, leaving damp prints on the unyielding wood.

Desperate to hold out against the madness, he banged the side of his head against the door, hard, so sparks of pain danced before his eyes. He welcomed it, focused upon it to keep his shuddering trapped inside. For a moment, he was victorious. He could think, he could feel—*Yusn*, his hand hurt! What had he done to it? He was aware, too, of Amanda staring at him as if he were a lunatic. *Oh, God.* Just like that, lucidity was gone, swallowed up by the churning panic. He couldn't hang on. Things faded, darkened. The band about his chest closed, hurting. He was floundering in a wash of raw emotion. His words gushed out between his frantic gasps for breath.

"I can't do it. I can't hold on. Don't shut me in here! Don't leave me! I'll die in here!"

Amanda was stunned. She watched as his fingers curled to claw at the edge of the door frame, tearing like a wild thing trying to dig its way out of a trap without thought to injury. She gave up trying to make sense of his behavior; there was no way to explain it. She only knew she had to quiet him, to keep him from hurting himself. She heard Will Bass's cold summation. *He's crazy*. She didn't want to believe that. She was afraid to. She had to depend upon Harmon Bass. She couldn't afford not to trust in him.

"Harmon, stop. The door's locked. You can't open it from in here." She reached around him, grasping both wrists, tugging his arms down to his sides. He stood in the circle of her arms, rigid and shaking for a long second. Then he gave a low, moaning cry.

"I can't breathe."

And hoarse, strangling sounds tore from his throat to emphasize it. She didn't argue. It didn't matter that there was no danger of them smothering in the small tack room. That he believed it was enough.

Amanda looked around frantically. Soon it would be too dark to see the hands in front of their faces. Why was she certain that if things seemed bad now, they would get much worse then? She didn't care to wait and see. There were no windows and the door sealed tight, yet she noticed a distinct whisper of cool air in the stifling space. Searching for that source of ventilation, she was surprised to see that Harm had indeed cracked one of the wall boards. She went to examine it. Bending close, she found he'd struck the board where it was weakened by a knothole. It was an exterior wall and she could feel the coolness of the night through the split in the board.

"Harm, here. See what you can do."

Once he felt the fresh air on his palm, he was quick to act. He drove the heel of his hand against the weak spot. Another crack. Then his fist smashed through. He went to his knees, face crammed into the small opening so he could suck in the saving coolness of the night in desperate gulps. After several long minutes, he sank down and

255

sagged back against the wall, his eyes closed, his breath shivering.

Amanda knelt down beside him. Because she didn't know what else to say, she asked, "Is it better now?"

He nodded.

"Let me see your hand." He didn't resist when she lifted it and unwound the sweat-soaked shirt. Her touch was very gentle as she prodded the back of it and worked his fingers. She couldn't believe they weren't shattered. It seemed a miracle that nothing was broken. Nothing but his composure. She kept his hand, holding it lightly, scrubbing over his bruised knuckles with her thumb. Gradually, his fingers curled until he was clutching hers with a fearsome strength.

"Are you going to be all right, Harmon?" she asked softly, fearfully.

He licked his lips nervously. "No." His gaze surveyed the now-too-familiar circumference of the room. "Not as long as I'm in here." The tempo of his breathing quickened, and when he felt her questions gather, he said harshly, "Can we talk about something else?" Then his tone eased. "Tell me about the East, with all those buildings and all those people. I can't picture such a place. What's it like? What are the people like? Would I like it?"

Amanda laughed quietly. "I don't think so. Have you ever been to a city?" He shook his head and she smiled, trying to picture him in New York. "It's noisy and dirty and fast . . . everything moves fast. There's no sense of space or beauty there. Not like there is here."

"It sounds lonely."

"Lonely?" She'd never thought of it that way, but he was right. Even with all that civilization packed around her, she'd been achingly alone. Yet here, where the horizons stretched from sunrise to sunset, there was no feeling of emptiness. It was as if the land held her in a fond embrace. It might be hostile and unforgiving, but there was a warmth in its sun and sky and endless space. Or was it Harm that made it seem so?

"Why are you going back?"

His question surprised her. She hadn't wanted to think about returning to New York. She'd been hoping for an invitation to stay here. But that was an impossible wish. There was no one who wanted her in West Texas any more than there was anyone waiting in the East. She couldn't tell him that.

"There are no snakes in New York City."

She heard his soft chuckle and her heart clenched tight. There were no real heroes in New York City, either. Just those on the printed page. With twenty-twenty hindsight, she knew why he'd done what he had at the bathhouse. Not out of cowardice, but because it was the prudent thing to do. Blind courage got men killed quick. He'd been thinking far ahead, with a survivor's instincts. Those, she had yet to develop. She was still thinking from the heart, not from the head, and that's why her reckless acts kept ensnaring them in trouble. He would undoubtedly be glad to be rid of her once his job was finished. If it wasn't finished for them first thing in the morning. But she didn't want to dwell on that now. Because she was anxious, she began to talk—about the East, about cities and the people in them, about anything that came to mind. When the unchecked flow of her words brought back her sense of calm, Amanda grew more aware of the man beside her.

Shadows thickened, melding into an impenetrable blackness. As Harm's breathing became rapid and rough, she realized she was losing him once more to whatever demons this small room had released inside him. Because she didn't know the cause, Amanda was afraid of those demons, too.

"Well, I've talked for long enough," she announced abruptly. "Now it's your turn." No response. "Harmon?"

"What?" That was said with an unnatural hoarseness.

"It's your turn to talk."

She heard him swallow noisily. His hand was kneading hers with damp, spasmodic fingers. "About what?"

"Tell me about Will."

"Will?"

"He said you would have made a good Texas Ranger."

"Did he?" Harm sounded surprised. And pleased. "He was a good lawman. One of the best. At one time, I wanted to be just like him." He made a soft deprecating noise. "Imagine that."

"Yes, I can. Why didn't you?"

"Because his idea of justice isn't quite the same as mine."

No, she couldn't imagine the solid, law-abiding Will Bass roasting a man's mental faculties over an open fire. Nor would he see slitting a man's throat as anything but murder. Why she didn't agree wholeheartedly was somewhat of a mystery to her. Every grain of decency inside her decried what she'd seen Harm do, yet still she made excuses for him, even when he would not. Was it because she loved him or because she couldn't see his soul as evil? Was the savageness in him inherited from the Apache or a product of this ruthless area known as the Big Bend? Or did it stem from something else altogether?

"Tell me how you came to live with him."

"He and his wife took us in after—after our mother died. Mrs. Bass, she was very kind, very frail. She was real fond of Becky, said she was like a daughter to her. Becky helped her out with things when she got sick and couldn't see to them herself. It was a good home for her. They took good care of her and saw to—to things. Most folks wouldn't have been so generous with their attitudes. Considering . . ." His words trailed off into silence.

"What about you?"

"Me?"

"Wasn't it your home, too?"

"I—I couldn't stay there."

"Why? They wouldn't let you?" What a horrible thought, a ten-year-old boy turned away from the home that took in his sister. But somehow, she couldn't believe that of Will Bass. Not after the way he'd talked about Harm with such respect.

"They said I was welcome to but I couldn't stay under their roof."

"So where did you stay?"

"Close by, in case Becky needed me. Sometimes in the hills with the Apache."

"Then Mrs. Bass died."

"Yes."

"And Will married Becky."

"Yes."

That single word was full of agitation. Amanda wished she could see his face. She listened to the quiet pant of his breathing and realized it was more revealing than any expression he might betray. She knew she was prying, pushing perhaps too far, but she had to know.

"And you didn't like the idea of them marrying." When he didn't answer, she asked, "Why?"

"She wanted to marry him. She said she loved him. She said he was good to her. She wanted a home of her own, a father for her child—her children. Why would I mind? It was what she wanted."

"Why do you?"

His breathing was rushed and irregular, as if he was fighting with that answer even now. "He was good to her.

259

He gave her a home. He took care of her . . . when I couldn't. He gave her three beautiful children."

Three: Sidney, Sarah, and Jeffrey. She remembered Will's harsh words at the table. *Your father's bad blood.* "Harmon, who was Jack's father?"

He bolted up from the floor beside her and stalked out into the dark center of the room. "Don't ask that. It doesn't matter now." She could hear the air seethe through his teeth. After a moment, he said thickly, "I love that boy. It's not his fault."

"No," Amanda agreed softly. "Of course, it's not." In spite of all the confusion, she felt she was very close to understanding what was at the heart of Harmon Bass. For a fleeting second, she wondered if she should just let it go, if she really wanted to know what darkness moved his soul. What if she wasn't strong enough to hear it? Something terrible had happened to the boy he had been, scarring him emotionally the way it marred him physically. But what was it? She knew it was all tangled up in his violence toward Will Bass and in his terror of this room. It had to do with Rebecca and Jack and the man he'd been torturing in the desert. She knew suddenly that was a part of it, too.

"He hurt her. I trusted him and he hurt her."

The words were so faint, she almost missed them. "Who, Harmon?"

"I told her not to. I begged her not to. She wouldn't listen to me. She told me it would be all right. She said he wouldn't. Why did she lie to me?"

"Rebecca?"

"He hurt her. She wouldn't let me stop him."

"Harmon? Who hurt her? Will hurt Rebecca? He beats your sister?" She couldn't believe that. She'd seen too much love between Will and Rebecca to believe it.

260

With his explanation came a whole slew of new confusions.

"He hurt her. Like I hurt you."

Amanda searched but couldn't see so much as a shadow of him in the darkness. Just the raw sound of his breathing as evidence of his pain. Then that tortured pattern broke with his moaning lament.

"Becky, oh, Becky, I'm sorry. I should have been there. I should have done something. I should have been able to stop it. I'm sorry, so sorry. No one will ever, ever hurt you again. I promise. I promise you." Then the frantic desperation was back. "I've got to get out of here. I can't breathe. Don't shut me in. Don't leave me alone. Oh, God! I can't get out. Don't leave me!"

"Harmon?" She heard him stumbling about in a blind panic. Amanda groped in the blackness until her fingertips brushed his knee. She stood, touching his hands, his forearms, his shoulders, and finally taking his damp face between her palms. "Harmon!"

He gasped and went rigid as death. She heard him take another convulsive breath before he whispered in stark horror, *"Mama?"*

"No, Harmon. It's Amanda. Amanda."

"Ammy?" He repeated it as if he couldn't believe it. Then his knees gave way and he went down on all fours, dragging her with him. Her arms went around him, holding tight, pulling his head against her. He clutched at her frantically.

"Don't let go."

"I won't, Harm."

"Don't leave me."

"I won't," she soothed, hugging him closer still.

"I'm sorry, Ammy. I'm sorry. I didn't want to hurt you. I won't ever do it again. Don't be afraid of me."

"I'm not afraid. I love you, Harmon."

She didn't know if he actually heard her. She didn't know if he had any grasp on reality at all as he huddled in her lap, his knees tucked up tight and his breathing ravaged by an awful internal dread. She held him, rocking slowly, wondering wildly what in God's name had happened to young Harmon and Rebecca Bass.

Chapter Sixteen

Harm slept fitfully in the curl of her embrace. Her own rest was intermittent, broken by his sudden startling cries when he'd wake to find himself in darkness. The sound of her voice reduced them to low panicked whimpers in the back of his throat and a ramble of Apache words laced heavily with Spanish and English. She wasn't sure she wanted to know what he was saying in those desperate rantings that were half entreaty, half threat. Then he would speak her name and become quiet, eventually drifting back to a restless sleep.

In the darkness while he slumbered in her arms, Amanda sat lost to dreamy threads of exhausted thought. Methodically, she stroked his black hair, then slowly that touch became a light caress along the line of his jaw. His face was warm and surprisingly smooth. The Indian blood in him, she supposed. She should have been worrying over what the morning would bring or over all the mystifying things he'd said, but she was much too tired to think. Feeling was easier, and he felt so good. She let her palm explore the hard swell and curve of his shoulder and upper arm, squeezing gently to revel in the strength packed so tightly within her little Texan.

"I love you, Harmon," she said again, liking how it

sounded and the way it felt to say it. Because it was true. If their future extended beyond the morning, she could easily see herself spending it with him. Not because he was the heroic legend, but perhaps because he was not. No man of legendary perfection would need her, and she liked the fact that Harm did. Maybe not much, but enough to make her feel wonderfully useful.

She did sleep then, deep and dreamlessly, until the heat of daylight made her stir on the hard floor. What woke her was the emptiness of her arms.

Harm was standing by the door, staring at that barricade as if sheer force of mind could tear it open. He'd put his shirt back on but hadn't tucked it in his pants, so its loose tails swaddled his lean hips. When he rubbed his palms along his thighs, she caught a glimpse of badly bruised and swollen knuckles.

"Good morning."

He didn't turn nor did he respond. Was he uncomfortable because she'd witnessed his weakness? She hadn't expected him to thank her but this cold indifference would not do at all. How dare he snub her after keeping her awake half the night feeding frantically off her consoling words?

"Are you feeling better?"

"Yes."

She waited but that was all he'd offer. Scowling, Amanda got to her feet, and after stretching the kinks from her back and shoulders, she walked over to him. He gave a slight start when she lifted his battered hand for examination.

"Anything broken?"

"No."

He pulled it away and scrubbed his palms together. He hadn't looked at her yet. His profile was stony and severe, as if he were angry. Why would he be angry with her?

Except for the obvious reason that her foolishness had landed them in this awful spot, but she thought he'd gotten over that last night. What then?

He took an unsteady breath and asked hesitantly, "Last night, did I do anything to . . . disgrace myself?" His gaze canted quickly to her, then away. It was then she realized he probably didn't know what had gone on during those hours of panicked darkness.

"No," she told him with a feigned innocence, as if she had no idea what he was talking about. "Not that I recall." He shot her another look, one that was shrewd and sharp. Frowning, he looked away again.

She was lying. Harm knew it. He had very clear recollections of her struggling to keep him from punching his way through the wall and of wailing like a madman in the circle of her embrace. Why would she lie?

To protect him. That was the only answer. To help him salvage some of his tattered pride. He looked at her then, studying her the way he had while she was yet sleeping, with intensity, with longing, with a wry smile. He had a memory of other things, too. And of one in particular, one he held close and fragile to his heart, as if it was really true and not some figment invented within a fevered mind. *I love you, Harmon.* Of course, he didn't believe she'd said that, but he didn't want to ask, either.

"If you think nothing was out of the ordinary, you must have been more out of your head than me."

She rewarded him with a faint smile that plowed through him like an emotional steam train.

Quietly, he said, "I hope I didn't frighten you."

"I wasn't afraid," she lied again, but so sweetly he couldn't fault her for it. She glanced at the door. "But I am a little worried about what happens now." She gazed up at him through those big dark eyes. "They aren't going to let us go, are they, Harmon?"

265

He didn't answer, which, of course, was her answer.

She chewed her lips for a moment, then told him, "I'm sorry I got you into this. I know you're going to think me terribly silly, but as much as I hate to think about dying, if it has to be, I'm glad it's here with you."

His head jerked away. A ragged sound was cut off by the sudden thickening in his throat. For a moment, he couldn't even see and he had to blink hard to focus.

"I told you it was silly," Amanda muttered miserably. She gave a little gasp as his palm fit under her chin, lifting it so his mouth could slide over hers briefly before he gathered her close against his chest for an engulfing Apache embrace. She melted into him with a sigh of his name.

He pushed his face into the golden spill of her hair, closing his eyes, opening his guarded heart wide. "I don't think you're silly," he murmured gruffly. "I think the world of you, Amanda. I would die for you without complaint."

Before she could tell him she didn't want to collect upon that grand gesture, the lock grated and the door swung in toward them. Harm pushed her from him and immediately was squared and stoic.

"Out," was all the guard said as he waved his rifle toward the sunlight pooling in the yard.

Placing himself between her and the surly cowboy, Harm led the way out of the barn. He was breathing in deep draws of warm air until he was nearly light-headed. Behind him, he felt Amanda close on his heels. Then he forgot about reveling in his relief and began thinking hard and fast about how he was going to get her away from the McAllister ranch alive.

It didn't look promising when Tyrell Cates greeted him with a shattering blow to the jaw. Harm slammed back

266

against Amanda, stunned, then cursing himself for being caught unaware.

"You weren't playing straight with me, Mr. Bass," Cates said in a tone of mild annoyance. "The barber tells me you spent a goodly amount of time with the late Mr. Dexter before he was taken rather suddenly to Glory by the little lady here."

Harm shook off the effects of the punch and regarded the sheriff unblinkingly.

"What did he tell you?"

Harm just stared at him.

This time, he was ready. When Cates swung, he was lithely dodging back. Air whistled by his nose. Only Amanda's presence kept him from lunging for the sheriff's throat. He might get the pleasure of breaking the man's neck before they killed him, but that would leave her at their mercy, and that he wouldn't do. He straightened and glared, for a second letting all his hatred glitter before he veiled his eyes with the droop of his lids.

"Tie his hands," Cates snapped, and his men were grabbing at him, lashing his wrists together with cruel jerks and tugs. He didn't fight them. There was no point in it. A length of rope was tossed up and run through a large pulley suspended from the peak of the barn. Generally, it was used to lift heavy loads into the storage loft. This morning, its wheel sang as the rope slid through, then pulled taut from the hanging weight of the little Texan.

The tear at his arm sockets was fierce but Harm was able to carry some of his weight on his toes. They'd hung him too high for a flat-footed stance. His body was vulnerable and he waited, breathing slowly through his nose as he'd been taught, for them to do their worst.

Cates studied him for a long moment, as if measuring the tolerance of taut flesh and muscle. He'd seen a lot during his years on the Texas plains. He'd seen death and dying in all its varying forms, and he could usually guess at how much a man could take. With this tough little half-breed, he wasn't sure. It was going to be interesting.

"What did Dexter tell you?" he repeated. He didn't expect an answer, nor did he get one—yet. He nodded toward his men and they let loose with a flurry of punishing blows. For the next few minutes, it was oddly quiet except for the grunts of effort from his men and the solid sounds of fists upon tightly compacted body parts. He watched as Bass accepted the beating without flinching, letting himself swing on the rope to absorb the vicious shocks. The slitted stare locked his in challenge, never faltering. Cates looked away, suddenly angry with the man's fortitude.

Bass's woman . . . and Cates was not such a fool as to believe they were nothing to each other, stood silent as well. She was pale and trembling. An occasional tear traversed the anguished set of her features as she watched the brutal pummeling, but she didn't cry out, not in horror, not for pity. A woman as strong as she was soft. An intriguing compliment. As intriguing as her womanly contours. He let his gaze linger there, thoughtfully.

Spinning on the tether of his bonds, Harm used the pain to keep himself focused. He could see the way Cates looked at Amanda, with a ravening interest. Fury and sickness roiled inside him. He wanted to scream from his own helplessness, when pain couldn't force so much as a whimper past his rigid control. It wouldn't take long for a man like Cates to find that weakness in him. Then, he would shift from the abuse of his hard, well-conditioned body to the torture of her tender form, and that he could not endure. Not for a second. Never could he allow his

268

brave and beautiful Amanda to suffer a monster like Cates. He had to distract him away from her.

Grabbing the rope that held him, Harm supported himself by the strength in his arms and kicked out savagely at his attackers. He managed a few well-placed contacts before a shattering blow to the kidneys made his world go momentarily black and whirling. It was Cates himself who stopped the dizzy spin by catching him with hands on his waist, halting him so that they were eye to eye. Shaken by nausea and giddy from the brunt of vicious blows, Harm confronted his worse nightmare. In that merciless ice-blue stare he could see all the horrors reflected back. Memories of torment and ceaseless pain flooded up so strong that his teeth clattered and he couldn't stop them. Vividly, as viscerally clear as the pain, he remembered the fear, the incredible terror of being helpless, of being a victim, of being a witness to things so horrid they dazed his mind even now, so many years later.

With grim purpose, he invited those memories back, as awful as they were, finding power in the rage and a cold fearlessness in what had been a child's dread. He stilled his shaking. He calmed his raw emotions. And very slowly he smiled at Tyrell Cates.

Cates's gaze narrowed. "Who are you?"

"Send them away, cut me down, and I'll show you."

The sheriff gave a mirthless chuckle. "I don't think so, Mr. Bass. Here's the problem. The late Mr. Dexter had some information we wanted. He's not in any shape to tell us. I want to know what he told you. I'm asking now. I can make you tell me."

Harm's smile didn't falter. "No, you can't."

The hard slap made him blink. The return blow split his lip. Gingerly, he licked the blood away and continued to glare at Cates with an arrogant defiance, goading him to strike again. But Cates began smiling, too. He calmly lit one of his favored cigarillos and blew the smoke from it in Harm's face. The scent filling his nose was bitter and familiar. Cates puffed on it for a long moment, studying Harm's impassive features, then he withdrew it from the cruel twist of his lips and blew on the glowing tip. Harm was clenching all the muscles in his belly even before the man's fingers clenched in his hair, jerking his head back and his neck taut.

"Talk to me, Bass."

He was ready, but even so, the pain was so sudden and severe, he almost twisted away from it. Almost. Then all that was Apache steadied him. He remembered the challenges of his youth when, to test courage and endurance, they would place dry sage upon the bare skin of their own forearms and ignite it, letting it burn without flinching until scars were left behind as proof of personal strength. He had many such scars because he'd had much to prove. To his Apache peers and to himself. The stench of scorching flesh thickened as Cates pressed the cigarillo beneath his jaw, but he didn't move. He kept the pattern of his breathing slow and even, kept his mind focused on his hatred of this man until he could block the agony writhing through him like internal fire. He could stand it. His hatred was stronger than any physical torture.

"Stop it!"

The sound of Amanda's frantic cry nearly broke his concentration. Pain was throbbing in every bone and muscle. He continued to glare rebelliously at Cates until his features swam and welcoming darkness came. His eyes rolled back white, closing, and his body slumped at the end of his tether. And Tyrell Cates withdrew the cigarillo, crushing it beneath his heel in an effort to deny his feelings of awe and anger. He released his grip on Harm's hair.

The dark head bobbed forward and rolled slackly from side to side. From all around him came the uneasy mutterings of his men. They were a hard lot to impress, but impressed they were.

"You're one tough little customer, Mr. Bass," he said softly to himself, mystified that a man could endure pain past the brink of unconsciousness without a betraying sound. He'd only seen that kind of stubborn bravery once before, long ago, and the comparison bothered him. But of course, that was impossible. "Get some water," he barked irritably.

Awareness returned with a sudden shock. Harm coughed and shook his head. Then he looked up, immediately alert. Cates was watching him. It was a cold, cunning gaze and Harm was wary. He knew the man was fiendishly clever when it came to inflicting cruelty.

"I could probably fry your flesh right down to bone and you wouldn't so much as open your mouth, would you?" he mused.

Harm stared back, unblinkingly.

Cates drew his knife from the sheath on his belt. He studied the blade, then met Harm's gaze. Both were equally lethal. "You know, Mr. Bass, I heard tell that when you were tracking for the Rangers, they caught themselves a wounded prisoner and to get information from him, you nearly skinned that man alive. Is that true?" He waited but got no answer. "It doesn't matter. You're part Apache. You know all about them kind of things, don't you? You have a pretty fair idea of what I can do to you. Don't that scare you?"

"I'm not afraid of you."

"No? You should be."

"I'm not afraid of dying. I know you're going to kill me. What can you threaten me with?"

Cates ran the tip of his blade beneath Harm's jaw. It

was so sharp, Harm felt the warmth of his blood before he felt the pain. "But I can keep you alive for a long, long time."

"Only as long as I let you," he taunted softly.

Cates laughed. "I wish I had the time, Mr. Bass. We'd see, wouldn't we? But, unfortunately, my employer is rather eager to regain some lost property and I need to know where it is. I'm assuming that you're not such a fool as to pretend you know something when you don't. If Dexter hadn't told you anything, you would have said so by now. Wouldn't you?"

Harm smiled thinly and said nothing. Then agony exploded through his face, through his head, as the sheriff's fist sent him spinning wildly in circles, his toes cutting the dust in smaller circles. Faces of the hard group of men gathered about to watch like hungry wolves ran together into one ugly sneer. It took some time for him to focus, then everything was indecently sharp: Tyrell Cates standing in front of him holding an ashen-faced Amanda at his side. No! God! He let awareness slip away from him, grateful for the numbing peace of it, but too soon another dash of water brought him sputtering back to life. He concentrated on breathing, dragging air in through his nose and expelling it with a hiss through his teeth. His bloodied features were carved from native stone. Only his pale gaze showed any animation. And it was fixed upon Amanda.

"Maybe the little lady here knows something worth telling," Cates crooned.

"She doesn't know anything," Harm growled.

"But you do?"

"Harmon, don't tell him anything," Amanda cried out suddenly. She was clearly terrified, but angry, too. And an angry Amanda was dangerous to friend as well as foe.

272

While he was awed by her courage, Harm feared what else she might say. He gave her a hard look of warning but she missed it, too absorbed in the sympathetic study of his ravaged face. Her eyes teared up. Her soft mouth trembled, then firmed with a fierce belligerence. She was going to get them both killed.

"What's it going to take for you to tell me, Bass?" Cates prodded. Amanda gave a sharp gasp as his hand snaked around to the curve of her breast and squeezed roughly. She swallowed hard and tried to pull away. When she couldn't, she stood stiffly and endured his crude caress without a sound. Then her big dark eyes flashed to Harm.

"Don't tell him anything, Harmon," she said with a soft thread of steel.

Don't tell him anything. Yusn! Did she have any idea what Cates meant to do to her if he kept silent? She didn't understand. She couldn't, and yet ask such a thing of him. She was staring at him through wide eyes. He could drown in the fear he saw pooling there. Yes, she knew. She knew and she was willing him to allow her to make the sacrifice. He closed his eyes, wanting to wail in pain. *Oh, God, Amanda, I love you. You can't do this.* His fingers clenched about the rope that held him helpless. He fought the urge to pull against it, to lunge at Cates, to howl in rage and beg for some nonexistent mercy. But he didn't. Because he knew it would do no good. The only thing he could do for Amanda was to escape the trap of senseless fury Cates was trying to provoke him into. *Trust me, Amanda. Trust me.* Then he opened his eyes and stared impassively at Tyrell Cates. He ignored the others; they didn't matter.

Cates frowned. Bass unnerved him and he didn't like it. So he turned instead to the fiery little temptress Bass claimed as his wife but who was more likely his mistress.

273

She glared at him, too, but it was a kittenish bravado. She lacked the strength and experience to do more than hiss and scratch.

"So, Mrs. Bass, while your 'husband' is thinking things over, why don't you show me the rest of what you were teasing me with at the breakfast table yesterday?"

He caught the front of her shirtwaist as his men shouted encouragement and gave a hard yank. Fabric tore. Amanda screeched in fright and was immediately all spitting, clawing fury. Her nails sank into his upper arm hard enough to draw blood and her taloned fingers just missed scooping out his eyes. He hit her. It wasn't a chastising slap but rather a closed-fingered blow that landed against her cheekbone with a stunning force. She crumpled without a sound.

Breathe. Breathe. Breathe. Don't react. Don't fight. Harm chanted those things to quiet the killing rage tearing through him. He saw Amanda move and that was enough to get his mind working again. He would kill Tyrell Cates for what he'd done and for what he was doing now. But first, he had to get Amanda to safety.

Amanda's head was swimming. For a moment, she feared she was going to throw up. Cates dragged her to her feet and she swayed upon watery legs. His hand wedged beneath her chin, his fingers crushing her fragile windpipe until hot spots and blackness whirled. She vowed not to, but still she heard herself whimpering for Harm.

Satisfied, Cates eased up and looked to the stoic half-breed. "Well, Bass, found your tongue yet? Or do we have to take her right in front of you, one at a time?" Then he smiled. "Or all together."

"Take her." He said it with a flat indifference. He heard Amanda's small cry and continued harshly. "I've

274

already had her and it wasn't worth going back for seconds." He met Amanda's wounded stare with a glare of cutting truth. "What did you expect? How do they put it in your stupid books? 'For duty and honor not for hope of reward'? Well, you can't live on that. It's just for the money, Amanda. I told you. That's all I care about. The money."

Cates laughed uneasily as Amanda sagged in shock. He studied the other man. "Bass, you can't be that big a sonuvabitch."

"Harmon?"

Harm ignored her, addressing himself to Cates with a coldhearted clarity that gave even the hard cases surrounding them a shiver. "I need the money for my family. I don't care where it comes from and she's not in a position to pay. I let you punch me around for a reason, to let you know that you can't make me tell you where Dexter hid those jewels. But I can be cooperative if you make it worth my while."

Cates gave Amanda a shove away from him as if she were no longer important as a bargaining tool, but he continued to hold on to her wrist. "What would make it worth your while?"

"Living, mainly. That and the thousand dollars she promised for my pay. I think I've more than earned it."

Cates gave him a twisted smile. "You're a piece of work, Mr. Bass. I'll give you that."

"And let her go."

"Why? If she don't mean nothing to you."

Here's where he had to be very careful. Cates was studying him intensely. If he scented weakness, it would be all over. "She doesn't. But she's a woman and I don't hurt women."

"A conscience? From someone who'd skin a man alive?"

"I figure any man out here has done something to deserve it. She hasn't. It's not her fault she's too trusting for her own good."

Cates chuckled. "You're probably right."

"Let her go then, and I'll take you to the jewels. First, she rides out . . . alone. What can she do? She's just a stupid eastern girl. She'll probably wander in circles out there until she's buzzard food. She can't do anything to hurt you. But I can. Let her go."

"You ain't in much of a spot to be giving orders or making threats, boy." But Cates felt it just the same, a hard, forceful, right-for-the-throat challenge, all the more dangerous because it was so seemingly impossible. A feeling of the familiar crept over him again but he shook it off as a distraction. "Tell you what. I'll go up and ask the judge. Don't go away."

The instant his grip on Amanda lessened, she flew at Harm with a howl of rage. Her slap set him swinging before her arms were caught by one of the guards and she was hauled back.

"I hope they kill you, you coward! You traitor!"

Cates was laughing. "Hell, if the judge says no, I just might give the little lady my knife and let her have at you. I heard tell that a society female scorned is more vicious than any Apache on the warpath." He continued to laugh all the way into the house.

Harm hung loosely by his wrists. He felt the heat of the sun and the ache of his many bruises. The worst, though it hadn't been anywhere near the hardest, was the side of his face where her hand had left its mark. That was the pain he felt clear through to his soul. With that pain came the bittersweet knowledge that hating him would save her. He'd had to say the words that would hurt enough to

276

drive her away from him. Because staying with him would mean death. No matter what decision Tyrell Cates brought back from the main house, he was going to die and he knew it.

Judge Russell McAllister listened to his hired gun's speech without once looking up from his newspaper. When he finally spoke, it was with an annoyed effort.

"Get the jewelry, then kill him."

"Yes, sir, Judge. What about the woman?"

"Let her ride out. When Bass is dead, track her down and kill her, too. No loose ends. She can't get very far on her own." When this was met with silence, he lowered the paper and stared at his duly appointed sheriff through cold blue eyes. "Have you got a problem with that, Cates? I've never known you to be reluctant when it comes to dealing with women."

"I ain't got no problem with that, Judge. You know me better than that."

"Then what?"

He hesitated. It was Bass who bothered him, but he didn't say so. His boss would think he'd gone loony if he said Harmon Bass made him think of a boy who'd been dead and buried for fourteen years. He shook himself mentally but the nagging remained. "I'll see to it for you."

"That's what I pay you for." Then the paper snapped up in curt dismissal.

They brought her Fandango, all saddled and ready. Slapping away the offer of aid, Amanda climbed up and with one last piercing look at Harm slashed back with her heels.

Watching her ride away without betraying any emotion was the hardest thing Harm had ever done. She'd probably hate him forever and would curse his memory. Fine. At least she'd be alive to do it. *Ride hard and fast and far, shijii, and don't look back.* The best thing he could do to prove how much he loved her was to keep Cates and his gang of cutthroats busy riding in circles long enough for her to escape. He knew they'd go after her once they killed him, but hopefully, if she was smart, they wouldn't be able to catch her.

Amanda, be smart. For once, be smart.

"Cut him down," Cates commanded. "Get the horses."

Harm spilled down onto all fours, then onto his face when his overstrained arms refused to hold him. He hurt all over. All he wanted to do was lie there in the warm sun until the misery subsided. But Cates wasn't about to let him.

"Get up, Bass."

His eyes opened. He could see a pair of fancy stitched boots and heavy silver roweled spurs. And the rage began to build inside him. Now that Amanda was no longer his priority, he had things to attend. Slowly, his gaze climbed, just as his hatred climbed. He started breathing through his teeth. And he saw through a heart filled with blackness. He knew he'd find a way to send Tyrell Cates to hell before they killed him.

It would be worth it.

"C'mon. You're taking us on a treasure hunt. And I don't need to tell you what's in store if it begins to look like a wild-goose chase instead."

Harm smiled flatly. No, he didn't need to tell him anything. He sat up, then lifted his bound hands. It wasn't a gesture of supplication.

"I don't think so, Mr. Bass. I feel a lot more comfortable with you trussed up."

Harm continued to smile. Bound hands wouldn't stop him or even slow him. He stood, making his movement purposefully awkward and wobbly, as if his strength were uncertain. He hugged one arm against his ribs as if they'd been broken. And his eyes missed nothing. The .45 Cates carried on an empty chamber, the big bladed knife tinged with his blood riding on his hip, the Winchester stuck in the scabbard of his fancy tooled saddle. *I'll get you with one of them, you* cabrón, *or with my bare hands, but I'll get you.*

He led them without hesitation toward the foothills where he'd found Randy Duncan. He didn't know how much Dexter had told them, so he would have to stay close enough to keep them fooled. The longer, the better. With every mile he led them, it was a mile closer to freedom for Amanda. He rode sloppy in the saddle, as if the pain from his beating had come close to breaking him. His eyes were watchful, charting the terrain, keeping track of the five who rode with them. If he could get one of the guns, he might have a chance of escape. But then, he might not get Cates and he wanted him more than he wanted to get away. Amanda was lost to him now. He had nothing except his pledge for vengeance to sustain him. Will Bass would be glad to be rid of him. Becky would cry but she'd get over it. And she'd be glad, too, because he knew what he reminded her of every time he came to her door. He had no reason to look beyond the base of Tyrell Cates's neck. One quick, hard pull and it would be done. It would be a relief to escape his hellish existence. Maybe he'd find peace at last.

Cates was riding beside him. He could feel the ice-blue eyes upon him in hard scrutiny.

"Bass," the sheriff mused. "You any relation to the Ranger? No, huh?"

"I'm not any relation to anybody," he bit out tersely.

"Harmon . . . Harmon . . . Seems I'd remember a name like that, it being kinda uncommon and all. Harmon. Harmon Bass. Where the hell do I know you from?"

"When we get to the end of this, I'll tell you."

Cates frowned. The little feller spooked him and he didn't spook easy. What was that kid's name, the one they'd kilt all them years ago? He tried to bring it back but he just couldn't grasp on to it. Wasn't it something like Harmon? He could remember the mother screaming it over and over. He couldn't be sure. He wanted to be sure. Before he killed him, he'd find out. He didn't like loose ends, either.

They were going through a narrow canyon, Harm in the lead. It was hot. The sun baked down, glancing off the sheer rock faces and hard-packed ground with an almost-blinding intensity.

"It someplace close by, Bass?" one of the men grumbled as he mopped his brow.

"Closer than you think," Harm answered evenly.

His thoughts were moving with deadly precision. Where the canyon widened, he'd make his play. He'd let Cates catch up to him and lunge to knock him from his horse. Before the others could gather up their questionable wits, he'd cut the villainous sheriff a new smile. And after that, it didn't much matter to him.

Harm was mentally and physically tensing, getting ready to spring. His heart was beating with a savage excitement, and his mind was clear and calm. He eased his right foot out of its stirrup. He'd go up and over the saddle, bowling Cates to the ground. He could smell blood. He could imagine the taste of his foe's terror. And it was good.

And then, just as he was beginning to breathe deep and slow, Harm caught a glimpse of flashing metal from up in the flanking hills that could only mean one thing.

Damn that girl! Couldn't she ever do anything right?

Chapter Seventeen

Trust me.

I would die for you without complaint.

"Harmon Bass, you will do no such thing!"

Amanda wiped her eyes upon her sleeve. She'd been weeping like a ninny ever since she'd ridden out of McAllister's compound, but now was the time for cool, clear thought.

She never believed it. Not for an instant. Well, there was just that fraction of a second when she thought her entire world had caved in through the hole in her heart. Then he'd looked at her with that fiercely indifferent stare and she'd seen right through the bluff of it. He'd promised to see her safe. A man like Harmon Bass kept his promises. So she pretended to go along with him, pretended to be shattered by his deliberate cruelty. She felt bad about slapping his poor, sore face, but she supposed he had it coming for the one he'd given her at the hotel in Perdition. Playacting, he'd said. Well, she could playact, too. But it was time to stop playing and see to some acting. Harm had seen to her freedom; now it was time for her to rescue him.

That was her plan. But how to go about it?

She hauled in Fandango's reins. She'd been heading

away from the ranch, but now she turned and retraced her steps. She'd need a gun if she was to effect a rescue. She had surprise on her side and Harm would be expecting her move to save him . . . she hoped. She had no great experience in daring do, so she relied upon expert advice. As she urged Fandango in his spine-jarring trot toward the ranch, Amanda went over the plots to every novel she'd read, counting on Erastus Beadle, Norman Munro, and Frank Tousey, among others, to come to her aid.

Then she saw the high surround of the ranchero and a single guard walking the length of its front wall. The idea came in a flash, from *Bordertown Bountyman*. Wouldn't Harmon be pleased! Perhaps not. She wrenched a stout branch from one of the scrubby Texas trees and kicked Fandango into a mad gallop. Swooping down low along the wall, she was upon the guard before he had a chance to turn. The branch, wielded like a club, whacked him in the side of the head. He dropped immediately. Then Amanda was faced with the problem of stopping her eager mount. She dragged back on the reins until he was lying back upon his haunches. Finally, he tunneled his hooves and she went flying gracelessly over his head. Fortunately, Fandango stood quiet and she was quicker to recover than the sentry. She wobbled over to where he was sprawled and reached for his rifle. When he groaned, she murmured a faint, "Oh, I'm so sorry," and bashed him a good one. He didn't make any more noise.

Rifle triumphantly in hand, she limped back to her horse. "We won't mention that dismount to Harmon, will we, Fandango?" she muttered as she crawled back up into the saddle and settled her aggrieved backside slowly. Now she'd have a big bruise to go with the scattershot of scars. After a moment of wondering where they might have headed, she started for the mountains. It was hard to miss them. Harm would lead them away from where she was supposed to be going. He would be taking them into the hills where they thought Randy had buried the jewels. Not for a moment did she think Harm actually knew the whereabouts of the stones and had kept it from her. His honesty was the one thing she could believe in.

After all, he'd once wanted to be a Texas Ranger.

And she wanted to marry him.

Why couldn't she ever do as she was told?

Harm watched the glints of light from an ineptly handled rifle. No professional gunman would be so careless and it was only a matter of time before someone else noticed. He had to do something fast before she gave herself away. He didn't mind dying in this canyon; he just didn't want to do it for nothing. Thoughts of self-sacrifice were gone. He had to escape and get Amanda to safety. Cates would have to wait.

He jerked up on his reins. Cates pulled up beside him with a questioning look.

"This is as far as we go," Harm announced.

"Well? Where is it?"

"Damned if I know. I haven't seen a goose to chase all morning."

"You sonuvabitch!"

Cates's boot heel caught him in the ribs, skewing him in the saddle. With his hands tied, he couldn't halt his fall. Harmon had the air knocked out of him on impact with the hard ground. He heard gruff laughter from the sweaty men who cursed him for dragging them on the long, useless ride, and as he lay gasping, he heard the angry hiss of Tyrell's spurs. The cold-eyed sheriff bent, winding his fingers in Harm's shirtfront to hoist him to his feet.

"You think this is some big joke?"

Harm smiled at him. He kept smiling even as the black bore of a Colt .45 pressed between his eyes.

"I'm going to blow your friggin' head off!"

"Go ahead," Harm challenged softly. "Only this time make sure I'm dead before you bury me."

Tyrell Cates blinked and took a step back. His jaw went slack with understanding. The pistol sagged as he put his other hand up to the scar on his face. He remembered a dark-skinned boy with eyes of blue fire leaping at him from out of nowhere and the sudden pain scissoring up his face. "Goddamnit, it is you!"

Harm grabbed the knife from Cates's belt and, with an awful cry, slashed upward, hoping for his enemy's throat. Instead, as Cates feinted to the side, the blade tip tore up his unscarred cheek, opening a new and terrible gash. Seeing the tide turn from the favor of their boss, the cowboys shook off their amused lethargy and went for their guns. Cates howled and struggled to level his pistol. Just then, a shot exploded between their feet. The riders forgot about the dangerous little Texan in their midst and scanned the high cliffs for a greater threat. Tyrell clasped his bloody cheek, screaming with fury.

"Bass! Damnit! Get Bass!"

And in two strides and a leap, Harm was on his horse and he was gone.

He had no trouble finding her tucked in amongst the rocks. He jerked up his mount and took a moment to reverse Cates's knife in his hands, to saw through the ropes at his wrists. By then, Amanda was standing beside him, her hand on his knee, her anxious face uplifted. He started to yell even as he swung down.

"Of all the stupid, harebrained things to do! Why

didn't you ride out when I told you to? You should be in Terlingua by now instead of—"

The minute he touched down, her arms whipped around his neck. And she was kissing him. Hard. Taken off guard, he twisted back far enough to stare at her. The moment her mouth was free, she was talking.

"I'm sorry it took me so long but I had to get a gun, and then I couldn't find you, and oh, Harmon, I thought he was going to kill you!"

His anger melted. All the scolding words were forgotten. He touched her tear-streaked face with gentle fingertips. "Shh, *shijii*, you did just fine. That was quite a shot."

Her features crumpled up. "That's not where I was aiming," she confessed miserably. "I almost shot you myself."

He smiled, a sudden burst of white against his bloodied, dirty face. It hurt terribly but felt good at the same time. Just as being alive felt good when he was with this woman. She had saved his life. Her timely appearance had saved him from a vengeful suicide, but no way was he going to tell her that. He'd never hear the end of it. "Oh, Ammy, what am I going to do with you?"

Her dark eyes pooled with unmistakable yearning and that unspoken answer undid him. His palms captured the loveliness of her face between them as his mouth came down over hers. The kiss hurt him worse than the smile but it was worth it. She said his name softly as her arms hugged about him and her supple body pressed close. A hunger like he'd never experienced took control of him. His mouth slanted, opening wide so his tongue could plunge in to possess her. His hands tightened with the intensity of his desire, until she whimpered quietly. It wasn't a sound of protest. When he broke away for a shaky draw of breath, she was kissing his face, touching lightly over the many bruises with an impatient tenderness. The fact that danger was closing fast upon them only rushed the flow of need.

"Harmon. Oh, Harmon."

Then she returned to his mouth and he was lost. The tidal force of her passion took him right down to his knees with Amanda wrapped around him. There was no trace of the dreamy, hero-worshiping girl in that scorching tribute. Her kiss was pure woman to man and every bit as ravenous as his had been. For a long moment, he responded as wildly and fully as she could want, then he pulled back. He stroked her face, her hair, her shoulders. There was so much emotion crowding him, it hurt. His voice was hoarse.

"I never thought I'd see you again."

Amanda looked surprised. "You didn't think I'd come back for you?"

He shook his head slightly and the feelings just kept getting stronger. "You should have thought to save yourself. That's what I wanted you to do."

"But Harmon, I love you," she told him with a heart-shattering candor. "I couldn't just leave you."

He sucked in an uneven breath that seemed to lodge halfway down and swell into an achy obstruction. He stumbled to his feet, dragging her up with him. His hands crushed the softness of her upper arms. He started to look around them, started forcing his mind to work again. And all the while, his heart was hammering frantically.

"Well, we'd best be making tracks instead of making love, because they can't be that far behind me."

Amanda stood silently, watching his expression. Had she made a terrible mistake in blurting out the truth? She could feel him withdrawing, could sense his panic, and she didn't know how to reach out to him. There wasn't time to explore the reason for his tension or the trembling of his hands. For once, she just obeyed him, striding to Fandango and climbing into the saddle.

They rode hard all day. Harm stayed ahead of her and he never once looked back. She began to wonder if he was running from their enemies or from her impulsive declaration. It was the exhaustion of the horses that finally forced him to slow and at last to stop. She was surprised to recognize Blue Creek and pleased, too, because it meant she was getting familiar with his homeland. Pretty soon she would be reading the various buttes and wallows with the ease of New York street signs.

Harm rolled down off his horse and began to busy himself with his mount's care. Determined not to be ignored by him, Amanda shinnied off Fandango and went to press the reins upon him. He looked up at her through wary eyes. She wanted to give him a clutching hug but instead said brusquely, "Here, you see to the horses while I gather up some firewood. I hope you can rustle up something for supper. At this point, I don't care if it does crawl on its belly. While you're getting our dinner, I'm going to take a bath and then I'm going to see to you."

She paused and he just stood there, staring at her with an amazed blankness of expression, as if he'd never imagined she would take charge of their camp. As if he was stunned by notions of what seeing to him would entail.

"Well?" she snapped at him. "I'm hungry."

"Yes, ma'am." The corners of his mouth quirked slightly and he turned his attention to the horses.

Later, as he made a small fire from the wood she'd found, Amanda borrowed his knife to dig and chop yucca roots while he watched with the same curious expression. Then she carried her pseudo-soap and shampoo down to the edge of the creek and, without a trace of modesty, shucked her dusty clothes right down to the skin and waded in. Harm sat paralyzed by the fire. His senses were dazed by that brief glimpse of her fair skin. His breathing began to jerk with an uncommon urgency. Abruptly, he stood. Time to go hunting. He stalked off into the gathering darkness, not even bothering to walk quietly.

He was roasting his catch on a spit when she came up from the creek. He let his gaze lift cautiously and was relieved to see she'd dressed. She crouched down on the opposite side of the fire, not beside him, and he was grateful for that, too.

"What's on this evening's menu?"

"Sorry, I couldn't find you any snake. Rabbit all right?"

"Rabbit's fine."

She took the meat he passed her and blew on it before tearing into the tasty feast. He ate more slowly, distracted by the way the firelight played along the loose ripples of her freshly washed hair. Like sunshine on water, he thought, then shook his head. He could hear her teasing voice. *You're a romantic, Mr. Bass.* He was a fool.

They dined in silence, both of them hearing her words too clearly to speak around them. Both of them tortured by memories of that night in the hotel. Tension was razor-sharp. When their meal was reduced to bones, Amanda told him to go wash up while she took care of the dishes. He smiled at that. She smiled back. Then he all but ran for the safety of the water.

The cold current felt good on his battered and over-heated body. Amanda had ground enough yucca for him to use and he lathered up vigorously, glad to feel clean again. Then he simply soaked, letting relaxation steal away his caution. And thoughts of Amanda slipped in unguarded.

Harmon, I love you. For a moment, he allowed himself to cherish those words. A strange warmth spread through him, a satisfaction of heart and soul that was totally foreign to him. He let the sense of contentment ride over him, the way it had in their shared camp. It felt good having her there, taking charge, as she should. As she would if she were his woman. He was Apache enough to still believe in that division of labor. Though he'd been taking care of himself for most of his life, there was something so pleasing about having a woman want to do it for him. As a fierce warrior, an Apache man kept himself for masculine pursuits: hunting, care of his weapons, and of course, the use of them in warfare. A woman did the rest, as was expected. She kept his home, bore his children, gave him comfort. Made him king, a hero like the western men in Amanda's books. Arrogantly, he thought it a very nice arrangement. Then he smiled to himself. Amanda would probably demand to accompany him on the warpath. She would make a lousy Apache squaw. She didn't have that quiet control of the spirit the Indians possessed. But she would make a fine Texas wife.

A sudden night sound startled him from his musings. It was an owl. He felt his skin tighten and break out in a rash of dread. Apache believed the ghosts of the dead entered the owl, that its hoot was the voice of that ghost speaking in their tongue, uttering threats against the living. Exposure to that night bird brought on the dreaded ghost sickness that could often prove fatal unless treated at once by the local shaman. He'd thought himself too white to believe such superstitious things, but he was shivering and uneasy in his soul. Was it a warning for him to cast off all thoughts of Amanda? Or a whisper of dangers to come? He suddenly wanted the security of the fire and the calming presence of the woman waiting there.

But she wasn't at the fire. When he emerged from the creek, sleek and naked, to reach for his clothes, she was there, kneeling at the water's edge. He froze. She stared fixedly, and not at his face. Her breathing rattled. As surprised as he was, as suddenly bashful as he felt, his body stirred beneath the heated intensity of her stare. She wouldn't look away and he was abruptly angry.

"What are you doing down here?" he growled, grabbing for his pants.

"I was going to wash out our things." How breathless she sounded. She swallowed hard and murmured, "Oh, my goodness."

He gave a low Apache curse and turned away from her to step into his jeans, jerking them up until she could no longer admire the hard curve of his flanks. He was wildly upset and unsure of what to do about it. Then he turned back and she rose up to flatten herself against him. Her lips devoured his. Her hands were eager in their movement over his bare chest. As much as he wanted it, as much as he wanted her, he grabbed her shoulders and pushed her away. His breathing labored.

"No!"

"Harmon . . ."

"Stop it, Amanda. Don't do this. You're asking for more than I can give. Please. Stop."

She let her hands drop away. She let him stride back to the fire and huddle there with his scarred back turned to her, with his scarred heart closed to her. Yet she refused to be discouraged as she bent back down and scrubbed his shirt and her outerwear clean.

He heard her moving about in the black night. There was no longer a hesitation in her step. She walked easily, as comfortable in the desert darkness as she'd once been timid. He heard her spread their clothes to dry, listened to her picking up sticks for their fire, heard her rustling about in the underbrush for a long while before she came into the circle of light. First, she fed the fire, then she turned and fed the flame of longing in his heart.

Her hair was down, fanning in glorious golden waves

about her shoulders. She was wearing only the thin undergarments. She'd managed to pull the bodice of her chemise together and tie it where Tyrell Cates's rough hands had torn it open. It was an awkward closing, leaving a patch of bare white belly below and a curve of browned bosom above. He felt every muscle in his body pull taut as she came to him and knelt, her knees to his knees.

"Here. Let me take care of your cuts." It wasn't until he watched her crush the thick sap from a fleshy mescal leaf that he realized she'd come to heal him, not to seduce him. Still, he was dreadfully uncomfortable.

"No. I'm fine."

"You're not fine."

He flinched back from her extended hand, eyes going dark and apprehensive. "No."

She gave an aggravated sigh and snapped, "Don't be stupid. Sit still."

He sat still.

Very gently, she rubbed the cool ointment on a split at his cheekbone. The muscles of his face twitched. His eyes closed.

"Am I hurting you?" she asked softly.

"No." A whisper.

Carefully, she applied more of the soothing agave to the sundry swellings, lingering over the spot where she'd struck him. She hadn't left her mark the way Cates and his men had, but he winced slightly and she knew he still felt the sting of her slap.

"I'm sorry."

He turned his head ever so slightly and she felt his lips graze her palm. She continued her attentions, the terrible ache of remorse lifting. Cupping his chin, she tilted his head to tend the thin gash the sheriff's blade had scored beneath his jaw. He tensed. She let her thumb rub lightly across his mouth. He relaxed all but his breathing. That had grown faint and fast. Hesitantly, she dabbed the salve to the raw burn. He didn't move but her eyes filled up with anguish. How could he have stood it? She wanted to weep just thinking about his stoic bravery. She moved on quickly, cautiously pressing the bruises along his ribs, relieved when he didn't show any reaction. Would he? Even if they were splintered like dry kindling, would he betray it? His tolerance awed her and frightened her at the same time, because it was so indicative of the hard life he'd led. She shifted her attention to his hands, treating his scraped and torn knuckles, massaging the abrasions around his wrists.

His eyes were open. He was watching her. The caution was gone. A curiosity remained.

Slowly, so he could resist if he wanted to, she brought one of his hands up and nudged her face into his palm. He was very still. With her hand covering the back of his, she guided it over the smooth contour of her cheek, then gradually released him. His fingers continued to rove the soft curves, tucking strands of her hair behind her ears, stroking back through the thick, golden mane of her hair.

Then a frown came to his expression. He clutched a handful of her hair to hold her head immobile, then reached up his other hand to gently touch her other cheek. A sudden pain surprised her. She gasped and tried to pull back.

"Easy, *shijii*."

As she watched anger darken his features, she remembered the feel of Tyrell Cates's fist crashing into her face. She'd truly forgotten it until this moment, but from the way fierceness turned the blue of his eyes as hot as inner flame, she knew he hadn't. And he wouldn't. For just an instant, she was glad. She wanted the satisfaction of knowing the man would be punished for hurting her, for hurting him. If Harm wanted to string him by the heels, she would gladly tend the fire. That bit of savagery should have appalled her. Such violence was not in her nature. But a sense of justice was. And Tyrell Cates was a man who needed to be brought to justice. He was the law of Perdition, but he was not above the law of this harsh and vengeful land.

Amanda didn't want to think about Cates or vengeance, not now. And she didn't want Harm distracted by it, either.

"What does it mean?"

"What?"

"The name you called me."

He glanced down and awkward color came to his swarthy face. "I don't know how to translate it into English." He was lying. She thought Apaches didn't lie.

"Is it an endearment?" she asked with a provoking smile.

"Yes," he growled, glaring up at her with a formidable surliness.

"Oh," was all she said. Then she stood and went into the shadows.

He could hear her washing her hands in the stream. He was shaking with tension. Angrily, he stalked to their saddles and untied their bedrolls, spreading hers on one side of the fire and his on the other. Then he lay down on his, unhappy with the arrangement and at himself for wishing it could be different, still tense, still angry as she came back from the creek. She paused to study the position of their bedding. He gritted his teeth, waiting for her to comment. *Coward,* he called himself.

Without a word, Amanda walked over to her blankets. Without hesitation, she picked them up, carried them around the fire, and laid them out right next to his, so close, in fact, that they overlapped. Then she sank down with a weary sigh and put her back to him.

"Good night, Harmon."

He stared at her for a good long minute, breath suspended, tension at a breaking point. She was making him crazy! But of course, that was what she intended. Sullenly, he settled in his blankets, scowling, cursing her under his breath in Apache, in Mexican, but not in English. He tossed onto his back and stared up at the stars. But all he could see was the longing in her dark eyes. He closed his, only to be taunted by the memory of her pale figure gliding into the water.

Harmon, I love you.

A rumble of objection growled deep inside him; not because he didn't want her to, but because he couldn't let her.

"Did you say something?"

Before he could deny it, she rolled onto her back, then up onto her elbow to look down at him.

"No. Just trying to get comfortable."

Another lie, she thought. *Shame on you, Mr. Bass.*

"I can't sleep. Are you tired?"

"Yes," he grumbled, closing his eyes. That lasted all of ten seconds. He could feel her stare on his face. It was like trying to ignore an itch. He glowered up at her and she smiled.

"I thought we might talk. If you can't sleep, either."

He sighed irritably. "About what?"

"Tell me about your mother."

He blinked, so startled he couldn't even respond.

"Was she pretty? I bet she was."

"Yes. Very pretty. Like Becky." Slowly, his breath released, and with it his tension.

"She must have been very brave and strong to raise two children by herself."

The admiration in Amanda's tone touched something deep in him. A well of tender memories he'd forgotten he possessed. He reached for them carefully, handling them the way he would something fragile and precious, something he feared he could break and never replace. "Yes," he said quietly. "She was. We had a ranch. Not much of one, but it belonged to Becky's father and she was so proud of it. She wasn't ashamed to work hard. She was half Apache."

"Why didn't she go to them? Wouldn't that have been easier for her? For all of you?"

He was silent for a time, then he told her, "Most of them died of illness and starvation at Fort Sumner in New Mexico. There was nothing easy about living as an Apache."

"Yet you chose to, at least sometimes."

"I lived in a house of women. I had to learn how to protect them."

She touched her fingertips to his bare middle, to call him back from the sudden melancholy that settled in his expression. The sensation burned all the way to his backbone. "She must have loved you very much to have given you such freedom."

"Yes." His answer was simple and certain.

"And now you have Rebecca and her family to care for. Haven't you ever wanted a family of your own?" Her palm had begun a slow rotation over the flat plain of his abdomen. He didn't object so she didn't stop.

"Children. I'd like children." Then he gave a sudden start, as if surprised that he'd spoken that out loud.

"The Apache may not know how to kiss, but surely they know how to make children. Or do the Apache men spend too much of their time making war to remember how to make babies?"

He scowled at her and said testily, "The sense of family

is everything to the Apache. One spends most of his life in the company of his relatives. Once a man has proved himself in raids or during battle, he's expected to take a wife and join her clan. Failure to marry is a rare and a pitied state amongst the Apache. Childlessness is a great misfortune and reason for divorce." Then he paused. "Are you making fun of me?"

"No," she soothed, and was quick to ask, "How do an Apache man and woman get together to avoid this dreadful state of independence?"

"Such things are usually arranged by the parents. A man does not spend his time in the company of women."

Amanda smiled at the haughty way he said that. She wondered if the fierce Apache warriors were all reduced to shy boys in the company of the opposite sex. She didn't want to bruise his dignity by asking. Instead, she crooned softly, "And what does an Apache man look for in a mate?"

"If a man has special feelings for a woman, he's not usually attracted by the beauty of her face. He looks at her industry, her strength, her childbearing qualities, her sweetness of temper and congeniality."

"What about love? Is there no love among your people?"

"There is respect and affection that grows with the years, and a sense of equality." He stared up at the timeless stars, pretending he was speaking of things as far removed as those glimmering heavens. Pretending he wasn't painfully aware of the touch of her fingertips on his bared skin. And of the hot cravings growling through him. He spoke as if he never considered these personal things as they might apply to him. To him and her, together.

"The union of a man and woman brings their spirits together as one in life and after death. Each sustains and completes the other with their knowledge, their abilities, and their powers. They do not ever seek to humiliate, weaken, or dominate the other. A man surrenders all he owns except his horse and weapons to go live amongst the family of his wife. He is a virtual slave to her parents and he would fight to the death for them without thought, without fear."

"What does the Apache man call his wife?"

"The term for mate is companion or 'the one with whom I go about.' "

"The one with whom I go about," she repeated in a whisper. "That's beautiful."

Her hand skimmed up to form a vee beneath his chin, holding him lightly as her lips touched his, once; briefly, twice; slowly, a third time; deeply. Then she moved away before he could protest, settling upon her bedroll on her back. He pursued without thought, without wisdom, rising up on his elbow, then bending over her, unwilling to relinquish the sweetness of her kiss. He continued to caress her, with soft, searching sweeps of his mouth, with the restless inquiry of his hands, one lost in the silken luxury of her hair, the other stroking from shoulder to wrist again and again. Passion built quietly, powerfully, until it was impossible to pull away. Still, he tried.

Looking down at her was like gazing upon his every sweet dream. She didn't try to coax him back to her, not with words or with touch, but her liquid eyes were all eloquent invitation. His will shuddered and began to collapse, along with all the vows he'd made. Torment writhed inside him, the wanting, the shame, all twisting into a terrible knot of guilt.

"Ammy, don't let me hurt you. I don't want to hurt you."

She reached up to rub the taut angles of his face. "Does

this hurt?" Her hand eased around the back of his neck, drawing him down to her soft kiss. "Does this hurt?" He looked at her through eyes so wounded and wary, she wanted to wail, *Harmon, why can't you trust me? Why can't you trust yourself?* But, because she had to earn that fragile trust, she asked gently, "What is it you want, Harm? Whatever you want." She waited, knowing if he backed away, she'd have to let him go.

He drew an uneven breath. His tortured gaze detailed her lovely features and swept down the tempting un-knowns of her body, always a threat before but maybe . . . maybe not now.

"I want . . . I want to touch you. I want to feel the softness of your skin."

She took his hand and he let her guide it to the outer curve of her breast. It stayed there unmoving, warmth radiating through the thin fabric of her chemise. He looked uncertain and a sudden thought struck her.

"You've never done this before."

Her tone of amazement made his eyes narrow, as if she'd challenged his masculinity. But she didn't laugh at him. She took up his hand again and moved it beneath the cotton barrier, so it rested on bare flesh.

"I think it will feel better under here."

She wasn't prepared for his frown or his dark growl. "Did you learn this from the same man who taught you how to kiss?" He started to pull his hand back and she caught his wrist, restraining him.

"I didn't learn it from personal experience, if that's what you mean, Mr. Bass. You can learn a thing or two from reading the right kind of books."

He didn't look convinced. So she smiled at him.

"Besides," she added, "I've never wanted to do this with anyone but you. I'm afraid we're both going to be fumbling a bit blindly. But I suppose that half the fun is in fumbling."

When he didn't respond, she pursed her lips cajolingly. "Shall we find out, Mr. Bass?"

Chapter Eighteen

Harm bent down. Amanda's lips parted expectantly but his fell, not there upon that ready dampness, but instead in a light brush on her forehead. Then a graze down the bridge of her nose. A caress to either cheek. A peck upon her chin. By the time he pressed his mouth to hers, she was nearly moaning with impatience.

He kissed her long and lavishly, until she was half mad with wanting . . . more. She gasped as the thrust of his tongue timed to the first feel of his hand upon her bared breast. His palm was rough, his fingers gentle. The contrast was wonderful. He shaped the fullness of her with his hand, waking its peak from its placid state to a hard nub of yearning with the slow revolutions of his thumb. When he stopped, she wanted to cry out in protest. He lifted up slightly, his stare penetrating hers right to the soul.

"I want to see you."

With fingers shaking in their haste, Amanda untied the makeshift fastening and drew the fabric away. As he took his fill with that intense gaze, a restlessness came over her body. She wanted to rub against him, to arch up for his touch, to ask him to please, please satisfy the inner craving she didn't understand. She'd thought this slow tenderness was what she wanted from him, but now she longed for some of the heat, some of the hurry, even some of the hard-edged desire he'd displayed in the hot hotel room in Perdition. She shifted in agitation, needing his touch, needing something she didn't know how to ask for and could only pray he knew how to give. Her skin was burning, alive with sensation.

When he caressed her breasts, she gasped and shut her eyes tight. When she felt the dampness of his mouth upon one aroused crest, she thought she'd perish from the sharp pleasure of it. Amanda moaned his name. And he stopped.

She met his hesitant gaze with a shaky little laugh. "I'm liking this very much, Harmon. Please continue."

Her eagerness, her honesty, emboldened him to sample what he'd coveted for so very long. He stroked her and she trembled. He tasted her and she pushed up against him. She made a soft, whimpery female sound that had nothing to do with distress when he dragged his tongue across that excited puckering. Her fingers drove into his hair and clenched tight as he tugged with his lips and grazed with his teeth, laving her soft skin generously until she was saying his name with each moaning breath.

She smelled good. She tasted good. So soft, so warm. He'd never felt so compelled by anything in his life as by this desperate need to know her fully, to touch her, to please her. The womanly little noises she made shook him to the very edge of control, and it was an effort to balance there between that heaven and hell of giving and wanting.

She was shivering when he lifted up. Her eyes stayed closed as he rose to kiss her. Her lips parted sweetly. Her breath raced lightly against his. He said things to her, quiet things of the heart, spoken in the Apache tongue because he didn't know how to phrase them any other way. A quiet poetry filled with longing, steeped in love. She didn't understand the words but responded to the tenderness of tone by kissing and stroking his face, by holding his head to her shoulder when he nestled it there within that welcoming curve.

He watched his hand move down in an outline of her shape. His skin was dark and brown against her fairness. He loved the pale pearlescence of her, the way she felt like fragile, expensive cloth. He adored her with his touch, creating a quivering beneath it. His hand eased down along the contour of her thigh and her legs dropped open of their own accord, coaxing him to that heated apex, to that place of mystery and darkness. When he touched her there, her body shuddered. He started to withdraw but her hips lifted, pressing against him so he thought perhaps it was all right. He moved his palm against her, surprised by the feeling of heat, of moisture, even through the barrier of cotton.

She made an impatient sound and released him for a moment as she reached down to shinny out of her drawers. Then there was nothing between them. Her breathing had altered into funny little hitches that increased in tempo the minute he brushed over the golden tangle of curls, then stopped altogether at his first careful overture. He delved into the soft folds of her femininity, exploring gently, and the breath exploded from her lungs in a rush of unbearable delight to become a quick panting. Her agitation beckoned him, the rhythmic rock of her movements instructed him in the ways that best pleased her. The more he learned of her, the more unfamiliar his own body became to him; so hard, so full, all taut and desperate throbbing. He didn't dare brush against her, afraid that fierce tension would overrule his stringent control.

But Amanda had no such worry. Her control was gone. Her movements were ungovernable, led by impulses and instincts that evolved quite naturally on their own. His touch freed them and encouraged them to expand beyond her wildest imaginings. This was what Rose had hinted at with her smug smiles and veiled speeches about rampant raptures of the body. She felt sensation build and heat pool, and Amanda knew she was close, so close to discovering all. Then he pushed his fingers inside her. She cried out. She couldn't help it. The shock of it, the delicious thrill of it. And he jerked back, going completely still.

"No . . . Harmon, please don't stop. Not now!"

Her whole being vibrated with anticipation. She couldn't seem to catch her breath. And then she felt his hand trail down her belly, his touch cautious then, at the sound of her whispery cry of expectation, sure and swift. As swift as her sudden eruption of response. She gasped in surprise as hard shocks of exquisite feeling rolled through her from that one pulsing center, surging upward, outward, until every extremity was flushed and tingled with an elusive vibrance. She clutched at Harm, hanging on to him, shuddering against him until the wild tremors eased to a fitful trembling. Then it was a relief to just sag down upon her blankets, relishing the glorious aftershocks that shivered through her system.

Finally, the daze of pleasure lifted. Amanda opened her eyes to see Harm staring down at her, his expression impenetrable. She smiled faintly and raised an unsteady hand to his cheek.

"Oh, goodness," she whispered with a marveling euphoria. "Oh, Harmon, I had no idea."

Neither had he. He let her lead him down to her. He kissed her sated mouth, her warm cheeks, the flutter of her eyelids. *He'd* had no idea. And suddenly he felt very powerful, very pleased, and very humbled.

Her hand slipped down from his warm face, down the hard curve of his ribs, reaching for the band of his Levi's. He intercepted, curling her fingers into his palm, holding them there, then bringing them up to the press of his lips. She could feel the tremors of tension shivering through him, and now that she realized what it was he'd experienced in their first rough mating, she couldn't deny him the chance for satisfaction.

"Harm, you can—"

"Shhh. No." He kissed her knuckles and rubbed them to his taut cheek. "This night is yours, *shijii*. My gift. Don't insult me by refusing it. Sleep well and safely."

Though he felt ready to rip out the seams of his denims, he forced his own needs to subside beneath the strength of his vow and he held her, cherishing the frailty of her, the softness of her, the mystery.

"I love you, Harmon. Oh, how I love you."

His embrace tightened until his arms shook. Already, she was relaxing against him, shifting, snuggling, nuzzling close with a sigh of trusting contentment. Emotions massed inside him, convulsing into an agonizing ache.

"Ammy, what am I going to do with you?"

He closed his eyes, trying to shut out the answer he didn't want to acknowledge.

He was going to send her home.

Amanda woke with a wonderful feeling of restfulness. She stretched in her blankets and was startled by the sensation of rough wool on bare skin. Lots of bare skin. Then she remembered how she arrived at such a state and she smiled her satisfaction. Mmmm . . . Harmon. Her hand pushed out of her covers and touched . . . cold ground. His bedroll was gone.

"Harm?"

With blankets clutched about her, Amanda sat up. She saw him immediately and relaxed. He was with the horses, putting the final tug to Fandango's double girth.

He didn't look around when he called, "Get dressed. We've got to get moving."

No fond good morning. No lover's greeting. No kiss. No tender glance. This morning, like last morning, he was . . . Harmon. Amanda shouldn't have expected anything different. With a sigh, she threw back her blanket and reached for her underclothes. She had her drawers up to her bent knees when she felt his stare. Glancing up, she was momentarily stunned by the hunger in his gaze. Then he expelled a rough breath and turned back to the horses. She finished dressing and rolled her blankets tight. By the time she'd washed her face in the clear creek water and swished her mouth clean, he was leading the animals up to her. He spoke crisply, unemotionally.

"We'll head for my sister's. We can get supplies there and head for Fort Davis."

She stared up at him. "Fort Davis?"

He swung up on his horse, mentioning casually as he did, "I'm putting you on the stage there."

"You're—" It hit her hard. He was sending her away. Angrily, she jumped to her feet. "You are not!"

"Don't argue, Amanda. I'm not going to change my mind."

"Your mind? What right do you have—"

"Every right! Because I don't want to see you in the middle of this. I don't want to bury you. And I don't want you to be there when they bury me. Get on your horse. Let's go."

He jerked his reins to the side, putting his mount's rear end to her to finish the discussion. Amanda huffed for a second in sheer disbelief. The gall of him!

"Harmon Bass, if you think I am going to let you dictate—"

He kicked his heels back and set his horse into a canter. It was mount up or be left behind. And she had no

306

intention of being left behind. Not ever. She urged Fandango to follow, steering him so that they came abreast. Recklessly, she reached out to snag Harm's reins, pulling him to a stop.

"I'm not going back to New York. Not until I'm finished here."

"You're finished here," he said bluntly. "Any more finished and you wouldn't be breathing. Do you think they're just going to forget the whole thing? Do you think they're just going to shrug off the loss of all that money and let you go? Or me? They're going to track us down until they find us, and then they're going to kill us."

"But you don't know anything."

"That's not going to matter."

"Harmon, I won't leave you."

His head snapped around. His stare pinned hers with a sudden harsh fury. "Listen to me, little girl. You're getting on that stage and then the train, and you're going to get the hell out of here. Then I'm going to burrow into those mountains so deep they'd need dynamite to find me."

"I'll go with you."

"I don't want you to! Don't you get it? I don't want you with me! I can't be bothered with you. I've got enough to do just keeping myself alive. I don't need you making it worse. You understand?"

His reins dropped from her hand as Amanda withdrew from a pain so deep it numbed her. Just as if he'd taken his knife and severed all the links to her emotions. She nodded stiffly. Oh, yes. That she understood quite clearly. She'd heard it every place she'd gone since her parents died.

Harm looked away from her stricken expression. He couldn't bear it. Didn't she understand that it was her own stubbornness that forced him to say such things? She had to go. For her own safety. Because he wasn't going into hiding. He was going hunting. He couldn't do what he had to when he was consumed with worry over her. He had to be free to move, to think, to act swiftly and without mercy. She was a fetter about his heart that would slow him down. He couldn't afford it. Not now. Maybe not ever.

"Let's go."

Amanda nudged Fandango into a smooth gallop and she didn't look at him. Not once until they reached Rebecca and Will Bass's ranch. He pulled up in the yard and was off his horse before it came to a complete stop. Then he was striding for the house, ignoring his sister's cry of "Harmon, your face! What happened?"

"We need supplies to get us to Fort Davis," he told her as he let the door bang shut behind him. Through the window they could see him jerking open the low trunk where he kept his meager belongings. He pulled out his spare carbine and began to load shells with grim purpose.

Rebecca looked up at the weary young woman and said gently, "Climb down, Amanda. Wash up for supper. You'll need some fresh clothes and a hot bath."

"No time for that," Harm snapped as he burst from the house. He was carrying his carbine. Two extra cartridge belts were looped bandolier fashion across his chest. He looked set and dangerous. "We'll need water."

Rebecca caught his arm. "She needs rest. So do your horses. Harmon, stop. Think. You're safe here. Stay the night and get an early start tomorrow."

He didn't respond right away. Indecision warred in his features. He cast a glance toward the way they'd come and a more stealthy look at Amanda. And Rebecca wondered what he was pushing to escape from—the danger that pursued or the threat of what he possessed.

"Climb down, Amanda," she restated firmly. Her grip

turned into a caress along her brother's arm. "There's grain for the horses in the barn. Dinner will be ready soon."

"I don't want anything to eat," he growled softly.

"I'm not interested in what you want. You need a hot meal. The children will want to see you. Take care of what you have to and come up to the house. If you don't, I'll come get you."

He scowled and grabbed up the reins to their horses. "What are you making?"

"Chicken and dumplings. And peach pudding."

Harm weakened but wasn't ready to give in. "No peas. I hate peas. I won't eat them."

She smiled. "No peas."

"All right." And he stalked down to the barn.

The hot bath, the change of clothes, the filling meal; none of them made Amanda feel any better. She sat quietly at the table, no longer a part of the group gathered there. She didn't feel anything but emptiness. She listened to the children's laughter, to Rebecca's fond scoldings, to Will's stern corrections, and Amanda mourned for the sense of family she would never have. She'd only been fooling herself with the difference between fact and fiction. She didn't belong.

Harm was equally withdrawn and watchful. She could sense his gaze upon her but she didn't look up. She didn't want to read of his restless desire to have her gone. All her life she'd been an unwanted burden to someone. Well, she didn't want to drag on his sense of responsibility. She could take care of herself. She'd have to.

"What's in Fort Davis?" Rebecca asked as she poured coffee.

Amanda answered her with a surprisingly even tone. "The Overland. I'm going back to New York."

"New York?" Rebecca looked between her bowed head and her brother's stoic features. She'd thought . . . she'd hoped . . .

"It's time I was leaving," Amanda continued. "My family must be out of its mind with worry by now. I'm sure they'll be happy to have me back."

Only Harm would recognize the tang of sarcasm, and he said nothing.

"Well, it certainly has been a pleasure having you here. Hasn't it, Harmon?"

Harm never flinched beneath his sister's penetrating stare. "Yes," he replied shortly.

"Thank you. That's very kind of you to say." Emotion threatened. It thickened in her throat and threatened behind her eyes. Since she could think of nothing else to add, Amanda pushed back from the table. "If you'll excuse me, I'm very tired. We've got a long ride ahead of us tomorrow."

"Of course. Jack, would you take Miss Duncan to her room."

"Sure, Mama."

The boy rose at the same time she did. Their eyes met across the tabletop, his such a pale, odd shade of blue. Like ice water. Like . . .

Amanda gasped in sudden shock. She was quick to recover, but not before Harm saw the way she was looking at his nephew. With a horror of recognition.

She knew but she didn't understand.

Tyrell Cates was Jack Bass's father.

The scent of approaching rain was heavy in the air, lacing it with a stickiness only a downpour could wash away.

Harm stood on the front porch, eyes watchful, posture

tense as the massing clouds. Rain would be good. It would quench a dry land and rinse clear the signs of their passing. He didn't think any of McAllister's men were good enough to track after a sweeping storm. That would take a special talent. It would take someone like the legendary Harmon Bass. He allowed a grim smile to shape his lips. And Harmon Bass wasn't available.

"Hey, Uncle Harmon."

"Hey, yourself."

The curve of his mouth softened as he looked to Jack. The boy came up to stand beside him, gazing up at him through unashamedly awestruck eyes. He put out his hand to lightly touch the back of his nephew's head.

"Can I ride with you when you take Miss Duncan to Fort Davis?"

"Not this time."

"But—"

"Not this time," he repeated.

Jack sighed and tried to hide his crestfallen expression by ducking his head. "I was hoping you could teach me some more things."

"You've got a lifetime to learn the things you need to know."

"But I want you to show me now."

"What's the hurry?"

"When you come back through again, I want to leave with you."

"Leave with me?" He hooked his thumb beneath the boy's chin to angle it up. "You want to spell that out a little plainer?"

Jack looked him straight on, his features determined. "I don't want to be a rancher. I don't belong here. You're my family, Uncle Harm. I want to be like you."

Harm drew a breath, then he laughed softly. Jack stiff-

311

ened up at the sound, afraid his ambitions weren't being taken seriously by this man he idolized.

"Son," Harm corrected quietly, "you don't want to be like me."

"Yes, I do."

"No. Hush now. You listen. You got everything here a man could want. You got family, you got belonging, you got ties to the soul. You can't just tear up those roots and blow off on a wind."

"But, Uncle Harm—"

"Listen! I know you look around and see nothing but hard work and long hours, and you feel like a dog staked out on a short rope, just wanting to break loose, to run free. But once you start running, son, you got no place to go. I'd give anything to have what you have—a future so clean and bright, it's like tomorrow's sunrise, a chance to grow to be a man like Will, a good man. Don't you ever sell that off cheap or I won't even want to know you."

He could see the boy didn't understand. But he would. Some day he would.

"But you said I did good. You said I could ride with you anytime. Didn't you mean that?"

Harm cupped the somber face in his palm. "Oh, yeah. I meant it. There's nothing I'd like better. But you're not mine to take. I can't do it, Jack. This is where you belong. If you want to look up to someone, don't look to me. I'm nothing. You look to Will. You look to him and you learn good, and you'll know everything there is to know about being a man. And then someday, when you're standing, looking out over your own place, and you got your own house full of a wife and kids, I'll come by now and again to sit at your table, and you'll look at me and then at them and you'll thank God you decided to stay put."

Jack frowned, his eyes filling up with a frustration of youth. Then he bolted from the porch and ran down toward the barn, as if he were running from an unpleasant truth. Harm watched him go, leaning into the porch post as an ache of isolation swelled up inside. Then he felt a gentle touch and the familiar shape of his sister leaning into him.

"It's hard for him," she stated softly. "I try, Will tries, but he still feels like he's on the outside. He's such a good boy, Harmon. He shouldn't have to feel that way."

"I know."

"Those were beautiful words, Harm. It must have cost you dear to say them."

"They needed saying."

"Maybe you should do more than say them. Maybe you should listen, too." When he said nothing, she looked up into the stark loneliness of his features. "It's not too late for you, Harmon. But it will be if you send her away."

Every tendon in his body went taut. "I don't—"

"Yes, you do. You know exactly what I'm talking about."

His features were molded by a staunch reserve. He wouldn't look at her. "A man does not discuss such things with his sister."

"Don't you hide behind that Apache arrogance with me, Harmon. You need to talk to someone. Talk to me or talk to her."

He flashed her a quick glance. "She would never understand."

"She loves you."

"She doesn't know me."

"I think she does."

"If she did, she would never have let me—" He stopped, remembering himself, drawing in a ragged breath and drowning in the sense of shame.

His sister's question slipped between his ribs and headed right for the heart.

313

"Are you in love with her?"

The pain was awful. His answer was flat. "It doesn't matter."

Rebecca readied an argument, but before she could speak, a slender figure wiggled between them.

"Good night, Mama. Good night, Uncle Harmon."

Sarah's arms reached up to him, and without a pause, Harm lifted her into a snug embrace. He kissed her baby-soft cheek and pressed his against her black curls, his eyes screwing up tight in a poignant agony. Pulling together a tight smile, he set her down and rumpled her hair with a gentle hand.

"G'night, *shijii.*"

His unguarded stare followed the child to the house, then lifted to meet the unwelcomed insight of his sister's.

"Are you going to tell me you don't want that for yourself? That you don't want it with Amanda?"

He jerked away from her and began to pace the porch, his movements fast and tight with agitation. "It doesn't matter what I want. It can't matter. You know why."

Rebecca caught at his sleeve, tugging him up short. "No, I don't. I don't think you do, either." He tried to pull away but her grip strengthened, just as her tone strengthened. "Harmon, don't send her away. You need someone just like I needed someone to help me get over the pain and the remembering. I have Will—"

A harsh growling sound worked its way up from the painful compression of his chest. He jerked free and stalked to the opposite edge of the porch. When he didn't return, Rebecca went to him, trying to gentle his emotions with the light rub of her palms along his rigid shoulders. She could feel him shaking all the way down to his boot soles.

"Harmon, haven't they taken enough from us already? Don't let them take this chance from you."

"Chance for what? Oh, God, Becky, I'm nothing she wants to mess with. I can't be what she needs. What am I supposed to do? Build her a nice cozy little house and not even be able to go inside to share it with her? You think she's going to understand why I want to sleep outside under the stars instead of in some nice comfortable bed? You think she's going to wait with a smile on her face while I do what I have to do?"

"Harm—"

"No! Becky, stop it! Stop it! I love her. I do love her, and I have to keep her safe. The only place I'm safe is out there alone. The only place she's going to be safe is far away from me. Don't you see? I can't be with her and not want her." He confessed that as if it were a tortured wickedness borne by a blackened soul. He drew a hoarse breath. "I can't protect her any better than I protected you. I can't protect her from them and I can't protect her from me."

"Harmon, don't—"

"I've got to get her away from me."

"Why? She doesn't need to be protected from you. You're not like them."

"I am," he argued fiercely.

"No—"

"Becky, I am! There's a darkness in me that won't go away. I can't control it. Something's not right in here"—he touched his temple—"or in here"—he put his hand over his heart. "I don't know what's wrong and I don't know how to make it stop." He took a hard, shuddering breath and was suddenly very, very still. His voice was glacial. "I don't want to stop it. Not yet."

Rebecca felt a chill grip her. "You've found another one of them, haven't you? Which one?"

Slowly, he turned his head, his gaze going down to the barn.

315

"Oh, Harmon."

He was holding her, holding her tight. Both of them were trembling.

"I'm going to take care of it, Becky."

Abruptly, she drew back. She seized his taut face between her hands so he couldn't avoid her penetrating gaze. "No. Harmon, no. No more. I was wrong, don't you see? I was wrong to think that killing them would take away the horror of what they did. I was wrong to feed your hate and encourage your need for retribution. Will was right. It's got to stop. Now. Can't you see what it's doing to you? To both of us? You can't change anything that's happened. We've got to let go. We've got to move on. I don't want to remember any more. I want to be happy with what I have."

"I can't forget!"

"You have to! You won't as long as you pursue this. Stop, Harmon. Stop before it kills you. I love you, Harm. My family loves you, but I can't stand by and watch you turn into something so hard and dangerous I can't trust my own children with you."

His features collapsed. "Becky! How could you think I'd hurt those kids!"

"I never wanted to think you'd try to kill my husband!"

"But he was—"

"No! No! He wasn't! He wasn't trying to hurt me. You're so confused by the poison they put inside you, you can't understand. And you never will. Until you stop. Please, Harmon. Let it go."

"I can't."

"Then don't come here again."

"W—what?"

"You heard me. I don't want you to come to my house with blood on your hands and hate in your heart. No more. I don't want to share this madness with you. I can't.

316

I love you too much to see you become . . . iike them."

The storm had closed on them. Lightning filled the sky directly overhead with dazzling flashes, striking in forked tongues along the nearby hills. The air became suddenly fragrant as the sound of raindrops pattered on the porch roof overhead.

Harm took a step back. He was panting with uncertainty and a tenuous disbelief. But Rebecca wouldn't relent from either stiffened stance or somber statement. She was searching his face, hoping for a sign. Then that smooth impassive Apache mask took control of his features and she knew she'd lost him.

"Oh, Harmon . . ."

He leaned forward, brushing one cheek with his palm, the other with his kiss. Tasting her tears.

"I love you, Becky. And I'm sorry."

Then he was walking away.

"Harm."

He kept walking.

"Harmon!"

He left the porch just as the heavens tore loose in a torrent and he was swallowed up behind that wall of bluish-green water. Leaving Rebecca Bass silently sobbing his name.

Chapter Nineteen

"Are you asleep?"

Amanda turned toward the soft voice. She could see Rebecca's figure silhouetted in the doorway. She sat up and moved back against the headboard. "No. Come in."

"I found this. I think it's yours."

Amanda reached out and felt the warm gold surface of Randy's pocket watch fill the cup of her hand. She clasped it tightly. "Yes. It was my brother's. Thank you." She rubbed her thumb over the contoured lid, feeling the fine etching, feeling the loss more keenly now than ever. Because this watch was all she had to take back to New York with her.

Rebecca started to turn back toward the door, then hesitated. "He loves you."

"Who?"

"Harmon."

Amanda was aware of a sudden quickening within her breast, a flutter of hope she couldn't contain. "Oh, Rebecca, I don't think so."

The older woman came and sat on the edge of the bed. Amanda couldn't make out her features in the dimness. "Amanda, if you want him, you're going to have to chase him down. He'll run because he's scared, not because he doesn't want to be caught."

She made a joke of it because she didn't dare let herself believe it could be true. "It's rather hard to catch a man who can run farther on foot than a horse during the course of a day."

"But if you're serious about it, you can find a way. You do want him, don't you?"

No hesitation. "Oh, yes. I want him."

"Good." She patted Amanda's knee and started to stand.

If you don't believe me, ask my sister.

Amanda remembered the words and she saw her chance—perhaps her only one before Harm packed her off on the stage—to find out why he was so determined to push her away. If indeed he really loved her. "Rebecca?"

"Yes?"

"What happened to Harmon?"

Those words hung, suspended by a tense silence. Then Rebecca made a quick movement toward the door.

"Please!"

She paused without turning.

"I do want him. I love your brother. But there's something so terribly wrong about him and I have to know what it is. I won't love him any less no matter what you tell me. I can't help him unless I know the truth. Please."

The quiet stretched taut.

"It's bad."

Amanda shivered in spite of herself. "Believe me, Rebecca, I understand 'bad.' "

"Not like this."

"Please. I know some of it already. I know Harm has killed men—horribly. I know he has scars on his back and probably ones that are much worse on the inside. I know he's afraid of closed in spaces and of—of being intimate. What I don't know is why. It has something to do with the sheriff in Perdition . . . Jack's father." She heard a rattly intake of breath and knew she was right. She had to press on. "Rebecca, what happened when your mother died? I know that's got to be it, whatever it is. Please tell me. Why is he so afraid that loving me is the same thing as hurting me?"

"Because he doesn't know there's a difference. All he knows is what he's seen. And what he's seen . . . oh, Amanda, what he's seen is enough to drive any man mad." Rebecca paused and drew a slow breath. "Are you sure you want to know?"

"Yes."

Harm's sister came back into the room, not to sit on the bed again but to stand at the window. Brilliant stabs of light from the storm outside illuminated her tragic features, glistening on the trails of dampness tracking her cheeks. She began to speak with a flatness of voice, as if trying to suppress the emotions associated with the words. She wasn't successful for very long.

"My father and mother owned a ranch up by Burgess Springs. He died when I was very small and she took to running the spread herself. She was young, too young not to want a man in her life, and then he came—the son of one of our neighbors. She fell in love with him and Harmon was borne between them. When her lover went away to a school in the East, it nearly broke her heart, but he said for her to wait, so she did. But when he returned, he would not marry her. He and his family had ambitions, and there was no place in their plans for a half-Apache bride. He would not marry her, but he could not stay away and she would not send him away when he came to visit.

"This went on for many years, until the rich neighbor

married. Then she turned him from the door and never spoke of him again. Because of her shame, my mother would not tell Harmon who his father was when he was old enough to ask. She was afraid he would try to see him, to claim a name he could not wear now that her lover was a powerful man. Because he was a boy, Harmon couldn't understand why his father would not claim him or show an interest in him. He was very hurt by this, and he turned more and more to my mother's Apache family." Rebecca gave a wry-sounding sigh. "He made a good Apache."

She paused for a moment, looking back across the years, seeing the tough, wiry little boy her brother had been. Amanda could picture him, too, all dark and sleek and wild, learning the things he would need to know to survive in an unfriendly land. To protect his family, he'd said. Such a great duty at such a young age.

"The Apache trained their boys to be sly and successful thieves. To them, raiding was a way of life. They didn't try to raise what they needed to live, they stole it—from the Mexicans, from the white settlers. But never from our ranch. Harmon once told me that the Apache refrained from killing all Mexicans because they wanted them to raise livestock for them to steal. Even when he was a boy, eight or nine, he would disappear for sometimes weeks and return with money and supplies. Mama knew he'd been raiding across the border but she never said anything to him. He was providing for us, as a man provides. They taught him to be hard, to be clever, and one very valuable lesson: that a man fights to protect what he loves but he submits when he has to. Bravery meant living to fight another day. They taught him well. He was as fierce as any warrior twice his age, but there was a gentle caring in him passed from my mother's white side that he could never overcome. Of course, he hated it, thinking such

321

sentiment a sign of weakness, but I think I loved him more because of it. Sometimes you can still see it in him . . . sometimes."

Her voice faded as those fonder memories faded. And Amanda tensed, knowing things were about to get "bad."

"Then he came back, my mother's lover. He came at night after we were in bed. We could hear him in the kitchen arguing with my mother. Harmon wanted to go down but I wouldn't let him, because by then they were no longer fighting. I was older. I knew what the silence meant; it meant she'd taken him back as a lover. He didn't stay long and Mama was very upset. He had talked to her about selling our land to him and she didn't want to. She was proud of our ranch and of what we'd done. She wanted it for Harmon so he would have a place to come back to. She wanted him to have a home.

"Then the man came back and brought others with him. Harmon was off in the hills, hunting. I wasn't supposed to be listening to their talk, but I did. He wanted the land. There was water on our property, and water out here is worth a fortune in gold. He told her he would take care of us, that he would see Harmon was schooled and accepted as his son. He lied. Mama wanted to believe him because I think she'd never stopped loving him, but he never loved her. She found that out the minute she signed the papers of sale. He laughed at her and he walked away from her tears. He got on his horse and he told the men who were with him to get rid of the three of us and all signs that we'd ever existed. He told them he didn't care how it was done. And then he rode away.

"By the time Harmon came home, they had made themselves comfortable in our house and had taken the first of their ugly pleasures from my mother and me. He's never forgiven himself for not being there sooner. Mama was screaming and the silver-eyed man, Cates, was coming out of the house when Harm jumped him with his knife. He cut his face and then he saw the other men. There were nine of them and he was ten years old. He stopped fighting. That was what saved him from being killed on the spot.

"They stayed for three, maybe four, days. They had whiskey. They made us butcher and cook up our livestock in a great feast. And they took my mother and me whenever they wanted, wherever they wanted, like animals down in the dirt."

"And Harmon saw all this?" Amanda asked in a soft, stricken voice.

"And he couldn't do anything to stop it. That was the hardest for him—seeing and not being able to do anything. They made him dig a big hole in the yard. We knew what it was. It was going to be our grave when the whiskey ran out and they finished with us. Harm asked the man with the cut face if he could build a coffin. The soil was hard and he couldn't dig down very far, and he was afraid coyotes would dig up our mama. He asked without tears or whimpering, with such dignity that they were all a little awed by him. He was told he could and he set to building it. I think his bravery shamed them, reminding them that they were the miserable coyotes preying on the weak. It got to bothering them that Harmon would do whatever he was told but he would never bend or beg. He'd fetch their drinks and pull off their boots and let them kick at him, trying to shelter us from as much abuse as he could by taking it himself. They were very drunk and very mean by then, and Mama and I were too worn to provide much sport. They began to bet on who could break Harmon's spirit. He was a boy, Amanda, a little boy, but he was more of a man than any of them." Her tone grew raw with the agony of remembrance. "They did . . . they did unspeakable things to him."

Unspeakable things.

Amanda's mind went crazy with imaginings.

"He never made a sound, not one. Mama couldn't stand it, watching them torture him. She begged them to stop and one of them hit her . . . killed her. Harmon lost all control. He got hold of a gun, shot two of them, but didn't kill them. Finally, they hit him, too. I thought they'd killed him. Then they tossed Mama into that box Harm had built and him in with her. And they buried them."

Buried them. But Harmon wasn't dead. The horror of it overwhelmed her: Harm waking to find himself in a shallow grave, shut in an airless darkness with the cold body of his mother. God above, no wonder he'd gone half crazy in the little tack room overnight.

Rebecca was silent, staring out into the night. Her features were still and strong. The dampness upon them betrayed her inner anguish.

"What happened then?" Amanda asked faintly.

"Two of them took a fancy to me. Thought they could make good money selling me south of the border. So I went with them when the others split up. And Harm followed. He dug himself out, and he made himself a bow and arrows, and he tracked us on foot for more than sixty miles. And he killed them. But not right away. I watched him. I encouraged him. Because I had wanted to do it myself and wasn't strong enough. Harmon was strong enough, so he made them pay for what they'd done."

Because she couldn't stand the terrible images that crowded in the second there was silence, Amanda asked, "When did Will find you?"

"A few days later. We were in pretty bad shape by then, on foot, with no water, sucking stones to stay alive. He took us home, he brought us here. Mrs. Bass was so kind and I was so tired. But Harmon . . . he wouldn't come into the house. He'd crouch out there in the dark and keep watch over me. He'd changed into something so wild and so frightened it was like trying to coax a starving wolf up to the door. They left him alone, put out clothes for him, food, water, and he finally got so he'd trust them. He'd follow Will around the yard like a half-tamed pup, and when Will rode out with the Rangers, it didn't take him long to find out how useful Harm could be. They got to be close after a fashion—not like father and son or friends, but respectful of one another."

"And then you found out you were pregnant."

Rebecca nodded. "I was so afraid to tell Harmon, but oddly enough, I think he loves Jack more than any of the children. Maybe because he didn't know his own father."

"Rebecca, who is Harm's father?"

"That is one thing I plan to take to the grave with me. I won't tell him. No good can come of him knowing his father arranged for our deaths. And it's better if neither of us are discovered to be alive."

Amanda understood and she agreed. There was no reason for Harm to know.

"And then Mrs. Bass died," Rebecca continued. Her voice held such sadness, even now, that Amanda knew how much affection must have grown between the two women who would love the same man. "I stayed on to cook and care for Will's house. Harmon didn't mind it at first. I had the baby and Will was kind. And then we realized we had fallen in love. He was lonely and he was so good to me."

"But Harmon didn't take it well."

"Oh, no. Harmon didn't take it well. He argued with me, he pleaded with me. He was so sure Will would hurt me the way the men at the ranch had hurt me and our mother . . . the way he thought all men hurt women. Nothing I could say would convince him that I had nothing to fear. We married, and on our first night together, Will was so gentle with me. I will love him for the rest of my life for that tenderness. But I must have made some outcry, because Harm burst in and went for Will's throat with his knife. He almost killed him, Amanda.

"Will talked about locking him away someplace, but Harmon wouldn't have been able to stand it. He said because of what had happened my brother would never be right again, but I wouldn't believe him. I was sure he'd understand about Will and me when he began to mature. He was just a little boy, younger than Jack is now. Will tried to talk to him. I tried to talk to him but he wouldn't listen. After that, he disappeared for a long time and I started to hear through Will that the men who'd stayed at our ranch were turning up dead. Not just dead, but mutilated in the way of the Apache. And I was glad. In my heart, I was glad."

Again, the taut silence fell. Amanda realized how much of the same darkness dwelt in Rebecca Bass as in her brother, Harm. And she could see how necessary it was— that hardness, that anger that allowed them to survive such horrible circumstances. Someone softer wouldn't have. Someone weaker couldn't have. She wondered if she, herself, could have endured and felt the answer to be no. She admired Rebecca at that moment as much as she loved Harmon.

"When Will was shot, Harmon came back. He kept a careful distance at first, but finally, because he loved me and Jack and the children I bore Will, I got him to come in to our table. And that's when he started showing up with money to pay for repairs, to buy supplies, to purchase shoes for the children and new dresses for me. Will was furious at first, but I told him that to refuse the gift of an Apache is the greatest insult a man can give. So finally, to make peace with me, he took what Harm brought and said nothing. He saved my life, Amanda. He's saved this family. And now I have to do something to save him."

Amanda was immediately all ears.

Rebecca came to her then, sitting down facing her, taking up her hands for a firm press. "Will saved my soul from the same hell my brother is in. Loving him and my children brought me back to life again. Harmon is lost and he can't find his way back alone. Amanda, if you love him, help him. Stop him from going after Cates and the three others that still live. He thinks that when he's killed them all, his life will be back in balance. I'm afraid that when he's killed them all, he'll have nothing to live for. He's a man worth saving. He hasn't gone over that edge . . . yet. But I'm so afraid for him. He could fall either way. I want my brother back and I think you can give him to me. I think he'll come back for you."

There was nothing stranger than a Texas rainstorm. It fell in isolated strips that could soak one side of a fence and leave the other arid and untouched. One could stand in warm sunshine and reach into a torrent raging at arm's length. A light half-hour rain could start a small stream running. A continuous downpour could build a roaring wall of water. But whenever it fell, however violently it ravaged the land, it was always welcomed. As Amanda welcomed its coolness when she stepped off the porch with a blanket tented over her head. Everywhere was the scent of dust being wet down as she sprinted across the damp grasses of the yard.

She found him right where Rebecca said she would, tucked in beneath a canopy of gnarled brush, out of the weather. A flash of distant lightning illuminated her figure and cast his uplifted features into stark relief. He didn't look happy to see her.

"What are you doing out here?"

"The rain feels good. And I was looking for you."

Amanda crouched down and wiggled beneath his shelter. She settled on her knees, facing him. She could hear him breathing light and fast.

"You didn't come out here to argue with me, did you? Because if you did, you're wasting your time."

"I didn't come to argue." She let the blanket slip down and fall purposefully open. Her hair was about her shoulders in a thick spill of gold. She was wearing one of Rebecca's thin nightdresses. She could feel his gaze scorch over her in a hard, angry, wanting sweep. "I just wanted to talk."

"I didn't think you'd have much to say to me."

Amanda made a soft sound of amusement. "I'm sure that's what you were hoping." Then she sighed. "Well, after tomorrow, you won't have to worry about listening to me ramble."

He was silent for a long while, then his voice came like a whisper. "I haven't minded it all that much."

"You're lying, Mr. Bass."

"All right, you drive me crazy. But I've sorta gotten used to it."

"My, that's a mighty compliment. Considering."

From out of the darkness, she felt the graze of his fingertips. She wanted nothing more than to seize his hand, to rub her cheek into its rough palm, to press kisses there, but she held herself still. When she didn't respond, he pulled away.

"You'll be safe in New York."

"I'm sure you're right about that, Mr. Bass. You're usually right about everything."

"I want you to be happy, Ammy."

"I want the same for you, Harm, but it doesn't look as though either of us will get our wish. Don't give it another thought. I'll do just fine. I've always gotten by on what I've been given, and if I've learned anything from being here with you and your sister and the Lowes, it's not to complain."

His touch moved up and down her chill arm in a restless caress. Frustrated by her lack of reaction to it again, Harm drew back.

"It won't be that bad for you."

She said nothing.

"I'm sure your family has missed you."

Again, silence, damning him with its unspoken refute.

"And your friends."

"I have more friends here then I ever earned there."

Harmon made a growly noise in the back of his throat and he jerked her up against him. His face pushed into the fragrant waves of her hair. His heart was pounding against the soft press of her bosom. His hands roamed the curve of her back and shoulders in an agitated discontent.

"Damnit, Ammy, what do you want from me?"

She didn't move. She leaned into him but she didn't touch him. It was hard to hold back but she did. "I want you to tell me you don't want me to leave."

"I don't want you to leave." Before she could expand her intake of delight to its fullest degree, he concluded, "But you have to go."

Amanda moved out of his arms. She had to struggle to do it. He didn't want to release her. But he did. "So you can hunt down those men and kill them." She stated it as a calm fact, not as an accusation. That confused him. He'd expected . . . something different.

"Amanda, you don't understand."

"Yes, I do, Harm. If I had understood then, I would have basted that man while you cooked him."

The ferociousness in her tone set him back. She could almost feel his wariness, his tension building there in the darkness.

"What did Becky tell you?"

"Everything."

She heard his breath drag in. "Everything?"

Unspeakable things.

What had they done to him?

"Enough to make me feel so angry and helpless I don't know whether I should hold you or paint for war beside you." Her voice shook and thickened with tears she refused to shed. She would not hamstring him with her pity. He didn't deserve that from her. She wasn't quite sure what he needed until he spoke very quietly.

"Hold me."

She brought his head down to her shoulder with an easy curl of her arms. She wanted to weep and wail over him but she was silent, just holding him with a simple, strong support.

"They killed my mother," he said suddenly.

"I know."

"I couldn't do anything to stop them." That came out low and punishing. She couldn't stand to let him torture himself any longer.

"Yes, you did. You stopped them by staying alive. You stopped them when you saved your sister. And you'll stop them by not becoming like them."

His breathing came in savage jerks. She could feel his resistant tension hardening along the length of him like the cooling of molten steel. "They have to pay for what they did."

"Yes, they do."

"Did Becky send you down here to ask me to let it go?"

"Yes. She loves you, Harmon. She's afraid for you."

"Well, I won't. I can't."

"I know."

"I'm going to kill them."

"I'm not going to stop you."

That threw him so hard, he could think of nothing to say.

"Harmon, you do what your honor demands. But you do it in the name of honor, for the sake of justice, not just for the ugly satisfaction of watching them die. That's what makes you different from them. Control it, don't let it control you. You're a good man, Harmon Bass."

His head shook in a brusque denial but she continued firmly.

"The best man I know, and I'm not alone in thinking that. If it wasn't true, so many people wouldn't believe it."

"No," he moaned so low and rough, it pained her to hear it. Because he believed it. "I'm not. You don't know."

"I know enough."

"You don't know anything. I'm crazy, Amanda. My head's all wrong inside. I'm a danger to everyone who loves me."

"Only to yourself, Harm. And if you're crazy, so am I . . . about you. I love you, Harmon."

He made a hoarse sound, a wild, panicky sound, and tried to pull away. She clutched him tighter.

"I love you, Harm."

"No. You can't. You don't know. They hurt me, Ammy. They—they—"

Oh, God! Don't tell me! Please, don't tell me, Harmon. She hugged him fiercely, absorbing the shocks of tightly repressed horror. They shook through him in tiny spasms.

"Shhh! Don't. It doesn't matter. You were strong enough to survive it then and you're strong enough to rise above it now." She buried her face in his sleek black hair and told him with a gentle conviction, "I can't change what happened to you, Harmon. If I could, dear God, if I could, I would."

Harm quieted. The trembling eased but the tension remained; a terrible, self-denying tension. When Amanda leaned back, he sat up so that they were facing one another. It was too dark to see each other's expression. She reached out to read his with the sensitive stroke of her fingertips. He was all hard angles and taut lines.

"Harmon, I can't change things but I can take some of the hurt away."

Her kiss was soft against his mouth, softer still along his torn jaw and warm throat, where she could feel his frantic swallowing. He sat unmoving, breathing in quick little snatches. She put her hands on his shirtsleeves, rubbing the coarse cotton where muscle corded tight. His head tilted back so she could touch her lips to the channel where his blood crowded through in hurried beats. He said her name and she could feel the flutter of its vibration beneath her kiss.

She plucked at his shirt. "Take this off."

"It's cold." That was said more for protection than out of protest.

"I'll keep you warm."

He shucked it off.

Her palms skimmed his bare chest. Skin jerked taut like a sheet on a clothesline snapped by a sudden breeze. Her hands moved in slow expanding circles, and as they did, his lungs constricted.

"Oh, Harmon, you feel so good," she murmured along the rigid set of his shoulder, and that hard range shook as if by a sudden earth tremor. She leaned against him and he allowed her to take him down onto his back. One slender leg rode across denim-clad thighs, shifting in a provocative rhythm. She was snug against his side, and the heat was ample to chase off the chill of the ground and the misty air. Her wet mouth traced delicate patterns upon his chest and he started panting.

"Harmon, I want to touch you. Will you let me?"

His hand closed over hers with a crushing strength, yanking it down and fitting it over the thick ridge within his Levi's.

"Oh, goodness," she exclaimed breathlessly. And then her hand began to move with a curious adoration.

It was torture of the worst kind. His arms flew up over his head, stretching out even as his toes reached down, pulling every fiber like the strain of an Inquisitor's rack. His knuckles rolled helplessly in the damp soil, his palms filled with rain. Then he felt the surprising coolness of the air upon hot flesh. The contrast made him gasp. The light brush of Amanda's fingertips made him moan. He had no idea, none at all, that sensation could burn through him like fire, on tongues of pleasure instead of pain. Heat coiled inside him. His boot heels furrowed dry ground. And with one mind-blanking surge of darkness, control was gone.

Amanda gasped at the hard clamp of his hands about her upper arms. With a single twist, he was up and had knocked her over upon her back. The pressure of his hips ground over hers, mashing her into unyielding earth. But it was the harsh seethe of his breathing that frightened her into sudden rebellion.

"No!"

He didn't listen any better than he had in the stuffy hotel room. She fought him. It was no longer an issue of passion but one of power. He was stronger and she couldn't stop him from taking by force what she was eager to give with love. The violence in him scared her into tears but her anger rose up to challenge. Not an anger at him, because he didn't understand why what he was doing was so wrong, but a cold, unforgiving fury toward those who had impressed a young mind with images of domination instead of tenderness.

Her words cracked like a slap.

"Harmon, you're hurting me. Stop it."

He was off her in an instant, backing into a protective, bristling huddle. "I thought it was what you wanted," came his low, ragged growl.

"It is, but not like that," she corrected quietly. Amanda sat up and reached for him. He struck away her hands and retreated farther.

"And I suppose you know all about how it's supposed to be from reading your stupid books." His breathing was labored and Amanda saw right through his caustic words. He was scared and he was running from her as fast as he could go. And she didn't know if she could catch him.

"No, Harmon," she told him candidly. "I learned from you, last night."

Silence stretched out between them. She took advantage of it to scoot close to him, to touch his face. He reared back to avoid it. His breathing started up again in a quick, hard shiver. He said nothing, so she continued.

"You showed me you could be gentle and I want that from you. I won't let the past cheat us out of it. I want you too much. I love you too much." She was able to capture his face between her hands. He didn't resist her kiss. But he didn't respond to it, either. "I'm not afraid of you, Harm. I'm not afraid of this. Please trust me."

Still, he was silent.

Not knowing what else to do, Amanda gave his lean features a last caress and his thinned mouth another kiss.

"I'm going inside. You think about what it is you want. If vengeance is all you need to sustain you, I'll get on that stage tomorrow. If you want more . . . if you want me . . . you know where I'll be."

With the blanket tugged back over her head, she backed out into the rain and ran for the house, leaving him in his solitary darkness.

Chapter Twenty

It was cold. However, it wasn't the seeping chill that had Harmon shivering. It was the seeping memories.

He sat tucked back into darkness, hugging to still the shake of his knees, his eyes squeezed shut against stark images. Violent scenes. Violent sounds. His soul shriveled up tight to protect against them.

I can take some of the hurt away.

Please . . . oh, please . . .

The sense of aloneness was terrible. He shared the Apache dread of separation. Family was the root of all things. His family loved him. He'd always had the comfort of that knowledge, even when he chose to stay away. But now those doors were closing to him, shutting him out, shutting him away. How could he exist without them?

Becky, don't make me go. It's not my fault. It wasn't my fault.

She was right to fear him. He was afraid of himself, afraid of the humanity being sucked from him with each blow he struck in retribution. It wasn't supposed to be like that. Where was the sense of justice? Where was the return of his self-worth? Instead of getting stronger, he was weakening, losing his foothold against the evil he confronted. Becoming more like it even as he fought to destroy it.

Control it, don't let it control you.

I can't! Don't you see? I can't.

I don't want to.

That was the truth that shook him to the core. He didn't want to stop. He didn't want to face the savagery he'd indulged in for the last fourteen years. He wanted to lose himself in darkness because there was safety there. He could strike out with like viciousness against the terrors that held him hostage. He was like them. Just like them.

But that wasn't true.

Hadn't he just learned that? Hadn't he just discovered that difference? Before, there'd been such fear, such confusion. He'd been drowning in it. Not anymore. Now he had no excuse. He knew the difference. He knew what he was doing was wrong. He knew he could stop, should stop. He had a choice.

Don't look away, boy. He could hear the sinister silkiness of Tyrell Cates's voice brushing against his ear. *That's what you are, too. That's what it means to be a man; to have power, to take what you want. If you had a man's length on you, you'd be joining in the fun. Don't think you wouldn't. 'Cause you're just like us. No different at all. No different at all.*

No . . .

I love you, Harmon. You know where I'll be.

He hugged his knees and rocked, harder, faster, until the momentum propelled him forward, to his feet, toward the house, up onto the porch where he paced restlessly. It was dark inside. He stalked up and down, hands working convulsively at his sides.

If you want more . . . if you want me . . .

He was through the door before he had time to talk himself out of it. All was quiet except for the hoarse rasp of his breathing. He could hear his heart beating. He could almost hear the sweat breaking out along his forearms. The need for escape swelled to the point of suffocation. *I can't do this. I can't do this.*

"Harmon?"

The sound of her voice broke through the pattern of his panic. It gave him the strength to cross the room, to sweep her up, to hold her close.

"Oh, Harmon."

Her lips were warm against his sore face. Her cheek was damp where it pressed to his. He felt her tremble at his gruff whisper of "I want you, Ammy."

She stepped back and the feeling of separation was almost crippling. His palms grew damp. His gaze moved anxiously about the contained corners of the room. His breathing quickened, then was jerked to a sudden halt when Amanda pushed her nightdress off her shoulders. His gaze tracked its fall to the floor, then rose slowly, up every perfect inch of Amanda Duncan.

Yusn.

By the time he met her liquid stare, she was wrapped around him, kissing him senseless, touching him until he was engulfed in a sensory madness.

"Undress," she ordered huskily.

He started maneuvering out of his boots. "My family . . ." It was a vague objection.

"Are all asleep. Be quiet and shut the door. I'll turn up the light."

The soft glow of the lamp guided him to where she waited at the bedside. They'd shared it before, but this time it would be very different. He scooped her face into his palms, holding her for the gentle ravishment of her mouth. She moved in close, and the feel of hot flesh to flesh was an exhilarating surprise. Her arms stole about his middle. Her hands stroked his back, his shoulders and, without a trace of shyness, the curve of his flanks.

338

"Make love to me, Harm. It's going to be wonderful."

"Yes," he said to both things.

She went down with him onto the bed without the slightest reluctance. It was then she felt his weight and the staff of his manhood wedged hard and full between them. She couldn't block out the memory of pain from their first rough union and it scared her, even as she vowed she would bear it without a sound. Loving him was more important than any physical distress. It wouldn't matter. She wouldn't let it matter. She forced the cords of tension from her body, making herself relax, urging her arms around him, holding him close, closer.

Then he was kissing her, deeply, absorbingly, wetly. A shudder of helpless abandon shook her. Oh, how she did like kissing him. If only the other could be as nice. She gave a little moan of expectation as his hand curved up around the outer swell of her breast. She shifted so that his palm captured it completely and gave herself over to the exquisite handling. He was moving atop her, rubbing her in an insistently arousing manner. His knee was nudging upward and hers opened wide to receive him into the cradle of her thighs. It hadn't been like this before. She hadn't been so intensely aware of him as a man; of the hard bunching of his thighs, of his broad chest deliciously crushing her bosom, of the crisp furring of his abdomen scraping her soft belly. And oh, it was exciting.

Her hands clutched at the firm rack of his shoulders, kneading them in anxious spasms as she felt him begin to press his fullness against her. He pushed. She couldn't help the tensing, the preparation for the pain. But never did she expect such sudden paradise.

They were nose to nose. His hands clasped her face between them so she couldn't turn away. He was studying her expression with an almost-fierce concentration, searching it in an apprehensive dread. Her breath sucked in sharply. Her body stiffened. Her beautiful brown eyes squeezed shut and he knew a moment of horrible shame.

"Ohhh!" Her breath expelled in a rush, followed immediately by a gusty, "Ooooo!"

Harm hadn't moved. His every muscle locked with strain. His breath raced lightly against her parted lips as he waited for a sign.

Then her eyes came open, glowing darkly. And her lips curved upward. "Oh, Harmon!" That sweet sigh of satisfaction drove a shiver to his soul. She reached up with an eager mouth, taking him with a wide-open, tongue-thrusting taste of passion. She moved beneath him, rocking her hips slowly to experiment with the feel, stroking him with heat and exquisite fire. Urgency shook through him but he resisted, letting her tease him and coax him with those small movements until he was dazed by the strength of pleasure. He closed his eyes, letting the sensations flood over him, wreathing him with degrees of pleasure that shocked the body and stunned the mind. He moaned softly, purely amazed.

Abruptly, Amanda shifted. Driven by half-understood longings, she tumbled Harm onto his back and rode astride him. There she found the freedom to move unrestricted, to sample, unchecked, the strength and the wild delight of him. She lifted and plunged, consumed by the tempting knowledge of what awaited, hurrying to get there. Harm's hands fluttered along her rib cage for a restless second before dropping, palms up, to the mattress. Tension bowed his body and shaped his features into a stark relief of strong, shadowed angles. A dark, sensual image that sent Amanda beyond the brink of discovery.

She cried out and Harm's eyes snapped open in alarm. But there was no mistaking the cause of her taut trembling for anything other than spectacular delight. Her back arched, casting her pale breasts into glorious silhouette.

Sharp, pulling spasms closed around him as she took her pleasure, and it was enough to wring his senses in an explosive response.

Amanda lay panting upon the rapid pulse of his chest. She had no desire to move—ever. Then she felt his hand against the spill of her hair, brushing it back, following its silken path along the delicate tremble of her shoulders. The need to read a similar satisfaction in his face brought her up to her elbows. He was staring up through wide, bright blue eyes. She couldn't tell what he was thinking. His fingertips eased down the curve of her jaw.

"I thought I was going to make love to you, not you make love to me."

The thought that she might have displeased him with her boldness was devastating. Perhaps the Apache in him didn't appreciate her grabbing up control. She felt a moment of despair but no regret even as she told him, "I'm sorry. I didn't mean to. I guess I got carried away."

"You carried me with you. It wasn't a complaint." Then he smiled, a small, well-contented smile that melted her heart right down into a warm pool of devotion.

"Oh, Harmon, it was wonderful, wasn't it?"

"Yes."

"When can we do it again?"

She rode the rumble of his laugh. He murmured something soft in Apache, and before she could tell him she didn't understand, his eyes were closing with a languid ease. Now would be the perfect time to tell him.

"I'm not leaving, Harm."

He sighed and slipped into a blissful state of relaxation. "I never wanted you to."

That was all she needed to hear.

* * *

Harm drew a breath. The sound of it rattled in and expelled upon a moan. The scent of damp earth was overpowering. He could feel the closeness on his skin, prickling there. He could see nothing, hear nothing, over the heavy pounding of his heart. He couldn't move. *Oh, God, I can't get out. They've buried me alive.*

Gentle fingers brushed over his chest and he choked on his scream.

"It's all right, Harm."

"Mama?"

"No, it's Amanda."

Shivers ran the length of him as he repeated her name in a dull sort of disbelief.

"I'll get the light."

His hands groped wildly, finding warmth, finding a familiar form, clutching tight. "No. Don't leave me."

"I won't ever leave you, Harmon."

She gathered him close, feeling the rivulets of disoriented fright coursing through him. She stroked his dark hair. She kissed his brow. And she spoke to him softly.

"Don't be afraid. Don't be afraid. I'm here. There's nothing keeping you inside. The door's open, Harm. You can leave if you want to. It's your choice."

She knew exactly when he started to listen. His breathing altered, growing deep and full. She knew exactly when he started to believe. His palm moved upon her bared breast. That cautious touch became a slow, sensuous revolution, prompting a hardening of response—in her, in him.

His caresses kindled flame. His kisses—on her mouth, on her skin, in her hair—encouraged a spiraling anticipation. He touched her knowingly and she moved against him. He settled over her and she welcomed him with anxious arms winding tight around his neck, around his

342

ribs. Her legs spread in invitation and he answered with a smooth, deep entry that had her gasping into his kiss.

It took longer this time. Amanda relished each added second. Every push and pull intensified the building rush of readiness. She loved everything about it: the quivering tension bunching low in her belly; the restlessness that had her legs twining and stroking his; the feel of Harmon, hard and disciplined above, hot and deliriously stimulating within. The rough, quick sound of his breathing was a stimulant, as was the light pant of it against her neck. She turned her face to his and his mouth scattered distracted, hungry kisses all over in the dark.

Then the tempo of his breathing changed, becoming thick and raspy. He tucked his head into the cove of her shoulder and she held it there with desperately grasping fingers. He said her name, low and raw-sounding, as the rigid coil of his muscles began to shake from strain. He thrust extra hard, pushing beyond the boundaries of pleasure, and startled, she was completely undone. Her body dissolved into a series of clutching tremors. Within that blinding delight, she felt his hard rhythmic shudders pulse up through her, engulfing the last of her subsiding shivers with a possessing force.

Time was measured by the beat of Harm's heart, easing from a hurried rush to a soothing repetition. He lay in total collapse along the yielding length of her body and Amanda held him, loving it, loving him. Finally, he gave a sated murmur and shifted off her, ending their union with a soft groan of regret. He stretched out on his back with a sigh and a moan of "I am such a fool."

Uncertain of his meaning, Amanda was cautious. "Why is that?"

"To think we could have been doing this, enjoying this almost from that first night."

She poked him in the ribs. "Think again, Mr. Bass," she huffed indignantly. His arm slipped beneath her waist and rolled her up flush against him, where she curled in complete contentment. "I was too tired that first night," she explained primly. "Besides, I didn't know how much I wanted you until—"

"Until?" he prompted, nosing the softness of her hair.

"That first night at Blue Creek."

"So, it was my healing powers that swayed you."

"No, not quite. It was the way you looked in those wet blue jeans."

Harm's laugh was deep and delighted. He was so relaxed, he could have sunk right through the mattress to the floor below. It was a bone-melting lethargy, a sense of peace that surrounded his spirit with harmony. It was Amanda. He gave her a squeeze and let weariness overpower him. Never once did his anxiety over the darkness reassert itself. He was too drained to pay it any attention.

"So," Amanda began with a slight edge to her voice, "am I going to have to start cutting the noses off every woman you come across from now on?"

"Why would you?" He was completely, maddeningly sincere.

Amanda wriggled with embarrassed jealousy. "I just thought that maybe now you would be looking—"

"I'm not looking for anything," he corrected. Harm came up on his elbow. His fingertips caressed her cheek. *"Shijii,* I have everything I want right here."

She sucked a constricted breath and cried, "Oh, Harmon, I love you."

"Then quit talking and let me sleep." He brushed her lips with a quick kiss and rolled over onto his side. She was quick to fit along the curve of his backside, issuing a soft little purr of happiness. Harm was smiling as he hugged her forearm to his chest and closed his eyes.

He must not have moved for the rest of the night, for Amanda found him lying in that exact same spot the next morning. She opened her eyes to daylight, the brown of his back, and exquisite memories. The first thing she wanted to do was wake him and read the truth of what had transpired in the Texas blue of his eyes. Surely everything had changed. She was about to reach out to touch him, when her attention was absorbed by the scars marring his flesh.

Unspeakable things.

A shiver took her. Oh, Harmon, how they must have hurt you, she thought with a tender shift of emotion. The significance of what he'd allowed to happen between them rose to awe her. Together, they'd conquered his fear of the flesh and the anxiety of his mind. Would his heart follow? She'd told him she loved him more than once, yet not a single time had he replied with his own feelings. He'd claimed her as his in a physical sense twice, three times counting that first dreadful encounter, yet he hadn't claimed any emotional relevance to those acts of passion. He'd begged her to stay but had given no reason for it. Her elation began to fade before stark realities. Harmon Bass was far from being hers. They'd just touched upon the first complex layer of the barriers guarding him and she had no idea how deep she would have to go to reach the heart of him. However far, however long, she vowed.

It wouldn't be easy. Harm was not going to let her in without a struggle. And once there, what would she find? What if he couldn't shake the violence that directed him? What if there was nothing inside Harmon Bass that could love? She didn't believe that. She wouldn't believe that.

He loved his family and she wanted desperately to be included in that circle. She thought of Rebecca's dire words, about the tenuous balance he walked, and made up her mind to grab on hard and haul with all her might so that he would make the right choices. Unconsciously, she was binding herself to this dark-souled man, taking on the burden of his pain without knowing if she was strong enough to bear it. She was risking all upon his fragile hold on goodness and upon the hope that he would want her, need her enough to keep her with him.

Then what?

The threat of Tyrell Cates would not go away. The unresolved stain of guilt still damned her brother. She was all alone in the world except for Harm, and she was in terrible danger as long as she remained with him. Those were the facts. And it was impossible to rest easy with them preying on her mind. Suddenly, she envied Harmon his deep, exhausted slumber.

The gold of Randy's pocket watch caught her attention from where it sat upon the night table. She lifted it, cherishing the familiar shape of it. The knowledge that she would never see her brother again still stunned her, that sense of surprise returning all the pain of loss. *Oh, Randy, how unfair this was to you. It should never have happened. You shouldn't have had to die.* How she would have liked the chance to share this adventure with him. He'd had so little excitement in his carefully regimented life. Why did he have to choose that one fateful moment to be brave?

Harm sighed and muttered sleepily beside her. He rolled from one side to the other so that he was facing her. One brown hand slid across her thighs and tucked casually between them. The warmth of his rough palm caused a ripple of heat to rise and settle in her most female places. His unintentional touch could unnerve her almost as drastically as his caresses. She took a moment to enjoy the

346

study of his dark features. He looked young when he slept, as young as she. But his expression didn't soften. If she touched him, she knew he would spring awake in an instant. He was on guard even in his sleep.

You don't need to worry over me, Randy, she communed in the quiet of her thoughts. I'm not alone. Harmon will keep me safe. Then she smiled. What would her sober, sensitive brother think if he could see her now, curled up with this tough Texas legend? He would probably never get over the shock. What would he think of her in her borrowed clothes, tanned skin, sporting a pattern of buckshot and snakebites? What would he do if he knew she'd killed a man? Please don't think too harshly of me, dear brother, she prayed. Then she smiled again. Knowing Randy, he was probably boasting of her courage to all who'd listen in heaven.

Amanda opened the watch and was confronted by her own likeness. How innocent she looked with her girl's smile and shining eyes. She frowned at the broken watch face. The crystal had been shattered and the bent hands pointed to nine-forty-five. Was that when he'd been killed? A tremendous swelling closed her throat. Then she swallowed. No. It had been in the afternoon. Absently, she rubbed at what she thought was a spot of rust and nearly wailed aloud. Because it was her brother's blood. Amanda started to close the case, unable to look at it anymore, when suddenly the makings dropped out onto the bed. Dismayed, she scooped up all the fragile gears and springs, ready to place them back inside, when she noticed the distinct scratches on the inside back of the watch. They had been hidden by the timepiece's mechanism. It was a picture, a sort of crude drawing, and she wondered what it meant. She studied it, frowning.

Not a picture. A map.

With a gasp of discovery, she turned her head, meaning

to wake Harm with the news of what she'd found. Her lips were shaped to say his name, when they were abruptly and quite thoroughly claimed.

He'd been awake for some time, watching her through slitted eyes. The play of emotions upon her face intrigued him. Her features read as easily and gushingly as her favorite books, no mystery whatsoever. Usually. But this morning, in the glow of daybreak, there was a pensive quality that bemused him. Her thoughts were secret, as was her occasional soft smile. He wanted to ask what she was thinking as those sometimes melancholy, sometimes smug, sometimes apprehensive shadows shaped her delicate brows and supple lips. About him? He wondered. And he liked believing that. After last night, she had plenty to think about. He knew he did.

She'd opened his eyes to many things—pleasures that had been mistakenly wreathed in darkness, a panic that could be controlled by a gentle touch. She'd knocked him from the destructive spiral he'd been plunging down for fourteen years, and for the first time this morning, he woke well rested and eager to meet the day.

He wanted to stretch luxuriously like a big, lazy cat. His body felt strengthless and completely at ease for the first time he could remember. The novelty of waking in a bed was nice. The fact of being within a room for an entire night amazed him. And the love he felt for the beautiful creature beside him pooled heavy and warm in his veins.

He wanted to make love to her again.

He wanted to spend countless nights as they had the last one and wake the next day with this same sense of satisfaction. Now he understood the terrible position he'd placed his sister in, between the loyalty to her brother and the love of her husband. And he knew that Will Bass had never, ever hurt her.

A lot to learn in one night.

He would have lain there absorbed in the study of her face and form all morning long, but when she turned to him with her features lit with animation and her sweet lips already parted, he couldn't resist. She tasted of a young boy's dreams and grown man's hopes—fresh, promising, and as sultry as the air after last night's storm. He wanted to breathe her in like springtime.

For a long moment, she enjoyed the sensual communication of mingled breaths and teasing tongues. She moaned his name as if in a daze, then said it again more sharply, as if coming awake.

"Oh, Harmon . . . Harmon!"

She wanted to pull back. He never wanted to let go. She pushed against his chest. He moved his hand between her thighs. Resistance fled. Amanda made a soft sound and arched to meet his touch. His pliancy became a hard stiffening. Her passions were so malleable, so quick to flame, her response to him stripped bare of guile or shyness. She was natural in her desires, unashamed in her want of him and in her pleasure of what he was doing. She took to making love as if she'd been instructed in it all her life. He was shaken by the knowledge that she would let him do anything. She would accept his touch, his kiss, the claim of his body, be it tender with care or rough with urgency. And she returned as good as she took. Hers was a humbling power. At that moment, thinking those thoughts, he was lost.

It took scant minutes for her to find release. Even as those complete shudders embraced her slender form, she was tugging at him, pulling him over her, opening to take him inside her in unabashed welcome. It was an impatient mating, a quick, hard race to a spectacular finish, and only afterwards, as he sagged atop her, spent and happily dazed by the force of their passions, did she murmur, "Good morning, Mr. Bass."

He lifted up far enough to smile down upon her. "Yes, it is, Miss Duncan."

Her thumb rubbed over that soft curve of his mouth. "Now isn't this better than going off to run in the hills?"

"Yes, ma'am."

He eased from her and she gave a voluptuous shiver. They lay curled close together, steeped in the awareness of the other, neither wanting to move or to wake from the heavy luxury of contentment. But even so, sounds of the outside world began to intrude, movement on the other side of the door, voices, muffled at first, then closer.

"I should go," Harm murmured against her hair.

"No. Not yet."

"I shouldn't be here."

"Not yet."

And he had no will or want to leave.

Then, too close, came Rebecca's voice.

"Sarah, see if Miss Duncan is awake."

The door flew open without preamble. There was a moment of stark silence, then Sarah Bass went running for the kitchen, calling, "Mama, she's awake. Uncle Harmon's with her, and—" she paused for dramatic effect, then blurted out, "they're both jaybird naked!"

Chapter Twenty-One

Breakfast at the Bass table was an awkward affair.

No one spoke except to ask for the passing of a platter or the refill of a cup. The children were fidgeting with curiosity, their lowered glances darting between their somber-faced uncle and his blushing lady friend. Rebecca kept a tight control over the conversation even as she struggled to conceal her own delight. She supplied a light kiss to her brother's temple as she poured his coffee. She hugged Amanda's rigidly set shoulders as she delivered up her plate. And she would allow for no snickering. The second it threatened, she stifled it with a severe look.

"Uncle Harmon, how come you and Amanda were sleeping in the same bed? You could have come upstairs with us. We had plenty of room."

"Sidney," Rebecca warned gently, casting a glance at her brother, seeing his jaw tighten and his eyes fix on his plate. "Eat your eggs before they get cold."

"Where were your clothes?" Sarah piped up quickly, grabbing for the chance to speak. "Mama won't ever let us sleep without nightshirts. Doesn't Miss Duncan have one?"

Color ran rampant up into Amanda's cheeks as she

351

nearly choked on her piece of toast. She wouldn't look up at Harm. She absolutely couldn't.

"Sarah, pass the biscuits," her mother interrupted firmly.

The youngest Bass had been silently considering the situation and arrived at his conclusion with a beaming smile. "Uncle Harm and Amanda must be married!" Jeffrey declared. That created an instantaneous clamor amongst the children. Jack, who felt himself too old to indulge in such gleeful speculation, covertly eyed the two very guilty-looking parties and decided they soon would be. He wasn't sure he liked it, though. He liked having his uncle's attention all to himself. But if his Uncle Harmon had to go and help himself to a wife, Amanda was a good choice.

"Are you our aunt, Amanda?"

"Are you going to stay here with us?"

"Does this mean we get to sleep upstairs all the time?"

"Children, hush. You are being very rude. Now finish your breakfast and get to your chores."

"Well, what do you expect?" Will growled from the head of the table. He was through holding in his two cents's worth. "Carrying on like this was some kind of cheap—"

"Will."

"Right under our roof with a houseful of kids."

"Will!"

"I would have thought you'd have more respect, not to mention sense, Harmon."

"Will Bass!"

Harm shoved back from the table. " 'Scuse me. I'm going to saddle up the horses. We've got a long ride."

Amanda's head shot up, her embarrassment forgotten. "Where are we going?"

"Fort Davis."

"No." Then she turned him from the door and never

He stared at her across the table, annoyed. He felt just about everything between him and Amanda had already been laid bare, figuratively and literally, in front of his family, and he wasn't about to argue. "We've been through this."

"Yes, we have," she agreed without a degree of hesitation. "And you agreed I shouldn't go."

His brows lowered into a stormy horizon. "Just when did I do that?"

"Last night."

"I don't recall—" And then he did. And he remembered exactly when he'd agreed. Heat flooded up into his face. He was suddenly aware of his entire family's interest and he closed his mouth tight. Muttering a dire Apache curse, Harm stood and stalked from the house, letting the door bang shut behind him.

Amanda sat tense and trembling inside. A terrible fright began to well up, pushing tears against the flicker of her eyelids and a thickness up into her throat. Rebecca's hand rested gently upon her shoulder.

"Jack?"

"Yes, Mama?"

"Is your uncle heading for the barn?"

"No, ma'am. He's on the porch."

"Take him his coffee, please. Children, get to your chores." Then Harm's sister leaned down to whisper approvingly, "You've run him to the ground, Amanda. Show no mercy. He wouldn't expect you to."

Harm sipped his coffee without much notice of the flavorful brew. His gaze was on the distant hills and plains, restless, watchful. He would not think of Amanda. He wouldn't torture himself with the stricken look she'd

353

had upon their discovery. He wouldn't see her scrambling for her clothes without looking at him, without speaking to him, as if she preferred he not exist. Or the stiff way she sat at the table, trying not to cringe with disgrace. He wouldn't consider his responsibility for her distress or the only solution to her shame. He wouldn't admit to himself that the obvious pleased him almost as much as it frightened him. He had no choice. He would have to wed her.

When he heard the scrape and thump of his brother-in-law's crutches, he went rigid inside, knowing he deserved the brunt of Will's anger. What he'd done was a disgraceful thing. The Apache called such clandestine affairs night crawling, and a man would be beaten if caught at it. While he knew Will would not chastise him physically— he never had, not once in all the years they'd known each other—if his brother-in-law chose to let loose a verbal punishing, Harm vowed to take it manfully. He'd shown an inexcusable lack of self-control and poor judgment, and he'd earned his family's contempt. It wasn't the last impression he wanted to leave with them. Because this was the day he would ride away from them and not return.

Will angled up beside the smaller man and let his crutches rest against the rail. He had enough strength to stand on his own for a time and he wanted to spend this moment on his two feet. He glanced at Harm. The stony profile gave nothing away, but then that was Harmon. Most of the time, Will still viewed his wife's brother as a boy, but not this morning. He wasn't that wiry half-breed kid who'd tagged his steps and worked so tirelessly to please him, nor the somber youth who'd gone into a dangerously sullen retreat rather than accept him as his sister's mate. This morning, he was an equal.

"Let me give you a word of advice, Harmon," Will began easily, man to man. "Guard your mouth when you're with a woman in the dark. All them pretty things just want to come gushing up from the soul, but remember, she won't ever be forgetting a single one of 'em. Them nice things might be motivated by the moment, but a woman don't understand that. She takes 'em as pure forever and ever gospel. Don't say anything lessen you mean it."

Harm was silent for a long moment, then he said soberly, "I'm sorry, Will. I've no excuse."

Will sighed charitably. "Guess you don't need one. She's mighty fetching. Best be keeping it behind locked doors, is all. You put me in a bad spot in there. What you and the lady do is none a' my business. You make it mine when you do it in the middle of a passel of nosy younguns. I don't care to hear the details discussed over my breakfast. They grow up fast enough as it is." Secretly, he was more than a little pleased. He'd always figured what Rebecca's brother needed was a good, long, lusty romp with a willing woman. In his own opinion, sexual self-control was what made the Apache male such a savage species.

Harm was staring into his coffee cup. Something was working on him, coming up slow and painful like a poorly digested meal. He spoke with a quiet ferocity. "I was wrong for what I did beneath your roof with Amanda. And I was wrong for fearing you would mistreat my sister."

Will blinked at the apology he'd never expected to hear. "Where the hell did that come from?"

"Experience."

"Oh."

"I've made things difficult between you and Becky, and I was wrong. I don't expect you to forgive me that. I didn't know—"

"You don't need to explain, Harm." No, he didn't.

Amanda had taken an emotional virgin and made him into a man. What was to explain?

Harm cleared his throat. "Is there anything that needs doing before I go?"

"I think you've done more than your share, Harmon."

"It's just that it might be a while before I get back this way." He let that trail off and Will understood. He wasn't coming back. The older man picked his words very carefully.

"This is your home, Harmon. I know I haven't always made you feel welcome and I'm sorry about that. A lot of it's to do with pride, some of it worry, but that ain't cause for you to stay away."

"That's the way Becky wants it."

"Now, son, I don't believe that for a minute."

Harm's dark head bowed. He said nothing.

Will looked at him long and hard—at the tough little kid who had slain two men at ten, had dragged his sister to safety, had suffered from a nightmarish situation and survived it, but not totally unscathed. At the boy who'd never asked anything of him except that he be allowed to stay close by where he could cherish the illusion of belonging to a family. The stark loneliness of that existence woke a paternal care in Will Bass that couldn't easily be shaken off. Suddenly, Harm wasn't as much a danger to his family as he was a part of it.

"I been doing some thinking, Harmon. 'Bout that windmill. Guess I wouldn't mind having you around for a time this summer whilst you put it together. Jack could help you out. I'll ask Becky what she thinks."

Harm sucked a ragged breath and, without looking up, muttered, "Thanks, Will."

The big ex-Ranger clapped his hand atop shoulders

that couldn't support quite as much weight as they pretended. "I can use all the cheap labor I can get."

Amanda waited until he was alone to approach him. She was nervous and angry that she should have to be after the ardent hours they'd spent in each others's arms. He was aware of her at once. She could tell by the way he straightened and stiffened with a familiar wariness. He was obviously uncomfortable with her. And just as obviously ashamed of what had happened. She wasn't. She'd wanted it—badly, desperately—and his withdrawal hurt. To keep her weak tears at bay, she adopted a gruff, impersonal manner as she joined him at the porch rail.

"I wanted to show you something."

He glanced at her cautiously and she fought the urge to scream in frustration, to strike at him in wounded anguish. But instead, she held out the watch in a steady hand.

"What's this?" He looked eager for the distraction.

"Randy's watch. Look at it. Closely."

Harmon turned to lean his rump against the rail, contemplating the broken timepiece. He spent a moment looking at the image of Amanda. He knew every line by heart. He'd engraved them there within his chest as he rode back with the news about her brother. "So? You might be able to get a watchmaker to fix it."

Amanda lifted it from his palm, aware of how he flinched at the brush of her fingertips. She tapped the mechanism into her other hand and extended the gold shell. "What do you make of this?"

He studied the crude scratches. An alertness firmed his features.

"A map?" Amanda tried not to sound too hopeful.

"I know this place."

A thrill shot through her.

"Let me see the watch face."

She passed it back to him wordlessly.

"Nine-forty-five. He must have set it to that time. But why?" Harmon frowned, thinking hard, trying to wedge himself into the expensive eastern shoes of a man who knew he was dying and was trying to convey one last message to his sister. He came off the rail with a sudden movement. "Unless it doesn't have anything to do with time."

"What, Harm?"

"Unless he meant for it to be a compass."

"Due west. Is that it? Is that what he meant? Was he trying to point the way to where he left the jewels?"

"Only one way to know for sure." He hollered down toward the barn. "Jack, saddle up my horse."

"Our horses," Amanda yelled. Then she faced his scowl and said simply, "I'm going, too."

"No."

"Yes."

"They'll be watching for us, Amanda." He let that linger with significance, and it touched off a spark of fear in her eyes. But it didn't sway her.

"Then you'll need someone to watch your back while you're studying the ground."

His hands gripped her upper arms, shaking her slightly in his effort to convey concern. "Ammy, I need you safe. I have to concentrate on what I'm doing."

"Would you concentrate better knowing I'm beside you, where you can keep an eye on me, or wondering when I'm going to blunder into the middle of everything and get you killed?"

Damn, she had a point there.

"Don't get in my way."

"No promises." She smiled suddenly, brightly, and his

heart dropped into his boots, wallowing there in a misery of longing he couldn't betray.

"If we're going, let's go."

Happily, she flung her arms around him. And he went stiff as a post. Amanda tried to pretend she was unconcerned as she loosened her embrace and stepped away. She was going with him. That was the main thing. Wasn't it?

He went back inside to pick up his gear and Amanda trailed in behind him. She'd be sorry to leave the comfort and companionship of the Bass ranch, but there were things to be resolved before she would feel welcome there again. Things like the vindication of her brother and the uncertainty of her relationship with Harm.

"You're leaving?" The quaver of Rebecca's tone implied there was much she wasn't saying, and Harm's crisp reply conveyed his understanding of those unspoken words.

"Yes."

"For Fort Davis?"

"No."

Rebecca waited for him to say more but he wouldn't. She looked to Amanda and found no answer with her, either. She watched her brother gather up his things as if he were painting for war. There was a hard determination in the way he checked his weapons and draped his cartridge belts. He passed Amanda a loaded pistol and the eastern woman took it without question, with the same grim set to her features.

"What kind of trouble you riding into, Harm?" Will asked from where he leaned against the sideboard.

"None I can't handle."

He was lying. His tension said it plain. Will had never known Harm to worry and he figured it was because of Amanda, because he had more than his own life at stake.

Loving someone did a whole lot of changing to a man's attitude and he had no doubt that his brother-in-law was crazy over Amanda Duncan.

"Harmon?"

The impassive face turned toward him.

"If you need help, don't be no hero. There's plenty who'd ride beside you if you but asked. And if you just need some plain old get-right-to-the-point advice, talk to Calvin. He's the best there is with such things and he'll steer you straight."

"No," Harm disagreed softly. "If I want words from the best there is, I would come to you." Then he continued to stuff his supplies, never seeing how greatly his confidence affected the crippled Ranger.

When Harm shouldered the pack of necessaries and picked up his carbine, he found his sister's arms around him in a tight embrace. He tried to hang on to his reserve but it couldn't withstand the wash of her silent tears. His arms came up to fold her close and his cheek leaned into the softness of her hair.

"Harmon . . ."

"Shhh, *silah*." And suddenly the years were gone, and it was just the two of them holding together against odds that should have overwhelmed and fears that would have humbled had they been other than who they were.

"I love you, Harmon. Think about what I said and please, please come home. I'll always need you."

So quietly she could barely hear the words, he whispered back, "I love you, Becky." Then he stood her away and strode for the door, glad the worst of the parting was over. Or so he thought until he stepped out onto the porch. All four of Becky's children were waiting for him.

"When you coming back, Uncle Harm?" Jack wanted to know as he handed over the reins to his horse.

"When I'm finished with what I have to do."

"Will it take a long, long time?" Jeffrey demanded from where he sat in his uncle's saddle.

Harm put up his arms and the littlest Bass slid down into them. He hugged the boy fiercely, his heart chugging as if he were laboring up the side of a mountain. "No, it won't take a long, long time. But until I get back, I want all of you to help out your folks. You do that for me?"

A chorus of "Yessir, Uncle Harmon."

"What do you want me to bring you?" he asked as he settled Jeffrey on the top porch step.

"A new book," Sidney said without hesitation.

"Anything but a Harmon Bass adventure," Harm agreed, ignoring the pout of his nephew's lower lip.

"Hard candy!" Jeffrey demanded.

"Some hair ribbons. Yellow ones. For me and my doll."

Harm touched Sarah's dark curls and smiled. Then he looked to Jack. "What about you, son?"

"Just come back."

Amanda watched him floundering helplessly in the riptide of emotion. This was the family he loved and she could see it was breaking his heart to ride away, possibly never to return. Because the dangers he warned of weren't exaggerated. She was slightly surprised by the warm little hand that pressed into hers and she smiled down at Sarah Bass.

"Are you coming back, too, Miss Amanda?"

"If I don't, it's not because I don't want to."

"When you marry Uncle Harmon, we'll be almost like sisters."

Amanda didn't know what to say, so she bent and hugged the child, thinking to herself, *Yes, we will, sweet Sarah.*

Harm rolled up into his saddle and Amanda climbed atop Fandango with what could almost pass for grace.

Without another word to his family, he jerked the reins around and kicked up a quick, distancing canter with Amanda at his heels.

The air grew unbearably humid as the moisture from last night's rain cooked up out of the earth. It lay along the surface of the skin in damp sheets and lent an uncomfortable thickness to the act of breathing. Thirsty ground seemed to yield up lush green overnight and bright blossoms of color were everywhere, too stubborn to wilt from the heat. Just like Harmon Bass.

Amanda envied him his Texas toughness. She watched his back mile after mile and never saw him so much as twitch in discomfort. He rode as if the intensity of the sun and the heaviness of the air somehow deflected off his bare black head and unstooped shoulders. Out here, he was part of the surroundings, moving with the horse in harmony, absorbing the heat the way the rocks and wiry plants did. But the same environment embracing him with a familiar affection fought to keep her out. It beat down to slow-cook her brain to a hazy mush. It wrung the sweat from her until she felt as parched as old leather. The constant shift of the saddle chafed every part of her that touched it.

Amanda had thought herself used to the harsh Texas clime, but as the sun beat down from directly overhead, she felt helpless against it. Her head pounded mercilessly, and instead of feeling flushed and hot, there was a strange clamminess to her skin, almost as if she was chilled. That alarmed her beyond the grip of pride.

"Harmon."

It was more a croaking groan than a call. He didn't turn. She wet her lips and tried again.

"Harmon . . ."

Dizziness swept her up. She was vaguely aware of him twisting in his saddle to look back at her. A curtain of blackness began to rise, swelling like a dark tide. Then she felt his hands pulling her down from Fandango, steering her toward the welcomed shade of some Texas scrub. She sank down and started to crawl back into those cool shadows, but he caught her shoulders.

"No. Not back there. That's the first place an enemy would look. Never go to the deepest shade. It isn't safe."

She didn't have the strength to argue. With a moan, Amanda collapsed in the dappled fringes of light and rolled onto her back. She couldn't seem to open her eyes without inviting in the giddy sensations, so she kept them closed, listening to Harm move about her. She felt his fingers loosening the neck of her blouse, his palm easing the wet hair from her forehead and neck. Then there was a delicious coolness dotting exposed skin surfaces and finally resting across her sore eyelids. His hand slipped behind her neck, lifting so she could sip from his canteen. Before she'd had near enough, he was taking it away. Then he lowered her down and she kept right on sinking.

Amanda had no idea how much time passed before a sense of focus returned. Reaching up an unsteady hand to push the cloth from her eyes, she discovered Harm sitting patiently at her side, eating canned peach slices from the blade of his knife. When he saw she was awake, he set them aside and bent over her, touching his warm hand to her brow.

"How are you feeling?"

"Did I faint?"

"Just a touch of heat. It'll pass. I wasn't thinking. Sometimes I forget you're still a newcomer."

She wasn't sure if she was being complimented or insulted. Her eyes closed again and the gentle comfort of his hand returned to soothe her face. Then it lowered, resting against the curve of her ribs, sliding up to cup the under-swell of her breast. His palm seemed to adhere to the stickiness of her skin right through the sodden fabric. She pushed his arm away with a plaintive movement and he withdrew completely, returning to his peaches, feeding his grim mood as well as his voracious appetite. She hadn't meant to hurt him. She'd only wanted to end the unpleasant contact as tacky heat made every surface bond to-gether. She felt she should explain or apologize.

"Harm—"

"We'll marry in Terlingua."

Amanda blinked stupidly. "What?" Surely she was sun-addled. He couldn't have said what she thought she heard, not in such a hard, angry voice. "What did you say?"

"I said we'll get married in Terlingua."

That's what she'd thought she heard, but it made no more sense hearing it a second time. All she could think to say was, "Why?"

"It's the proper thing to do."

Now she wondered if he was the one struck by sun madness. "Is that your only reason?"

He wouldn't look at her. "I've disgraced you before my family."

"I see."

She sat up and he risked a quick cant of the eyes in her direction. Her look wasn't promising. Why was she angry? She said she loved him and wanted to go about with him. What was her objection? It seemed the prudent thing to ask before a child was made between them. He had to admit that when she swooned from horseback into his arms, he remembered when Becky had suffered from similar weaknesses and he'd thought . . . he'd hoped that maybe a child . . . but no. It was too soon for hopes. Though the Apaches believed such things only happened

364

after many couplings and an accumulation of fertile blood passed from man to woman, he was not so sure. There was that night in Perdition to consider, though he wouldn't like to think their child had been planted during that regrettable union. Better during those blissful matings at his sister's house. Better still, within wedlock. He'd heard once was all it took, and he would protect Amanda and any child she might conceive if that should prove true.

Her blunt question had taken him by surprise, as had her brusque rejection of his touch. He said the first thing he could think of and now suspected it hadn't been a good thing to say. Logic sometimes didn't work with Amanda. He was at a loss with her.

"Then it's settled," Harm stated with what he hoped was confidence. He felt a sudden surge of anticipation. His wife. His to love and care for. Then she sliced right through his fragile dreams.

"I don't think so, Mr. Bass."

He stared at her through eyes as big and blue and unmasked as the Texas sky overhead. "You don't want to marry me?"

She scowled at him. "I would marry for a lot of reasons, but to save you from embarrassment is not one of them. I'm feeling much better now. Shall we go?"

Amanda scrambled out from under the cool shelter and crawled up on Fandango without another word. Trying to control his confusion, he ducked out after her. She pulled her horse's head away, so it was step back or be knocked down by the sudden powerful shift of the animal's hindquarters. Harmon was frowning direly when he got into his own saddle. He didn't understand her at all. She'd been chasing him for weeks, winding herself around his heart, and now that he was ready to admit defeat, she wanted no part of him. He was mystified and, at the same time, deeply frightened. What if she didn't want him as a husband?

Kicking up his mount into an aggressive gallop, Harm decided. He would think of a reason to return to his sister's . . . and soon. He didn't need advice from Will Bass on warfare. He needed to ask him how a man proposed marriage to the woman he loved.

Finding the jewels was ridiculously easy with Randy's crude map in hand. Harm dismounted and walked the same track he'd taken the day he found the young easterner's body. Physical signs had been washed away in the rains but he remembered the route. Amanda rode behind him, her gaze alternately watching him and nervously scanning the high ridges. She held her pistol at the ready and the grip was slippery in her palm. The fact that Harm was afoot and vulnerable made her uneasy. The fact that he'd stripped off his shirt and hunkered down over the trail with muscles swelling the tight denim over his thighs made her restless.

He'd asked her to marry him.

Never mind for a moment that it was all for the wrong reasons. He'd asked. Maybe she was crazy to hesitate. She wanted Harmon Bass as much as she wanted that hidden cache of gems. Both had irreplaceable value to her. If only she'd been more clearheaded and he hadn't dropped it on her from out of the blue. If only he'd mentioned love or need or anything that would hint that emotions prompted his unexpected declaration. But he'd mentioned honor, duty. Bland fare for romance. If he couldn't make himself say the words now, what chance would there be of her ever hearing them? And she wanted to. She wanted to hear someone other than her brother speak them, especially now that his voice was forever silenced. Maybe it was a petty thing. Rose would have called her a grand fool for not grabbing at what she wanted, circumstance be-damned. But Amanda was an incurable optimist. She'd held out for a tender touch from him and she'd gotten it. And oh, that had been well worth the wait! If she required a poetic sentiment, would she find herself waiting forever?

Amanda had been so intent upon her thoughts that she didn't notice Harm had stopped, and she nearly rode Fandango right up his back. She was all too familiar with his tense posture.

"What is it?"

"Three mounted men." He fingered the tracks upon the dusty ground.

"Cates's men?" Her eyes immediately flew over the stoic canyon walls.

"That would be my guess. They're either doing some looking on their own or—"

"Or what?"

He straightened and gave her a steady stare. "They're looking for us."

Chapter Twenty-Two

The thought of falling into Tyrell Cates's hands terrified her.

It must have shown on her face, for Harm's voice softened as he asked, "What do you want to do? It's your call. We can go back and try again, or we can keep on with it."

"If we stop now, they could find the jewels before us."

"Possibly."

"How dangerous is it to keep on?"

"They're about fifteen minutes ahead of us. No problem, unless they decide to backtrack and we meet them nose to nose."

Amanda stared down the trail. She fidgeted. So close. "Let's keep on."

Harm betrayed no expression one way or another. "All right. You stay close and don't go making any unnecessary noise. And do what I tell you." She started to open her mouth to agree and he waved off her words. "No. Don't waste them."

He went back to his study of the terrain and she pulled a petulant face behind his back. She was planning to listen . . . this time.

After a few more yards, Harm stopped again, looking

from the empty watch to the surrounding outcropping of rocks.

"Harm?"

He didn't respond. Instead, he made a ninety degree turn to his left and he smiled thinly. "Jackpot."

"What?"

"My guess is he didn't have a chance to slow down with Dexter chasing him, so he just gave it a toss from the saddle. That's why I didn't catch it the first time." Harm sounded pleased, as if his professional pride had been vindicated. "Then, when he had the chance, he scratched out the markings on the watch, hoping it would end up in your hands so you could follow his map to where he'd hidden them."

"Where?" She stood in her stirrups but couldn't see anything out of the ordinary.

But Harm was striding off the path, moving up into the rocks, bounding between them like some lithe mountain cat. Amanda watched with breath suspended as his slick-soled boots slid more than once. He paused to break off a sturdy stick, then reached the point of it up into the crotch of a Y-shaped rock. Amanda remembered the letter scratched into the soft gold of Randy's watch case.

"Catch."

Harm snagged the handle of a small travel case and swung it toward her. It flew off the end of his stick with a few lazy spirals and landed right in her outstretched arms. Anxiously, she flipped up the fasteners. There on top sat her brother's toiletry kit, with his brush, his comb, and his razor. The familiar scent of his cologne brought a lump of anguish to her throat. Tears massed and she couldn't blink them away.

Harm jumped down to the trail beside Fandango. He frowned up at her. "Ammy, what is it? Aren't they in there?"

"You look." She pushed the case at him, but before he could take it, he jerked away and stood rigidly poised. "What?" she hissed at him.

"They're coming back."

"I didn't hear anything. Harmon—"

But he had. Faint and very distinct. The sound of horses approaching. "Here." He snatched up the reins to his horse and passed them up to her. "Go. Ride for Terlingua and don't stop before you give those stones to Calvin Lowe."

"But you—"

"I'm going to wait here. Lead my horse with you. They won't be able to tell I'm not riding it."

"Are you going to ambush them?"

He was looking up, his face all etched into harsh angles. And he smiled, just that faint pull across bared teeth. "Something like that."

"I'll wait up ahead for you."

"No. I might have to trail them a while before I find a good spot."

"Good spot for what?"

"What I have in mind. Now go."

"Harm, I don't want to leave you."

"You said you wouldn't argue. Go! You've got the jewelry. Isn't that the important thing?"

"No." And it wasn't. "You are."

Her words kicked like the shoulder recoil of a Sharps buffalo gun. He tried not to be bowled right over. There wasn't time for it. "Ride straight into the sun. Don't stop. Don't worry about me. I'll meet you at Cal's."

"You're going to kill those men."

"I'm not going to let them catch up to you."

"It's not the same thing, Harmon, and you know it. Come with me. Now."

370

"No." The sound growled from him. He was looking up the trail. She could feel his tension, his anticipation.

"Harmon, don't do this. Please."

But he had his carbine unslung and his knife blade glittering in his hand . . . the way his eyes were glittering. "You got what you came for, now I'm going after what I want." And he was running, like a low, sleek shadow along the edge of the canyon. Running with the pounding of blood lust in his veins. Amanda gave a soft sob and kicked back her heels, startling Fandango into a hop, then a turf-gobbling stride. She didn't look back. This time, she would obey. Because what Harmon Bass was planning didn't involve her and she didn't think she could stand to see it.

He lay low. Sun-warmed rocks heated his bare belly as he stretched out like a basking basin lizard. Only there was nothing lazy about him. Sweat glimmered off tightly corded muscle. Boot toes buried deep to provide leverage for a sudden forward spring. And he watched, silent, stalking with immeasurable patience.

He heard them. They rode unconcerned, talking amongst themselves. Careless. Soon to be dead. He slowed his breathing until it eased in through his nose and blew out softly between slightly parted lips. Systematically, he calmed his breath, his heartbeat, his thought patterns, until all was channeled along a fine, deadly line. Then he saw them. Three riders in cowboy dress. One of them was young, not much older than Jack, smiling up easily at a man who had to be either father or brother, their features were so similar. And Harm knew a moment's pause. His fingers worked in agitation over the suddenly-wet gunmetal. He didn't like it—not the fact that he hesitated, not the fact that the kid was so damned young, and not the fact that he'd be killing one right in front of the other's eyes. He watched them for a minute longer, letting them come close, almost too close for him to launch his surprise. He liked it even less. He kept seeing Jack looking up at him through those big, expressive eyes, so eager to encompass the whole world in the next few moments. That boy's whole world was going to be his next few moments. If he fired.

If he fired.

Harm lay stunned. Choice. He had a choice. He could ease back and let the three riders pass. He didn't have to draw down on them. He didn't know for absolute certain that they were riding for McAllister or that they knew about the jewelry or him or Amanda. He didn't know any of those things, yet he'd been ready to bury them in an instant. And he'd told Amanda that he wasn't a killer.

What a liar!

He let out his breath in a shaky gust. Let them go. What did it matter? They gave no sign of even recognizing another pair of horses had come this way. Let them go.

Harm started to slide back, away from the need for bloodshed, when his gaze touched upon the third man. His gut felt as though it had been yanked out by the roots. The image was so clear: the sharp face, the long, greasy blond hair and thin moustache, the tooled pistol belt, the cold black eyes. That man he knew was no innocent cowhand. That man he knew deserved to die by his hand. He knew it because the third rider had killed his mother.

Rage clenched in his belly. It boiled up to explode through his chest in a great aching wave. Instinct gripped hold of him, vibrating savagely through every pore.

And then he heard the boy's laughter. Sweet, innocent laughter.

It's got to stop. Let it go. Becky. *I don't want you to come to my house with blood on your hands.* Becky, please! He squeezed his eyes shut. He could see that big doubled fist, swinging back into a vicious, fatal arc. His mama falling. Not moving. *Mama!* He shuddered with the memory. *Do it in the name of honor, for the sake of justice. Don't let it control you. Ammy, help me!* Will's rough voice. *Come on, you savage little sonuvabitch! Prove me right!*

Harm grabbed up the carbine and did the first foolishly white thing he could ever remember doing. He jumped up from behind cover to his feet and threw down a bead on the startled trio, calling with a deadly quiet that would make any Texas Ranger proud, "Don't move, gentlemen, or I'll blow you in two."

A tired, bedraggled Amanda showed up at the Lowes in the heat of late afternoon. They welcomed her like an old friend, opening their arms and their home to her. If they noticed her restrained mood, they said nothing of it. And they said nothing about Harmon, figuring one had to do with the other.

She settled into the extra room, first tucking the satchel far up under the bed, not wanting to open it until Harm was with her, then she washed up and went to the bank. She wired New York for five thousand dollars, realizing as she did that every one of her relatives would know their gold-mine niece was in some godforsaken place called Terlingua, Texas. It didn't matter. Then she established a line of credit and went to the mercantile to buy something pretty and feminine, something that didn't make her think of sleeping in bedrolls or toting an inch of Big Bend dust. She would not think of Harmon Bass and of what he might be doing at this very moment out in the West Texas heat. To distract herself, she relied on something she had learned in New York. Amanda went shopping.

She bought a lacy shawl for Elena, a bottle of the best wine Terlingua offered, which was probably a notch above spit, yellow hair ribbons, hard candy, a dime novel, strong coffee, and a case of canned peaches. With her new wearing apparel tucked under her arm and a promise that the rest would be delivered to the Lowes', Amanda started along the rickety boardwalk, oblivious to the stares she garnered. Until she bumped head-on into a strapping cowboy.

"Give you a hand with them there parcels, ma'am?" The voice was polite. The gaze was not.

"Thank you, but I'm not going far. Excuse me."

He made no effort to move out of her path. When she stepped to one side, he sidled that way, too. She stepped the other way, and he did, too. Amanda drew an aggravated breath and glared up at him. At one time, his hot gaze would have intimidated her. Today, she met it straight on and wondered if Calvin Lowe would clap her in jail if she blew a hole through the rude fellow's spleen.

"You are in my way, sir. Please move."

"Why, ma'am, must be we're fated to get together." He grinned. Amanda glowered, ready to pull her pistol. She'd give the lout one more warning.

"I would not give two cents for your fate if you don't leave me alone."

"Why's that, pretty lady?"

"Because my fiancé is *The* Harmon Bass and he would not appreciate it."

"Well, hell's bells, ma'am, Harm Bass ain't in these parts."

"He will be."

A drawling voice intruded over her shoulder. "Sooner than you think."

Amanda glanced back at Sheriff Lowe, then followed his nod to the far end of the street. She gave a soft little gasp of relief and was only vaguely aware that her accoster turned deathly pale and faded from the sidewalk like a water spot at midday.

Harm rode down the center of the street, his carbine resting easy across his knees. He led two other horses and shepherded three men on foot in front of him. He halted the procession when they came to Calvin, swinging his leg over the saddle horn to ease into a dismount. He didn't look at Amanda. His gaze was on one of the three prisoners.

"Whatcha got here, Harmon?" Cal asked as he gave the winded trio the once-over.

"Them two, I don't know about, but him, that one there, he killed my mother."

Amanda made a startled sound and Calvin Lowe looked no less surprised to find the man still breathing.

"That there's Ed Franks, a real hard case. Works for McAllister. Them other two are Cy and Tandy Bartlett. Can't imagine them mixed up with the likes of Franks unless it was for the money. They got a run-down place east of here, big family, hardworking. Cy, your wife know what you're doing?"

The older man was breathing hard from the long walk and his face was pasty with regret. He kept looking anxiously at his son. "Sheriff, we just hired on to help this feller find a missing travel case up in them there rocks. We didn't know we was doing something to run cross-grained of you. My Bonnie took real sick with our seventh. It's due next month and we was just looking for a way to put some extra aside."

Harm clenched his teeth against a sudden surge of sickness. God, he'd almost shot them down! He'd almost killed them for trying to earn money for their family.

Cal was looking at him strangely. "I can vouch for them, Harm."

"Let them go." His voice was raw. Then his gaze fixed on Franks, glittering with all manner of malice. "Him, I want you to hang."

"Why, Harm, that would be my pleasure."

The fellow in question spoke up for the first time, his voice angry, afraid. "You can't do this. I'm a duly authorized deputy for Sheriff Cates down in Perdition. When he hears about this, he'll have me out of your jail in a minute."

"You're safer in jail," Harm drawled, and the man shut his mouth tight.

Cal's hand slid along Harm's rigid shoulders in a companionable gesture. He was smiling. " 'Sides, wouldn't surprise me a-tall if justice was to move so fast in this case that you'd be cooling in the dirt by the time word gets down to Perdition. C'mon, Harm, help me herd this hard case over to the jail, then I'll stand you to a beer. Cy, you and the boy skedaddle. Amanda, tell Elena she might have to wait supper for a little bit."

"I'll do that, Sheriff."

Harm looked to her then, and she was stunned by the fatigue and strain dulling his gaze. He didn't say anything to her. He didn't have to. He'd kept his word and he'd kept his mother's murderer from roasting in the hell of his retribution. She couldn't ask for more than that. She smiled faintly and continued on to the Lowes', where she planned to bathe and dress for dinner. And to greet Harmon properly the minute she got the chance.

Harm responded to the bump in the ribs by glancing up from his third beer. Calvin was grinning at him.

"So when's the happy day?"

Harm stared up at him blankly. Cal grinned wider.

"Son, let me give you a word of warning: Don't ever

forget the date afterwards." He chuckled to himself and tossed back his whiskey.

Harm scowled. "What are you talking about, Calvin?"

"Why, you and Amanda."

"What about us?"

"Three beers and the man forgets he's getting married." Harm looked so startled, Cal began to wonder if he'd put his foot in the wrong way. A bit more judiciously, he asked, "You are, aren't you? That's what the lady said."

"She didn't say it to me," he growled, and grabbed onto his beer mug with both hands. They were shaking. He was shaking. *That's what the lady said.* She was going to marry him!

Calvin was vastly amused by his small friend's discomfort. He'd never seen Harm squirm before, and he was twitching like a worm on a line. "What? She say no when you asked?"

"I didn't ask. I told her we were getting married."

"Told her . . . Oh, boy. Exactly how did you put it?"

"I told her it was the proper thing to do."

"And?"

"She bit my head off."

"You're lucky she didn't chew you down to bone and spit you out. Dang, Harmon, but you surely are dumb when it comes to women. Don't you go squinting at me like you're fixing to see me on the end of your knife. You don't *tell* a woman something like that. You ask her. You beg. You might even try a little crawling. Only hurts the pride for a minute. Either that, or she'll have you on your knees for the rest of your life."

"I don't beg for anything," came his haughty reply.

Cal laughed at him. "See how long you keep that attitude once she's got you by the . . . Never mind. You'll find out soon enough. Wouldn't want to spook you off, seeing as how you're so dad-blamed skittery anyway." He continued to chuckle to himself, thinking poor old Harmon was going to have one tough time of it. Amanda was going to fillet out his arrogant hide. He thought about the miseries Elena had put him through their first few months of wedded bliss. She'd had him spinning so bad he didn't know day from night. But it had been worth it. Every humbling second of it. And Harm deserved the same.

"Pard, you'd best lay off the beer and come on home with me. I got me a feeling that little gal of yours will be wanting to hear something more than a bunch of big man Apache talk from you. And you'd best make it sweet and sincere, or she'll be blasting you right outta your boots."

"You're enjoying this, aren't you, Calvin?"

The big ex-Ranger put his arm about his wretched friend's shoulders. "You're damned right, I am. Let me give you the benefit of my advice. . . ."

For all his arrogant bluster, Harm was ready to drop right down to his knees the second he saw her standing at the Lowes' table. He tried to swallow but nothing would go down, and nothing would come out through the paralysis in his throat. So he stood frozen while she smiled at him, a mind-stunning vision of soft gold curls, pale lace, creamy silk, and bronzed shoulders. And he wondered wildly how long she would make him crawl before he could make love to her.

Calvin's shove nearly toppled him. He glanced back at him in a daze.

"Harm?" He was waiting for something. Harm blinked. "You want to get a move on so's we can get some dinner, or are you posing for a statue in front of my chair?"

"Oh. Sorry, Cal." He shuffled to one side but still hung

back. Calvin gave him a push toward his seat and rolled his eyes at his wife with meaningful hilarity.

"Sit down, Harmon," he prompted.

He plopped like a sack of cornmeal. And he responded to everything going on at the table over Elena's hot dinner like that bag of grain. The meal went on forever, while his anxious gaze feasted on Amanda's beauty and he starved from the need to touch her. She was chatting easily with Calvin, then her big dark eyes would flit over to him with a purely scalding speculation. He was writhing in his seat. Then she wet her lips and smiled in a way that drove him half mad with impatience. Never had he wanted anything to end so badly as that cordial dinner, then, when it was over, he was faced with another problem. It wasn't as if he could drop Amanda down right in the middle of the Lowes' dining room. Not that Amanda would mind it. He wouldn't put it past her to shuck him down to nothing right in the center of town if she was of a mind to. He had a little more self-control than that. But not much. Not with the way he was foaming with anticipation.

So if not at the Lowes', where?

He pushed back from the table, nearly upsetting his chair. "I'm going to get a room at the hotel."

Calvin stared at him. "Harm, I ain't never knowed you to ever spend a night indoors. Owww! Elena, what the—"

Elena was smiling, ignoring her husband's scowl. "Why don't you and Amanda stay here and enjoy the rest of this fine wine. It is such a pretty night, Calvin, I think we should take a walk," the lovely Mexican woman announced, gripping the lawman's arm with a no-nonsense tug.

Cal looked at his wife blankly, about to protest that he hadn't had his coffee or his pie, then he glanced at Amanda, who was sitting like a soft pastel flower, and at Harm, who was ten shades of red and about to expire on the spot. And he grinned wide. "Why, I seem to recall liking them walks. If our guests would excuse us for a few minutes . . ."

"An hour," Elena corrected.

"An hour?" He received his wife's glare like the double bores of a shotgun. "Right. An hour." And he managed not to do his grumbling until they were outside under the stars.

Amanda rose from her chair, feeling suddenly nervous at the obvious abandonment. She started to pick up her plates, then gave a soft gasp because Harm appeared beside her before she was aware he'd moved. She opened her mouth to speak and his was covering it, hungrily, hurriedly, without so much as a by your leave. Her palms pushed at his shoulders and finally he relented, stepping back but not letting go. His fingers started shakily down the row of buttons on the front of her gown.

"We've only got an hour," he panted, then he looked up in surprise when she pushed his hands away. She ducked under his arm and he waited, puzzled.

"Well then, we'd better get right to it, hadn't we?" she drawled. "You clear off a spot and we'll do it right there on the table linens."

"All right." He started frantically moving dishes.

"Harmon! I wasn't serious."

"I am."

She scowled at him and walked away. It took him a minute to catch onto her anger and then he didn't understand it. He trailed after her, trembling with impatience. When she stopped in the hall, he bumped up behind her, his face nuzzling against the nape of her neck where her hair was caught up in a comb.

"You smell nice. Do you smell this good all over?"

"Yes," was her inflammatory answer. He groaned at the thought of it. He started licking along the side of her neck, but she twisted away and began walking. Toward her room.

Good!

He fell in step, practically breaking lather in contrast to her odd calm. His mind was racing furiously for the right things to say. Sweet, sincere things, Cal had told him. "That's a real pretty dress. Let's make love."

Amanda jerked up short and glared at him. He immediately started kissing her . . . or trying to at least. She swiveled her face away and he ended up gasping against her temple.

"Amanda . . ."

"Harmon, would you stop. I want to talk to you."

"Talk? Can we talk after?" His hands were all over her, stroking her hair, massaging the curve of her bosom, heading for those tiny buttons again. She wiggled out of his clumsy embrace and he was ready to die. "Amanda, please!" Begging was good, Cal had told him. He had no more pride to worry about. She'd stripped it from him with her coy refusal. He couldn't stand it.

"Harmon, what are you doing on your knees? Get up." She looked more flustered than pleased. Maybe he wasn't doing it right.

"Let's get married right now, then I'll get us a room."

"What? You want to marry me so you can sleep with me, is that it?"

Sincerity. He looked up from the ignominious position at her feet and said a breathless, "Yes."

"Oh!" She stormed down the hall and slammed the door to her room. He stared at it for a long moment, then got up and went to tap on it.

"Ammy?" There was no sound of movement on the other side. He leaned against the wood, trying to guess what she was doing. Then she jerked it open and he almost fell in on top of her.

381

"I sent for your money, Harmon."

"What?" He straightened and took a semi-dignified stance that didn't involve groping or drooling on her.

"It should be here in a couple of days."

Then it struck him. His money for a job well done. He stood very still, heart pounding anxiously. "Good. Did you give the jewelry to Cal?"

"No, because he'd have to give it to McAllister. I want it to go back to New York so Randy's name can be cleared of any wrongdoing."

Asking was like swallowing fire. "Are you taking them back to New York?" Oh, God, she was going to leave him! Panic ran wild inside him. He'd never thought . . . somehow, he'd never taken it to this point, the point where she'd actually pay him and go. Just like that. He couldn't breathe. His frantic thoughts thickened up around one anguished idea: *How am I going to live without her?* "How long would you be gone? When would you get back?"

She was looking up at him with an odd intensity. She spoke softly, slowly. "If I go back, my guardians will grab on to me and throw away the key. I'm under age, Harmon, in their control, whether I like it or not. I've have no legal rights. They would never let me leave. I couldn't come back."

"Unless you were married to me."

"Yes." She still didn't sound too thrilled and he was getting desperate.

"God, Ammy, what do I have to do? You're making me crazy! I've crawled and begged and reasoned . . . you said you love me!"

"But you haven't said it."

Her quiet statement hardly fazed him.

"If I didn't love you, would I be making such a damned

fool out of myself? I love you so much I'm ready to strangle you!"

She drew a rattly breath and let it out. "Oh, Harmon!" And she was in his arms, sucking the sense from him with her kisses. He stood there like a steer struck stupid by lightning. "Oh, Harm, why didn't you say so?"

"Say what?"

"That you love me."

"Is that all you wanted to hear? I could have told you that right after we got snake bit. Was it that simple? After I did all that humiliating stuff?"

"Who told you to do that?" She was smiling at him, touching his face, nibbling his lower lip.

"Calvin. He said I should . . . He made a real fool outta me." Hot color flamed in his face and he ground his teeth with embarrassment, not knowing how he was ever going to look her in the eye again. Or face Cal's ribbing. Until she took all the mortification away with one sentiment.

"I thought you were sweet."

And he melted on the spot. "I love you, Ammy. And I need you. And right now I want you so bad I'm fixing to pop."

"Oh, we can't have that, now, can we?" She was all tender sympathy. Her clever hands were at the band of his jeans and the buttons on his shirt, stripping him down to sleek, brown skin while she was still all pampered lace and satin. The slippery slide of fabric teasing against him made him groan.

"How many buttons are on this dress?" he moaned.

"Too many."

His hands roamed restlessly over the fragile silk. "It's so pretty. I don't want to tear it off you." But he was reaching for his knife. Just one quick slit up the seam . . .

"We'll just leave it on," she panted against his mouth. "This time."

He was pushing her back toward the bed, kissing her wildly, deeply, passionately, murmuring, "I don't want to get it all wrinkled up."

"Then let's not." She turned so that he sat on the bed and then urged him up to lean back against the headboard. With yards and yards of pretty silk carefully gathered up above shapely knees, she settled over his lap, settled atop his painfully eager arousal and eased down.

He snatched a gulping breath and let it out shakily. She sighed with a wicked degree of contentment.

"You can start on those buttons now, Harmon."

And she began to move.

Later, when she was tucked in all naked and lazy beneath the covers, Harm pulled out the satchel. He sat close beside her as they went through her brother's intimate belongings. He kissed away her tears as they gathered along the fringe of her lashes, whispering of how much he loved her. And that took some of the hurt away.

Then they came to the jewels. Displayed in a three-tiered case, they took the breath away. Dazzling emeralds. Fiery rubies. Brilliant diamonds. Harm lifted one of the heavy strands and settled it about Amanda's neck. Then another. And another. Until she was draped in a fortune of gems. Then he held her face in the cradle of his hands to study her.

"You look more beautiful now than that first day I saw you. I love you, Amanda. Would you marry me and be my wife?"

Would she marry him?

She looked up at him, at the man who was so much more than legend. At the man who would give his life for her, who would trust the frailty of his soul to her, who would share his love and future with her. The past pain of not belonging fell away at his soft request. The loneliness of a lifetime disappeared. She saw Rebecca sitting on the arm of Will's chair, saw the way their gazes met and mingled in intimate communion. She imagined her and Harmon on their own porch, watching over their own children. And what lay ahead was her every dream.

Would she be his wife?

"Oh, yes."

When their hour was up, they were both decently clad and seated close but not touching on the front porch swing. Cal and Elena weren't too prompt in returning, and when they did, they looked a bit flushed themselves.

"Well?" Calvin demanded as he perched on the bottom step.

"Well, what?" Harm replied.

"Well, did you take my advice?" He canted a meaningful glance at Amanda.

"You mean, did I take all your sage wisdom to heart?"

Amanda reached out to run the back of her forefinger down Harm's swarthy cheek. "It was the poetry that did the trick, Calvin. A woman can't resist a man who recites poetry. Why, I never would have guessed you were such a romantic. When Harmon told me you wrote all those beautiful, flowery verses for Elena, why, I just thought she was the luckiest woman alive. I just love hearing my eyes likened to a starlit sky. Don't you, Elena?"

"I would not know." Black eyes cut to her husband. "Calvin has never written me poetry."

Cal met her furious glare in a panic. "Elena, I've never written a line of rhyming in my life. I swear! Harmon, tell her you're just funning."

Harm leaned back in the swing and smiled. "Could be you ought to practice some of your own advice there, Cal. You might start by doing a little crawling. Only hurts the pride for a minute."

Elena was prodding him, spewing out an angry spate of Spanish, and Calvin looked sorely aggrieved. "Harm, you got no sense of humor."

"I got a helluva sense of humor, Cal. G'night."

Elena stalked into the house, letting the door bang behind her. Calvin winced, thinking of how hard those floorboards were going to feel under his knees.

"Oh, and Cal . . . she said yes."

Try as Amanda would to convince him to stay, Harm refused to spend the night with her under his friend's roof. It was hard to settle down in the big bed alone, especially when the sheets were already more than a little rumpled from their passing passion. Mrs. Harmon Bass. Amanda smiled to herself and closed her eyes. She would ship the jewelry to New York. There was no way she was ever leaving West Texas. And when Randy's employers informed Judge McAllister that his merchandise had been returned, there would be no more looking over their shoulders for the shadow of Tyrell Cates. She hoped. That was one nightmare that would take a long time to go away, but if Harm could learn to sleep nights, so could she. As long as he was with her.

But she did sleep and soundly, for when she woke up she was surprised to find a message left upon her pillow. It was an odd one. It was a copy of *Harmon Bass and the Border Shift*. And it was signed. She smiled as she read the inscription.

Just so you don't forget what a hero I really am. I love you, Ammy. Be back soon. Harmon

And she continued to smile all day. It wasn't until darkness fell and he hadn't returned that she began to worry. Be back soon, he'd said. She tried to hold on to that with confidence. But inside, she began to panic.

It wasn't until Deputy Lon Pager from Perdition arrived with a writ for Cal's prisoner's release that she began to feel dread.

Where had Harmon gone? And why wasn't he back?

Chapter Twenty-Three

There was no way he was going to sleep. Just knowing his bride-to-be was curled up at Cal Lowe's was enough to put him on a restless edge. If he couldn't be curled up beside her, he wanted to be moving, to be doing something, anything, to fill the hours until they could be together again. Until they could be married and he wouldn't have to leave her side. Suddenly, he knew what he had to do, something he'd put off for long enough. Something he had to attend to now that he was going to take a wife.

He needed a last name.

Rebecca knew what it was. Or at least he always suspected she did. It had never mattered to him that much. When he was young, he didn't care. When he was older, Bass became comfortable. But the thought of having children of his own made him think of the man who fathered him. He felt like Jack, wondering, not knowing. Only in Jack's case, it was better not to know.

What was his own father like? What kind of man seeded a son and never watched him grow? What kind of man left the fate of his boy to strangers after the woman who bore him died? He never thought about it much, because looking back meant looking at everything that was past and that had been too terrible. Now, he could remember selectively without fearing all that would come crushing in. And as he thought about stirring life inside Amanda, he wondered about the man who'd lain with his mother to conceive him. To know what kind of father he'd be, he wanted to know what kind of father his was.

So he left Amanda a scrawled note, relying upon all his discipline to leave her once he saw her slumbering sweetly in the sheets they'd shared. And he rode into the darkness, not needing more than the stars and the moon to guide him because he was going home. To hear the truth.

Something was wrong. He knew it the second he saw the place. Harm drew up his horse and sat, studying the situation. He felt the short hairs crawl against the back of his neck. It was little things. Like half Becky's wash hanging. The barn door not open, not closed, but ajar. No kids in the yard. No sound of chores being done. And then came the sound that broke a sweat of terror.

"Good morning, Mr. Bass. Ride on in and have some coffee."

Then Tyrell Cates stepped out onto his family's porch holding Sarah in his arms, and Harm's world collapsed.

He sat for a minute, unable to move, shock shaking him so hard his breathing rattled. Crazy things tore through his mind, blind, brave, foolish notions, like rushing down with his gun drawn, blasting senselessly at any target that presented itself. But he knew who the targets would be. So, very slowly, with his hands spread wide and empty, he nudged his horse forward to carry him down into the yard of the Bass ranch.

They swarmed him, yanking him off the saddle, liberating his weapons. He let himself be manhandled. It didn't matter. His eyes were on the strong hand stroking a little girl's black curls. He strode forward, not glancing at the men who looked quickly to Cates for direction. The sheriff calmly motioned for them to let him come. Harm marched up to the steps and reached for Sarah. His face was emotionless. His eyes were lethal silver. Cates let her go.

With the warm little figure wound about his neck, Harm hugged hard. He didn't try to pretend anything. This was his family. No bluffs would work here. They had him by the frantically beating heart and they knew it.

"Uncle Harmon—"

"Shhh, *shijii.*"

"They hurt Daddy."

His mind went numb. *Yusn.* In front of the children. Dear God! He climbed the steps, brushing by Cates without looking at him, terrified of what he'd find inside but having to go in. He froze in the threshold. Several of McAllister's men lounged at the table, their dirty spurs gouging holes in the starched white linen. They looked up at him through eyes as dead and deadly as those who'd spent three days at a small ranch fourteen years ago; flat, unfeeling eyes of men who could torture and murder a woman and her children without a second of remorse. His insides began a terrible shivering.

"Uncle Harmon!"

He felt the impact of Sidney's hurtling body against his hip and he hugged the boy with his free arm. His eyes were on his sister. She was kneeling beside a big, inert form. Blood was pooling on the floorboards. Her eyes reached for his. They were dark and glassy but there were no tears. She stood slowly.

"Becky?" He asked everything with that question. *Are*

you all right? What happened? Is Will alive? Dear God, what have I done?

"Harmon." *I'm all right. Will's bad. Harmon, help us.*

Carefully, he set down his niece and gently kissed the top of her head. "Go to your mama, the both of you." They scampered to obey, clinging silently to Rebecca's skirts, big, frightened eyes tearing at the sight of their father's motionless shape.

With a sudden move, Harm grabbed one of the cowboys's ankles and flung his legs to the side. "Get your feet off the table." Then he stalked back onto the porch, where Tyrell Cates was waiting.

He was leaning on the porch rail, puffing one of his cigarillos. He smiled and waved a soft-bound book. *Harmon Bass and the Texas Twister.* "Everything I needed to know about you and your family right here in black and white. Including where to find them." He took Harm in with a lazy sweeping gaze. "Wasn't expecting you quite so soon. Sent my deputy into Terlingua to fetch you, but here you are. Thought we'd have time for a little fun while we waited, but I guess not. We'll have our fun later, just you and me."

"What do you want?" Harm snapped.

"You."

"Here I am. Let them go."

Cates chuckled softly. " 'Fraid not. See, that's what I want. My boss . . . he wants a little bit more. He wants his property back. And he wants you and your gal friend to bring it out to his ranch tomorrow."

"And you'll let them go?"

"Sure." He grinned, puckering the marks Harm had carved into his face, one old and weathered, one new and raw. "Hell, while you're there, you and your daddy can have a reunion. Kinda touching, don't you think? Father and son reunited. Not every day a man gets to meet up with the boy he ordered killed. Bet you'll have lots to say to each other."

Sickness swamped him. McAllister. McAllister was his father. "He knows who I am?" he asked faintly.

"Mr. Bass, you might say he don't give a damn. He'd stab his own mother if there was profit in it. Or rather, he'd have me do it. And you know me. Wouldn't bother me a-tall."

Then his cold ice-blue stare was distracted by the sight of Jack leading a whimpering Jeffrey up from the privy.

"Handsome boy."

Harm's belly turned to ground glass.

"Maybe I oughta take him with me. You know, kinda a father and son reunion of our own. Could be the boy'd learn a thing or two from his old man." He laughed, but Harm wouldn't be baited from his stoic stance.

"Uncle Harm," Jack said quietly, coming up to stand beside him on the porch. "Go on in to Mama, Jeffrey." He gave the child a push, then looked up at his uncle. His stare was worried but controlled. "What do they want?"

Harm cupped his hand behind the boy's head, rumpling the dark auburn hair. "I'm getting it for them, son. You take care of your mama and the kids till I come for you. Keep a level head."

"Yessir."

"What happened to Will?" he asked in a lower tone.

The boy's chin quivered, then firmed resolutely. "He wouldn't let them push him around. They shot him, Uncle Harm." A horrified dampness welled up and was quickly blinked away.

Damn Will and his heroics. Only a fool would challenge such odds. A brave fool. "Don't you give them any cause to be doing the same to you. Hear? A dead hero's just that, dead. Keep yourself and your family alive. Do whatever it takes."

"Yessir."

"You go on inside, too."

He started to nod, then with a great hitching sound, Jack was burrowed into Harm's chest, hanging on tight. "Don't let them kill you, Uncle Harmon."

"I'll do my best."

Then Jack broke away and strode into the house, with head high and shoulders squared.

Cates was smiling at him, a thin, sneering smile that ranked everything he held dear as contemptible. "Fine boy. Makes a man proud."

"You're no man. You for whom the demons copulated." That quiet Apache curse drained all the false good nature from Tyrell Cates's face. What remained was hard and ugly.

"I'm going to enjoy killing you, Bass. But first, I'm going to give your sister and that sweet little girl to my men. And I'm going to hang you up on the wall by the skin and do all those things I did when you were just a little runty kid to that pretty lady of yours while you watch. Remember what it was like watching? Only I don't think she's going to survive it like you did. What do you think?"

He made the mistake of coming close to gloat. They were eyeball to eyeball in willful challenge. Then in less than a heartbeat, Harm's hands shot up to lock around the other's throat, crushing with rending strength while Cates twisted and gurgled for air. The butt of a rifle slammed into the side of his head. Fingers slackened, and Cates rubbed the abraded flesh of his neck as Harm spilled down the steps into the dusty yard.

"Oh, yeah, Mr. Bass. I'm going to enjoy killing you."

* * *

393

Pain moved fluidly in ebbs and floods. He rode with it, letting it pull and push him back and forth across the boundaries of consciousness until he found the strength to stand firm against it. He was breathing in dirt and the thick scent of blood. His head ached massively. It was hard not to ball up in a knot of misery there on the ground and just whimper in defeat. Thoughts flowed back slowly, lapping against his awareness, teasing, vague. Then all at once, it rushed over him and he moaned mightily, knowing they were already gone. Knowing he might never see them again. Was there a reason to move?

Will.

Harm dragged himself up to hands and knees, letting his head hang low as blood banged between his temples. He thought of his sister's husband, his friend, the only father figure he'd ever known, and he wanted to cry in Apache fashion and chop off his hair. Grief was worse than pain. He'd have to bathe the body and see to its burial. He'd have to burn his own clothes and purify his body in sage smoke. He was thinking these things as he crawled up the steps and hauled himself to his feet. He wouldn't think about Becky and the children yet. He wasn't strong enough. He would see to the dead, then go about matters of the living.

He was weeping unashamedly. Mourning severed all need for control. Weak with emotion, he wobbled into the house, unable to see much beyond the watery shapes around him. He crossed to where Will Bass was stretched out on the floor and went down to his knees with a wail.

"Oh, Will, I'm sorry. I didn't mean to bring such trouble to your door. I'll take care of them for you, I swear." And he leaned forward dizzily to rest his head against the broad chest. Then he jerked upright. There was no chill, no rigidity of death. Harm slashed his sleeve across his eyes.

"Will?"

He put his hand to one side of the thick neck. Then he was up on his feet, running from the house down to the barn to hitch up the buckboard.

Will Bass wasn't dead.

"I didn't have no choice, Harm."

Cal kept an anxious eye on the too-quiet man staring into the empty cell. Feeling more wretched by the second, he muttered on.

"Pager had all the right papers. I had no legal means to protest. Lon . . . he may be kind of a skunk, but he is a lawman, more so than Cates. I hate to say it, but son, you should have blown Franks to hell when you had the chance."

"It's not your fault, Calvin." Harm turned away from the taunting sight of the open barred door. His voice was flat, deadened. "I need a couple of big guns, some hand pieces, all the rounds you can spare."

"Anything you want, Harmon, but you talk to me first."

"Got nothing to say."

Calvin gripped one tense arm. "You brought in a good friend of mine breathing on a prayer. You think I'm just going to let you walk on outta here with your jaws gripped shut? Think again."

"This has got nothing to do with you."

"The hell you say. I ain't talking to you as the law. I'm speaking as a friend, to you and Will. What is going on?"

"Stay out," he growled, pulling beneath the curl of his hand.

"No. You listen to me. Harm, listen! I ain't one for messing in nobody's business. I been letting you come and go for years without saying so much as boo to your doings, even after I heard some things I probably shouldn't have let slide by. You're tough and you're smart and you can get by on your own. You've proved that. But there comes a time when things get bigger than a man can stand off on his own. I'm guessing that time is now. You go on outta here and blast a bunch of folks to kingdom come, and I'm gonna come looking for you, Harmon, as the law. Since I don't think you'd ever shoot me down, someday I'll catch up to you. I don't want to go chasing you all over Texas and you don't want to run. You got yourself a fine little woman, a good family, and damn good friends. Don't do this thing on your own."

"You done?"

"I guess."

"Is Amanda still at your place?"

"Waiting on you."

"I guess there is something you can do for me, then, before I go over to see her."

"Best clean yourself up first or you're like to scare the wits outta her. Hold still." He dabbed his kerchief at the gore dripping from beneath his hairline. Harm didn't flinch. "Now, what can I do?"

"Ammy?"

Amanda heard the soft call of her name and woke with a cry of relief. "Oh, Harmon! Where have you been?" She sat up and in one move was in his arms, hugging him fiercely even as he settled on the edge of the bed. She kissed his neck, his cheek, and finally his mouth, lingering there until she had her fill of the taste of him. "I've been worried."

"I'm here. Just like I promised."

She couldn't see him in the darkness of the room, but he felt good and solid to the touch. "I thought maybe you'd gotten second thoughts."

"About what?"

"Making me Mrs. Bass."

"No. Come with me." He caught her wrist and started towing her out from under the warm covers. She pulled back.

"No, you come in here with me."

"Later. There's something that needs doing first."

She was padding on bare feet beside him as he opened the bedroom door and strode out into the well-lit hall. "Harmon! I'm in my nightclothes!"

"You look beautiful."

That mollified her for a moment. Until she realized he was taking her right into the front room where Calvin, a sleepy-eyed Elena, and a stranger were waiting. She gave a squeak of protest but his arm was around her waist, melding her into his side. When he dropped down onto his knees before the grumpy-looking visitor, Amanda had no choice but to join him there. The stranger began to speak.

"We're gathered here at this unholy hour in the sight of God, these witnesses, and the eyes of Texas to join this man and woman in matrimony."

"What?"

Harm squeezed the rest right out of her lungs.

The pastor yawned and intoned, "You, Amanda Duncan, take this here feller Harmon Bass as your lawful wedded husband?"

"Say yes," Harm hissed at her.

"Yes," Amanda breathed.

"Harm Bass, you take Amanda Duncan for your lawful wife?"

397

"I do."

"Anybody object?" Cal sat back grinning and Elena was all dewy-eyed. "Good. By the power vested in me by the Almighty and the great state of Texas, you're man and wife. Now, sign this and let's all get back to bed."

Amanda stared as Harm affixed his signature and passed her the document. It was dated and already signed by Cal and Elena. Her hand shook so badly her own name was almost illegible.

"G'night, all," the clergyman mumbled, blowing on the fresh signatures before folding the paper away. "See you on Sunday, Calvin, Mrs. Lowe."

"See you out, Reverend Baines. Gots me someplace to go tonight." Cal gave his wife a quick kiss and ambled, with his arm firmly about her waist, out after the preacher.

Harm leaned forward, brushing his mouth over Amanda's slack lips, whispering against them, "I love you, Ammy."

"Oh! Oh, Harmon!" She gave a wild sob of delight and was kissing him all over the face, finally finding and fastening to his lips with a frantic haste. When she eased back for air, her cheeks were wet with happy tears. Then she gasped. "Oh, Harm, you're bleeding!"

"Let's go to bed, Mrs. Bass."

And she forgot all about everything.

Harm stared up into the blackness with Amanda cuddled into his side. He was petting her hair and pressing occasional kisses to her brow as she sighed and murmured blissfully. He refused to think of anything beyond this moment, when his life held the illusion of being perfect. Suddenly, she began to chuckle.

"What?"

"Do I tell our grandchildren that the groom had a concussion and the bride wore a stylish nightgown?"

"I'll leave that up to you," he answered quietly.

"At least I don't have to explain to my new husband how I came by a pattern of buckshot in my behind."

"Or who doctored it."

"I can't believe we're married."

"Regrets?"

"Not a one. Except that your family couldn't be here."

"There was nothing I could do about that, *shijii*."

"I never thought to ask where we were going to live or—"

"Later, Ammy. We'll discuss all of that later. I just want to hold you and make love to you all night." A desperate desire began to stir again and he felt no need to suppress it. Not when the lady was his wife. His wife. Emotions plugged his chest up solid.

"Oooo! That's fine with me." She put up her arms and coaxed him down for a long, passion-drenched kiss.

"Are the jewels someplace safe?" he asked as he nibbled down her neck to the sensitive skin of her collarbone.

She clutched at his dark head, arching up. "Under the bed. I don't think we have to worry about anyone stealing them out from under our noses, do we?"

"No." And he rolled up over her, pushing her slender form down into the mattress with his weight, pushing his strength inside her. He let the hot sensations engulf him before saying gruffly, "Take what I give you and make a child, Amanda."

"A son?"

"A daughter. To carry on your family line. A beautiful girl like you. Someone for you to love."

"Then give me lots to work with, Harmon."

And for the remaining hours of the night, he did the best he could.

The whisper of his lips over hers woke her. She lay very still, pretending sleep. Something was wrong. She didn't know what, but she knew Harm.

He'd been awake all night. Not once, even after their many glorious couplings, had that alertness faded. He was as tense as a fence line. He made love to her as if there would be no tomorrow, and that got her thinking that perhaps he believed it. He didn't act like a man who'd just gotten wedded for a lifetime. He acted like the condemned living out his last requests. And Amanda was scared to death by his silence.

Where had he been? He never said. And where was he sneaking off to at this early hour right from the warmth of her arms? Was he planning to go after the killer freed from Cal's jail? Or was he going after Cates himself? She lay quiet, not needing to open her eyes to know what he was doing. She was familiar with the sounds. She heard him shinny into his snug denims and the soft sucking sounds of his feet settling into his boots. The splash of water and rasp of a towel on damp skin. The sigh of his cotton shirt. Then something odd. She heard him kneel and felt the bump of his shoulders against the bed frame as he reached beneath it. For the jewels.

What on earth?

She kept her breathing regulated. She could feel the caress of his gaze the way she'd felt the caress of his hands. His sigh was heavy, laced with a ragged regret. And he left. No note. No words. No goodbye.

She let him get as far as the front porch.

"Why, Harmon?"

If it wasn't already obvious that he was sneaking off with the fortune in precious gems, his expression condemned him completely as he turned to face her in the doorway, where she stood wrapped in their bed quilt. Guilt, dread, terrible anguish, all battled for prominence, but it was his stoic reserve that finally settled.

"I didn't think you would give them to me if I asked."

Her world caved in upon that single flat statement. Betrayal and horrible hurt blunted reason. She couldn't think. She could only feel. Harmon, the man she trusted, the man she loved. He was no better than any of those before him who pretended to care. Who coveted her wealth. She had never mattered to any of them. The agony of a lifetime of neglect and barren affection was too much to bear with any grace.

"Is the money that important to you?" Her voice thickened with misery. Maybe he didn't understand. Maybe she hadn't made it plain that he now owned her vast inheritance. And she hated it, hated that she would have to bribe him with cash, not the wealth of her love, into staying with her. "I would have given you everything I had. And I'm worth considerably more than what you're carrying."

"Yes," he agreed huskily. "Yes, you are."

"Why did you marry me, Harmon?" The words pulsed with fragile agony.

He could see she was the one who didn't understand. It was torturing him to do this, to walk away from everything he so desperately wanted in order to save those he so dearly loved. But how could he explain without telling her all? He stood there, looking at her through impassive eyes, with his hands full of stolen jewels, expecting her to believe him when he said, "Because I love you and it was the only thing I could give you."

"What? The name Bass? It's not even your name."

He winced at that but his composure didn't falter. "Because it's a married name. A legally wedded name. And I thought if I couldn't give you my love for the rest of your life, at least I could give you the choice to live the life you wanted." When her brow puckered, he simplified it. "They can't make you go back to New York now. Your future is your own. No one can control it. No one can hurt you with their disregard."

"No one but you."

His expression never altered. He reached deep down into his Apache soul to dredge up the courage it took to say, "I'm sorry. I have to go." And he turned away.

Amanda clutched the blanket tighter and she stepped out onto the porch. Panic threatened but clear thought finally prevailed. This was the man who'd made love to her all night, the man who'd given her his name. Would he steal from her? Would he just walk away? Her insecurities faded. No. Even if that's what he would have her think. "I don't believe you, Harmon." He drew up short and looked back at her. She began to frown. "This has nothing to do with money, does it?"

He said nothing.

"Harmon Bass, what are you involved in? You tell me and you tell me now!"

"I love you, Amanda. I would never risk you. Not for anything. Not for anyone."

She looked at the satchel. She looked up into the weary blue of his eyes. And she knew. "It's McAllister. You're taking it to him. Why, Harmon?"

"Amanda, please."

"Why?"

"Because he has Becky and the children."

"Oh . . . my God."

"Cates has them. He's going to kill them unless I bring

402

them the jewels. Now do you understand?" His words were harsh, unnecessarily cruel in his upset.

"Yes," came a strained little whisper. "I understand that you stole them because you thought I would value my dead brother's reputation above the lives of your family. Is that what you thought? Is it? Well, you go ahead and take them. And don't you come back. Do you hear? Don't you come back."

She turned, blinded by tears, blundering against the door in her haste to escape him. But his hands were on her arms, his mouth warm and tender against her cheek. She struggled, beginning to sob softly.

"Ammy, don't cry. I didn't mean to hurt you. I love you."

She glared up at him through shimmering eyes. "They're my family, too, Harm. I love them, too. And I would do anything for them. Randy is dead. Nothing will ever, ever bring him back, but they're alive. Do you think I care what a bunch of people I don't like think about my brother? Over saving the lives of people I love? How could you not trust me?"

"I do, Ammy. I do." Now. And forever.

She let him enfold her in his arms, hugging her close in a body-fusing embrace.

"They have my sister and her family," he said hoarsely. "If they had you, too, I couldn't stand it. I couldn't. You're mine, Ammy. Mine. I couldn't risk you. Please try to understand that. I was afraid if you knew where I was going, you would want to go, too and—"

"And you're not planning to come back, are you, Harmon?"

She lifted her head up off his chest. Her huge dark eyes demanded the truth.

"They're not going to let me live, Amanda."

He said that so matter-of-factly, it took a moment for the shock to sink in. She started shaking, terribly. "And you think they'll let Becky and the kids go?"

"No, I don't."

"Oh, Harm."

His hands rubbed over her damp cheeks, fingers spearing back into her loose golden hair. "That's why you have to be safe. You and our baby, if we're lucky enough to have started one. Will's over at the undertakers—oh, oh, *shijii*, no. I didn't mean that he's dead. He's been shot and he's being cared for there. I need to know that somebody I love is going to survive this."

Her hands clasped over his. Her stare intensified. "We all will, Harm. They are not going to do this to us. I—I just won't stand for it! I just got married! I'm not going to be a widow in less than a day!"

He smiled faintly at her vehemence and he kissed her with a soul-sapping tenderness. "Ammy, if anyone could give them hell, it would be you."

"Then let's give them hell, Harmon."

He'd meant to keep her distanced, to keep her safe, but Amanda . . . well, she was Amanda—bullheaded, big-hearted, not always sound-thinking. And she was also right. They were her family now. She had a voice in their well-being. After spending the night drowning in bliss and tortured by grief in the arms of the woman he loved, for the first time, he felt less alone as she regarded him with those passionate brown eyes. Not that she could actually do anything, but it relieved the burden of isolation from around his heart knowing that she cared. More than anything at that moment, he wished he had a lifetime to give her.

"Calvin has a plan, but the timing is going to be dangerously close." He confided this while stroking the tumble of her hair. He loved her hair loose and thick like sunlight in rich wheat. He wanted to lose himself in its softness, in its womanly scent, instead of riding out to meet such ugliness. He hoped she knew how much he loved her. All he could give her were words and a borrowed name. Enough. He had work to do. He had to pull away, and he used the blunt facts to shatter the tenderness of the moment. "I have to keep Cates and McAllister busy while he gets Becky loose. Then I'm going to kill them both."

Keep them busy. Amanda shuddered. She knew how Tyrell Cates would occupy himself if he got ahold of Harm. "You plan to ride in there with the jewels and think they won't just shoot you down?"

"There really isn't much of an option."

Her mind rebelled against that stiff logic. Her heart decried it. She would not just give him up to slaughter. Not after going through such hell to have him! From desperation came a cool cleverness. "Yes, there is. Remember what you said the last time we were there? With me on the inside and you on the outside, there would be a chance. I'm willing to take that chance. I'll take the jewels in."

"No!"

"Harmon—"

"Cates is in there and he has plans you don't want to know about. Ammy, this is not one of your book adventures. It may not work. If Calvin isn't on time, they just might kill us all. And if Cates touches you—"

"I'm not afraid of him."

He saw through her bravado. And he loved her fiercely for it. That she would do this, that she would risk so much for him and those he loved, humbled him. She had so much courage. So little sense. "Liar."

"Harmon, we have no choice. If I go in, you can protect me. If you go in, are you going to trust my marksmanship to rescue you?"

How he hated it when she was right!

Chapter Twenty-Four

Amanda rode slowly up to the adobe walls of the McAllister fortress. It was harder to be brave when alone. Her knees trembled against saddle leather as her gaze scanned the high surroundings. How was Harmon going to get in unnoticed? Past the guards, to where they were holding his family hostage? But then, he was *The* Harmon Bass and nothing was impossible. She would believe that. She had no choice. It was too late for doubts as the iron gates swung open to what could prove to be the bowels of hell.

No one approached her horse. A half-dozen well-armed men walked in escort as she rode up to the shady patio, where waters played musically in the small artificial pools. And there, lounging in the shadows like a deadly cold-blooded viper, sat Tyrell Cates. He got up from his chair and stood with a lethal grace, smiling even as his eyes scanned the yard and circling walls.

"Well, well. How nice to see you again, ma'am. And where might our quick-witted little friend be? I can't believe he'd let you waltz in here on your lonesome."

"I have what you want. You don't need to concern yourself with Harmon. Not yet," she added with a tight smile of her own. She reined in Fandango, fighting to sit tall and steady when Cates took the reins. He never took his cold, mesmerizing gaze from her as he yelled to his men.

"Look sharp. Bass is out there someplace and I want him. Bring him to me alive or I'll have your livers for lunch."

Then he reached up his hand in a gallant gesture, which Amanda ignored. She swung down, right into the circle of his arms. Terror shimmied up her spine as she felt his warm breath against the back of her neck and his big hands settle on her waist. She spun toward him, lunging back against Fandango.

"Don't touch me."

He smiled lazily. "Why, Miss Amanda, you'd best get used to it."

"It's Bass. Mrs. Bass." Saying the words gave her strength. She shoved his hands away but he didn't step back from his too-personal stance.

"Is that so? Married you, did he? I envy the man the bedding, but I pity him for putting up with the talking. Well, let me congratulate you, Mrs. Bass, on your nuptials and very short honeymoon. I'm sure you won't be too disappointed if I have to take over for him in that area."

Her gaze raked him from head to toe and back. "Disappointed? After being with Harmon Bass, you could only be considered a cruel joke."

His smile didn't falter. Only the increasing narrowing of his eyes betrayed his anger. "We'll see, won't we? Until then, let me be the first to kiss the bride."

He leaned down, aiming for her mouth, and his eyes sprang open when cold gunmetal clanked against his teeth.

"I don't think so, Sheriff."

He looked, without a trace of alarm, at the gun she held in both hands. But he did move back. Amanda took a shaky breath. He was scaring her into talking too much. That had to stop.

"I didn't come here to chat with you. I want to see Judge McAllister."

"Why, yes, ma'am, Mrs. Bass. Or should I be calling you Mrs. McAllister? Oh, didn't your husband mention that to you? I'm taking you to see your father-in-law. So show a little respect."

Surprise made her guard drop and Cates was quick to take the advantage. The pistol was wrenched from her and his hand curled with painful authority about her upper arm.

"Let's not keep Daddy waiting," he drawled, tugging her forward.

Harm hadn't told her. A terrible pain filled her breast when she thought what that knowledge must have done to him. Rebecca had been right. He was better off not knowing.

Amanda walked beside McAllister's man with as much dignity as she could muster. It was up to Harm now. She wasn't clever enough to hold her own against the shrewdly dangerous Cates. She didn't have to. All she had to do was stall for time.

The inside of the ranchero was deliciously cool after the baking West Texas sun. Their boot heels echoed on the floor tiles as they approached heavy double doors. Cates tapped once.

"Judge, got you a visitor."

He swung open the door and gave Amanda a propelling push. She marched to the massive desk without hesitation, waiting for the large high-backed chair to turn toward her. It was then she found herself confronted by a strong-featured man with Harmon's blue eyes. This was the man who had fathered him and ordered him killed. And she hated him for his wealth and his power and his heartlessness. He looked bored with her and coolly impatient.

"You have something for me?"

"She wasn't carrying anything, Judge."

"Thank you, Sheriff. Let me handle this. Now, Miss—"

"Mrs. Bass," she corrected.

"Mrs. Bass," he drawled very civilly. "I trust you haven't come all this way to waste my time. I would just as soon avoid any unpleasantness. I'm not exactly sure how you came to be involved in this—"

"My brother died bringing the jewelry from New York," Amanda explained tersely. "And I'm not letting anyone else's blood be spilled over it. You want it, you can have it, but Rebecca Bass and her children go free first. And then I'm walking out of here."

McAllister smiled benignly. "My dear, lovely Mrs. Bass, what on earth makes you think you are in any position to barter? We have them and we have you."

"But you don't have Harmon. And anyone who can read knows Harmon Bass is no one to mess with."

"Where's Bass?" McAllister snapped at Cates.

"My men will find him."

"No, they won't," Amanda stated with an unnerving confidence. "Harm's Apache. He moves like a ghost. You won't see him until he has his knife in your throat. All he wants is his family, untouched."

Cates chuckled. "You expect me to believe that? That a man like Bass is just going to turn his back and walk away, forgive and forget?"

Amanda stared at him. "Oh, no, Sheriff Cates. He's going to kill you. If not today, then someday. Soon. But then, you're not important." She turned away from him as if that was true, and Amanda could feel the heat of his fury. She focused her attention on McAllister, noting his

410

amused smile as he took in his hired man's fuming sense of insult. "I'm here to conclude my brother's business. I have your jewelry. Release the woman and children and I'll hand it over to you."

"I can make her give up the stones, Judge," Cates drawled.

Amanda refused to look at him, though her skin tightened all over. "You would trust him, Judge? When he couldn't even kill a ten-year-old boy for you? If he'd done his job then, you wouldn't have Harmon breathing down your neck now."

"What is she talking about, Cates?"

Amanda glanced over her shoulder. "You didn't tell him?" The glacial blue eyes narrowed with warning. "You didn't tell him that Harmon is his son?"

McAllister leaned back in his chair, not stunned as much as entertained. "So Bass is Leisha's boy."

"He's your son and I'm his wife. Surely that means something, even to a man like you."

"It means I paid my men to do a job and they bungled it. Cates, I trust you'll remedy that."

"Yessir, Judge."

Never had she believed such an inhuman creature could exist. Disgust roiled. Amanda suppressed her need to be violently ill. For just an instant, she considered what a man like McAllister could have made of Harmon Bass. It was frightening. But it gave her an idea.

"Why kill him? Harm could be invaluable to you."

McAllister raised a curious brow. She gushed on eagerly.

"You're his father. Family is everything to him. If you had a man like Harm, with his reputation, working for you, just think."

"I'm thinking, Mrs. Bass. Go on."

"I love my husband but I have no intention of living in

411

some squalid little town like Terlingua. Not when I could live like this. Between us, we could convince him that his future would be best if guided by your hands. Harmon's smart. He's quick, he's fast, he's—"

"Dangerous. Why you listening to this, Judge?"

"Shut up, Cates. You afraid I'm looking to replace you?"

Amanda smiled tightly and let her creativity take over. "Harm wants to take care of his family. If you were to let them go, to show them kindness, even apologize for their inconvenience at the hands of your overzealous bully here, he might be grateful enough to give you a lifetime of loyal service. He loves me. If I were to talk to him, he'd listen. A man like Harmon at your side. Think of it."

McAllister's eyes narrowed thoughtfully and Amanda knew hope. Maybe, just maybe, she could save them all without bloodshed.

"You argue a good point, my dear. Perhaps you should be writing that fiction your husband graces. Well, what do you think, Tyrell? You think a man like Harmon Bass would serve me faithfully?"

Cates grinned. "I think he'd cut out your heart and eat it raw the first time you blinked your eyes around him. I would, if I were in his place."

"I'm sorry, Amanda, dear. But I do have to agree."

"But—"

"Then there's the little matter of him being my son. Bad business, don't you know? You see, I have political ambitions. Those beautiful gems are a gift for a certain senator's daughter in Austin. She's going to be the second Mrs. McAllister. I can't very well propose to her with a half-breed bastard son running loose, now, can I?" He stopped smiling. "Cates, convince her to give me the jewels."

The minute his cruel fingers twisted in her hair,

412

Amanda relented. Harm had made her promise not to be a martyr. She was trying very hard to do exactly as he told her.

"Stop. McAllister, call off your scum."

He waved a well-manicured hand and the sheriff released her with obvious reluctance. Slowly, Amanda loosened the billowy shawl she had draped about her neck and shoulders. Against her throat glistened a fortune in precious stones. McAllister drew a quick breath and watched greedily as she unfastened them and laid them out on his desktop one at a time.

"Beautiful. Just breathtaking. Don't you think so, Tyrell?"

"Oh, yessiree, Judge." His eyes were fastened on the curve of Amanda's breasts.

"You have your merchandise, now let us go."

McAllister laughed. "Are you that naive, my dear? No one's leaving here."

She wouldn't betray the anxiousness those words brought to bear. Instead, she flung out her one cool, balancing threat. "Aren't you forgetting Harmon? Are you going to sleep nights knowing he's out there?"

"No, I'm not. I want Bass now and I want to see him dead today."

"Yessir, Judge." Tyrell leaned close, nuzzling the spill of Amanda's hair. "Mind if I take care of things my way?"

"Just get them done and spare me the details." He was busy examining the glittery stones.

Amanda stiffened as warm fingers stroked her cheek. McAllister had dismissed her and Harmon as if they were nothing, meant nothing. His indifference surrendered them to the villainy of Cates and that terrified her. She clung to her faith in Harm, praying fervently that their plans would unfold as cleanly and predictably as the plot in one of his namesake novels.

"Think your loving husband could watch me lay you down on the ground out there and take my pleasure off you?" Cates purred with a sinister softness.

She met his icy stare with one equally cold. "Yes, he could."

"Maybe. Maybe not. Shall we see? Or you think he might be more motivated to give himself up if we started shooting those sweet little children one at a time."

She didn't move. She wouldn't give him the satisfaction of knowing she was scared to death.

Cates grinned and strode to the door. "Charley, fetch me the woman and kids." Then to a rigid Amanda, "Like a glass of wine while we wait, Mrs. Bass?"

"Yes, please." Anything to delay the inevitable. McAllister seemed to have forgotten them, but she was foremost on Tyrell Cates's mind—she and her husband. Amanda took the glass he extended and was mortified when he had to steady her trembling hand so she could take a sip. He didn't laugh at her display of ungovernable fear. It made him all the more impressed by her bravery.

"Don't look so jumpy, Mrs. Bass. Why, if you were to call your husband in, I might be persuaded to be real nice to you. Could be I'd even keep you for myself. For a while. Long as you didn't do too much talking. I'm not such a bad fella when I want something."

"You only want me because I belong to Harmon." She took the glass in both hands to keep it level, just as her glare was level. She had a sudden insight into Tyrell Cates. He was interested as long as there was a challenge involved. If she showed the slightest weakness, he would kill her. Eventually.

"Now, ma'am, don't go selling yourself off cheap. You got more brass than the boot rail on a saloon bar. And I find that a mighty appealing quality. 'Course, if you ain't

414

interested, there's always the alternative: dying slow and real messy-like next to Bass."

"Of the two, I'd prefer being skinned alongside Harmon."

He chuckled. "Could be you'll be changing your mind."

"Could be Harmon will change your tune."

The doors pushed open and a rather breathless cowboy strode in. "They're gone, Sheriff."

"Who is gone?"

"That woman and the kids. Guards had their throats opened ear to ear. Never heard nothing."

"Bass."

"Harmon."

And then all hell broke loose.

He went over the wall in that same shadowed spot he'd noticed during their captivity, touching down without a whisper in his hard-soled moccasins. He was across the open yard like a cloud skimming the midday sun. McAllister's sentries were looking outward, preparing for a massive show of force, not within for a single enemy. And that was their fault for not understanding the nature of their foe. Harm had no such illusions. He knew exactly what he was up against. Time.

He grabbed the first man he came to, clamping his jaws shut and jerking him back beside the stables with one smooth move. His knife lined up below the man's bobbing Adam's apple.

"The woman and children, where are they?"

The man shook his head. Harm lowered the blade from his neck to the crotch of his denims.

"Talk to me now or talk in a lot higher voice." At the frantic nodding, he eased his hand away.

"They's in the barn, locked in the tack room."

Harm's system shivered in remembrance. Not an original place, but one that was hard to get in and out of without notice. He applied the hilt of his knife to the man's temple with enough force to turn him to mush and draped the body out along the shadows, lifting his hat, his sidearms, and his rifle. Then he trotted to the edge of the building to assess the activity in the open square. McAllister's men were everywhere, alert but not looking amongst themselves for danger. Boldly, Harm clapped the Stetson on his head and strode from his hiding place, walking casually along the fringe of the square. One of the cowboys led a saddled horse by him. Quickly, he grabbed on to the pommel and let himself drop, drawing his legs up behind the belly of the animal and hanging by the strength of his arms out of sight in an old Apache trick until they passed the barn. Then he let go and faded through the door.

After the noonday brightness of the yard, the barn was black and featureless. He moved by instinct and memory, making no more sound, as he crossed the straw-covered floor, than a dry Texas breeze. There were two men stationed outside the door flipping cards on a bale of straw. He didn't hesitate to take advantage of the seconds afforded by the surprise. Two quick slashes. He killed them. Then he pulled open the door.

He wasn't expecting an attack from within. A figure hurled out of the dim interior and Harm had to sidestep to avoid a collision. He had the man by the hair and his knife to a taut throat before recognizing the slight figure.

"Jack! Easy, boy. It's Harmon."

"Uncle Harm."

A hard embrace, then he pushed away. "Becky, you and the kids all right?"

She flew into his arms, hugging tight, kissing his cheek

and wetting it with her tears. "Oh, Harmon. Thank God."

"Shhh. C'mon. You've got to move fast. Head right for that door and wait."

Jack led the way with his mother behind him. Harm scooped up each child as they left the room, squeezing them and bestowing quick kisses. Then he trotted up to the door, eyes now accustomed to the dark and scanning quickly for anything that could be of use. He gave Becky the rifle and Jack the pistols.

"Becky, Will's alive, or he was when I left him in Terlingua."

Her eyes fluttered shut for a moment of silent thanksgiving.

"And Becky"—she looked up because he sounded suddenly shy—"I married Amanda."

"Harm, that's wonderful." She hugged him swiftly, then was all business. "Let's get out of here and we can celebrate."

"I'm getting you out of here, then I have to get Amanda. She's in there." He nodded toward the house. "Keeping Cates occupied."

Rebecca's hand crushed over his. She didn't need more words to understand the terror in his heart. His wife was inside lulling a serpent from inside its coils, and he couldn't like it much. How could he not be remembering? "What do you want us to do?"

Harmon glanced around, forcing clear, quick thought to supplant his worry. "Becky, drop your skirts and shinny into a pair of one of those fellers's pants. Jack, gimme a hand."

Together, they upended a barrel, spilling out the ration of grain inside. Then Sidney and Jeffrey were wedged down in the hollow cavern.

"It smells in here," Jeffrey whined. "An' I don't got no room to breathe!"

"Hush, now," Harm scolded gently. "I happen to know your Aunt Amanda bought a big bag of hard candy. Less you want it to go to some other little boy who knows when to be quiet, you'll grip your lips tight."

Jeffrey's dark eyes rounded and he nodded, wiggling against the brace of his brother's knees.

"No noise now," Harm warned, and settled the lid.

Rebecca had put on a baggy pair of denims and one of the cowboy's loose jackets. She turned the lapels in to hide the bright splashes of blood on them. Wordlessly, she stuffed her hair up under a hat. She looked grim and competent, like the young girl he'd dragged across a desert. And Harm's heart bobbed up into his throat. She'd gone through too much to let the past snatch it all away.

"Think you and Jack can tote this here cargo over to that far wall?"

"I'm sure we can."

"What about me, Uncle Harm?" Sarah demanded.

"You're coming with me, *shijii*."

And that sounded much better to the little girl than squatting in a barrel like her brothers.

"Go on and be careful." Harm gave his sister another kiss, then sent her and her eldest out into the daylight with their precious cargo. He watched for a second, then smiled down at Sarah. "C'mere, Sarah. Step in here." He pooled an empty grain sack on the floor, then lifted it up around her to tie it over her head. "Now you just lie still like you was a sack of meal."

She giggled softly as Harm hoisted her over his shoulder. When he swatted her squirming bottom, she went appropriately limp. Then he took a deep breath and strolled out into the open. From the corner of his eye, he saw one of the hands leave the house and hurry down to the barn. He didn't alter his stride even as sweat began to roll. Then the cowboy burst out of the door running, and Harm knew in a matter of minutes the whole place would be bristling with danger. *Cal, now would be a good time*, he thought anxiously. He reached the rest of his family, trying not to look apprehensive. He smiled at them encouragingly and avoided Rebecca's intense gaze. She could read him like a map.

They were far from safe. Anyone looking would see them upon close scrutiny. What they needed was a diversion so he could send them over the wall.

A rifle report and a loud shriek heralded the arrival of Calvin Lowe and the dozen Texas Rangers riding with him; there wasn't an available man who wouldn't saddle up for Will and Harmon Bass. That small group was more welcome than an army. The only force on earth that fought better was a handful of Apaches. Harm spared a quick grin as the main force of McAllister's men rushed to the gates to meet the charge head-on. He wasted no time, cupping his hands and tossing Jack up to straddle the wall, passing the children to him one by one so he could settle them safely on the other side. Then Rebecca was hugging him.

"Becky, head for cover and wait for me or for Calvin. He should have some horses for you. I'm going for Amanda."

"You be careful. I haven't had a chance to welcome her to the family yet." She put her foot in the bridge of his hands and was up and gone. And that left Amanda.

The Rangers had breached the gate fortifications and were in a pitched battle with those who stood to fight and chasing down those who chose to run. Harm paid no attention to the close quarters combat. For just then, from across the square, roared a single shout.

"Bass!"

Tyrell Cates stood at the entrance of the hacienda, the muzzle of his Colt pressed beneath Amanda's ear.

Harm started across the square at a brisk walk. His knife sang as it jerked free of its sheath. His eyes were on Cates and his blood was hot.

Cates watched him come. His grip on Amanda was paralyzing. The time had come for dying and both men knew it. It had nothing to do with McAllister or the jewels. Or Amanda. It was the sound of terror in Harmon's voice when he awoke to darkness. It was the awed anger in Tyrell Cates when he couldn't break the spirit of a ten-year-old boy. Each woke a sense of helplessness in the other and it was more than the pride could stand. Neither would ever rest knowing the other lived. And so the time had come to end it.

Harm showed no sign of using caution. Seeing that, Cates twisted his hand in Amanda's hair, forcing her to cry out in pain. He didn't slow. Cates pulled down on the hammer of his gun.

"That's close enough, Bass."

He didn't stop. "Are you going to hide behind my wife? Afraid you can't best anyone but women and ten-year-old boys? Come on, coward. Come on, you coyote. Meet me like a man if you are one!"

Amanda felt her captor bunch with rage. For a minute, she thought he would cast her aside in favor of a fair fight. Then, he tugged her in front of him, shifting the focus of his .45 from her to Harm. Cates was going to shoot him down.

Without thinking, Amanda flung herself within the restrictions of his grip. She went for the arm he had leveled with deadly intent, sinking her teeth through sleeve and skin and sinew. He let out a howl of surprise and shook her hard, but she wouldn't let go. His fingers opened and the gun fell. Harm started running toward them, and finding himself suddenly without a ready weapon, Cates did the only thing he could. He struck Amanda and thrust her hard, right into Harm's path. They collided with enough force to send him skidding and scrambling to his knees with his arms around her. And Cates fled.

"Ammy?"

She heard him through the ringing in her head. She couldn't focus her eyes and she wanted so badly to see him. Her mouth was full of the taste of soiled shirt, man's sweat, and blood—his and hers. Amanda thought her nose was surely broken, so intense was the pain. She sagged against Harm, feeling the scatter of his kisses along her temple and the solid strength of his shoulder beneath her brow. His name came out like a whimper. She couldn't seem to stop her shaking, until he levered his palm beneath her chin and lifted her head so he could kiss her deeply, desperately.

"Ammy."

His features swam and finally cleared—blue eyes so steeped in worry and drawn with lines of strain that hers were lost in them. Then a moment of concern surfaced.

"Rebecca? The children?"

"Safe."

She slumped in his embrace, losing herself in the comfort of his arms. He kissed her again, then she felt the change come over him. Purpose tempered his muscles with inflexible steel. Though he still held her, she no longer had his attention. His control was strung with a tension so thin it vibrated with every breath. She wrapped her arms around him, hugging tighter, trying to contain him, to contain what was building inside him. Knowing she couldn't, Amanda found the courage to let him go.

He was rising up the instant she released him, senses quivering like a wolf in its eagerness to begin the hunt. For one distracted second, he looked down where she was spilled at his feet and his expression softened with a love so powerful it rendered them both helpless. Then his fingertips brushed her cheek and he was gone, running after fate in the form of Tyrell Cates.

She stayed where she was, too weak to stand, too scared for him to think. Gunshots had dwindled down and the Rangers were busy herding McAllister's men into the center of the square. They paid no mind to one weepy woman huddled in the shade. She heard a quiet step behind her and wasn't concerned, until she heard the very definitive click of a revolver being brought to full cock.

"Mrs. Bass."

She looked up with a moment's panic. He was standing with his back to the sun. All she could see was the halo of light framing his head and the intensity of the blue eyes he shared with Harmon.

"Get up. You and I are taking a little ride together."

Chapter Twenty-Five

Harm moved from room to room, silent and stalking. He filtered out the noise of commotion from the yard, listening instead for the betraying whisper of a footstep or the rasp of a furtive breath. His own were soundless. Gliding down the hall with a catlike quickness, his own aggressive heartbeats were like Apache war drums urging retribution.

He paused at a fork in the hall, senses reaching with a delicate skill, humming with an awareness of danger. Cates. Hot rage scalded his thoughts and he forced it down. This was not the time for rabid vengeance. It was a time to seek justice.

Weighing his balance on the balls of his feet, Harm crouched, poised for a second, then he flung himself low through the opening. The viciousness of Cates's swing skimmed over his head, then they were facing one another over long points of wickedly bared steel.

They didn't speak. Volumes were conveyed when glares locked with each other. They were both breathing softly, both measuring the other for strengths and weaknesses, both handling their weapons with lethal cunning. Cates took the first jab, darting out for the jugular. Harm feinted back and countered with a tightly controlled arc.

Fabric ripped, skin tore, Cates cursed, and first blood was drawn.

They circled warily, patiently seeking an opening in the other's defense, hemmed in by the close quarters. A lunge by Harm, a parry from Cates, the clash of fine steel against steel, and they jumped apart, not breathing so quietly now. They were too good to waste motion and too respectful of the other to force opportunity over caution. A sudden shift, a vicious swipe, and Harm felt agony run from elbow to shoulder, immediately numbing his right arm. He didn't look to survey the damage as he automatically switched his blade to his left hand and rallied with a low slash, just missing Cates's vitals as his own blood splashed bright and unnoticed upon the elegant tiles of his father's home.

With an abrupt change of tactics, Cates distracted with the blade, then followed through in a roundhouse punch, catching Harm in the side of the head and sending him staggering back into a table. A priceless collection of porcelains shattered with a single sweep of elbows. The sheriff took advantage of Harm's daze, landing a second, even harder blow before using his knife. The blade sank deep just above Harm's knee and wedged there between bone and muscle. Crippled by the pain, Harm started to collapse, driving upward at the same instant to slide his knife between Cates's ribs.

Blackness swirled as Harm released his knife and crumpled to the floor. He lay there on his belly, unable to draw a decent breath, so swamped by pain he could hardly see. He heard Cates fall and then there was silence. An unsteady hand reached for the blade, thinking he'd pull it free, but when his fingertips brushed the hilt, excruciating hurt exploded upward. Better he leave it. Hazy thoughts turned to Amanda and the Rangers outside the door. He only had to make it that far. Harmon couldn't stand, so he fought down the need to surrender consciousness and began to crawl toward the far opening where light, pure and silvery, beckoned. He dragged his leg and useless arm, smearing a thick trail of crimson as he inched along the cool tiles.

Over the rasp of his breathing, he heard movement behind him, a low groan, the shuffle of feet. Cates. Still alive and coming for him. Awareness waned for a moment as he pressed his cheek to the floor and closed his eyes, struggling for a saving strength. The scuffling steps grew closer, but he couldn't get up and he couldn't call out for the help that was just yards away. At that moment, it wasn't the fact that Cates was going to kill him that struck a terror into his heart; it was the fear that Amanda would be the one to find him there as dead as a butchered steer. He couldn't do that to her. He couldn't. He felt the toes of Cates's boots nudge his side, then the cruel twist of fingers in his hair, lifting his head up off the tiles.

"C'mon, Bass. I want to see your face. I want to read dying in your eyes when I cut you open."

Cates hauled on his slack form to flip him over. Then Harm rolled fast, yanking the blade from his own leg with a harsh Apache yell as he bowled his surprised enemy down and came up astride his chest. Cates had time to draw one startled breath, his last, as Harm plunged down with all his strength. Again and again, lost to the wild fear of the boy he'd been and the hatred of the man he'd become, stopping only when he lacked the strength to lift his arm to wrestle the knife free. Then he simply sat, panting, dizzy, drained. A tremendous calm settled over him and his first thought was of Amanda.

"Bass?"

It was an incredible effort to raise his head. He was looking up the bore of a Smith & Wesson and, beyond it, into the eyes of the man who'd killed his mother. Ed

Franks smiled grimly as he thumbed back the hammer of his pistol. A coward by nature, he'd stayed well back of the confrontation outside and had waited to see who would emerge victor between his boss and his worst enemy. With Harm wounded and helpless, he was flushed with the power of life and death.

"You should have killed me when you had the chance, Bass. Tell your mama I said hello."

The report was deafening, roaring down the hall like a cyclone. Harm jerked back, striking the wall, pressing there with eyes closed as Franks dropped beside Tyrell Cates. It took him a second to realize he wasn't dead. Or even shot.

"Harm? Harmon? Dang, you look a mess, boy."

Harm curled his fingers around Calvin Lowe's hand, hanging on weakly. He dragged his eyes open. The law-man crouched down in front of him and nodded at the unrecognizable figure.

"That Cates?"

Harm managed a hoarse, "Yes."

"Good. Seems I owed you this one." He toed Franks's perforated body. "Think you can get up, son? We're all done here. Your sister's mighty anxious to fuss over you."

He lifted his sound arm and Cal slid it around his shoulders, pulling him up. Harm groaned and hung against his friend, boneless and bleeding bad.

"Ammy?"

"C'mon, Harm."

"Ammy." He started breathing faster, feeling consciousness slipping. He tried to close his fingers in Cal's shirt. "Ammy."

"Let's get you fixed up."

Something was wrong. He tried to focus. He tried to stand on his own. He couldn't do either. What wasn't Calvin telling him? Why wasn't Amanda here, hovering over him, giving him anxious little kisses? He wanted her. He needed her. Why wasn't she there?

"Calvin, where's Amanda? I need Amanda."

"Rest easy, Harm. You're in a bad way. We're taking care of it for you."

"Taking care of what?" He stumbled and set his heels, forcing Cal to face him. "What, Calvin?" Blood was thundering in his head, the beat swelling, intensifying. "Where's Ammy?"

"McAllister took her."

McAllister took her.

That's the last he was aware of as the pulse of darkness overtook him.

"Ammy?"

Pain. His arm was on fire. His leg throbbed in matching misery.

Harm shifted. He was lying down on something comfortable. A bed. Where, he didn't know. He opened his eyes, but everything was bright and blurry. A gentle hand brushed his brow and he moaned.

"It's all right, Harmon. You're going to be fine."

Soft, tender tones.

"Ammy."

He reached up to catch the hand that stroked him, pressing his hot cheek into its palm, pressing kisses there along slender fingers until he felt a thin circle of gold. He'd never had a chance to give Amanda a ring. Confusion made him restless.

"Amanda? Amanda!"

"Shhh. Harmon, quiet."

He knew the voice now, recognized the caring touch. "Becky? Becky, where's Amanda?"

"They haven't found her yet. Calvin has all his men looking."

He remembered. Amanda, her nose bloodied, her face streaked with tears, huddled on the patio. Where he left her to go after Cates. Where he left her alone to pursue his vengeance. And McAllister took her, took his wife.

With a tremendous groan, he started to sit up. Immediately, he felt a firmer grip on his good shoulder, pushing him back. He didn't have the strength to resist.

"Harm, you stay still," Cal scolded. "I don't want to have to close up those holes again."

He shut his eyes in helpless frustration and tried to garner mobility. A seemingly hopeless task. He felt Becky's kiss, cool and light, upon his forehead.

"Let me take care of you this time, *silah,*" came her quiet voice.

He didn't want anyone taking care of him. He wanted Amanda. He wanted to know why she hadn't been found, why she wasn't beside him, how he was going to get through another agonizing second without her. He heard his sister's no-nonsense voice.

"Jack, you sit with your uncle while I go check on the children. Don't listen to anything he says, and if he tries to get up, shoot him in the other leg."

"Yes, Mama."

"That's one tough woman, your sister," Cal vowed. "Bet she keeps Will in line." He squeezed Harm's shoulder and went to the open door, where he spoke quietly to one of his men. Harm could make out most of the words.

"Why not?"

"Hell, Sheriff . . . over solid rock. Only one man I know can track over that and he ain't much good to nobody right now."

"Hush! I want you and the others . . . until you find

something . . . I ain't gonna tell him. Less you want to, you'd best get back out there."

"Yessir."

"Useless sonuva—" Cal was muttering as he sat back on the edge of Harm's bed. His rough palm pushed the damp hair back from a fevered brow. "Harm, you still with me, pard?"

He blinked slowly and struggled to focus on his friend's concerned face.

"Attaboy. I'm gonna have the fellers rig up a buckboard and we'll get you back to Terlingua. How'd that be? Think you can make the trip all right?"

Harm nodded slightly and let his eyes close again. Cal sat for a moment longer, studying the worn features, then he sighed, angry at his own helplessness. Damnit, he'd just stood up beside the man at his wedding. He wasn't about to stand beside him at his wife's grave. There had to be more they could do. He saw the wiry little boy Harm had been, all sliced to pieces, bringing his Elena back to him. And he swore again, softly.

"We'll find her, Harm. We'll find her."

The second Calvin left the room, Harm's eyes flashed open and he swung up into a sitting position.

"Uncle Harm, you're not supposed to—"

"Gimme a hand, Jack."

The boy looked at him in an agony of indecision. His uncle appeared to be in a real bad way. He'd never seen so much blood or wounds that looked so awful. His mother had told him to see Harm stayed put.

"You ease on back there, Uncle Harmon. You ain't going nowhere. Mama'd beat me if I was to let you outta here."

"Oh, she would not. If you're not going to help, get outta the way."

Harm sucked in a deep breath and pushed up to his

429

feet. And went right down to the floor, curling around his wounded leg with a terrible cry. Jack was bending over him, his features pale and anxious.

"Now see what you did. Let me get you back up on the bed."

Harm's fingers clenched the boy's shoulder as he leaned into him, gasping noisily. "Get me up," he ordered.

"No. I'm calling Mama."

"No! Jack. No. Help me, son. Get me to a horse. I can't walk but I can ride."

"And you'll bleed to death!"

"Please . . ."

"Uncle Harm . . ."

"I'm the only one who can trail them. I have to find her. It's my fault. My fault. I didn't stay with her. Jack, help me."

"The sheriff said you wasn't to get out of bed."

"Amanda's not his wife."

Jack was silent.

"Please."

"Grab on tight. I'll try not to hurt you too awful bad."

Between the two of them, they made it down the hall. The bodies of Cates and Franks had been removed, but the stains of violence remained. The boy was close to buckling under Harm's dragging weight but he managed. The pain was close to incapacitating but Harm managed as well. Fandango was still tied out front, saddled and snoozing in the heat. He shied when Harm latched on to the saddle.

"Whoa, there, horse. Whoa, Fandango." He felt foolish calling an animal by that silly name, but the horse immediately quieted. "Gimme a boost, Jack."

It was a struggle but Harm was finally in the saddle,

fitting his injured leg into the stirrup iron, fighting not to swoon dead away.

"Have you got a gun, Uncle Harmon? Hang on a second and I'll fetch you one." He was back in less than a minute, handing up a carbine. "Now you be careful. You want me to send the sheriff out after you?"

"No," he said, gathering up the reins. "This is personal."

"You're not going to get away, you know."

"Shut up!"

"Harmon's the best tracker there is. He'll follow you over water. He'll track you over mountains. He'll trail you right into hell."

"Shut your mouth."

"If you let me go, maybe he won't be in such a hurry to peel your miserable hide."

"As tempting as the thought of silence is, Mrs. Bass, you are the only thing that's going to keep me alive if he is after us. Now, I have to keep you breathing but I don't necessarily have to keep you conscious. Either you be quiet, or I'm going to knock you over the head."

Amanda sniffed at that as she glared at the man who'd fathered Harmon Bass. He didn't look quite so smugly superior running with sweat and fleeing in fear. And the bulge of precious stones stashed in his pocket would give no comfort to a dead man.

They'd been riding for hours, deeper and deeper into desert territory, into the badlands area alongside the Comanche Trail, where the ground was so wasted that even the Indians avoided it as a death trap. It was mercilessly hot. Amanda had picked up a stone and was sucking it to keep the saliva moistening her mouth. And she watched for Harm. She wouldn't consider that he might be dead. She just wouldn't.

"What I wouldn't give for some water."

She looked thoughtfully at McAllister. "I can show you where to get water."

"How would you know, city girl?"

"Harmon showed me and he's Apache. Have you ever known an Apache to perish of thirst?"

He reined in. "How?"

"The desert provides. You just have to know where to look."

"Get down and start looking."

It felt good to get off the horse and stretch her cramped legs. Amanda went right to the business of finding water. She snapped off a hollow stalk and stuck it down into the basal leaves of a mescal plant, then sucked through it like a straw. Rain from nights ago still lingered near the pulpy heart of the plant, protected from the heat. Not enough to satisfy but enough to sustain. McAllister followed suit.

"Give me your knife."

He eyed her warily. Then he passed her the blade, bringing up the muzzle of his gun to keep watch while she chopped into the body of a barrel cactus and began to chew the pulp. When she cut into a second plant, the juices ran thick and milky. She looked at it for a moment, remembering Harm's warning, then hacked off a big slice and handed it to the judge.

"Here. Chew on this."

He did as he'd seen her do, sucking greedily. Then abruptly he spat, his stomach seizing up into cramps. He tossed the meat away. "Are you trying to poison me?"

"Sorry. That kind of cactus must not be any good." She gave a mild smile over gritted teeth, wishing it had been potent enough to kill in an instant.

"Get back on your horse."

"Let me wipe off my hands first. They're all sticky."

Amanda thrust her hands deep into the dirt, then flung handfuls into McAllister's face. While his arms flailed frantically, she ran for her horse, managing to get one foot into the stirrup before he grabbed her around the waist and threw her down. She glared up resentfully as the older man cleared his eyes with his sleeve.

"You're more of a savage than that little half-breed husband of yours."

"Thank you."

"No more tricks."

She put up her chin rebelliously.

"Try anything else and you'll be riding facedown over that saddle."

A mulish expression crossed Amanda's face as she got to her feet. McAllister stepped back to give her room as she advanced toward the horses. Abruptly, she flung up her arms and shouted as loud as she could. Startled, the horses reared back and wheeled away, running from the sudden fright.

It was worth enduring the back of McAllister's hand to see his look of aggravation.

"You little fool! Now we walk."

Now Harmon could catch up to them that much faster.

It had seemed like a good idea at first. But after trudging for countless miles, Amanda was less impressed by her own brilliance. What if Harmon wasn't coming? What if no one was following them into this wretched no-man's-land? She could well have condemned them. Without Harmon, would it matter? Her eyes began to burn. She'd be crying if there was any moisture left in her body. She was tired and she was fast losing hope of ever seeing the other side of this barren plain. Only the prod of McAllister's gun kept her moving. She guessed he jabbed her hard enough to make her wince because it made him feel better about her making a fool of him. At least she had the satisfaction of knowing this horrid creature who'd caused the man she loved so much pain would perish with her. That was the least she could do for Harm.

She thought it was a mirage at first, but then McAllister drew up beside her. A horse was cropping aimlessly at bunch grass. Then she saw it was not just any horse. It was Fandango.

Harmon!

She stood very still, refusing herself the luxury of casting about an anxious glance. If he didn't want to be seen, she wouldn't see him.

"We might just get out of this yet," McAllister was saying. He poked her with the pistol. "Sit down and don't you move while I catch our ride. And Mrs. Bass, you try anything, and I'm just riled enough to shoot to kill."

She sank down on the hard ground obediently. "I won't move."

That should have warned him, but he still didn't know Amanda Bass well enough to suspect her compliant moods.

McAllister advanced on the grazing animal. It had no saddle and was trailing reins. Those dangling ribbons held his attention as he stretched out his hand, murmuring softly. He froze as something round and hard jammed up into his belly.

"Don't *you* move."

McAllister had never heard his voice but he had no doubt when he glanced down at his feet that he would find Harmon Bass. Harm was flat on his back, flush with the landscape. The barrel of his carbine pointed to the standing man's midriff.

"Ammy, come get his gun."

She was up and sprinting toward them. Cautiously, she

434

removed the Colt that had been bruising her spine for the last few hours and leveled it on the judge with a smile.

"Didn't I tell you? Best tracker in the territory."

Then she looked down.

"Oh, my God! Harmon!"

All she could see was blood, encrusting his clothes, splotching his sleeve and pant leg in a wet pattern. So much blood!

"I'm all right, Amanda. Keep him covered for a second whilst I get up. If he twitches, blow him a new navel."

As hard it was, she kept her attention on McAllister while Harm groaned and thrashed awkwardly in his struggle to sit. Finally, he got one knee under him and levered up. He leaned into her. She could feel his weakness, his shaking, as her arm spanned his middle.

"Harm?"

His hand cupped her cheek, turning her face halfway toward him so he could kiss the corner of her mouth without obstructing her vision.

"I came as soon as I could," he panted.

"I wasn't worried."

His head rested on her shoulder and she supported him for a long moment. Then he rolled his forehead against her damp shirt and looked long and hard at Russell McAllister.

"So, you're Leisha's boy," the judge said quietly. "You look just like her."

"Shut up."

"I know I haven't been any kind of father to you, but it's not too late to remedy that."

Harm laughed, a low, raspy rumble. "I think it was too late the day you left your men behind to rape and murder us on the land you stole."

"I never told them to do that . . . Harmon."

"No? I guess a terrible mistake was made, then, wasn't

it? You really meant for Cates to help us move on over to your house so's you could take good care of us. Right?"

"I can do that now. If you let me go, I can see your family well provided for. I'm a rich man. You're my heir, Harmon, my son."

"Don't listen to him, Harmon," Amanda whispered into the damp blackness of his hair.

"My father," Harm muttered, and shook his head wonderingly. "I was always curious, but I know all I want to know now."

Slowly, he raised the barrel of his carbine and McAllister took a hasty step back. "You're not going to just shoot me down!"

"Isn't that what a son of yours would do?"

"Harmon . . ."

"This doesn't concern you, Amanda!"

The crack of his voice silenced her. The sudden rush of violence in him frightened her. But she held him up and held her tongue.

"I want you to dig."

McAllister blinked. "What?"

"Start digging."

"With what?"

"Your hands. There. Dig. Make it big enough for a grave. My wife prefers I bury my dead. Do it now!"

McAllister dropped and began to scoop the dry earth. He had no more luck with it than Amanda had when she'd tried to do the humane thing for a man who didn't deserve it. He was sweating. He was thinking feverishly of a way to escape his own execution. But the cold blue eyes that watched him allowed for no mercy.

"The ground's too hard," he said when his hands were raw and bleeding.

"Then I guess we'll just have to make do, won't we? Put your hands behind your head."

He did so, and he stiffened at the feel of cool metal against the base of his skull. His composure fractured. "You can't do this! I'm your father!"

"You're nothing to me! Nothing! The only father I've ever known is near to dying with one of your bullets in him! Don't you dare ask pity from me!" He pulled back on the hammer.

"Harmon . . ."

"For God's sake, you can't just kill me in cold blood! What kind of a man are you?"

"The kind you made me," came his flat reply.

"No, Harmon. No, you're not," Amanda pleaded.

"Ammy . . ."

"Harmon, don't do this. Please. You don't need to. What would Will expect of you?"

"Ammy, you don't know . . . you don't know what he did to us."

"Will killing him change any of that? Or will it push you into becoming just like him? Harmon, please. He's not going to get away with anything. Not now. I'll bring down lawyers by the boxcar if need be. He won't get away. If he doesn't go to prison, I'll shoot him down myself. Please, don't do this. First it'll be him, and then you'll be riding out after the two others. I want us to start our life together. You're not like them. If you were, I wouldn't love you."

The carbine lowered and McAllister expelled a noisy breath. Harm sagged against her. His knees gave and the pull of his weight carried her down with him.

"I'm going to rest a minute while we wait for Cal."

"All right, Harmon. I'll see to things for you." She cradled him in her lap, stroking his hair. Her pistol never wavered as it lined up on the back of McAllister's head.

"If he moves—"

"I'll dispatch him properly and promptly to hell."

"You're going to make me one helluva Texas wife."

"I plan to, Harmon. I plan to."

Epilogue

The nights were getting hotter, holding in the day's humidity like a big, dark sponge. Amanda escaped the heat of the house and went to join her husband on the porch. He was nursing a cup of coffee, gazing off toward the mountains.

"What are you thinking about?" she asked.

"Hmm? Oh, nothing." He lifted his arm and she sidled in close beneath its drape.

"Restless spirit?"

"Tired bones. Who'd have thought putting up a windmill could be so cussed hard."

"Don't tell me a little ole windmill's going to get the best of *The* Harmon Bass."

"*The* Harmon Bass is wishing he'd never mentioned it."

"Oh, but I'm so looking forward to taking a bath in that first tub of water. You might consider joining me."

"Right out in the middle of the yard?"

"Are you blushing, Mr. Bass?"

"I got over blushing around you a long time ago."

Silence settled comfortably between them just as married life had· once Cal Lowe had hurried McAllister through the courts and into serving ten to twenty, and they'd gotten back to the ranch. Will was up giving growly orders to all of them and Rebecca was spitting them right back at him. Amanda loved it. It was a feeling of family. And she loved Harm madly.

"Harmon?"

"Hmmm?"

"When you finish the windmill, can we start on our house?"

"Decided where you want it yet?"

"Someplace where there are no snakes."

"Someplace like Chicago, then?"

She chuckled and nuzzled warm skin. He was shirtless and freshly washed and quite delectable. "I was thinking Blue Creek?"

"Blue Creek?"

"Close to the mountains, close to here, close to Terlingua."

"Blue Creek isn't close to anything!"

"Distance is relative. And speaking of relatives, let's take a ride up there tonight."

"That's a fair piece of riding, Ammy. And what's it got to do with relatives?"

"Too many of them here. I want to go swimming and I want to roll around naked under the stars with you. Ahhh! You're blushing!"

"Ammy, I swear, you'd make a whore blush with some of the stuff you say." But he was smiling, and his fingers curved under her chin to lift it. Then his mouth was moving slowly, sensuously, upon hers. It was the only way he'd learned to keep her quiet. And he'd learned an awful lot about kissing in the last few months. When he leaned back, Amanda sighed and cuddled into the vee of his thighs, encouraged by the definite swell of his interest. They'd be on the way to Blue Creek in no time.

"Hey." The door banged behind them and Jack strode

out. "The kids want you to say good night . . . if you're not too busy, Uncle Harm."

The boy's drawl was one of pure cynicism, and Harm muttered, "I see what you mean about things being relative." Then he regarded Jack with a tolerant smile. "You want to help me build a house?"

"You gonna have yourself a mansion now that you got yourself a rich wife and don't have to work for living?"

"I'm gonna have myself your butt if you don't watch your mouth."

"Here. Sidney wants you to read this to him."

Harm caught a copy of *Shoot-out at Tornillo Creek, or; Harmon Bass rides to the Rescue.* "Why don't you read it to 'em and just fill in your own name?"

"If I was making up lies, it'd be *Jack Bass, Pride of the Texas Rangers, or; Son of a Legend.*"

"Sounds like a legend worth living up to," Harm mused.

"I'm proud of it."

"Should be. Tell the little ones I'll be in in a minute. And tell your mama and daddy that Ammy and me are gonna be riding out for a while. Be back late tomorrow. We're gonna be stepping off rooms for our mansion."

Jack grinned and disappeared into the house.

"I didn't ask for a mansion, Harmon," Amanda said softly.

"Can have one if you want. You're the one who's got to clean it. And pay for it."

She rubbed her palms along his chest, wondering how to ask, then just blurting it out in her usual fashion. "Harm, we don't have to take the money. I mean, if you'd rather we didn't, it's not that important to me." And she hoped she knew it wasn't that important to him. She'd never suspected that her accompanying fortune carried

441

any additional weight in the Bass household. And she wouldn't allow it to create any strain on her marriage.

However, Harm was ever practical. "Of course we'll take it! You think I'm crazy? I never turn down payment for something I've earned."

"Oh? And just what have you done to earn this particular windfall?"

"I've got to listen to you talk me into an early grave."

"Harmon!"

He caught her bunched fists and pulled her up close, kissing her until she was breathless and shifting impatiently against him. "Easy money," he murmured huskily and kissed her again.

"I love you, Harmon."

"Hah! Only because you like bedding down with a legend."

"I like bedding down with the man better." She took the book from his hand and gave it an indifferent toss into the yard. And then she was kissing him. And oh, it was nice. Almost as nice as the other things they'd soon be doing. She felt slightly guilty because she hadn't told him about the baby yet. Rebecca warned her to wait. She said Apache men had funny thoughts when it came to making love to their wives when they were pregnant or nursing a child. Since she wasn't about to do without for any longer than she had to, Amanda stayed wisely silent. Not that she didn't think she could convince him to forgo abstinence. To prove it, she stroked her tongue over his, feeling him shudder in response. Smiling, she indulged them both, until finally he twisted away, breathing hard.

"If we're gonna get to Blue Creek tonight, let's get a move on. Go on in and say your good nights while I get the horses saddled up."

He didn't have to tell her twice. And maybe she'd tell

him a thing or two . . . after they'd made love a time or two.

Harm smiled after her, then started from the porch toward the barn. *Yusn*, that woman drove him crazy! But it was a crazy he could live with without complaint. He paused and bent down, picking up the worn dime novel she'd tossed aside. He thumbed through the bold woodcut engravings and smiled again. Might not hurt to hang on to it, he thought, slipping it inside his shirt and striding on.

Just in case she ever forgot what a hero he really was.

HISTORICAL ROMANCES BY PHOEBE CONN

FOR THE STEAMIEST READS, NOTHING BEATS THE PROSE OF CONN . . .

ARIZONA ANGEL	(3872, $4.50/$5.50)
CAPTIVE HEART	(3871, $4.50/$5.50)
DESIRE	(4086, $5.99/$6.99)
EMERALD FIRE	(4243, $4.99/$5.99)
LOVE ME 'TIL DAWN	(3593, $5.99/$6.99)
LOVING FURY	(3870, $4.50/$5.50)
NO SWEETER ECSTASY	(3064, $4.95/$5.95)
STARLIT ECSTASY	(2134, $3.95/$4.95)
TEMPT ME WITH KISSES	(3296, $4.95/$5.95)
TENDER SAVAGE	(3559, $4.95/$5.95)

Available wherever paperbacks are sold, or order direct from the Publisher. Send cover price plus 50¢ per copy for mailing and handling to Penguin USA, P.O. Box 999, c/o Dept. 17109, Bergenfield, NJ 07621.Residents of New York and Tennessee must include sales tax. DO NOT SEND CASH.